bad machinery

THE CASE OF THE FORKED ROAD

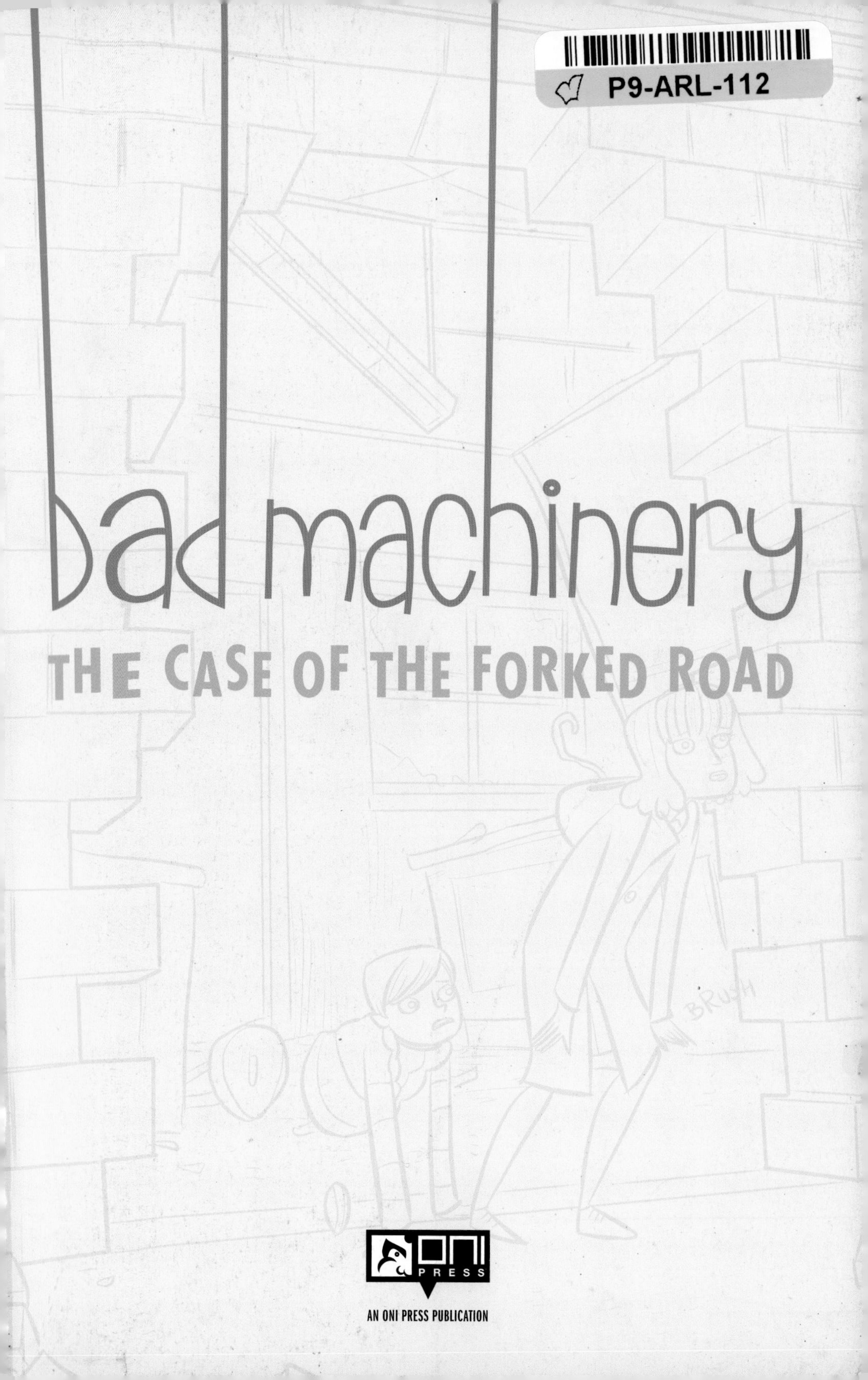
BRUSH

AN ONI PRESS PUBLICATION

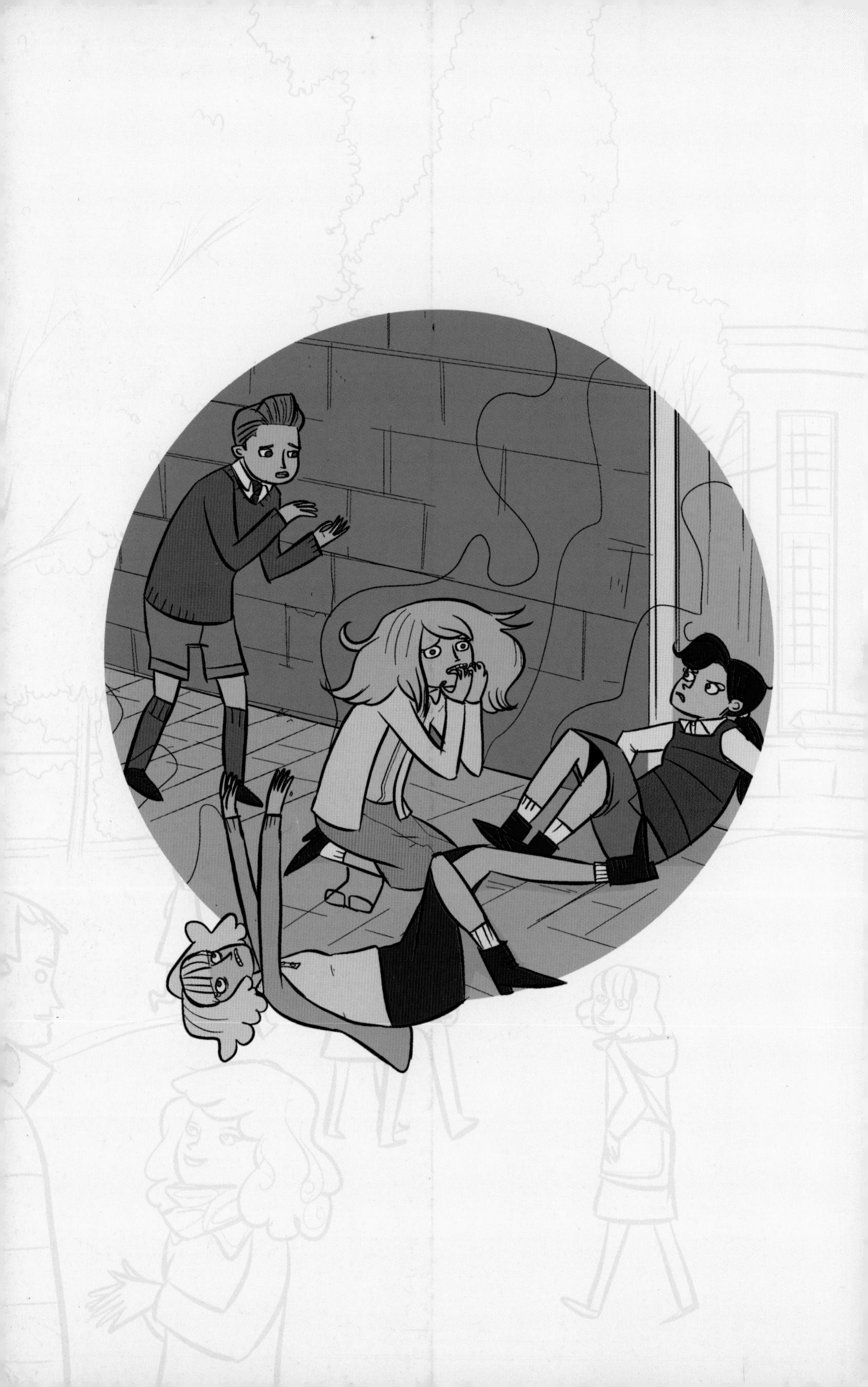

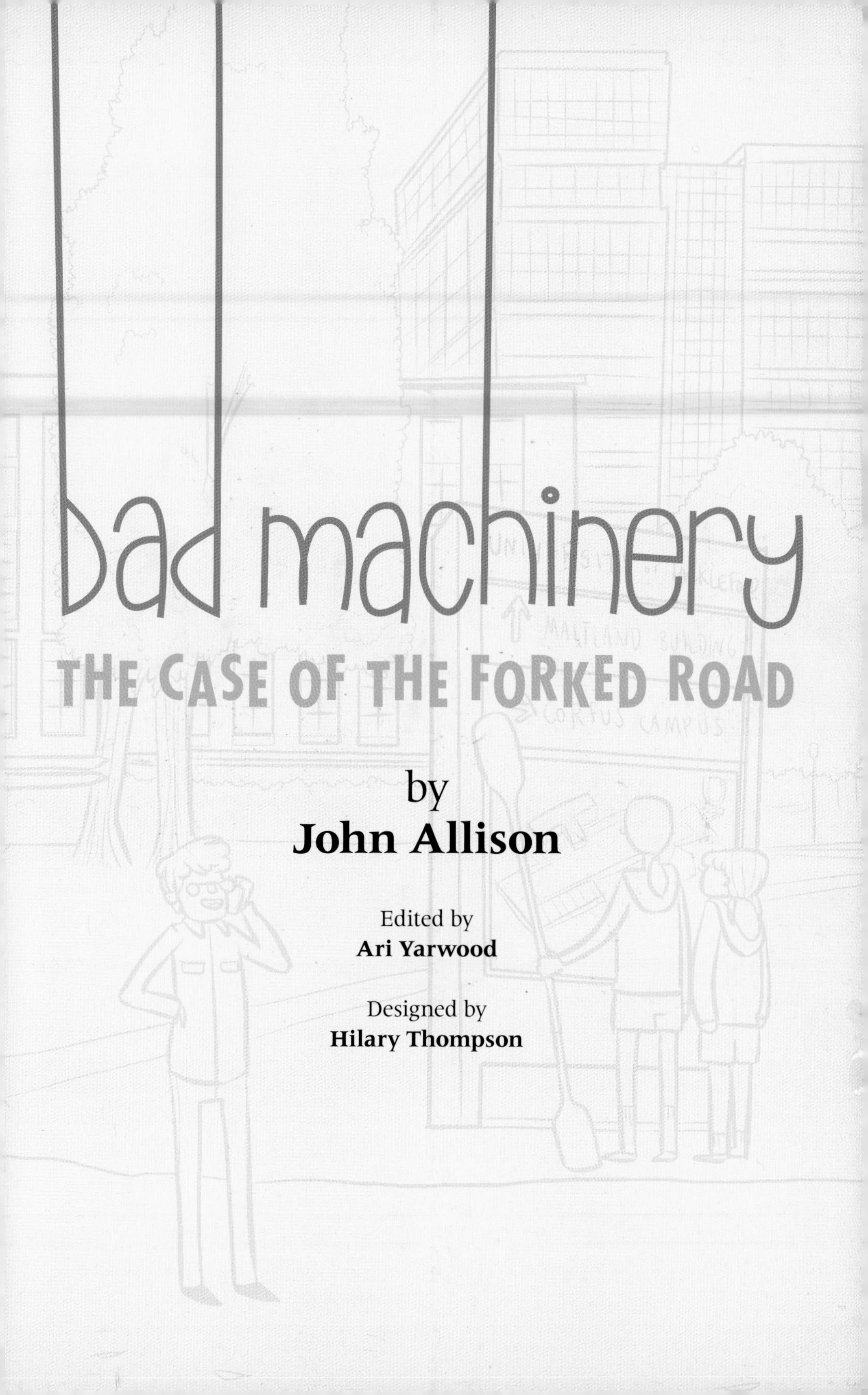
MAITLAND BUILDING
CORTUS CAMPUS

bad machinery

THE CASE OF THE FORKED ROAD

by
John Allison

Edited by
Ari Yarwood

Designed by
Hilary Thompson

PUBLISHED BY ONI PRESS INC.

publisher, **Joe Nozemack**
editor in chief, **James Lucas Jones**
v.p. of marketing & sales, **Andrew McIntire**
sales manager, **David Dissanayake**
publicity coordinator, **Rachel Reed**
director of design & production, **Troy Look**
graphic designer, **Hilary Thompson**
digital prepress technician, **Angie Dobson**
managing editor, **Ari Yarwood**
senior editor, **Charlie Chu**
editor, **Robin Herrera**
administrative assistant, **Alissa Sallah**
director of logistics, **Brad Rooks**
logistics associate, **Jung Lee**

onipress.com
facebook.com/onipress
twitter.com/onipress
onipress.tumblr.com
instagram.com/onipress
badmachinery.com

FIRST EDITION: MAY 2017

ISBN 978-1-62010-390-6
EISBN 978-1-62010-391-3

BAD MACHINERY VOLUME SEVEN: THE CASE OF THE FORKED ROAD, MAY 2017. PUBLISHED BY ONI PRESS, INC. 1305 SE MARTIN LUTHER KING JR. BLVD., SUITE A, PORTLAND, OR 97214.

PRINTED IN CHINA.

LIBRARY OF CONGRESS CONTROL NUMBER: 2012953355

1 2 3 4 5 6 7 8 9 10

CHARLOTTE GROTE
Maverick, profile writer

Likes: who can truly know my heart? Only I dear reader hem hem. I like mystery, and trouble. A summer's day. A baby's laugh. Pumpkin seeds!

Dislikes: when people put their shoes on the bed in TV shows. Take your shoes off, TV characters!

SHAUNA WICKLE
BFF (M/W/F/Su)

Likes: academic excellence, avoiding the glare of authority.

Dislikes: people who don't undertand brutalist architec-ture. "It's meant to look like that" she says. It looks like a big grey box to me but whatevs.

MILDRED HAVERSHAM
BFF (Tu/Th/Sa)

Likes: Mildred has a perverse interest in "science" and half the stuff she comes out with sounds at best well spurious and worst specially designed (by her) to fool the gullible eg me, la Grote.

Dislikes: enforced, lifelong veganism.

LINTON BAXTER
Youth sleuth

Likes: being right, all the time. Probably likes men's football and other typical man's things eg underground fight clubs and steaks.

Dislikes: being proved wrong and any subsequent victory celebrations.

JACK FINCH
Basic detective

Likes: the ladies. Jack is away with the fairies all the time thinking about whatever dame has crossed his path with her floral "scent" an enchanting "ways".

Dislikes: Jack has broad tastes but he doesn't have much time for moths.

SONNY CRAVEN
Naturally kind

Likes: Sonny is our angel, our special boy. His way of being basically decent in a world what is always getting darker (also perhaps "grim" and "gritty") suggests that he likes almost everything that is good in this world.

Dislikes: EVIL.

AMY BECKWITH-CHILTON
Sassy antiques expert?

Likes : ABC's likes are a mystery to me but seeing as how she has got mad tattoos all along both arms I guess she likes pain and Mr Harley Davidson's motorbikes.

Dislikes: I reckon she dislikes conformity and THE MAN.

RYAN BECKWITH
Teacher, husband, tired

Likes: Mr Beckwith is a simple soul who likes a cup of bad instant coffee, quiet in the classroom, and us not asking him questions that are maybe not related to what he is teaching us about. Also he probably likes his well nice wife.

Dislikes: there is a rumour that he once karate chopped a snake.

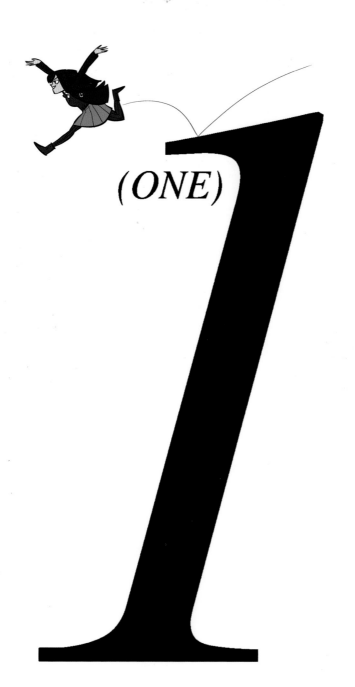

(ONE)

1

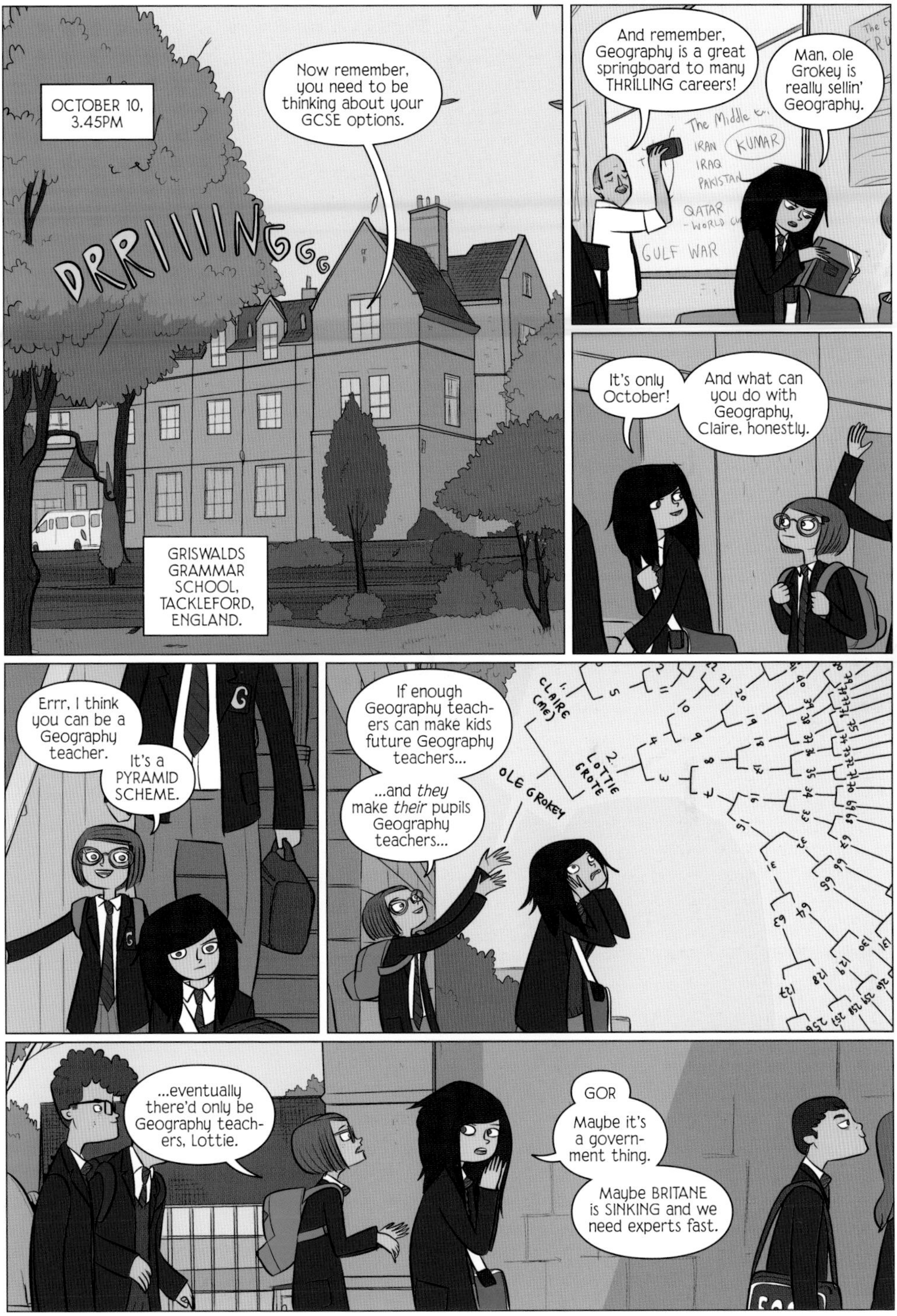
OCTOBER 10, 3.45PM
DRRIIIINGGG
Now remember, you need to be thinking about your GCSE options.
GRISWALDS GRAMMAR SCHOOL, TACKLEFORD, ENGLAND.
And remember, Geography is a great springboard to many THRILLING careers!
IRAN
KUMAR
IRAQ
PAKISTAN
QATAR
GULF WAR
Man, ole Grokey is really sellin' Geography.
It's only October!
And what can you do with Geography, Claire, honestly.
Errr, I think you can be a Geography teacher.
It's a PYRAMID SCHEME.
If enough Geography teachers can make kids future Geography teachers...
...and *they* make *their* pupils Geography teachers...
1. CLAIRE (ME)
2. LOTTIE GROTE
OLE GROKEY
...eventually there'd only be Geography teachers, Lottie.
GOR
Maybe it's a government thing.
Maybe BRITANE is SINKING and we need experts fast.

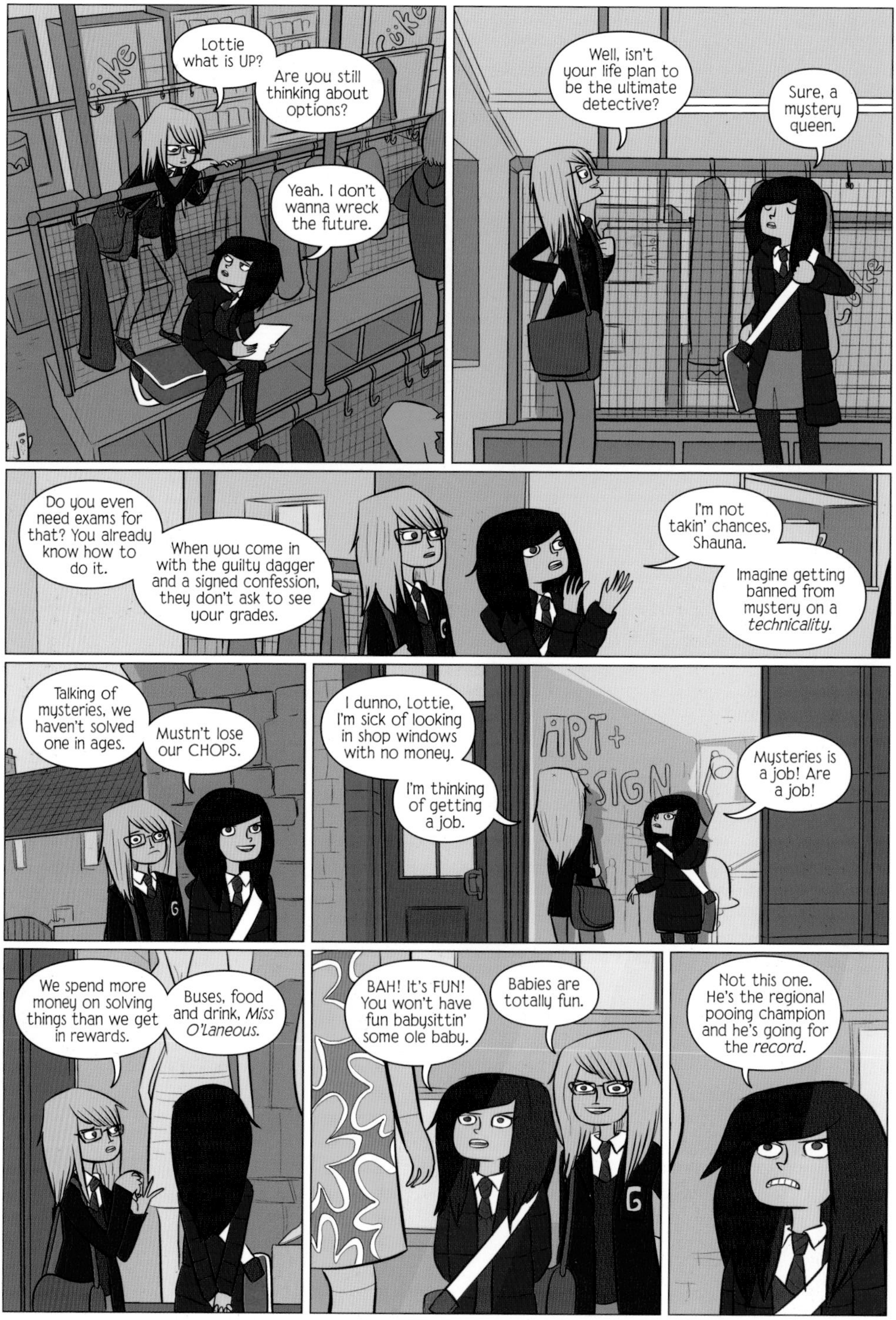
Lottie what is UP?
Are you still thinking about options?
Yeah. I don't wanna wreck the future.
Well, isn't your life plan to be the ultimate detective?
Sure, a mystery queen.
Do you even need exams for that? You already know how to do it.
When you come in with the guilty dagger and a signed confession, they don't ask to see your grades.
I'm not takin' chances, Shauna.
Imagine getting banned from mystery on a *technicality*.
Talking of mysteries, we haven't solved one in ages.
Mustn't lose our CHOPS.
I dunno, Lottie, I'm sick of looking in shop windows with no money.
I'm thinking of getting a job.
ART + DESIGN
Mysteries is a job! Are a job!
We spend more money on solving things than we get in rewards.
Buses, food and drink, *Miss O'Laneous*.
BAH! It's FUN! You won't have fun babysittin' some ole baby.
Babies are totally fun.
Not this one. He's the regional pooing champion and he's going for the *record*.

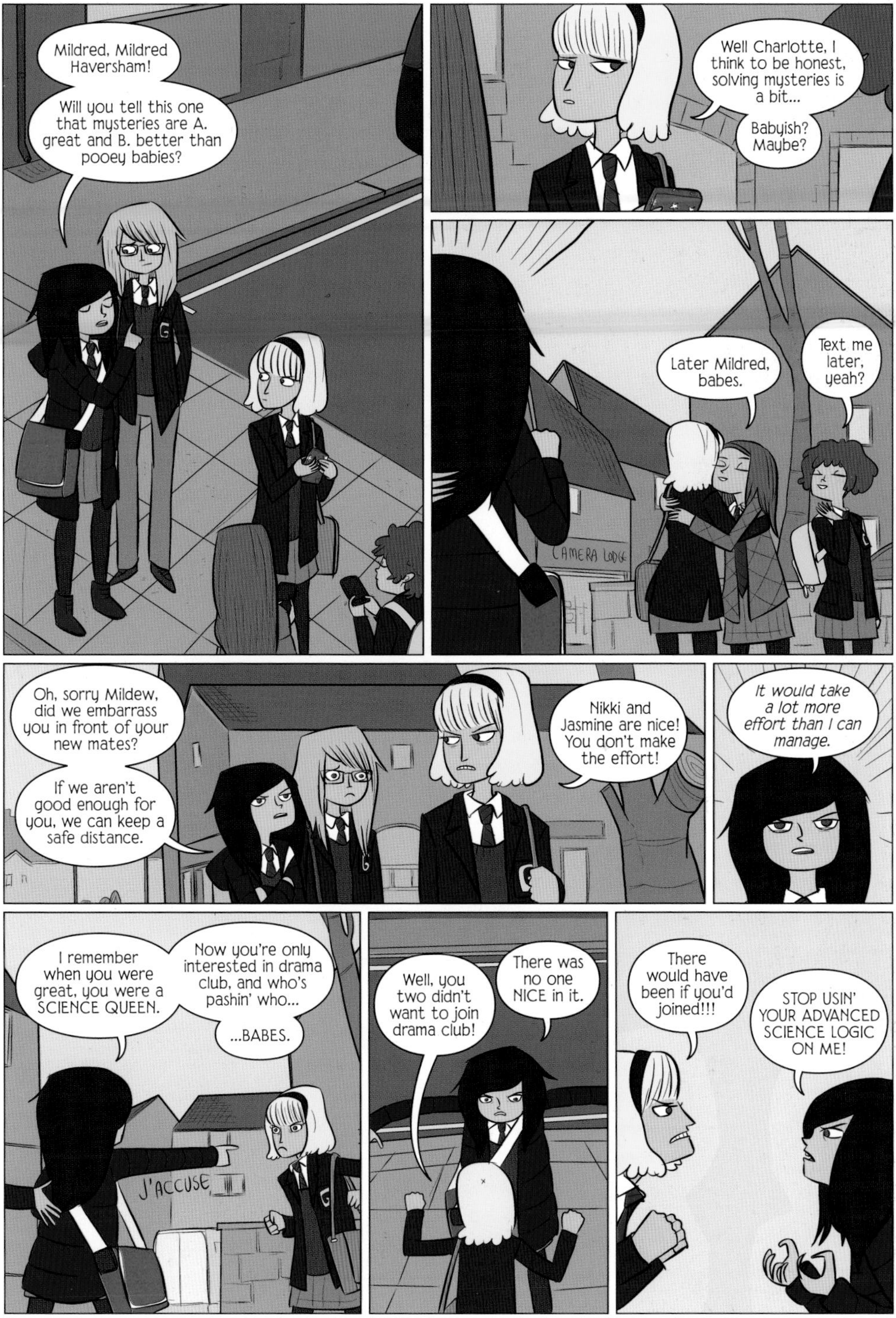
Mildred, Mildred Haversham!
Will you tell this one that mysteries are A. great and B. better than pooey babies?
Well Charlotte, I think to be honest, solving mysteries is a bit...
Babyish? Maybe?
Later Mildred, babes.
Text me later, yeah?
CAMERA LODGE
Oh, sorry Mildew, did we embarrass you in front of your new mates?
If we aren't good enough for you, we can keep a safe distance.
Nikki and Jasmine are nice! You don't make the effort!
It would take a lot more effort than I can manage.
I remember when you were great, you were a SCIENCE QUEEN.
Now you're only interested in drama club, and who's pashin' who...
...BABES.
J'ACCUSE
Well, you two didn't want to join drama club!
There was no one NICE in it.
There would have been if you'd joined!!!
STOP USIN' YOUR ADVANCED SCIENCE LOGIC ON ME!

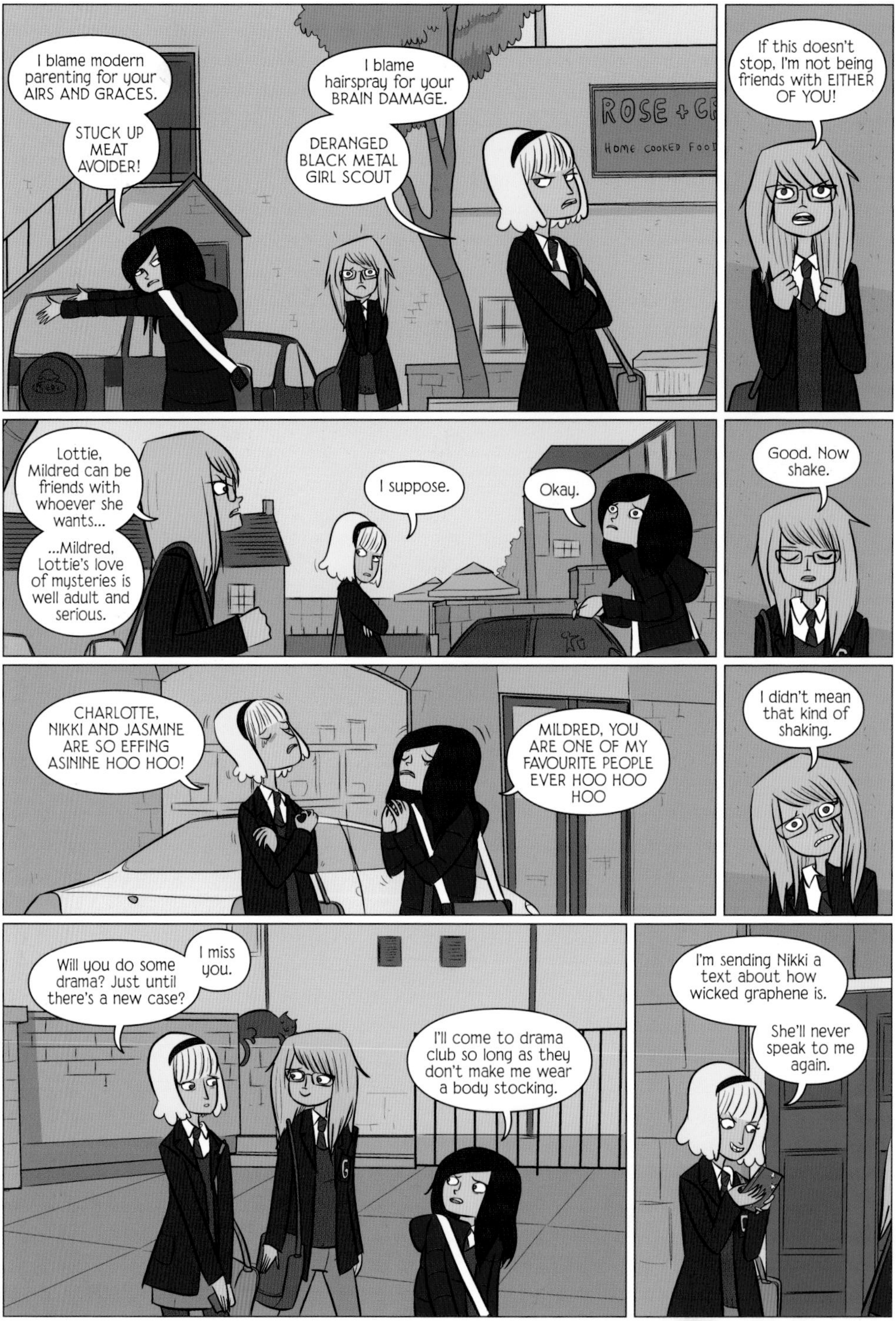
I blame modern parenting for your AIRS AND GRACES.
STUCK UP MEAT AVOIDER!
I blame hairspray for your BRAIN DAMAGE.
DERANGED BLACK METAL GIRL SCOUT
ROSE + CR
HOME COOKED FOOD
If this doesn't stop, I'm not being friends with EITHER OF YOU!
Lottie, Mildred can be friends with whoever she wants...
...Mildred, Lottie's love of mysteries is well adult and serious.
I suppose.
Okay.
Good. Now shake.
CHARLOTTE, NIKKI AND JASMINE ARE SO EFFING ASININE HOO HOO!
MILDRED, YOU ARE ONE OF MY FAVOURITE PEOPLE EVER HOO HOO HOO
I didn't mean that kind of shaking.
Will you do some drama? Just until there's a new case?
I miss you.
I'll come to drama club so long as they don't make me wear a body stocking.
I'm sending Nikki a text about how wicked graphene is.
She'll never speak to me again.

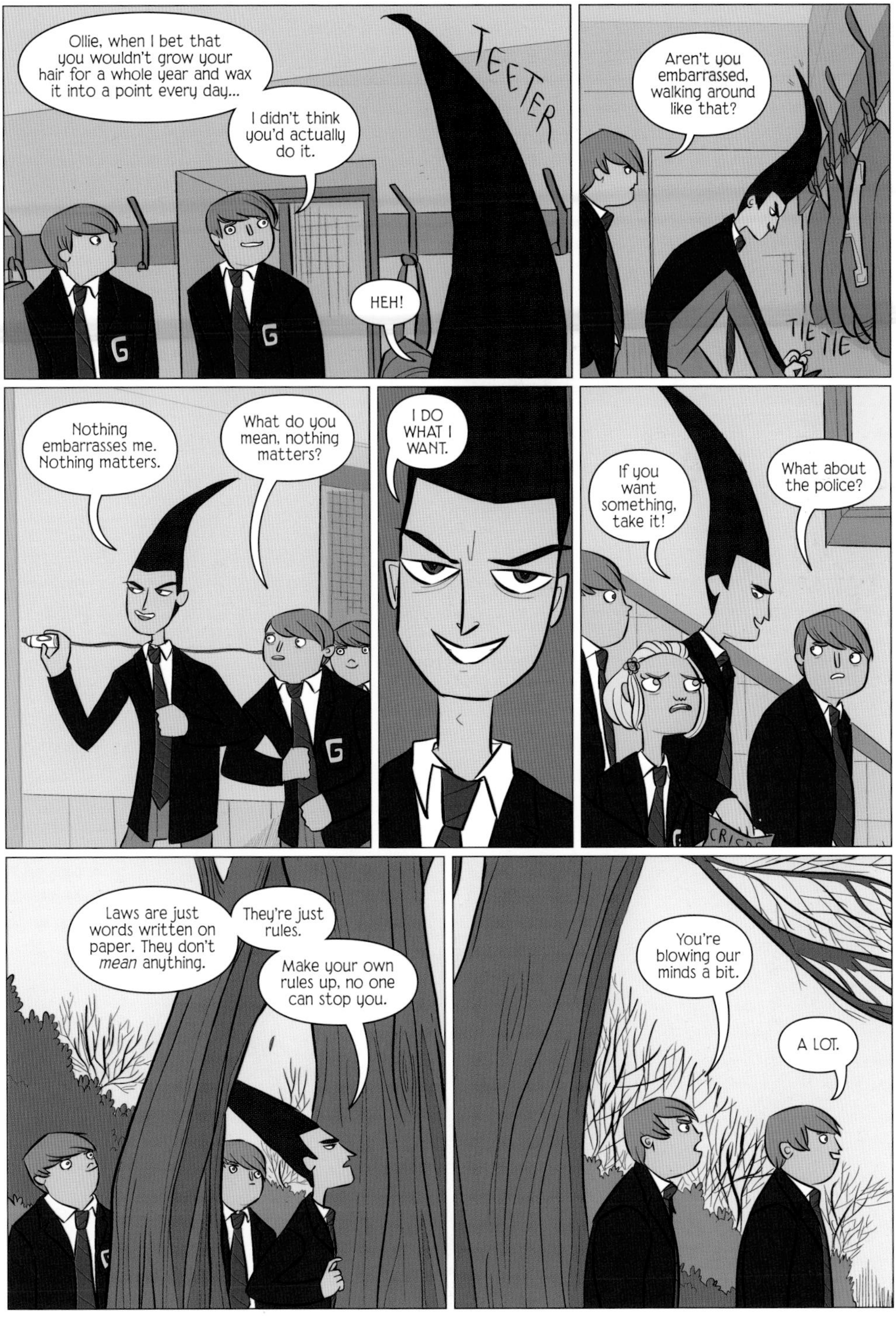
Ollie, when I bet that you wouldn't grow your hair for a whole year and wax it into a point every day...
I didn't think you'd actually do it.
TEETER
HEH!
Aren't you embarrassed, walking around like that?
TIE TIE
Nothing embarrasses me. Nothing matters.
What do you mean, nothing matters?
I DO WHAT I WANT.
If you want something, take it!
What about the police?
CRISPS
Laws are just words written on paper. They don't *mean* anything.
They're just rules.
Make your own rules up, no one can stop you.
You're blowing our minds a bit.
A LOT.

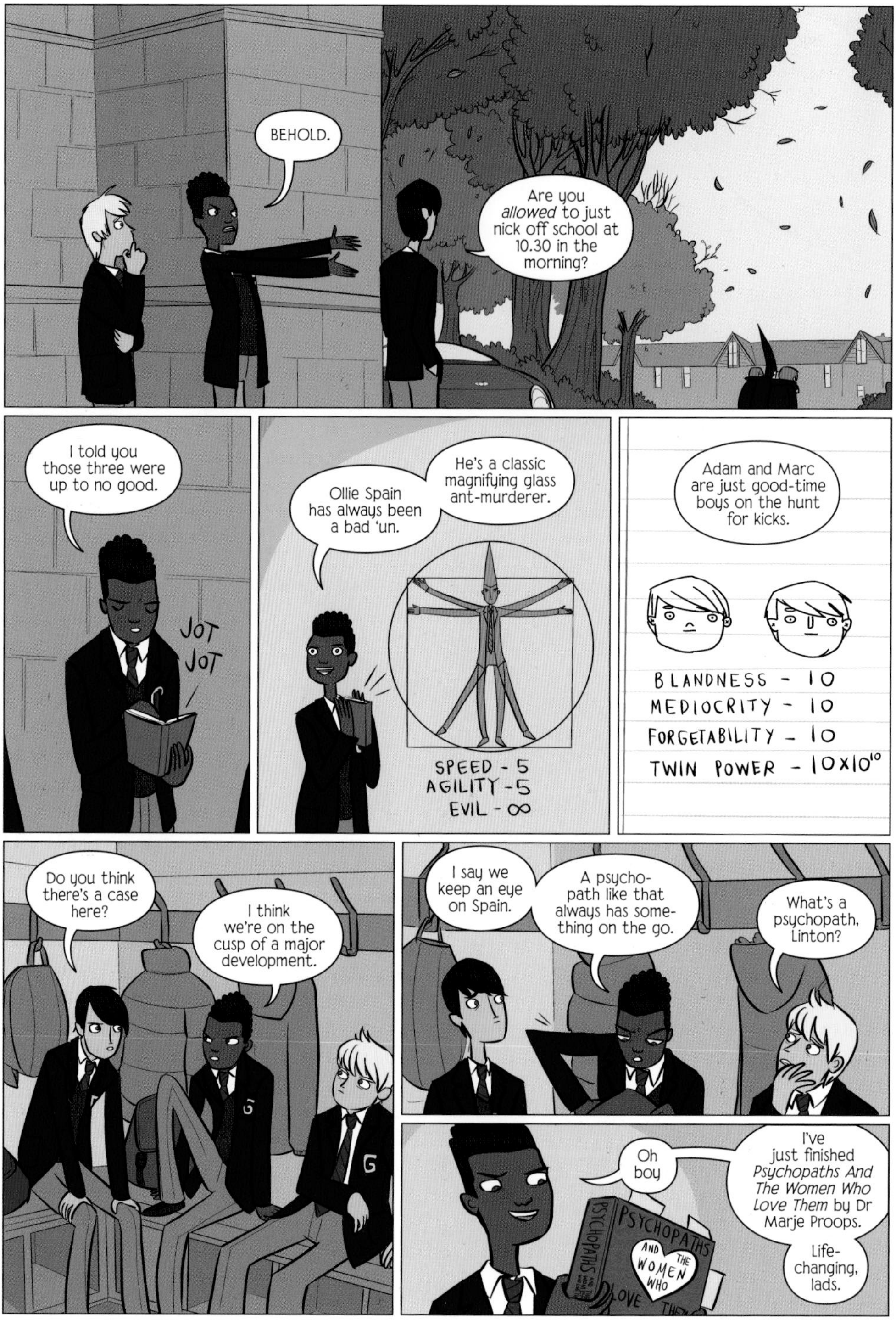
BEHOLD.
Are you *allowed* to just nick off school at 10.30 in the morning?
I told you those three were up to no good.
JOT JOT
Ollie Spain has always been a bad 'un.
He's a classic magnifying glass ant-murderer.
SPEED - 5
AGILITY - 5
EVIL - ∞
Adam and Marc are just good-time boys on the hunt for kicks.
BLANDNESS - 10
MEDIOCRITY - 10
FORGETABILITY - 10
TWIN POWER - 10x10[10]
Do you think there's a case here?
I think we're on the cusp of a major development.
I say we keep an eye on Spain.
A psychopath like that always has something on the go.
What's a psychopath, Linton?
Oh boy
I've just finished *Psychopaths And The Women Who Love Them* by Dr Marje Proops.
Life-changing, lads.
PSYCHOPATHS AND THE WOMEN WHO LOVE THEM

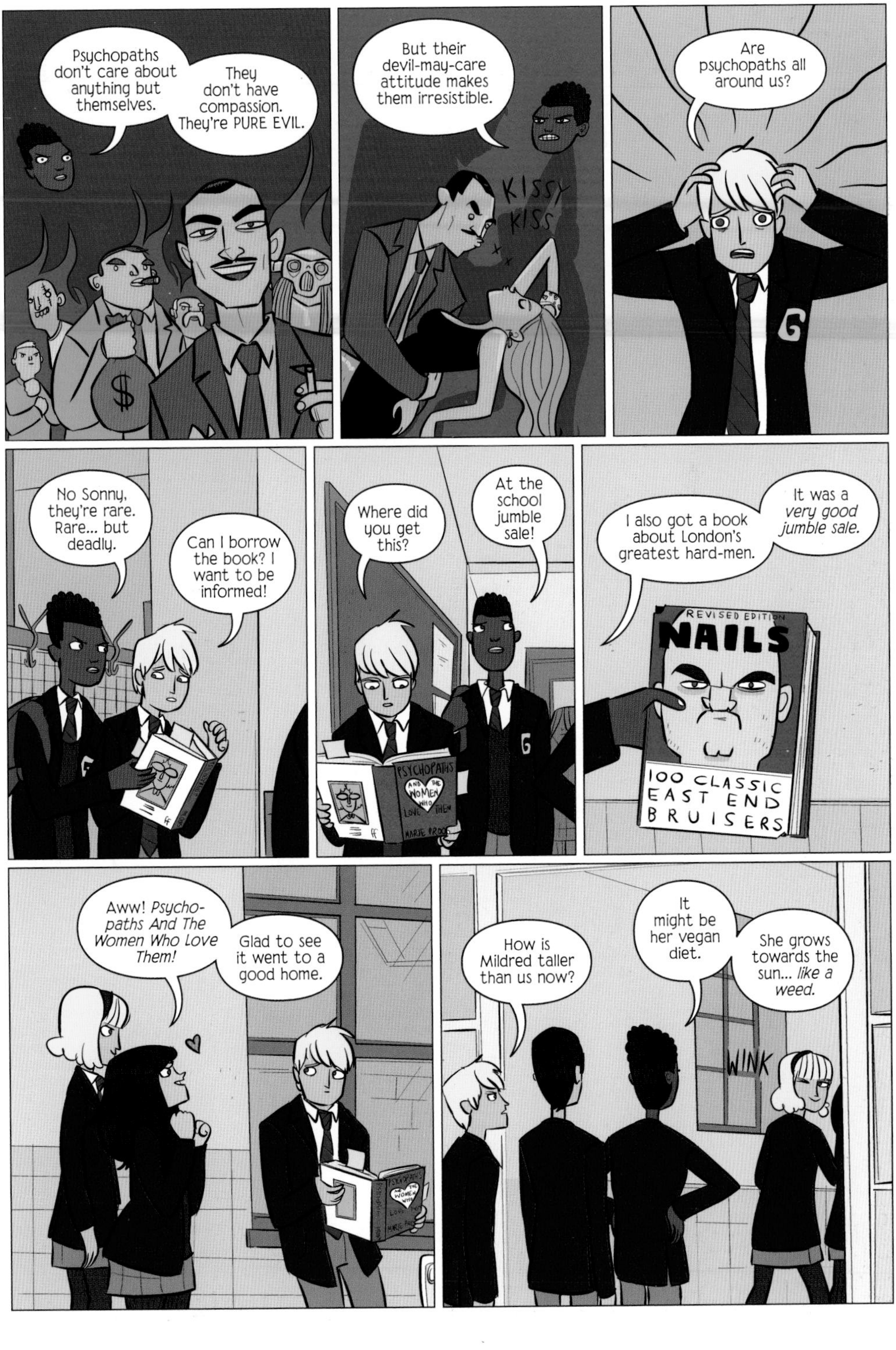

Psychopaths don't care about anything but themselves.
They don't have compassion. They're PURE EVIL.
But their devil-may-care attitude makes them irresistible.
KISSY KISS
Are psychopaths all around us?
No Sonny, they're rare. Rare... but deadly.
Can I borrow the book? I want to be informed!
Where did you get this?
At the school jumble sale!
PSYCHOPATHS AND THE WOMEN WHO LOVE THEM
I also got a book about London's greatest hard-men.
It was a *very good jumble sale.*
REVISED EDITION
NAILS
100 CLASSIC EAST END BRUISERS
Aww! *Psychopaths And The Women Who Love Them!*
Glad to see it went to a good home.
How is Mildred taller than us now?
It might be her vegan diet.
She grows towards the sun... *like a weed.*
WINK

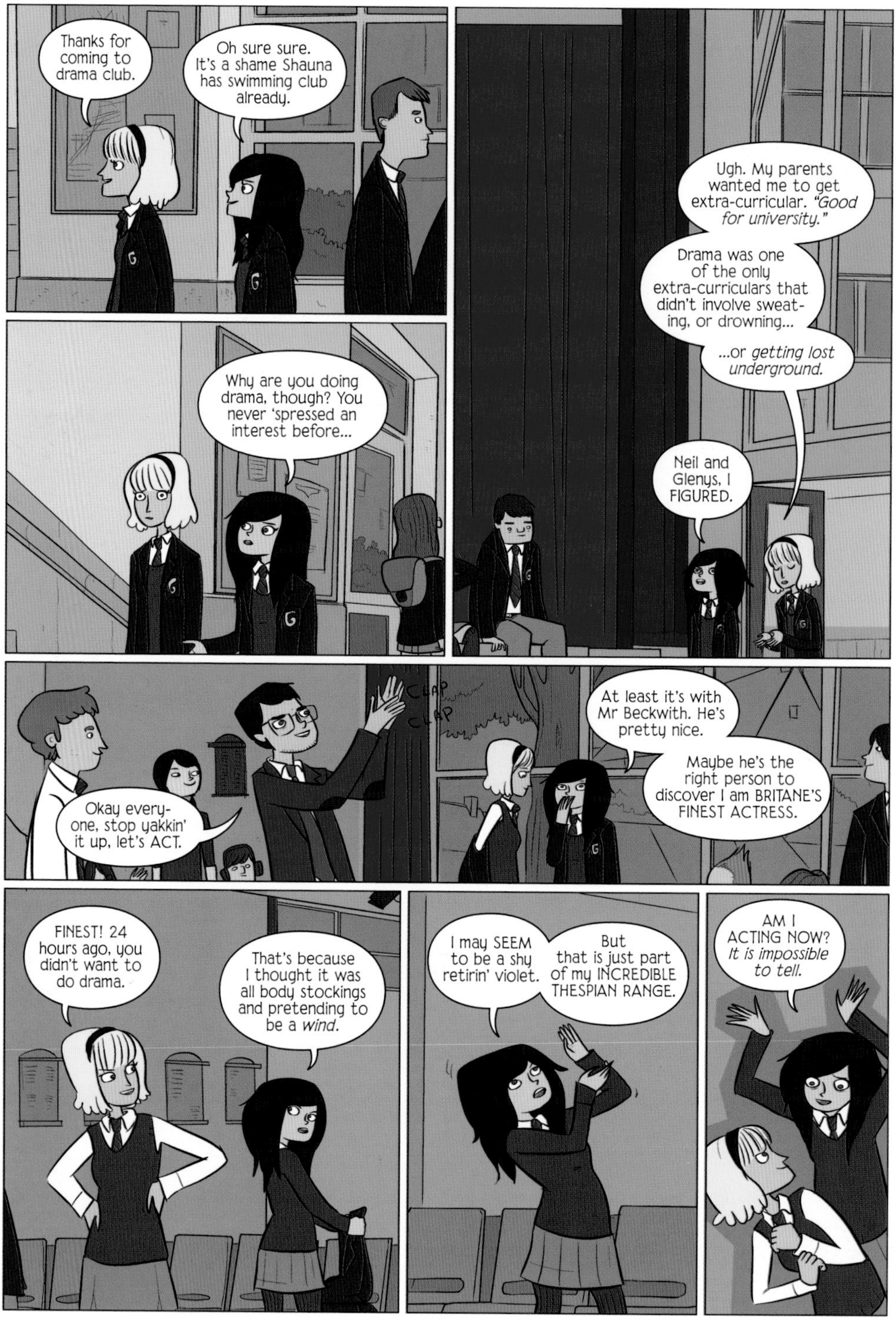
Thanks for coming to drama club.
Oh sure sure. It's a shame Shauna has swimming club already.
Why are you doing drama, though? You never 'spressed an interest before...
Ugh. My parents wanted me to get extra-curricular. *"Good for university."*
Drama was one of the only extra-curriculars that didn't involve sweat-ing, or drowning...
...or *getting lost underground.*
Neil and Glenys, I FIGURED.
CLAP CLAP
Okay every-one, stop yakkin' it up, let's ACT.
At least it's with Mr Beckwith. He's pretty nice.
Maybe he's the right person to discover I am BRITANE'S FINEST ACTRESS.
FINEST! 24 hours ago, you didn't want to do drama.
That's because I thought it was all body stockings and pretending to be a *wind.*
I may SEEM to be a shy retirin' violet.
But that is just part of my INCREDIBLE THESPIAN RANGE.
AM I ACTING NOW? *It is impossible to tell.*

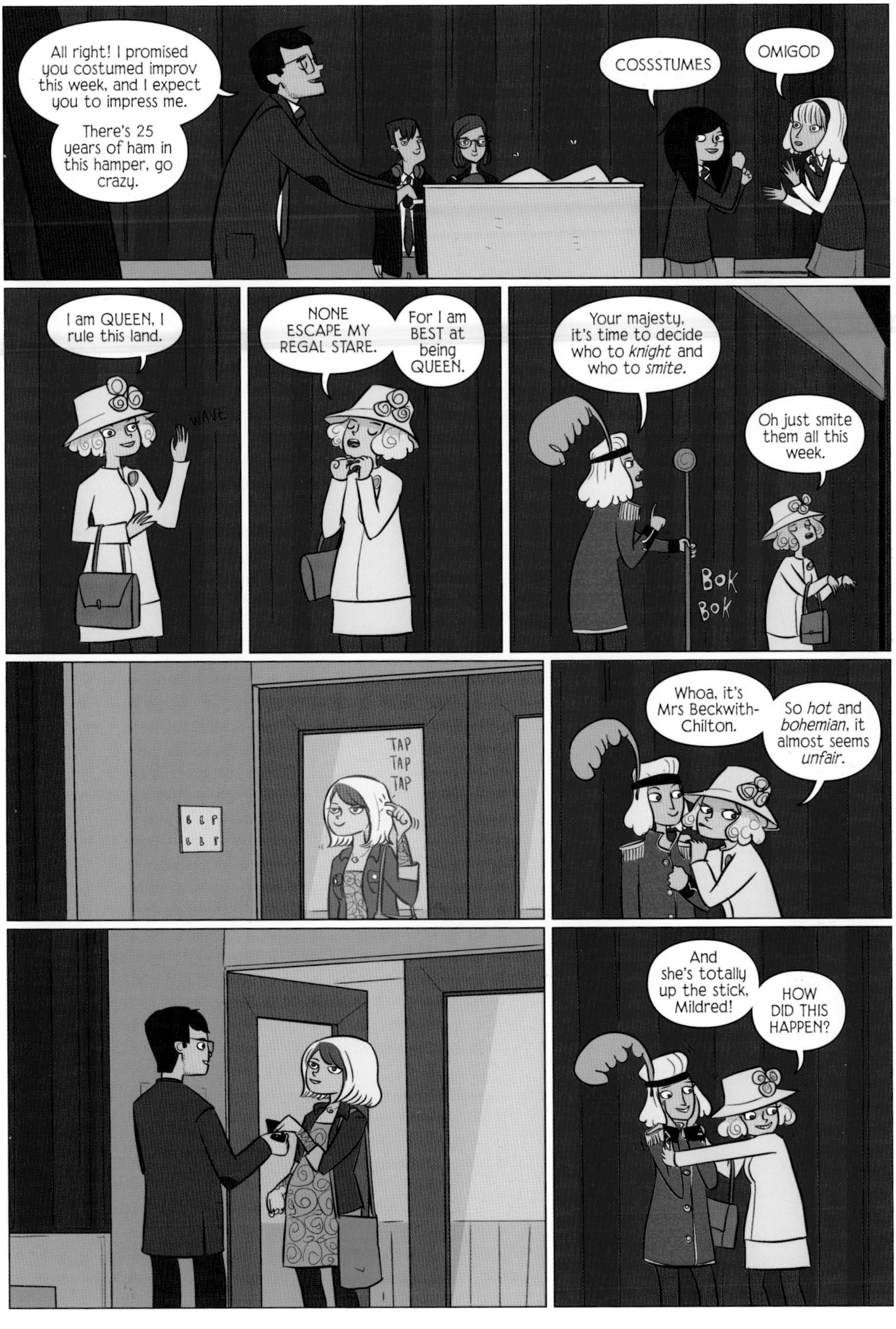
All right! I promised you costumed improv this week, and I expect you to impress me.
There's 25 years of ham in this hamper, go crazy.
COSSSTUMES
OMIGOD
I am QUEEN, I rule this land.
WAVE
NONE ESCAPE MY REGAL STARE.
For I am BEST at being QUEEN.
Your majesty, it's time to decide who to *knight* and who to *smite.*
Oh just smite them all this week.
BOK BOK
TAP TAP TAP
Whoa, it's Mrs Beckwith-Chilton.
So *hot* and *bohemian*, it almost seems *unfair*.
And she's totally up the stick, Mildred!
HOW DID THIS HAPPEN?

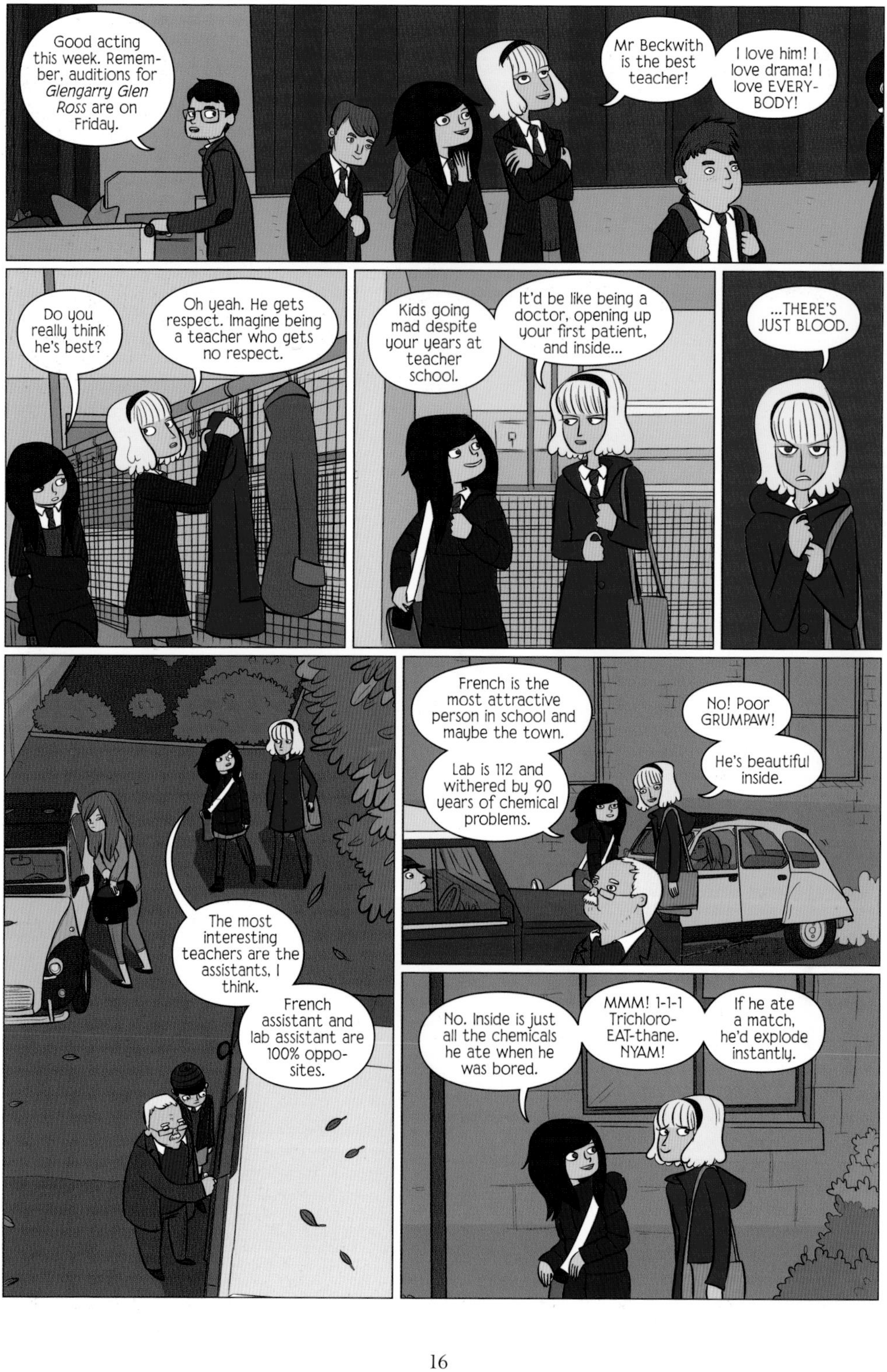
Good acting this week. Remember, auditions for *Glengarry Glen Ross* are on Friday.
Mr Beckwith is the best teacher!
I love him! I love drama! I love EVERYBODY!
Do you really think he's best?
Oh yeah. He gets respect. Imagine being a teacher who gets no respect.
Kids going mad despite your years at teacher school.
It'd be like being a doctor, opening up your first patient, and inside...
...THERE'S JUST BLOOD.
The most interesting teachers are the assistants, I think.
French assistant and lab assistant are 100% opposites.
French is the most attractive person in school and maybe the town.
Lab is 112 and withered by 90 years of chemical problems.
No! Poor GRUMPAW!
He's beautiful inside.
No. Inside is just all the chemicals he ate when he was bored.
MMM! 1-1-1 Trichloro-EAT-thane. NYAM!
If he ate a match, he'd explode instantly.

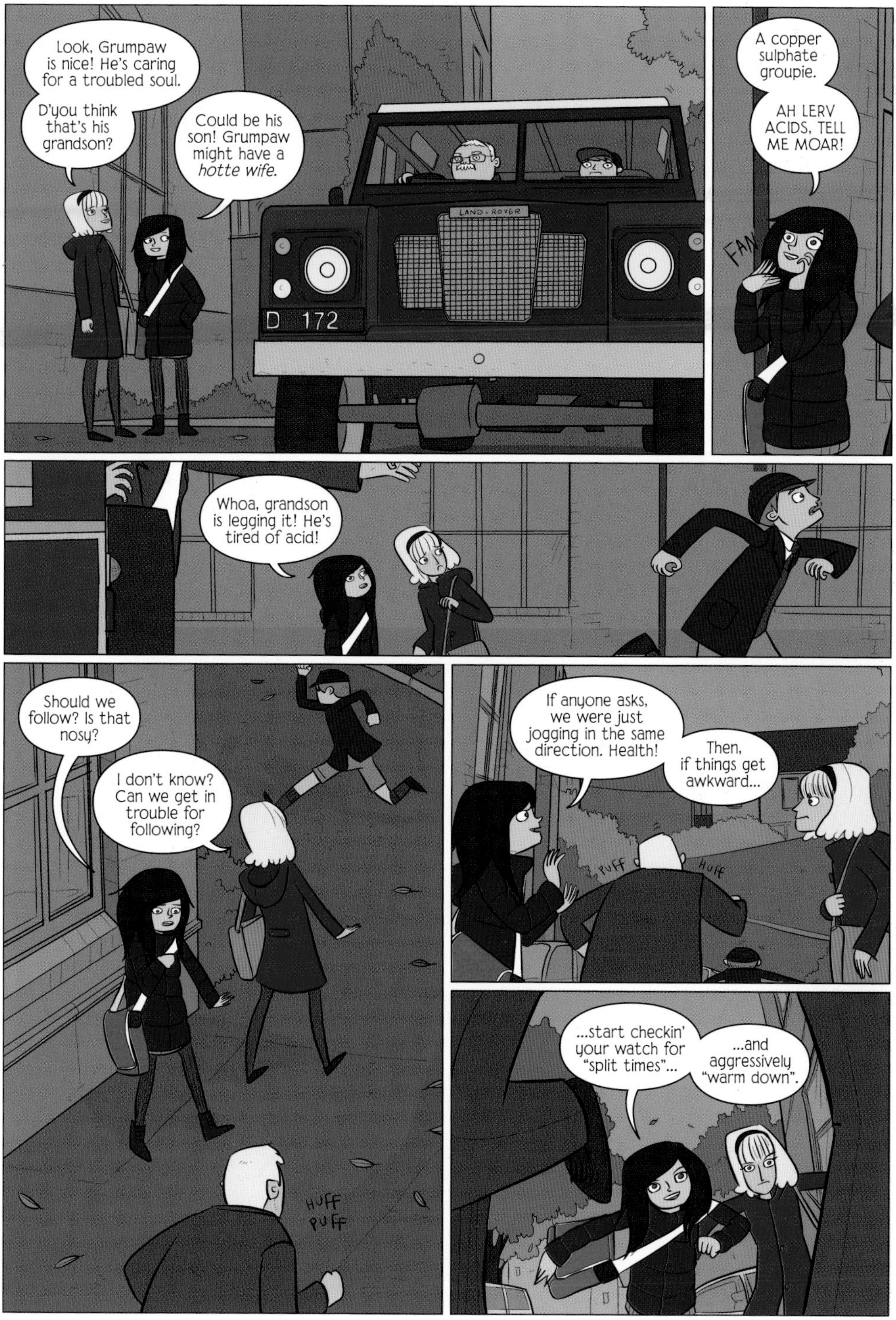
Look, Grumpaw is nice! He's caring for a troubled soul.
D'you think that's his grandson?
Could be his son! Grumpaw might have a *hotte wife.*
LAND ROVER
D 172
A copper sulphate groupie.
AH LERV ACIDS, TELL ME MOAR!
FAN
Whoa, grandson is legging it! He's tired of acid!
Should we follow? Is that nosy?
I don't know? Can we get in trouble for following?
HUFF PUFF
If anyone asks, we were just jogging in the same direction. Health!
Then, if things get awkward...
PUFF
HUFF
...start checkin' your watch for "split times"...
...and aggressively "warm down".

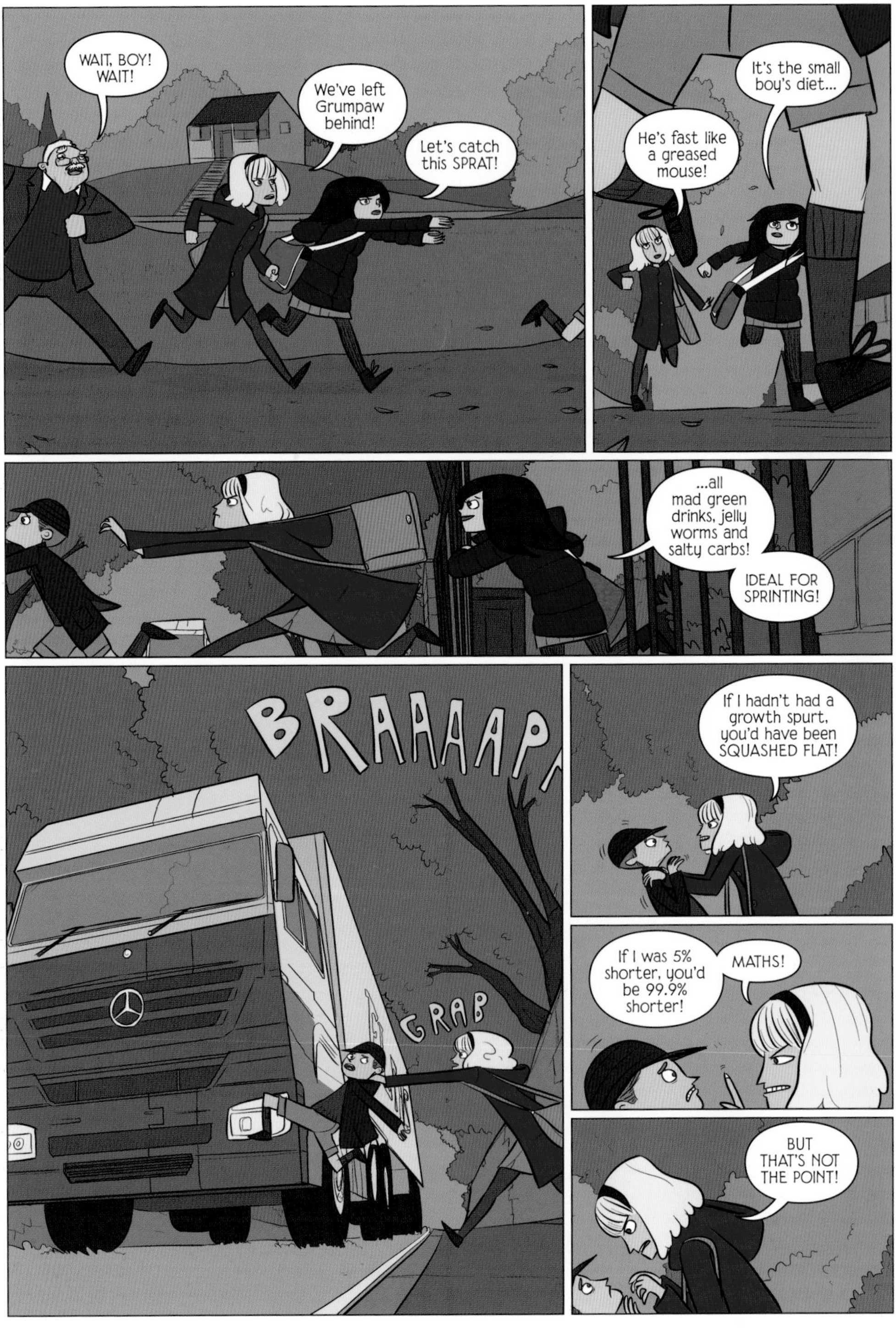
WAIT, BOY! WAIT!
We've left Grumpaw behind!
Let's catch this SPRAT!
It's the small boy's diet...
He's fast like a greased mouse!
...all mad green drinks, jelly worms and salty carbs!
IDEAL FOR SPRINTING!
BRAAAAP
GRAB
If I hadn't had a growth spurt, you'd have been SQUASHED FLAT!
If I was 5% shorter, you'd be 99.9% shorter!
MATHS!
BUT THAT'S NOT THE POINT!

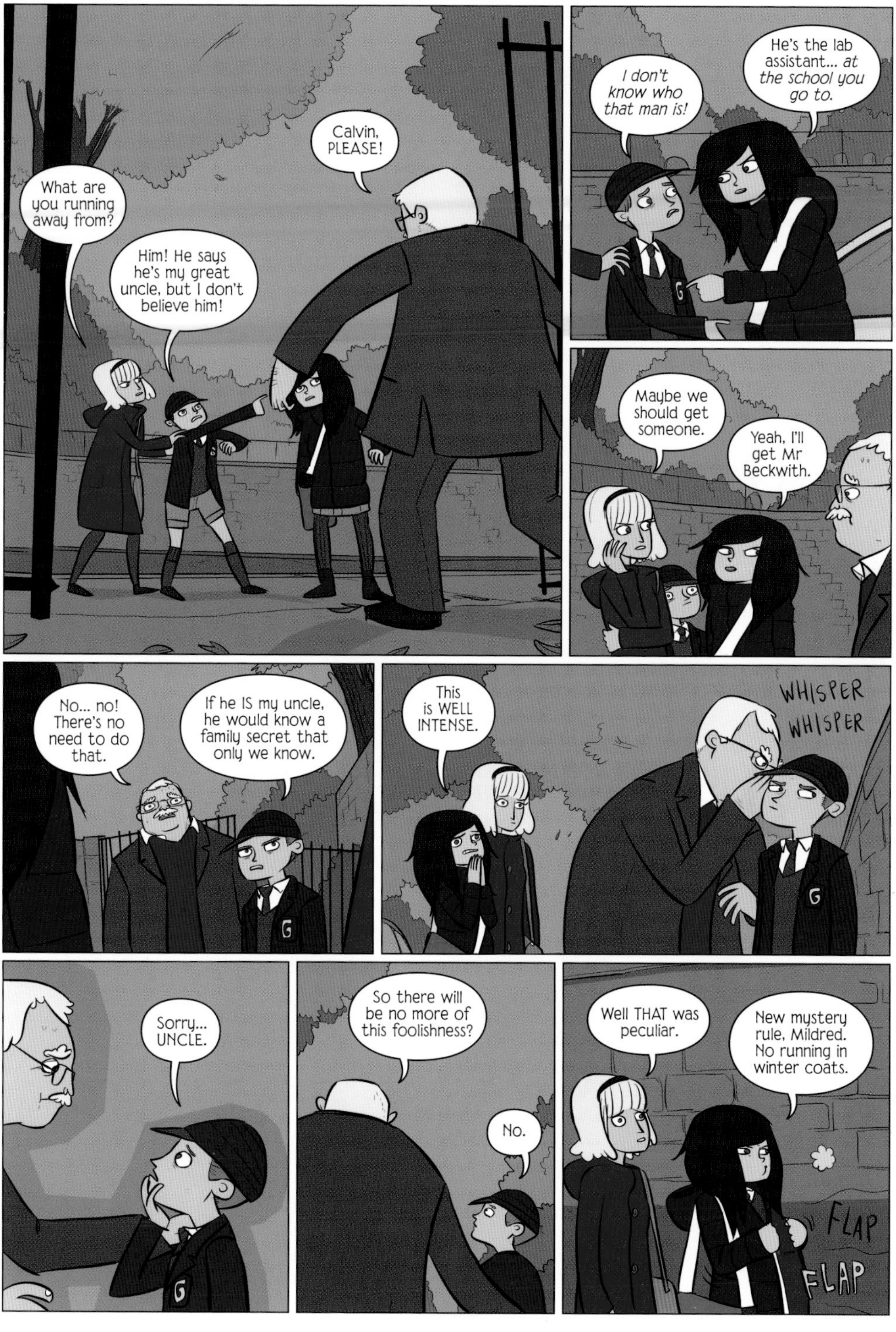
What are you running away from?
Him! He says he's my great uncle, but I don't believe him!
Calvin, PLEASE!
I don't know who that man is!
He's the lab assistant... at the school you go to.
Maybe we should get someone.
Yeah, I'll get Mr Beckwith.
No... no! There's no need to do that.
If he IS my uncle, he would know a family secret that only we know.
This is WELL INTENSE.
WHISPER
WHISPER
Sorry... UNCLE.
So there will be no more of this foolishness?
No.
Well THAT was peculiar.
New mystery rule, Mildred. No running in winter coats.
FLAP
FLAP

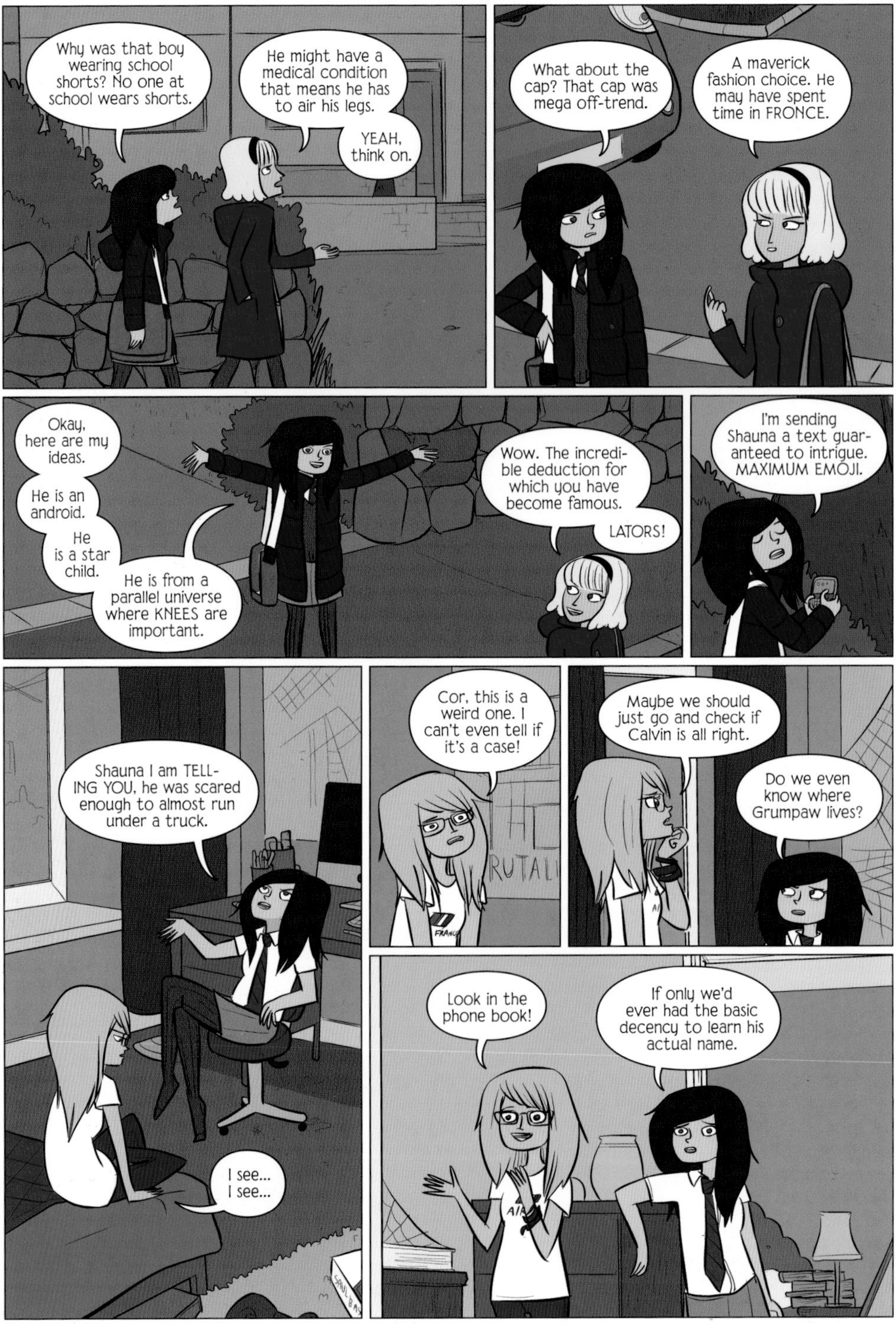
Why was that boy wearing school shorts? No one at school wears shorts.
He might have a medical condition that means he has to air his legs.
YEAH, think on.
What about the cap? That cap was mega off-trend.
A maverick fashion choice. He may have spent time in FRONCE.
Okay, here are my ideas.
He is an android.
He is a star child.
He is from a parallel universe where KNEES are important.
Wow. The incredible deduction for which you have become famous.
LATORS!
I'm sending Shauna a text guaranteed to intrigue. MAXIMUM EMOJI.
Shauna I am TELLING YOU, he was scared enough to almost run under a truck.
I see... I see...
Cor, this is a weird one. I can't even tell if it's a case!
Maybe we should just go and check if Calvin is all right.
Do we even know where Grumpaw lives?
Look in the phone book!
If only we'd ever had the basic decency to learn his actual name.

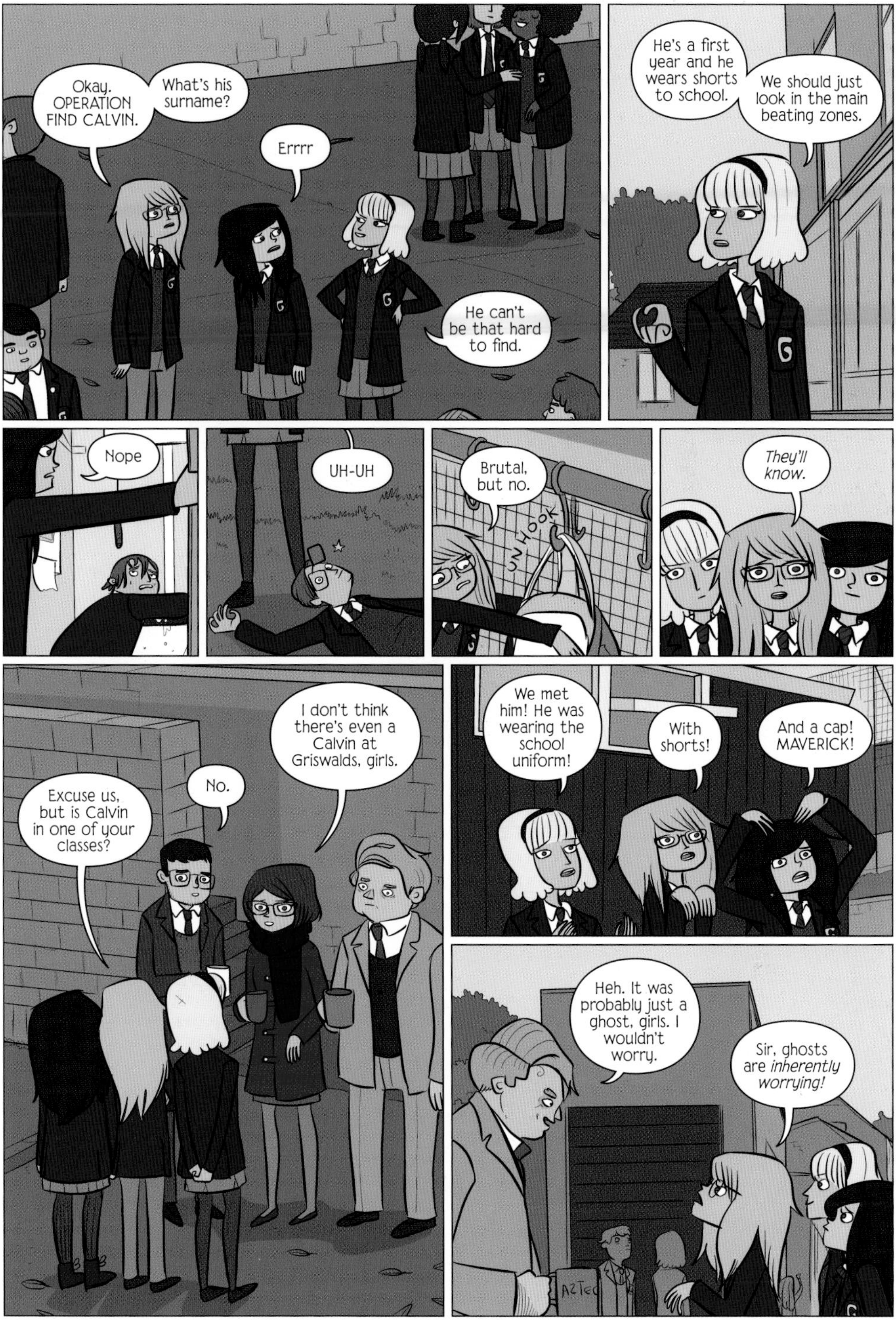
Okay. OPERATION FIND CALVIN.
What's his surname?
Errrr
He can't be that hard to find.
He's a first year and he wears shorts to school.
We should just look in the main beating zones.
Nope
UH-UH
Brutal, but no.
UNHOOK
They'll know.
Excuse us, but is Calvin in one of your classes?
No.
I don't think there's even a Calvin at Griswalds, girls.
We met him! He was wearing the school uniform!
With shorts!
And a cap! MAVERICK!
Heh. It was probably just a ghost, girls. I wouldn't worry.
Sir, ghosts are inherently worrying!

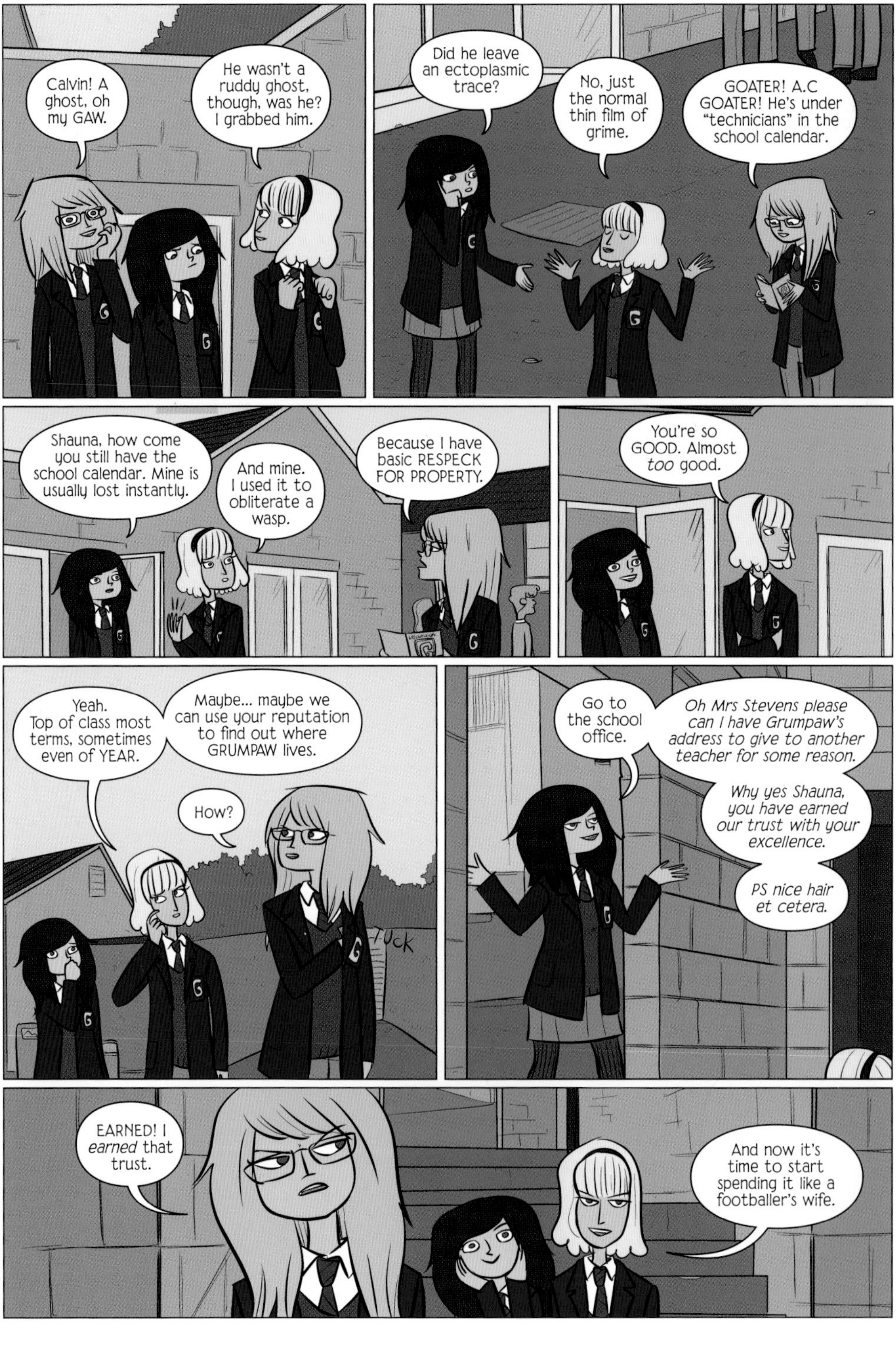
Calvin! A ghost, oh my GAW.
He wasn't a ruddy ghost, though, was he? I grabbed him.
Did he leave an ectoplasmic trace?
No, just the normal thin film of grime.
GOATER! A.C GOATER! He's under "technicians" in the school calendar.
Shauna, how come you still have the school calendar. Mine is usually lost instantly.
And mine. I used it to obliterate a wasp.
Because I have basic RESPECK FOR PROPERTY.
You're so GOOD. Almost *too* good.
Yeah. Top of class most terms, sometimes even of YEAR.
Maybe... maybe we can use your reputation to find out where GRUMPAW lives.
How?
Go to the school office.
Oh Mrs Stevens please can I have Grumpaw's address to give to another teacher for some reason.
Why yes Shauna, you have earned our trust with your excellence.
PS nice hair et cetera.
EARNED! I *earned* that trust.
And now it's time to start spending it like a footballer's wife.

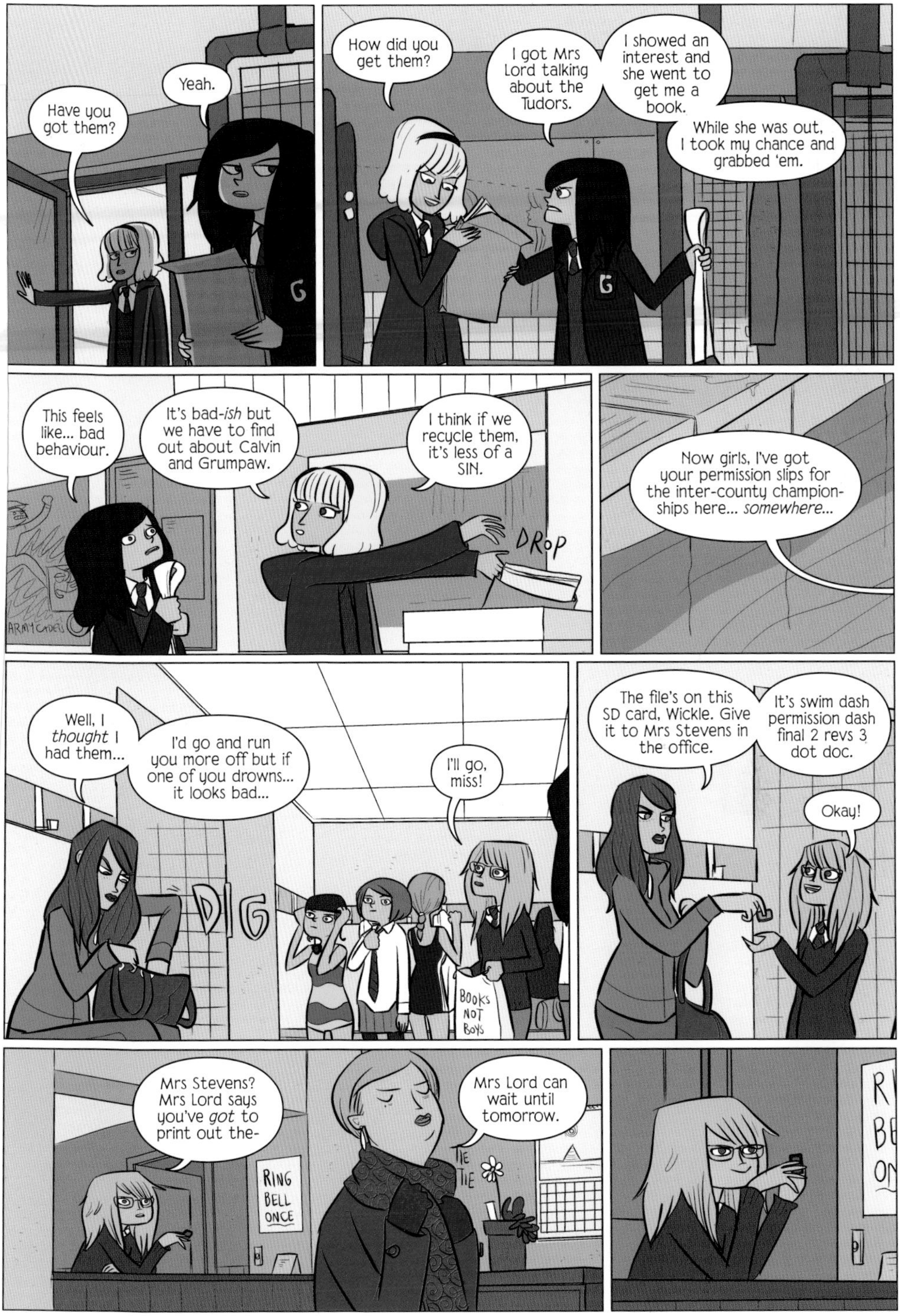
Have you got them?
Yeah.
How did you get them?
I got Mrs Lord talking about the Tudors.
I showed an interest and she went to get me a book.
While she was out, I took my chance and grabbed 'em.
This feels like... bad behaviour.
It's bad-*ish* but we have to find out about Calvin and Grumpaw.
I think if we recycle them, it's less of a SIN.
DROP
ARMY CADETS
Now girls, I've got your permission slips for the inter-county championships here... *somewhere*...
Well, I *thought* I had them...
I'd go and run you more off but if one of you drowns... it looks bad...
DIG
I'll go, miss!
BOOKS NOT BOYS
The file's on this SD card, Wickle. Give it to Mrs Stevens in the office.
It's swim dash permission dash final 2 revs 3 dot doc.
Okay!
Mrs Stevens? Mrs Lord says you've *got* to print out the-
Mrs Lord can wait until tomorrow.
RING BELL ONCE
TIE TIE

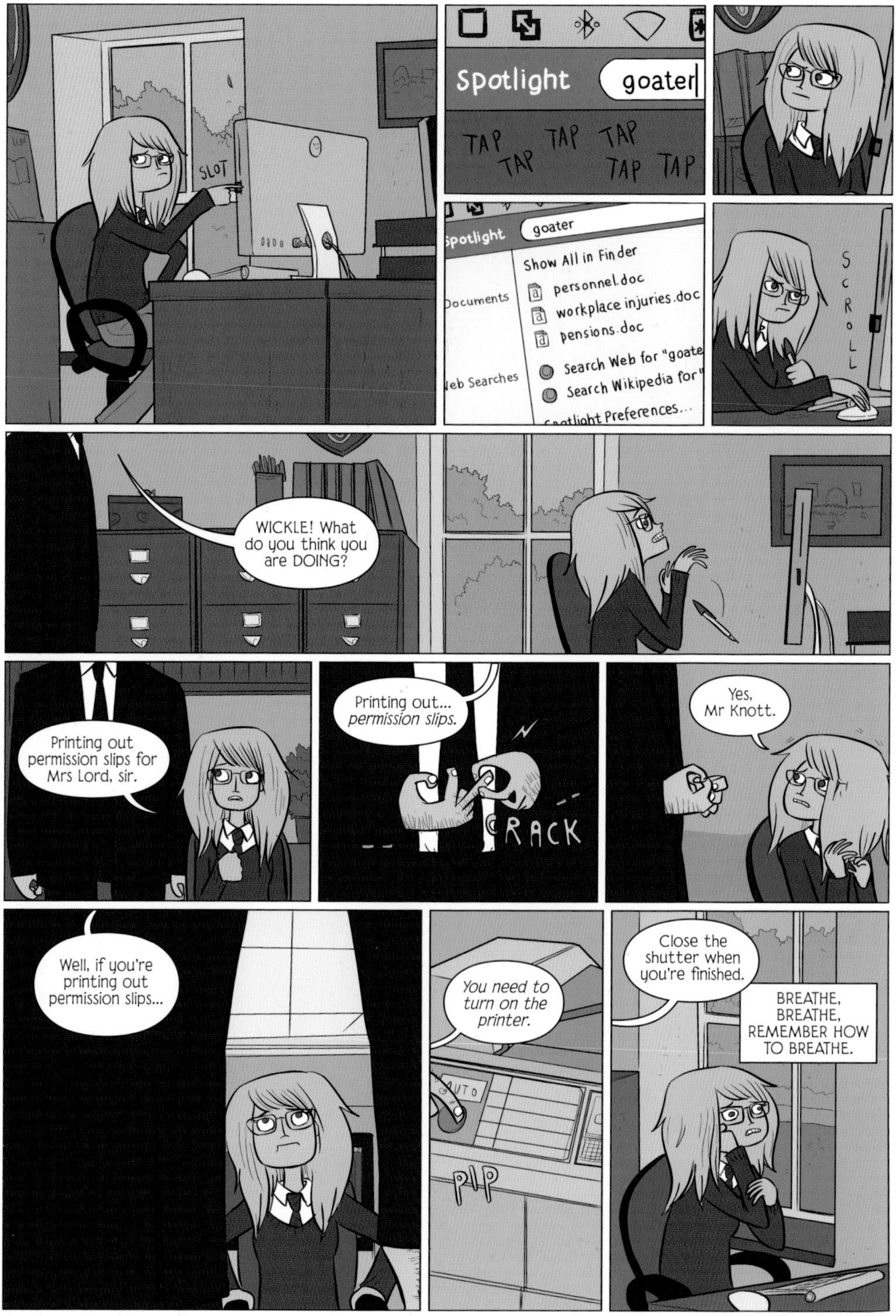
SLOT
Spotlight goater
TAP TAP TAP TAP TAP TAP
Spotlight goater
Show All in Finder
Documents
personnel.doc
workplace injuries.doc
pensions.doc
Web Searches
Search Web for "goate
Search Wikipedia for "
Spotlight Preferences...
SCROLL
WICKLE! What do you think you are DOING?
Printing out permission slips for Mrs Lord, sir.
Printing out... *permission slips.*
CRACK
Yes, Mr Knott.
Well, if you're printing out permission slips...
You need to turn on the printer.
AUTO
PIP
Close the shutter when you're finished.
BREATHE, BREATHE, REMEMBER HOW TO BREATHE.

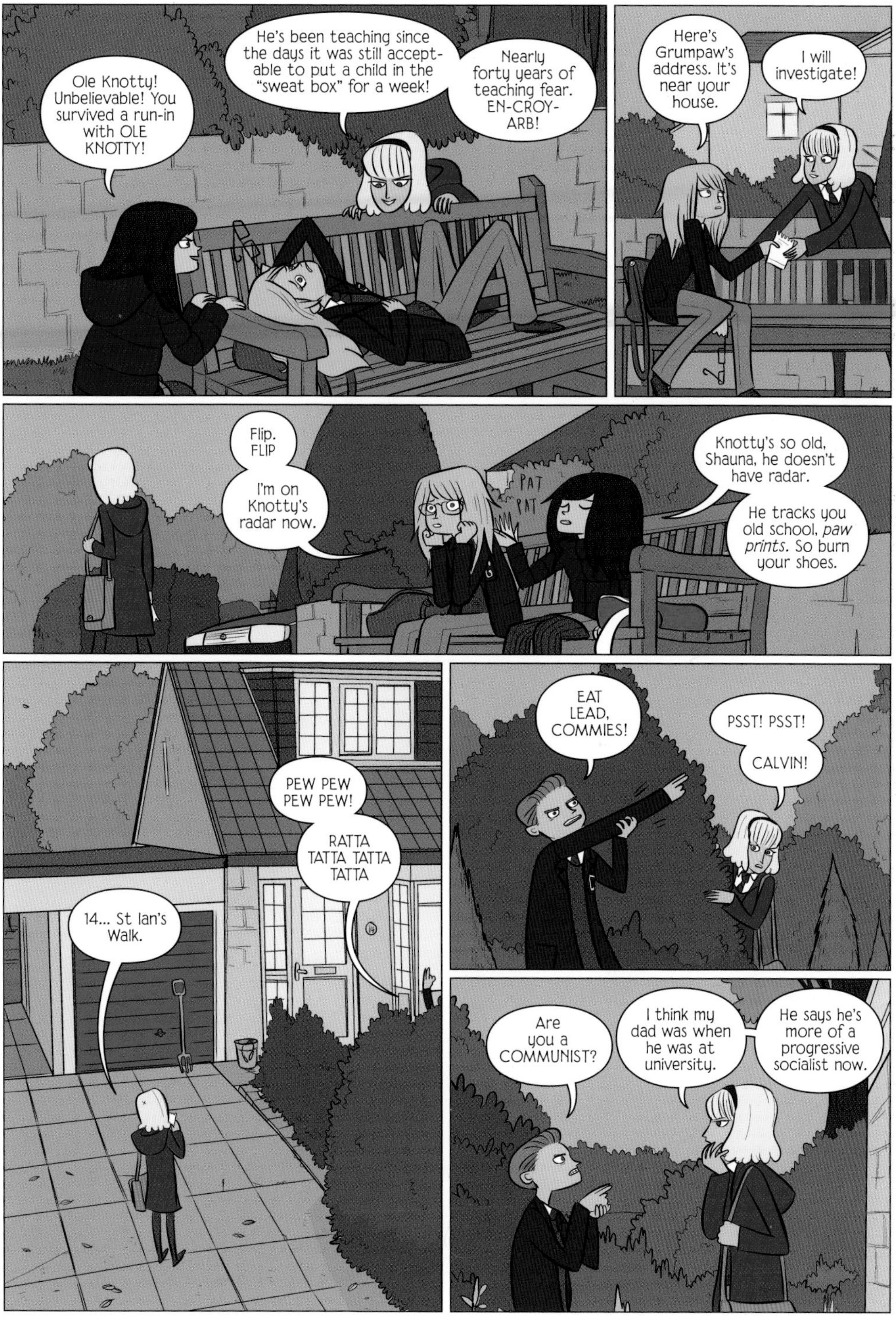
Ole Knotty! Unbelievable! You survived a run-in with OLE KNOTTY!
He's been teaching since the days it was still acceptable to put a child in the "sweat box" for a week!
Nearly forty years of teaching fear. EN-CROY-ARB!
Here's Grumpaw's address. It's near your house.
I will investigate!
Flip. FLIP
I'm on Knotty's radar now.
PAT PAT
Knotty's so old, Shauna, he doesn't have radar.
He tracks you old school, *paw prints.* So burn your shoes.
14... St Ian's Walk.
PEW PEW PEW PEW!
RATTA TATTA TATTA TATTA
EAT LEAD, COMMIES!
PSST! PSST!
CALVIN!
Are you a COMMUNIST?
I think my dad was when he was at university.
He says he's more of a progressive socialist now.

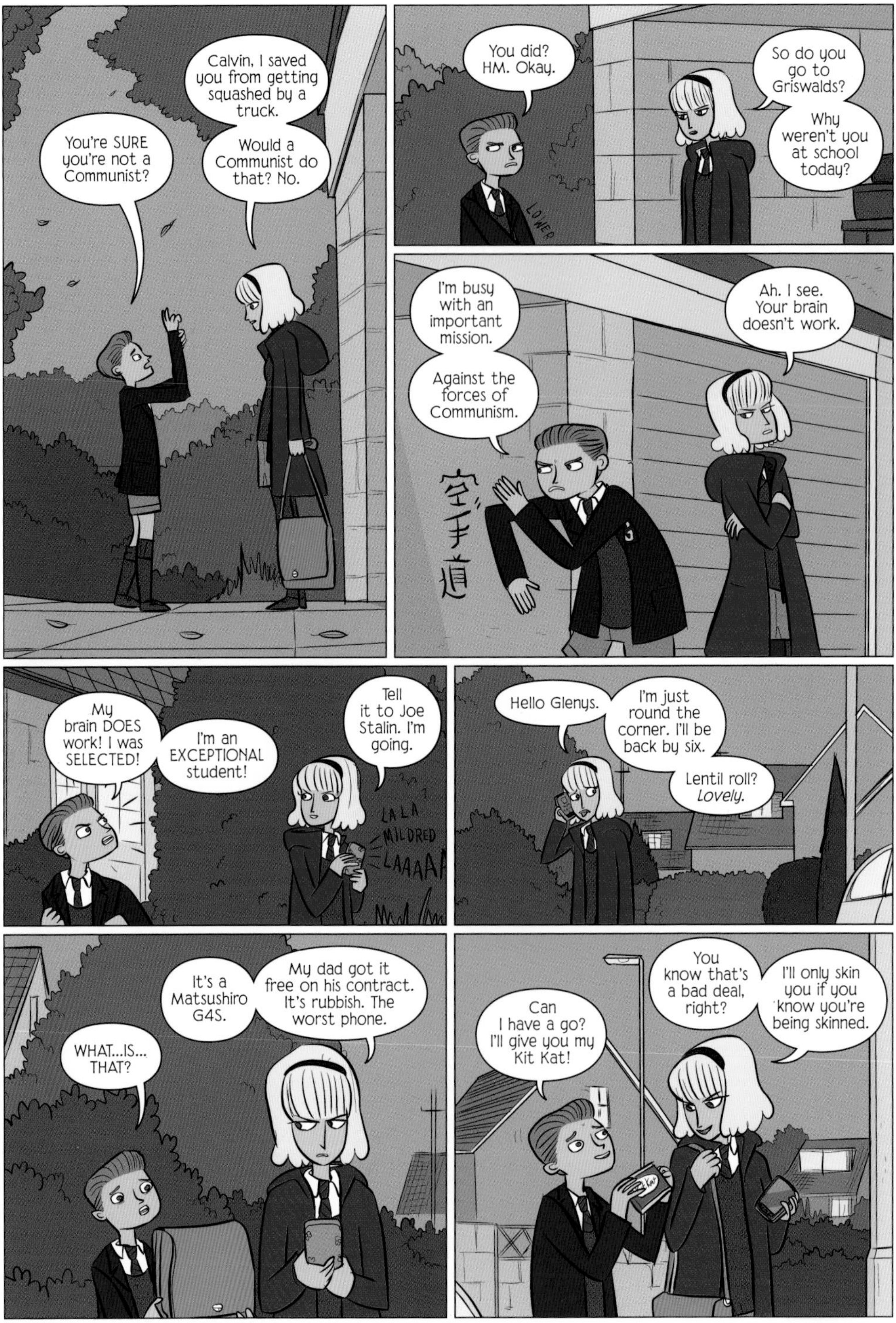
You're SURE you're not a Communist?
Calvin, I saved you from getting squashed by a truck.
Would a Communist do that? No.
You did? HM. Okay.
LOWER
So do you go to Griswalds?
Why weren't you at school today?
I'm busy with an important mission.
Against the forces of Communism.
空手道
Ah. I see. Your brain doesn't work.
My brain DOES work! I was SELECTED!
I'm an EXCEPTIONAL student!
Tell it to Joe Stalin. I'm going.
LA LA MILDRED LAAAAA
Hello Glenys.
I'm just round the corner. I'll be back by six.
Lentil roll? *Lovely.*
WHAT...IS... THAT?
It's a Matsushiro G4S.
My dad got it free on his contract. It's rubbish. The worst phone.
Can I have a go? I'll give you my Kit Kat!
You know that's a bad deal, right?
I'll only skin you if you know you're being skinned.

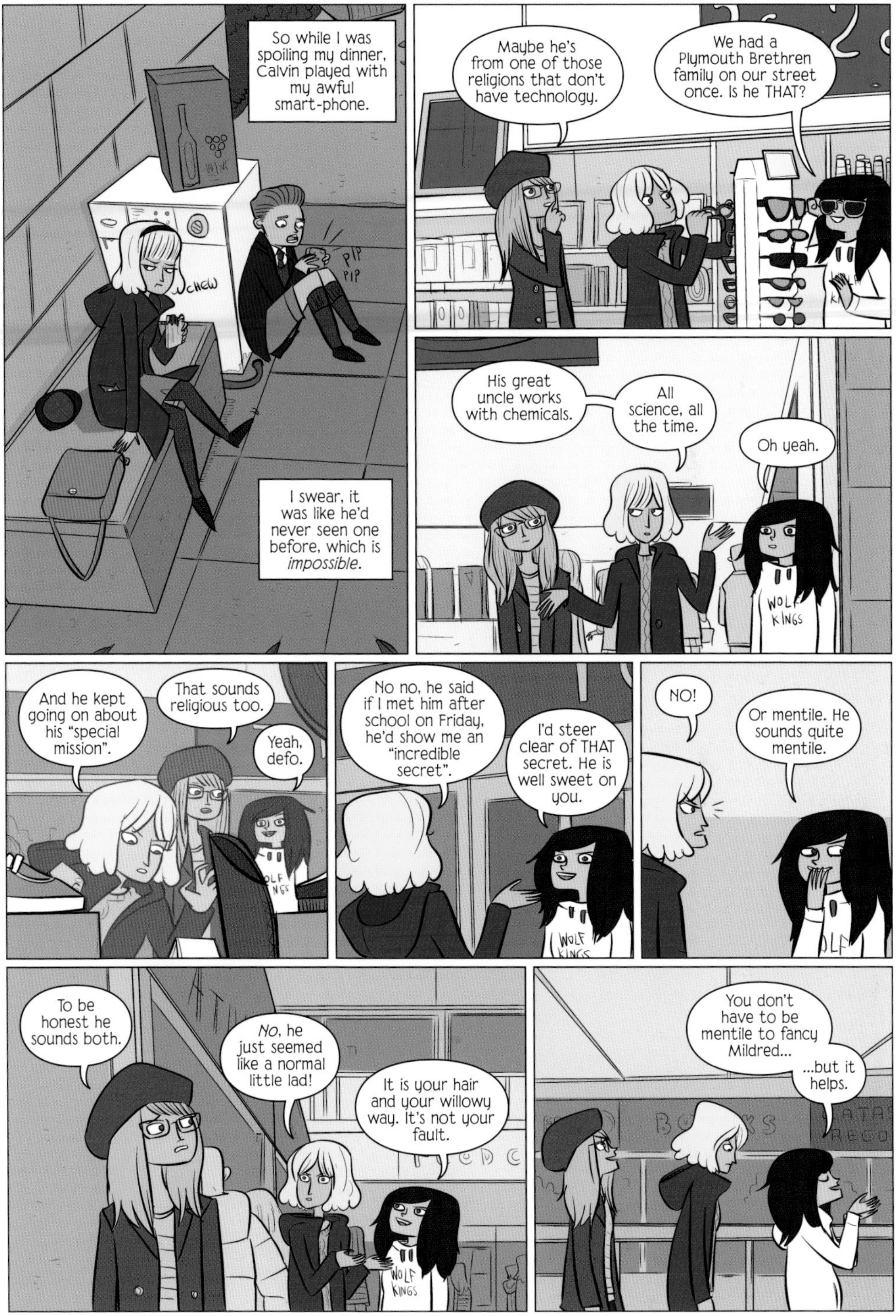
So while I was spoiling my dinner, Calvin played with my awful smart-phone.
CHEW
PIP PIP
I swear, it was like he'd never seen one before, which is *impossible*.
Maybe he's from one of those religions that don't have technology.
We had a Plymouth Brethren family on our street once. Is he THAT?
His great uncle works with chemicals.
All science, all the time.
Oh yeah.
WOLF KINGS
And he kept going on about his "special mission".
That sounds religious too.
Yeah, defo.
No no, he said if I met him after school on Friday, he'd show me an "incredible secret".
I'd steer clear of THAT secret. He is well sweet on you.
NO!
Or mentile. He sounds quite mentile.
To be honest he sounds both.
No, he just seemed like a normal little lad!
It is your hair and your willowy way. It's not your fault.
WOLF KINGS
You don't have to be mentile to fancy Mildred...
...but it helps.
BOOKS

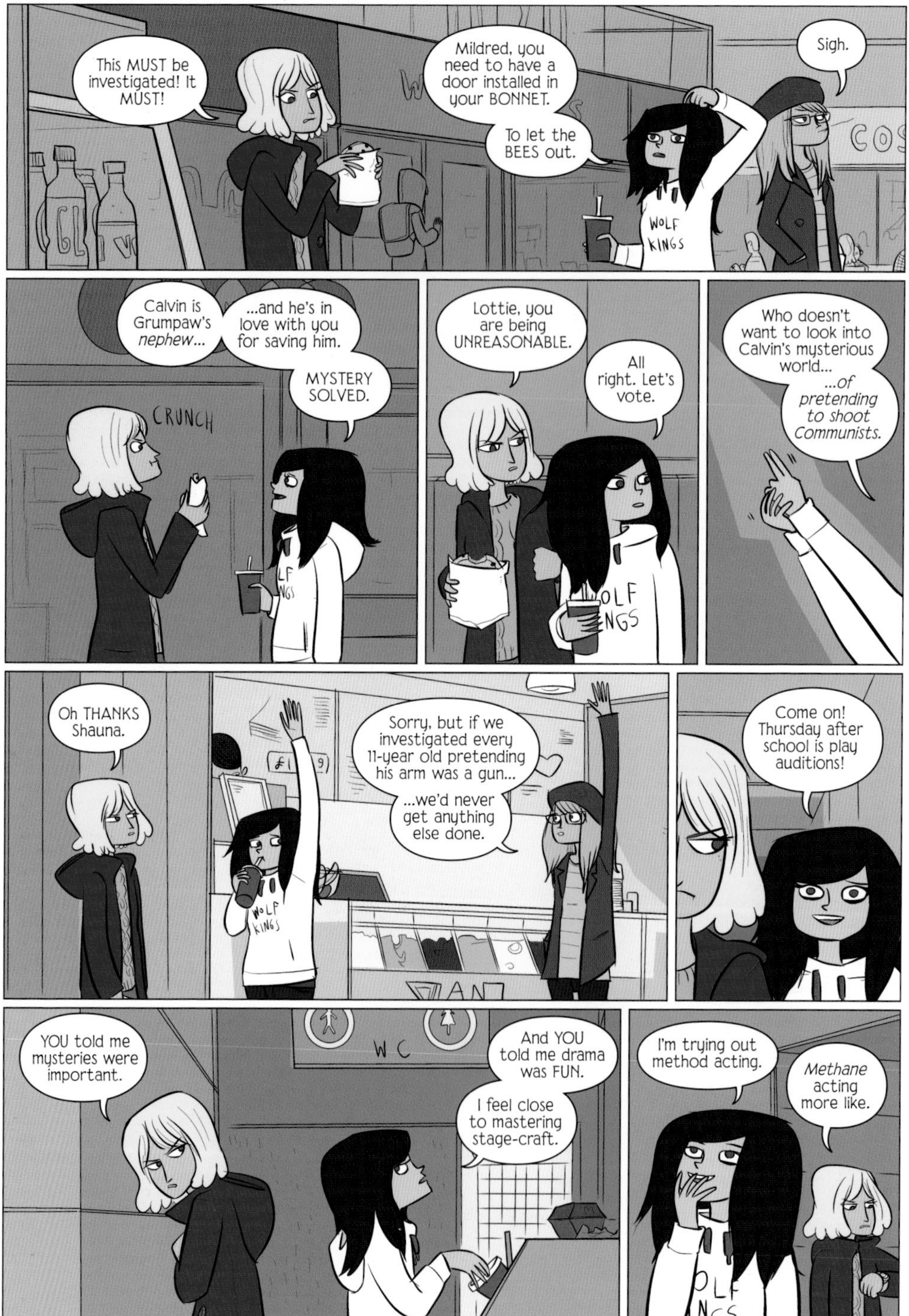
This MUST be investigated! It MUST!
Mildred, you need to have a door installed in your BONNET.
To let the BEES out.
Sigh.
Calvin is Grumpaw's *nephew*...
...and he's in love with you for saving him.
MYSTERY SOLVED.
CRUNCH
Lottie, you are being UNREASONABLE.
All right. Let's vote.
Who doesn't want to look into Calvin's mysterious world...
...*of pretending to shoot Communists.*
Oh THANKS Shauna.
Sorry, but if we investigated every 11-year old pretending his arm was a gun...
...we'd never get anything else done.
Come on! Thursday after school is play auditions!
YOU told me mysteries were important.
And YOU told me drama was FUN.
I feel close to mastering stage-craft.
I'm trying out method acting.
Methane acting more like.

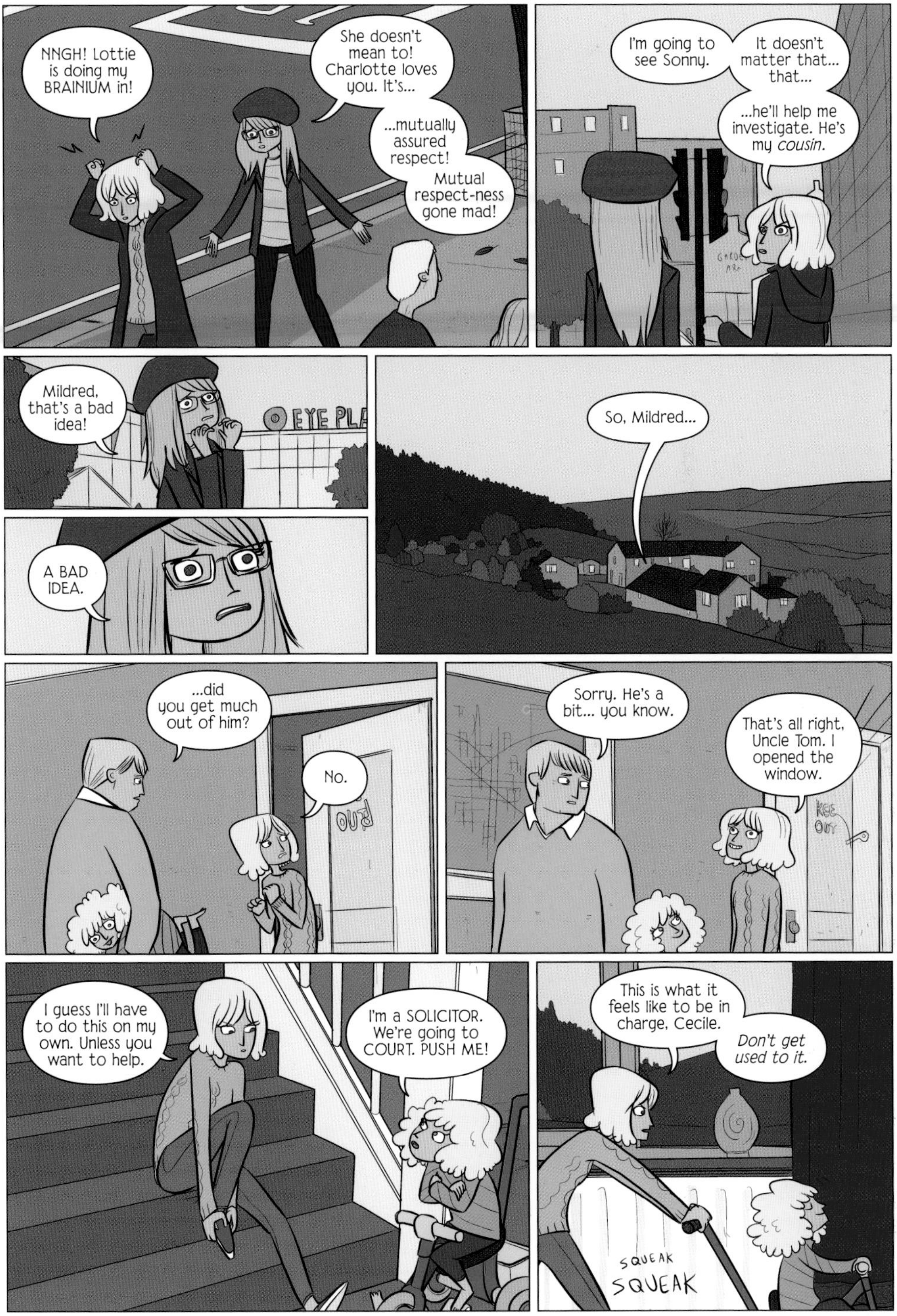
NNGH! Lottie is doing my BRAINIUM in!
She doesn't mean to! Charlotte loves you. It's...
...mutually assured respect!
Mutual respect-ness gone mad!
I'm going to see Sonny.
It doesn't matter that... that...
...he'll help me investigate. He's my *cousin*.
Mildred, that's a bad idea!
EYE PLA
A BAD IDEA.
So, Mildred...
...did you get much out of him?
No.
Sorry. He's a bit... you know.
That's all right, Uncle Tom. I opened the window.
I guess I'll have to do this on my own. Unless you want to help.
I'm a SOLICITOR. We're going to COURT. PUSH ME!
This is what it feels like to be in charge, Cecile.
Don't get used to it.
SQUEAK
SQUEAK

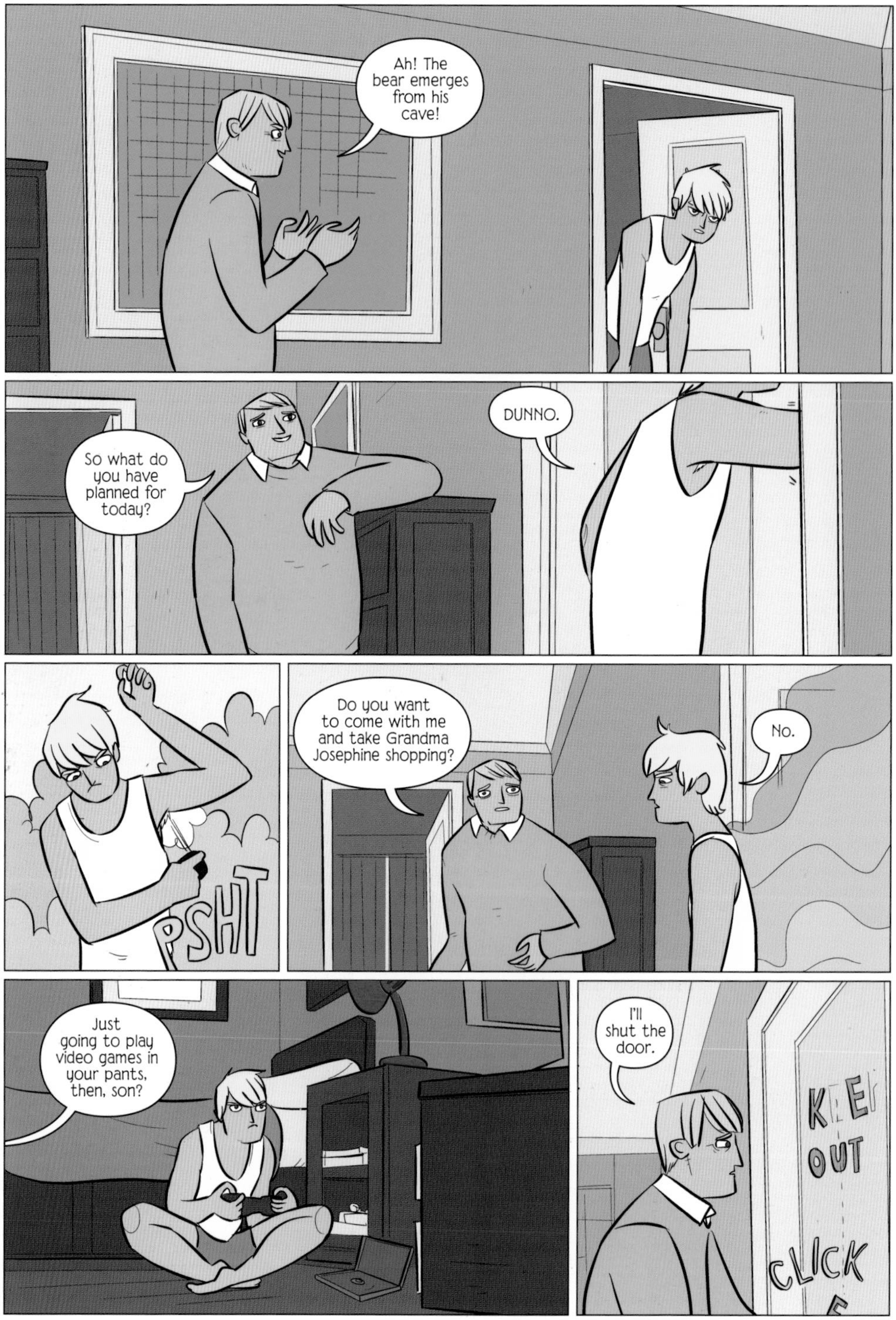
Ah! The bear emerges from his cave!
So what do you have planned for today?
DUNNO.
PSHT
Do you want to come with me and take Grandma Josephine shopping?
No.
Just going to play video games in your pants, then, son?
I'll shut the door.
OUT
CLICK

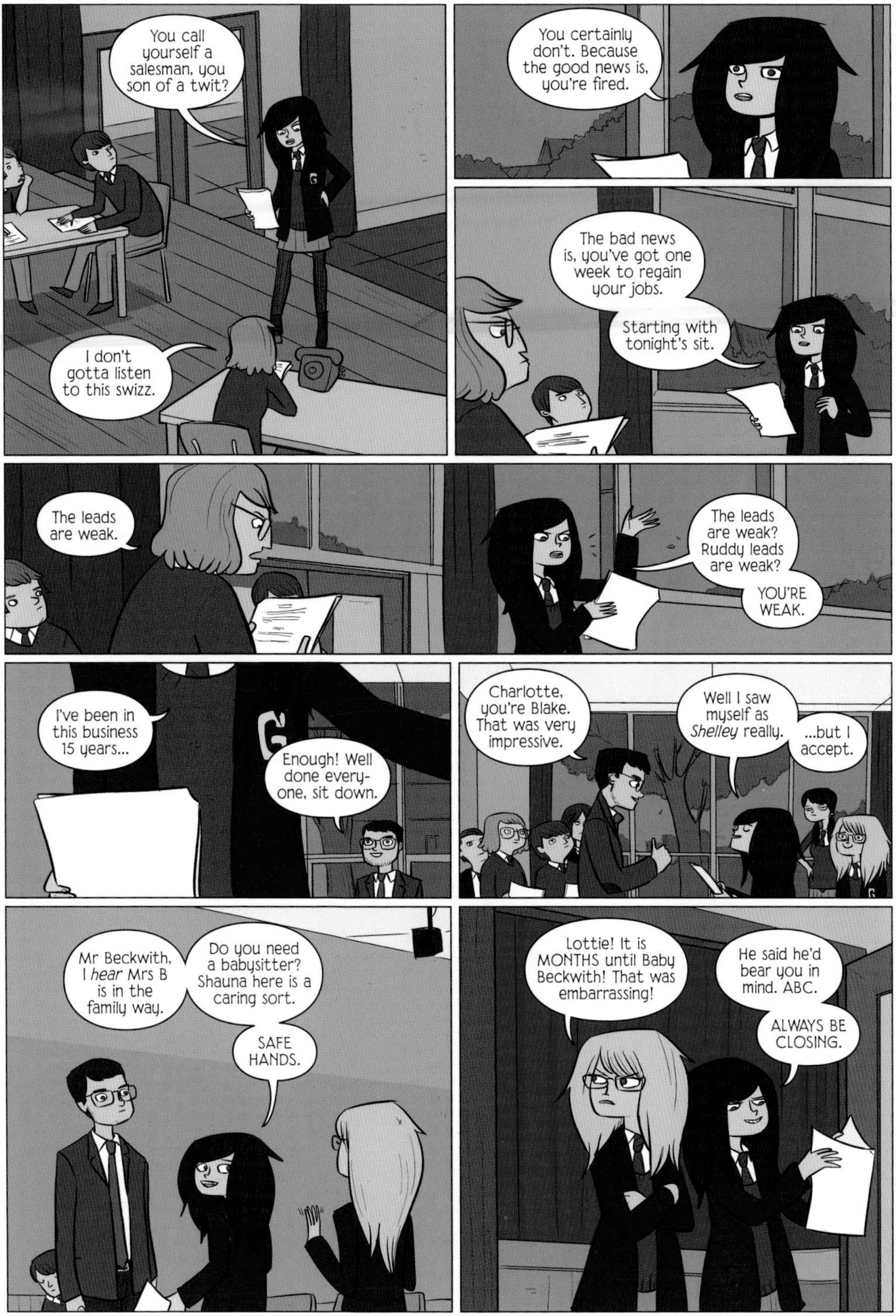
You call yourself a salesman, you son of a twit?
I don't gotta listen to this swizz.
You certainly don't. Because the good news is, you're fired.
The bad news is, you've got one week to regain your jobs.
Starting with tonight's sit.
The leads are weak.
The leads are weak? Ruddy leads are weak?
YOU'RE WEAK.
I've been in this business 15 years...
Enough! Well done every-one, sit down.
Charlotte, you're Blake. That was very impressive.
Well I saw myself as *Shelley* really.
...but I accept.
Mr Beckwith, I *hear* Mrs B is in the family way.
Do you need a babysitter? Shauna here is a caring sort.
SAFE HANDS.
Lottie! It is MONTHS until Baby Beckwith! That was embarrassing!
He said he'd bear you in mind. ABC.
ALWAYS BE CLOSING.

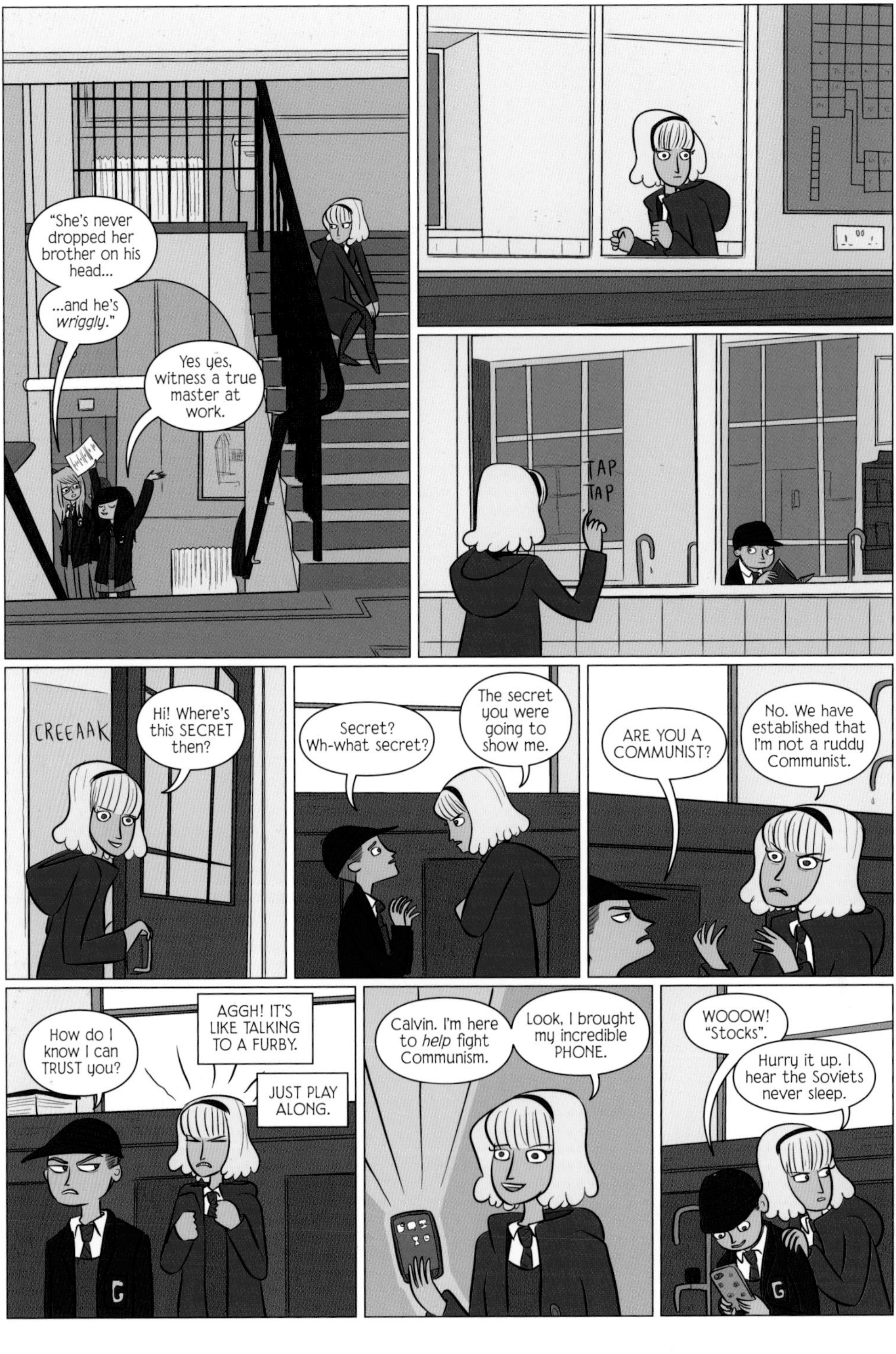
"She's never dropped her brother on his head...
...and he's *wriggly*."
Yes yes, witness a true master at work.
TAP TAP
CREEAAK
Hi! Where's this SECRET then?
Secret? Wh-what secret?
The secret you were going to show me.
ARE YOU A COMMUNIST?
No. We have established that I'm not a ruddy Communist.
How do I know I can TRUST you?
AGGH! IT'S LIKE TALKING TO A FURBY.
JUST PLAY ALONG.
Calvin. I'm here to *help* fight Communism.
Look, I brought my incredible PHONE.
WOOOW! "Stocks".
Hurry it up. I hear the Soviets never sleep.

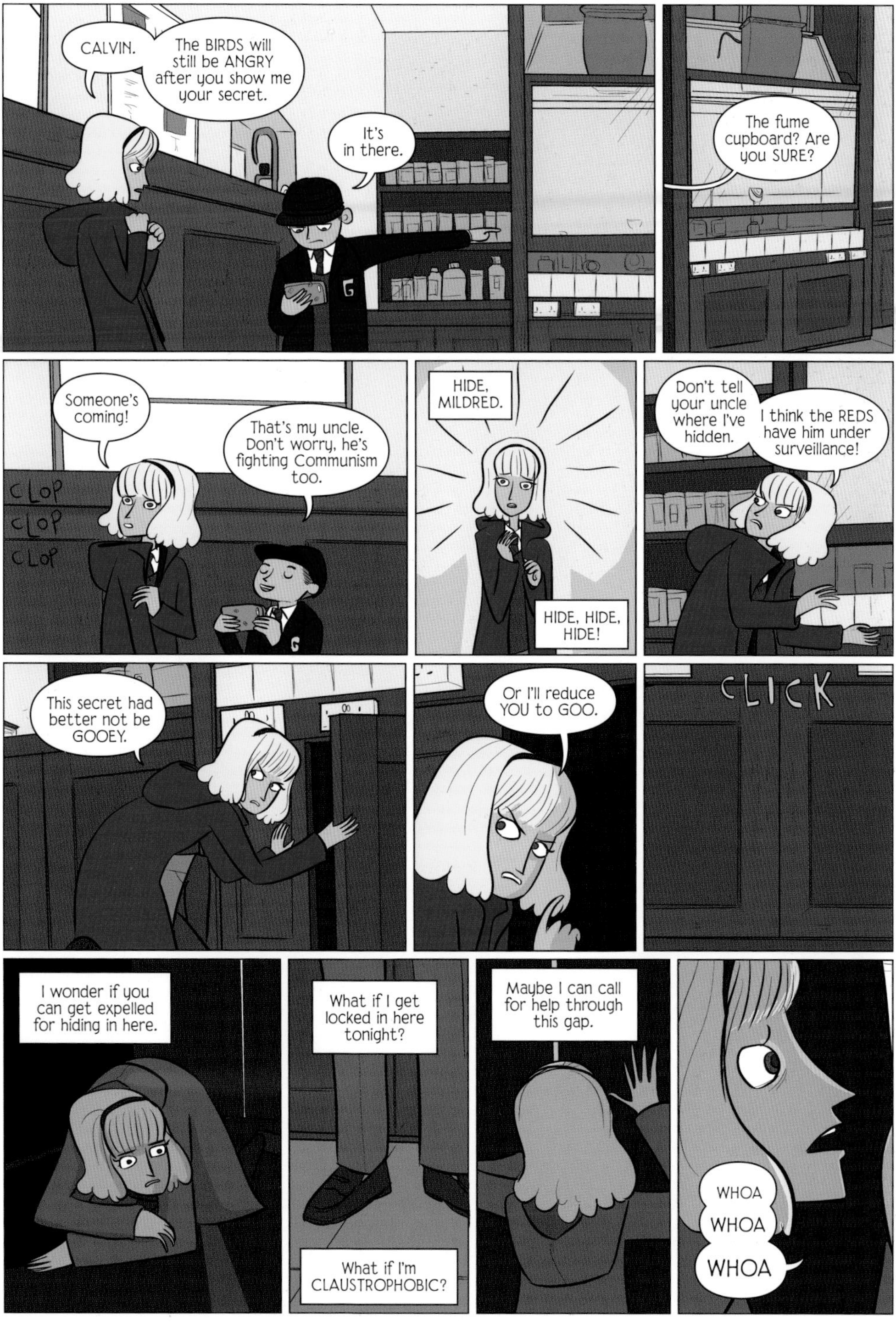
CALVIN.
The BIRDS will still be ANGRY after you show me your secret.
It's in there.
The fume cupboard? Are you SURE?
Someone's coming!
CLOP CLOP CLOP
That's my uncle. Don't worry, he's fighting Communism too.
HIDE, MILDRED.
HIDE, HIDE, HIDE!
Don't tell your uncle where I've hidden.
I think the REDS have him under surveillance!
This secret had better not be GOOEY.
Or I'll reduce YOU to GOO.
CLICK
I wonder if you can get expelled for hiding in here.
What if I get locked in here tonight?
What if I'm CLAUSTROPHOBIC?
Maybe I can call for help through this gap.
WHOA
WHOA
WHOA

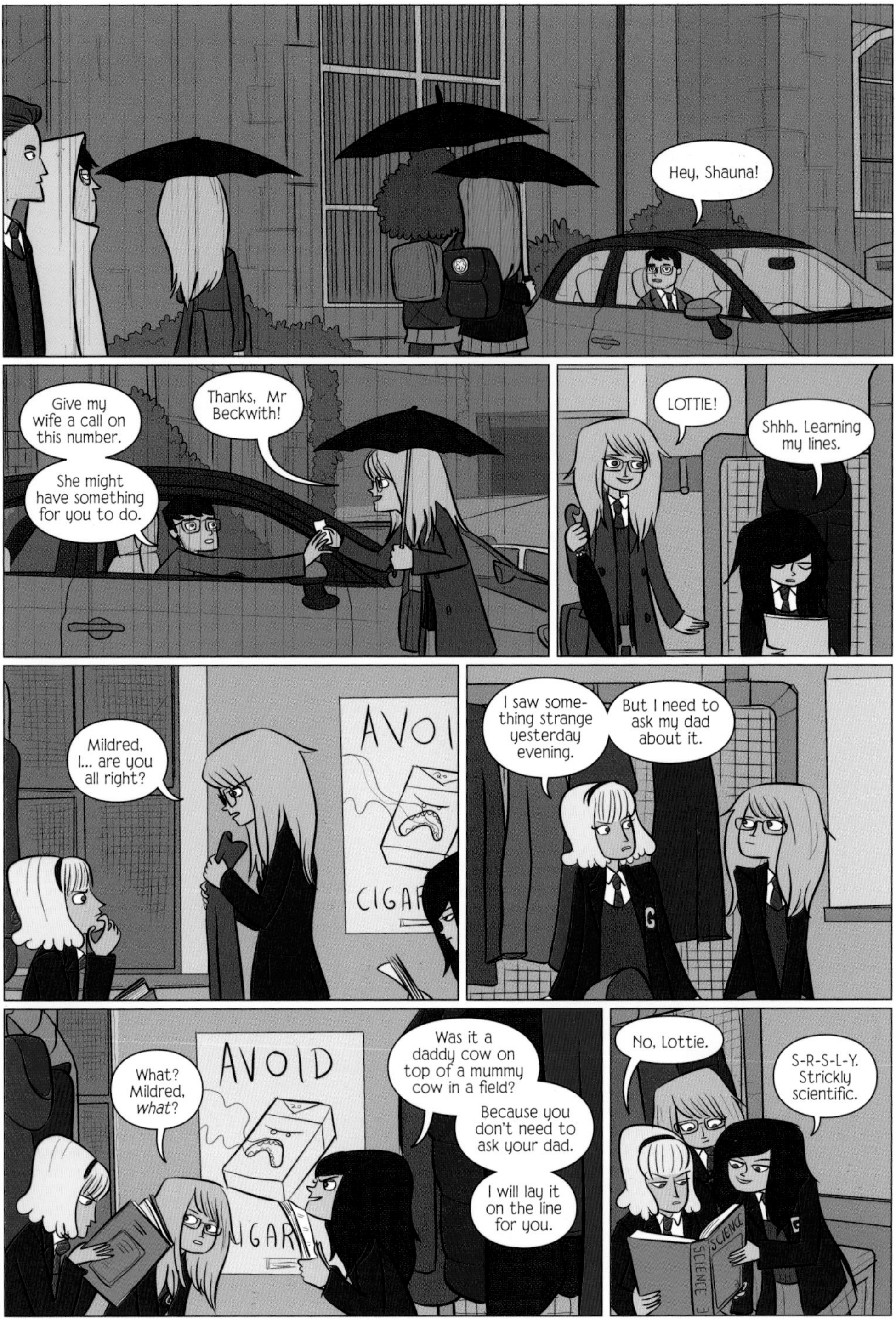
Hey, Shauna!
Give my wife a call on this number.
She might have something for you to do.
Thanks, Mr Beckwith!
LOTTIE!
Shhh. Learning my lines.
Mildred, I... are you all right?
AVOI
CIGA
I saw something strange yesterday evening.
But I need to ask my dad about it.
AVOID
GAR
What? Mildred, *what*?
Was it a daddy cow on top of a mummy cow in a field?
Because you don't need to ask your dad.
I will lay it on the line for you.
No, Lottie.
S-R-S-L-Y. Strickly scientific.
SCIENCE

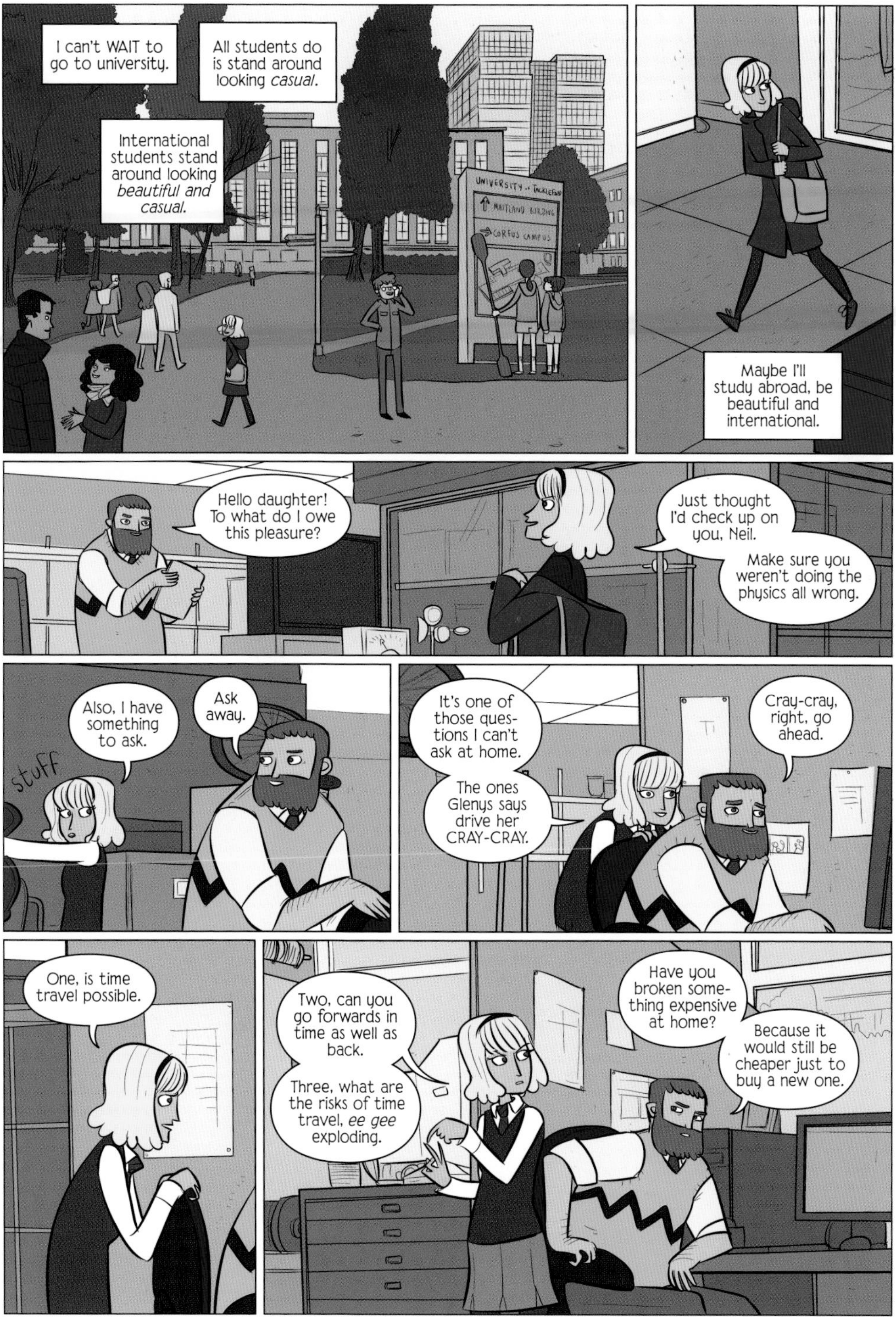
I can't WAIT to go to university.
All students do is stand around looking *casual*.
International students stand around looking *beautiful and casual*.
UNIVERSITY of TACKLEFORD
MAITLAND BUILDING
CORFUS CAMPUS
Maybe I'll study abroad, be beautiful and international.
Hello daughter! To what do I owe this pleasure?
Just thought I'd check up on you, Neil.
Make sure you weren't doing the physics all wrong.
Also, I have something to ask.
Ask away.
stuff
It's one of those questions I can't ask at home.
The ones Glenys says drive her CRAY-CRAY.
Cray-cray, right, go ahead.
One, is time travel possible.
Two, can you go forwards in time as well as back.
Three, what are the risks of time travel, *ee gee* exploding.
Have you broken something expensive at home?
Because it would still be cheaper just to buy a new one.

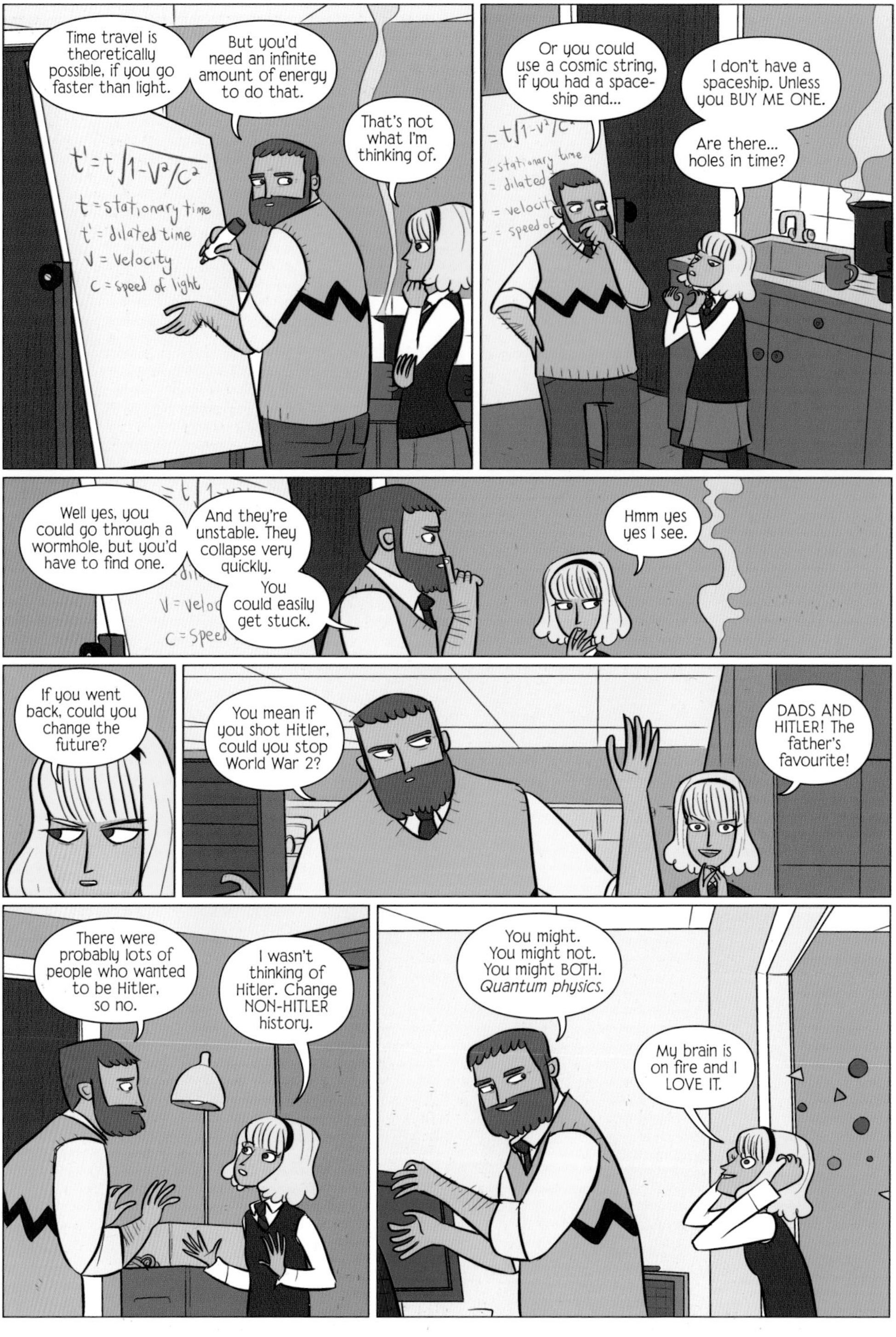
Time travel is theoretically possible, if you go faster than light.
But you'd need an infinite amount of energy to do that.
$t'=t\sqrt{1-v^2/c^2}$
t = stationary time
t' = dilated time
V = Velocity
C = speed of light
That's not what I'm thinking of.
Or you could use a cosmic string, if you had a spaceship and...
I don't have a spaceship. Unless you BUY ME ONE.
Are there... holes in time?
Well yes, you could go through a wormhole, but you'd have to find one.
And they're unstable. They collapse very quickly.
You could easily get stuck.
Hmm yes yes I see.
If you went back, could you change the future?
You mean if you shot Hitler, could you stop World War 2?
DADS AND HITLER! The father's favourite!
There were probably lots of people who wanted to be Hitler, so no.
I wasn't thinking of Hitler. Change NON-HITLER history.
You might. You might not. You might BOTH. *Quantum physics.*
My brain is on fire and I LOVE IT.

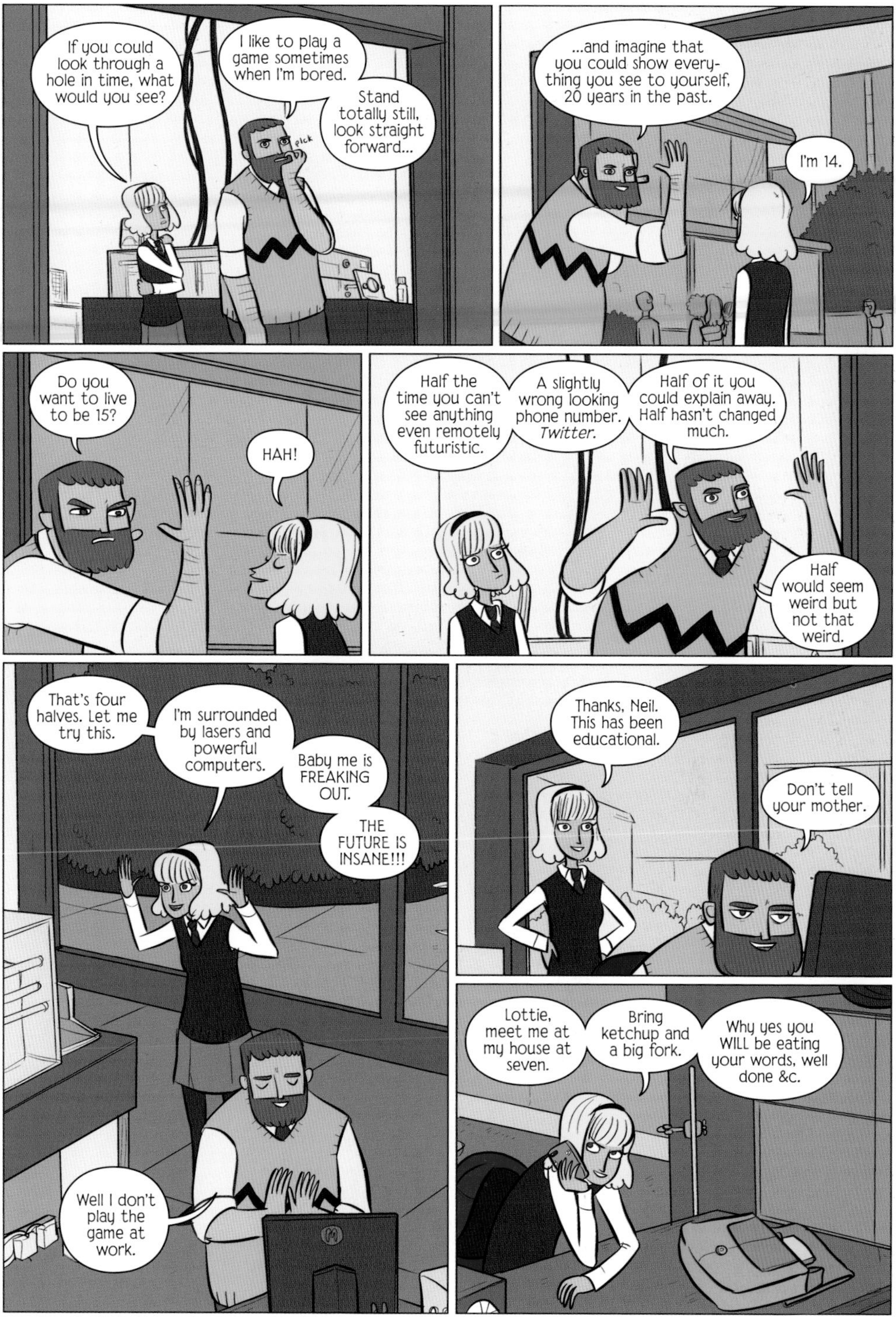
If you could look through a hole in time, what would you see?
I like to play a game sometimes when I'm bored.
Stand totally still, look straight forward...
pick
...and imagine that you could show every-thing you see to yourself, 20 years in the past.
I'm 14.
Do you want to live to be 15?
HAH!
Half the time you can't see anything even remotely futuristic.
A slightly wrong looking phone number. *Twitter.*
Half of it you could explain away. Half hasn't changed much.
Half would seem weird but not that weird.
That's four halves. Let me try this.
I'm surrounded by lasers and powerful computers.
Baby me is FREAKING OUT.
THE FUTURE IS INSANE!!!
Well I don't play the game at work.
Thanks, Neil. This has been educational.
Don't tell your mother.
Lottie, meet me at my house at seven.
Bring ketchup and a big fork.
Why yes you WILL be eating your words, well done &c.

(TWO)

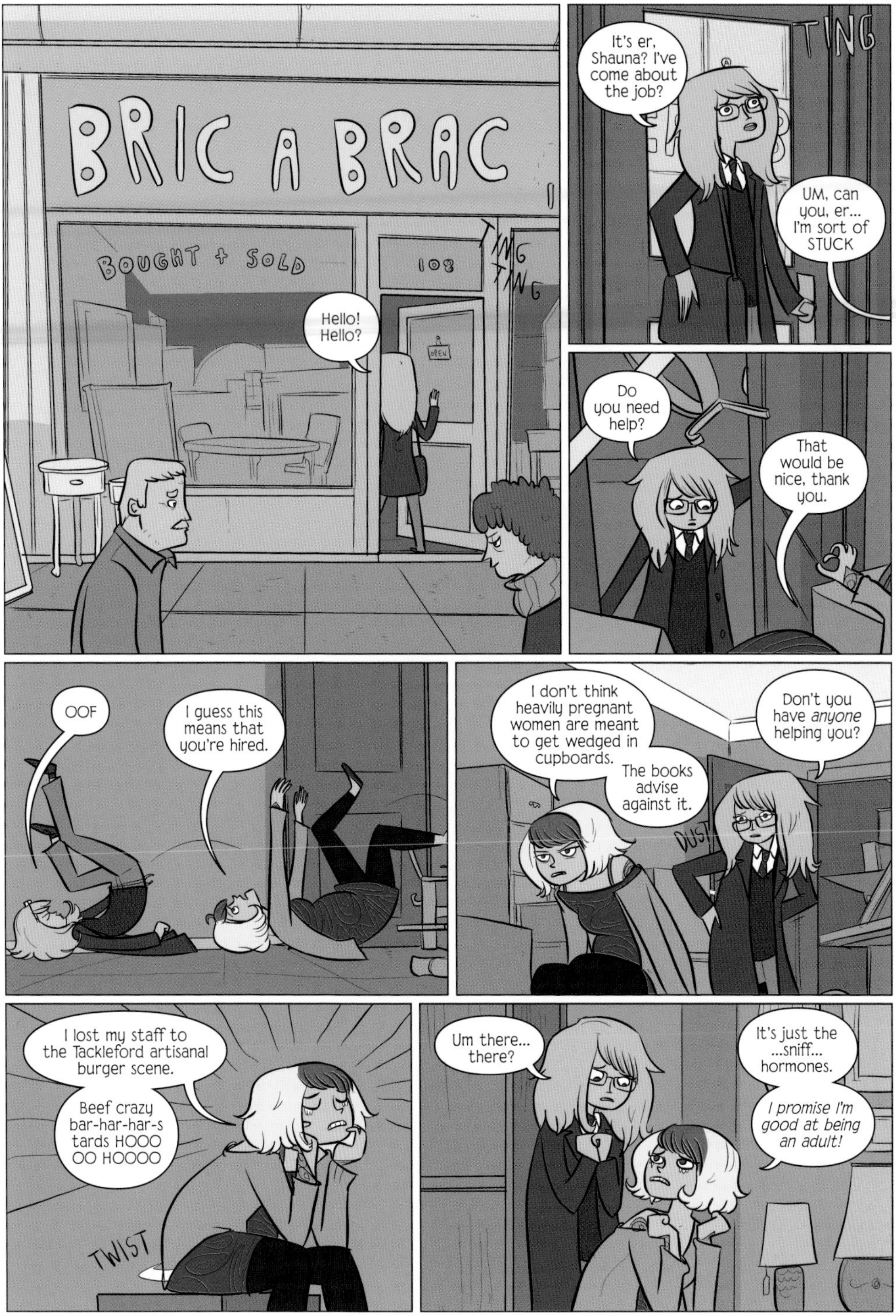
BRIC A BRAC
BOUGHT + SOLD
108
TING TING
Hello! Hello?
OPEN
It's er, Shauna? I've come about the job?
TING
UM, can you, er... I'm sort of STUCK
Do you need help?
That would be nice, thank you.
OOF
I guess this means that you're hired.
I don't think heavily pregnant women are meant to get wedged in cupboards.
The books advise against it.
DUST
Don't you have *anyone* helping you?
I lost my staff to the Tackleford artisanal burger scene.
Beef crazy bar-har-har-s tards HOOO OO HOOOO
TWIST
Um there... there?
It's just the ...sniff... hormones.
I promise I'm good at being an adult!

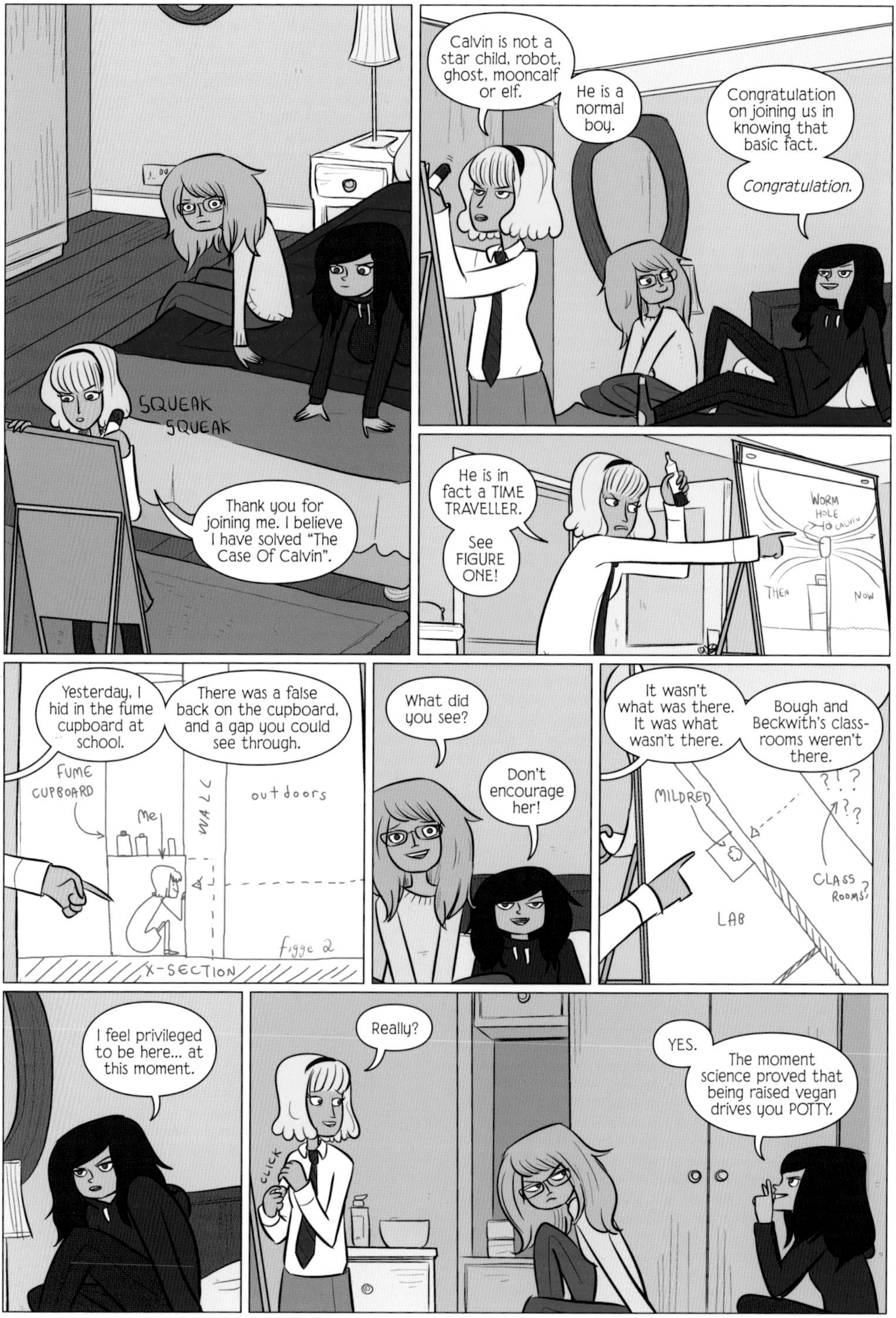
SQUEAK
SQUEAK
Thank you for joining me. I believe I have solved "The Case Of Calvin".
Calvin is not a star child, robot, ghost, mooncalf or elf.
He is a normal boy.
Congratulation on joining us in knowing that basic fact.
Congratulation.
He is in fact a TIME TRAVELLER.
See FIGURE ONE!
WORM HOLE
THEN
NOW
Yesterday, I hid in the fume cupboard at school.
There was a false back on the cupboard, and a gap you could see through.
FUME CUPBOARD
me
WALL
outdoors
figge 2
X-SECTION
What did you see?
Don't encourage her!
It wasn't what was there. It was what wasn't there.
Bough and Beckwith's class-rooms weren't there.
MILDRED
LAB
CLASS ROOMS?
I feel privileged to be here... at this moment.
Really?
CLICK
YES.
The moment science proved that being raised vegan drives you POTTY.

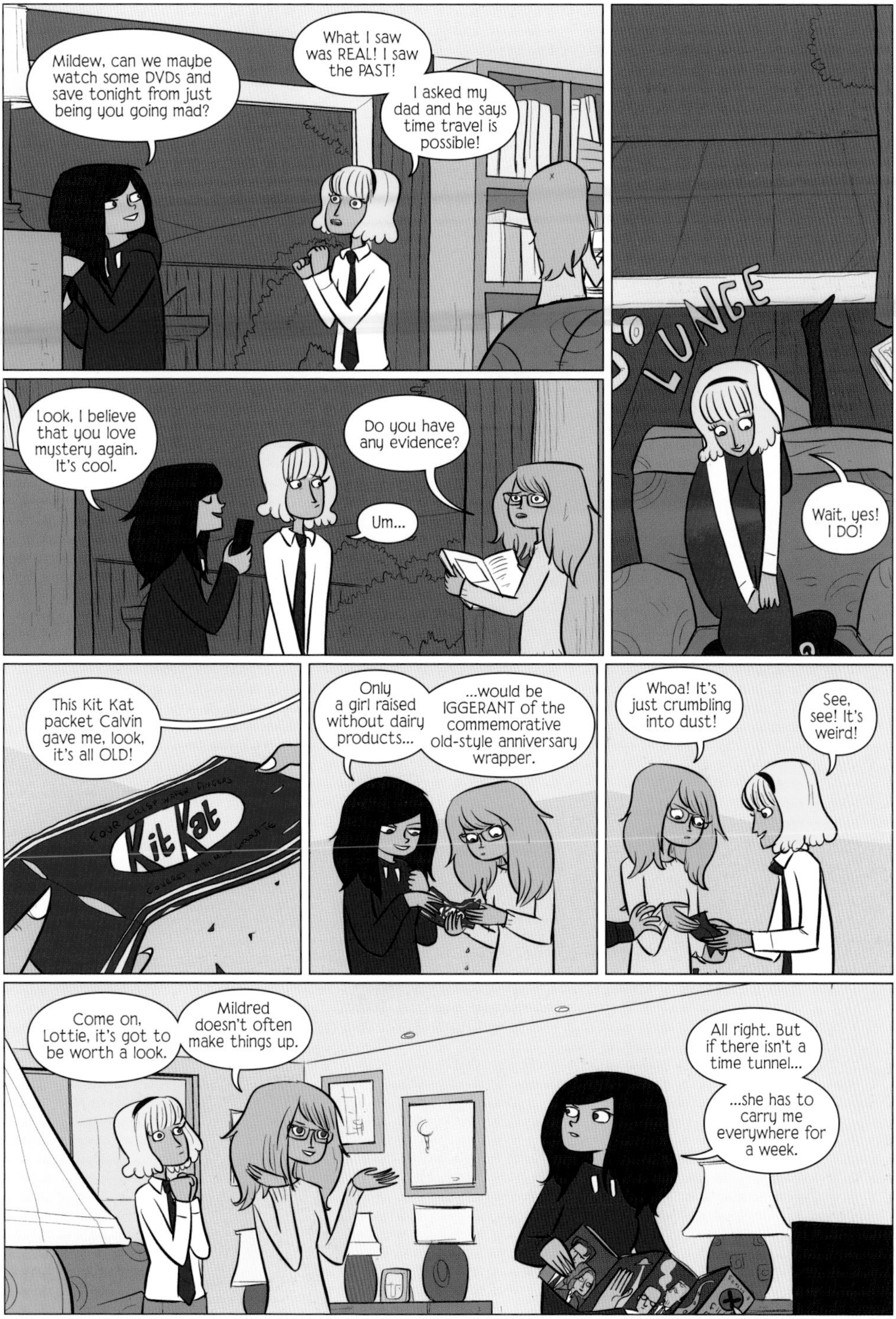
Mildew, can we maybe watch some DVDs and save tonight from just being you going mad?
What I saw was REAL! I saw the PAST!
I asked my dad and he says time travel is possible!
LUNGE
Look, I believe that you love mystery again. It's cool.
Do you have any evidence?
Um...
Wait, yes! I DO!
This Kit Kat packet Calvin gave me, look, it's all OLD!
Kit Kat
Only a girl raised without dairy products...
...would be IGGERANT of the commemorative old-style anniversary wrapper.
Whoa! It's just crumbling into dust!
See, see! It's weird!
Come on, Lottie, it's got to be worth a look.
Mildred doesn't often make things up.
All right. But if there isn't a time tunnel...
...she has to carry me everywhere for a week.

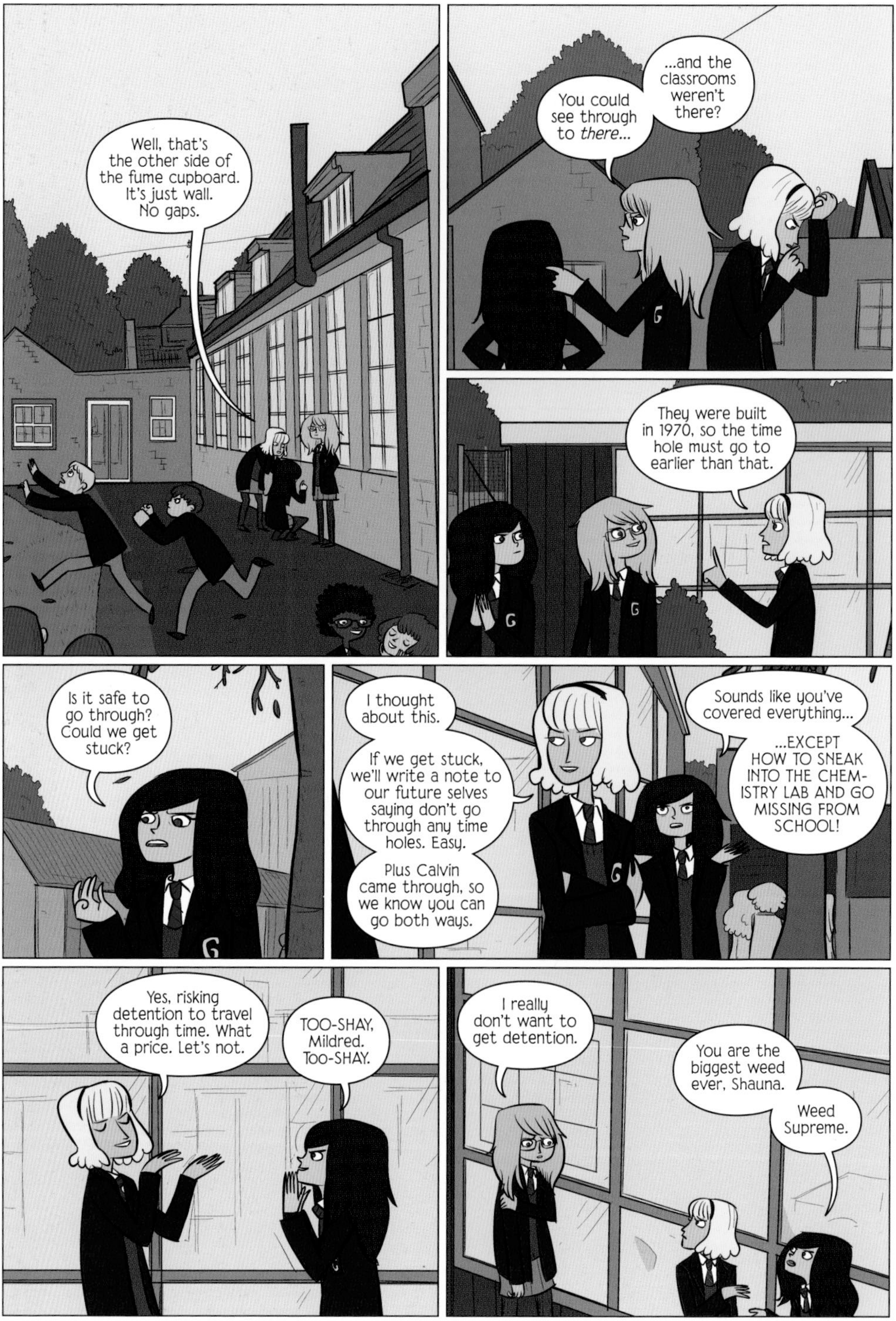
Well, that's the other side of the fume cupboard. It's just wall. No gaps.
You could see through to *there*...
...and the classrooms weren't there?
They were built in 1970, so the time hole must go to earlier than that.
Is it safe to go through? Could we get stuck?
I thought about this.
If we get stuck, we'll write a note to our future selves saying don't go through any time holes. Easy.
Plus Calvin came through, so we know you can go both ways.
Sounds like you've covered everything...
...EXCEPT HOW TO SNEAK INTO THE CHEMISTRY LAB AND GO MISSING FROM SCHOOL!
Yes, risking detention to travel through time. What a price. Let's not.
TOO-SHAY, Mildred. Too-SHAY.
I really don't want to get detention.
You are the biggest weed ever, Shauna.
Weed Supreme.

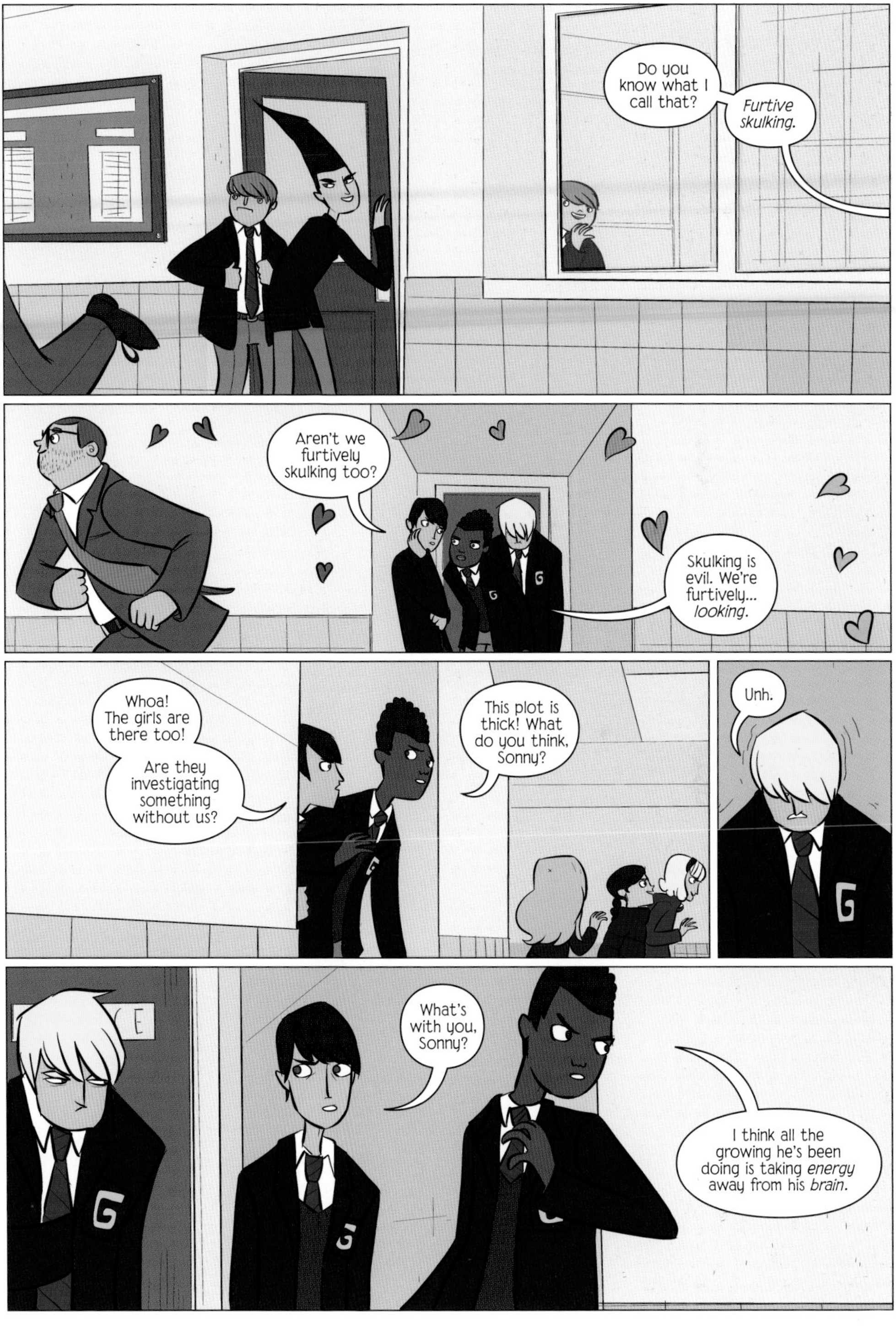
Do you know what I call that?
Furtive skulking.
Aren't we furtively skulking too?
Skulking is evil. We're furtively... *looking.*
Whoa! The girls are there too!
Are they investigating something without us?
This plot is thick! What do you think, Sonny?
Unh.
What's with you, Sonny?
I think all the growing he's been doing is taking *energy* away from his *brain.*

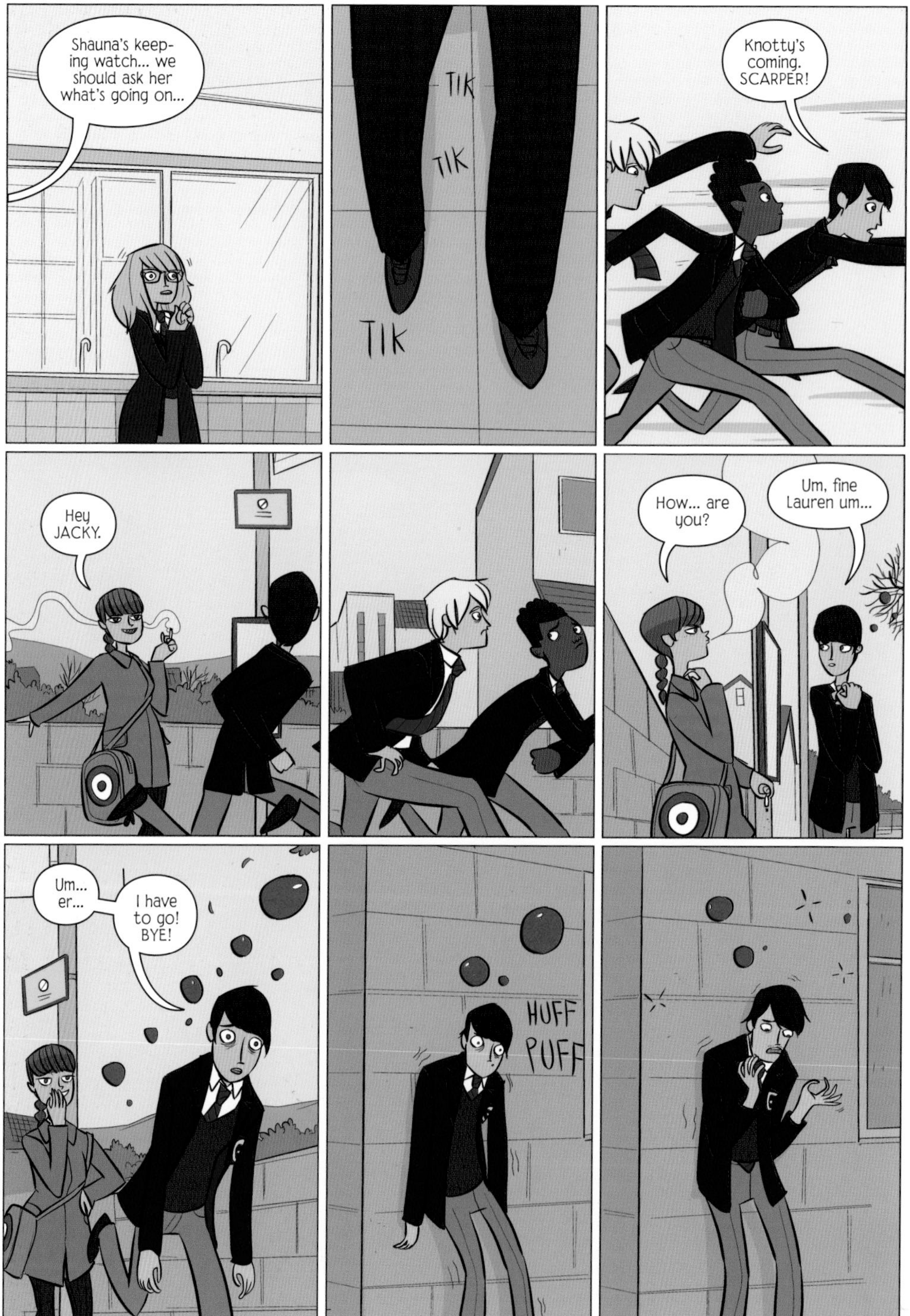
Shauna's keeping watch... we should ask her what's going on...
TIK
TIK
TIK
Knotty's coming. SCARPER!
Hey JACKY.
How... are you?
Um, fine Lauren um...
Um... er...
I have to go! BYE!
HUFF PUFF

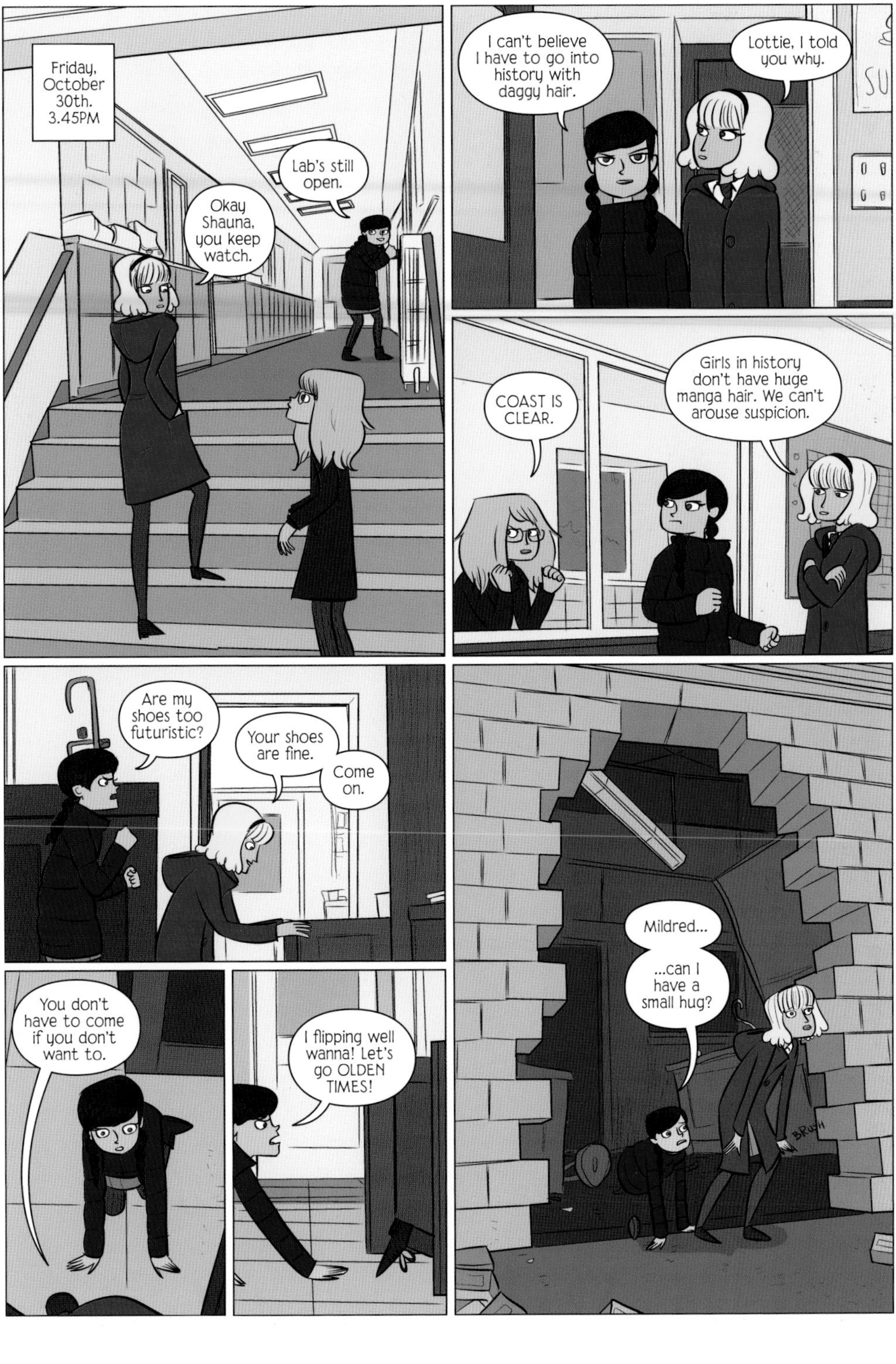
Friday, October 30th. 3.45PM
Okay Shauna, you keep watch.
Lab's still open.
I can't believe I have to go into history with daggy hair.
Lottie, I told you why.
COAST IS CLEAR.
Girls in history don't have huge manga hair. We can't arouse suspicion.
Are my shoes too futuristic?
Your shoes are fine.
Come on.
You don't have to come if you don't want to.
I flipping well wanna! Let's go OLDEN TIMES!
Mildred...
...can I have a small hug?
BRUSH

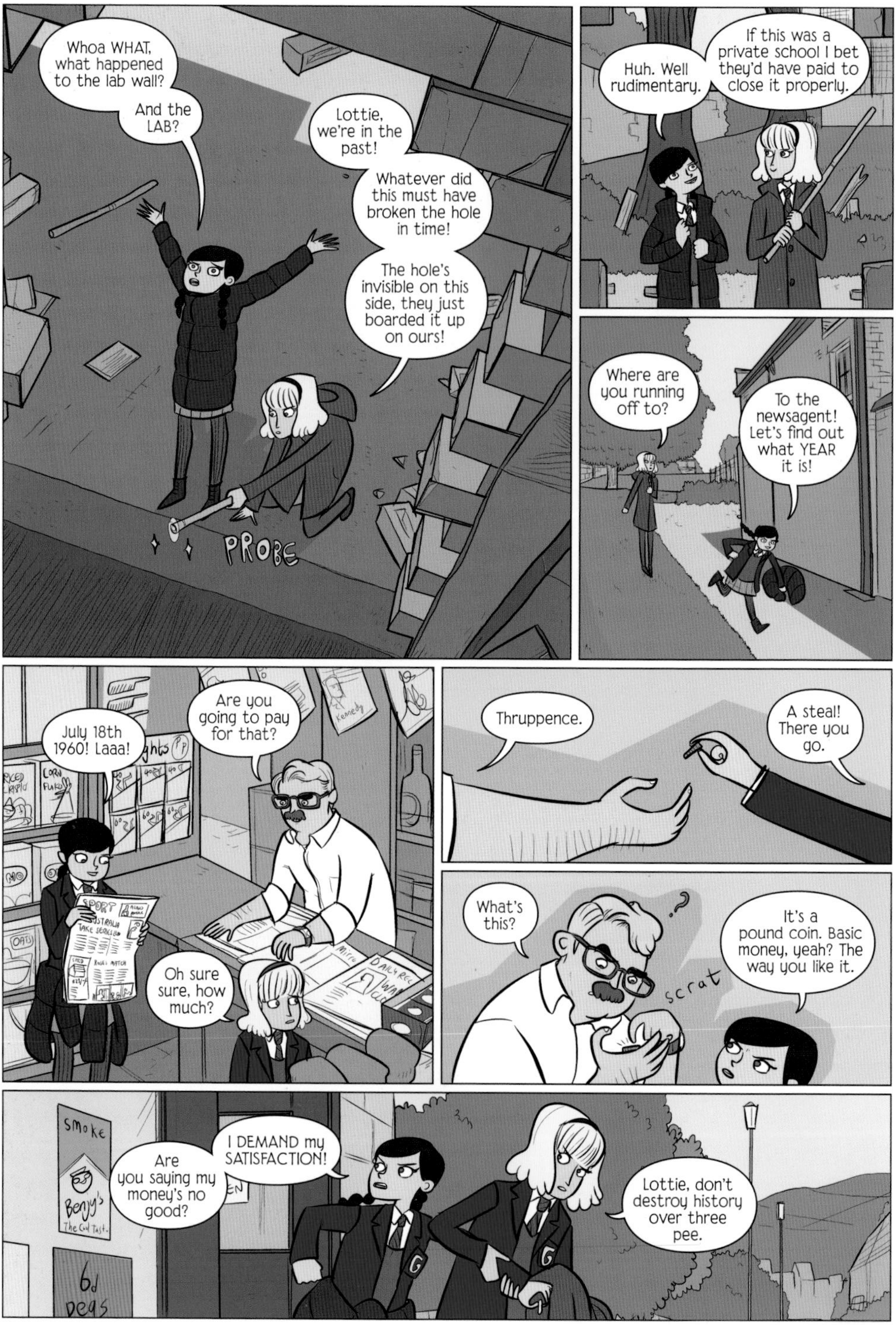
Whoa WHAT, what happened to the lab wall?
And the LAB?
Lottie, we're in the past!
Whatever did this must have broken the hole in time!
The hole's invisible on this side, they just boarded it up on ours!
PROBE
Huh. Well rudimentary.
If this was a private school I bet they'd have paid to close it properly.
Where are you running off to?
To the newsagent! Let's find out what YEAR it is!
July 18th 1960! Laaa!
Are you going to pay for that?
Oh sure sure, how much?
Thruppence.
A steal! There you go.
What's this?
It's a pound coin. Basic money, yeah? The way you like it.
scrat
Are you saying my money's no good?
I DEMAND my SATISFACTION!
Lottie, don't destroy history over three pee.

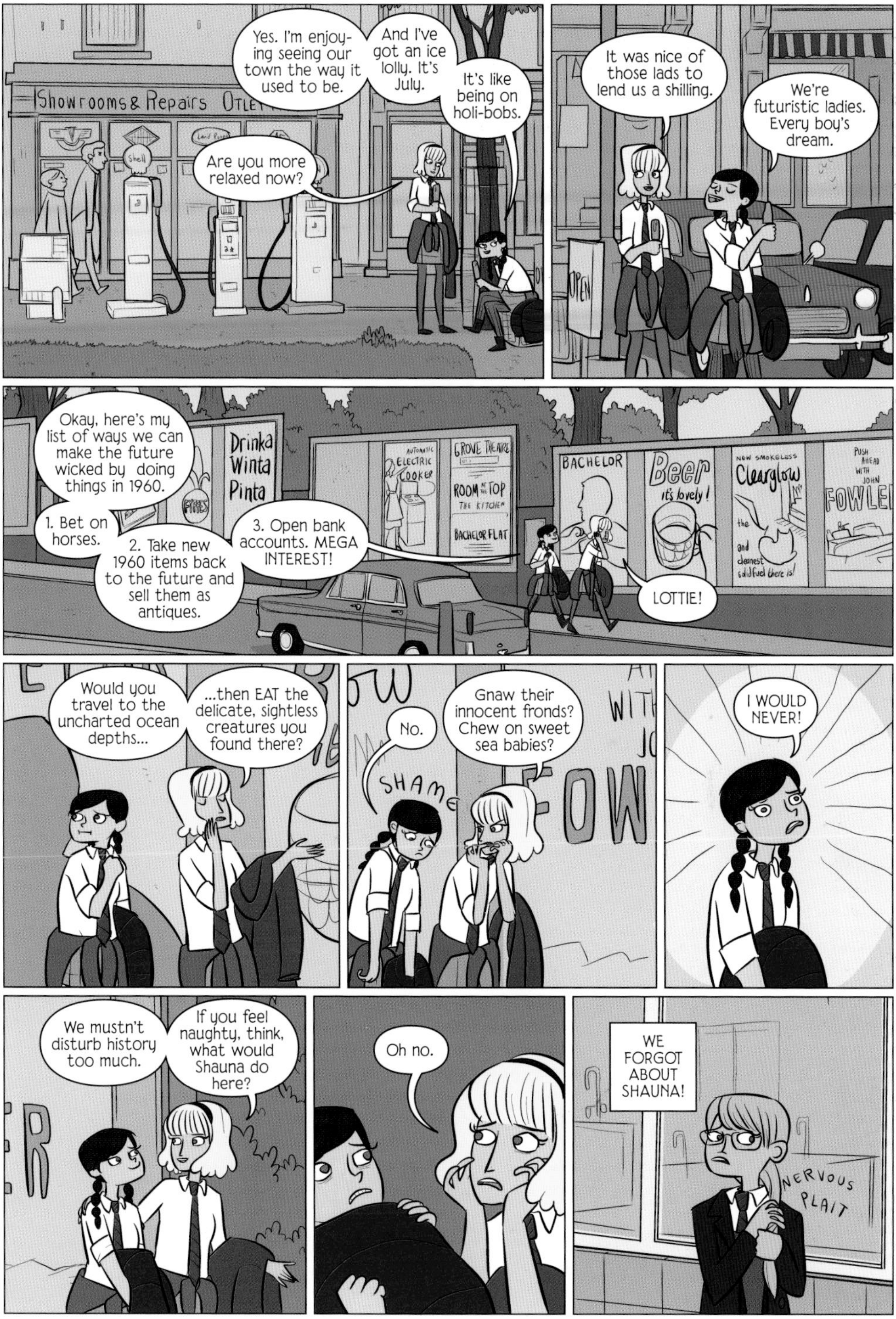
Showrooms & Repairs
Shell
Yes. I'm enjoying seeing our town the way it used to be.
And I've got an ice lolly. It's July.
It's like being on holi-bobs.
Are you more relaxed now?
It was nice of those lads to lend us a shilling.
We're futuristic ladies. Every boy's dream.
OPEN
Okay, here's my list of ways we can make the future wicked by doing things in 1960.
1. Bet on horses.
2. Take new 1960 items back to the future and sell them as antiques.
3. Open bank accounts. MEGA INTEREST!
Drinka Winta Pinta
AUTOMATIC ELECTRIC COOKER
GROVE THEATRE
ROOM AT THE TOP
THE KITCHEN
BACHELOR FLAT
BACHELOR
Beer it's lovely!
NOW SMOKELESS Clearglow the cleanest solid fuel there is!
PUSH AHEAD WITH JOHN FOWLER
LOTTIE!
Would you travel to the uncharted ocean depths...
...then EAT the delicate, sightless creatures you found there?
No.
SHAME
Gnaw their innocent fronds? Chew on sweet sea babies?
I WOULD NEVER!
We mustn't disturb history too much.
If you feel naughty, think, what would Shauna do here?
Oh no.
WE FORGOT ABOUT SHAUNA!
NERVOUS PLAIT

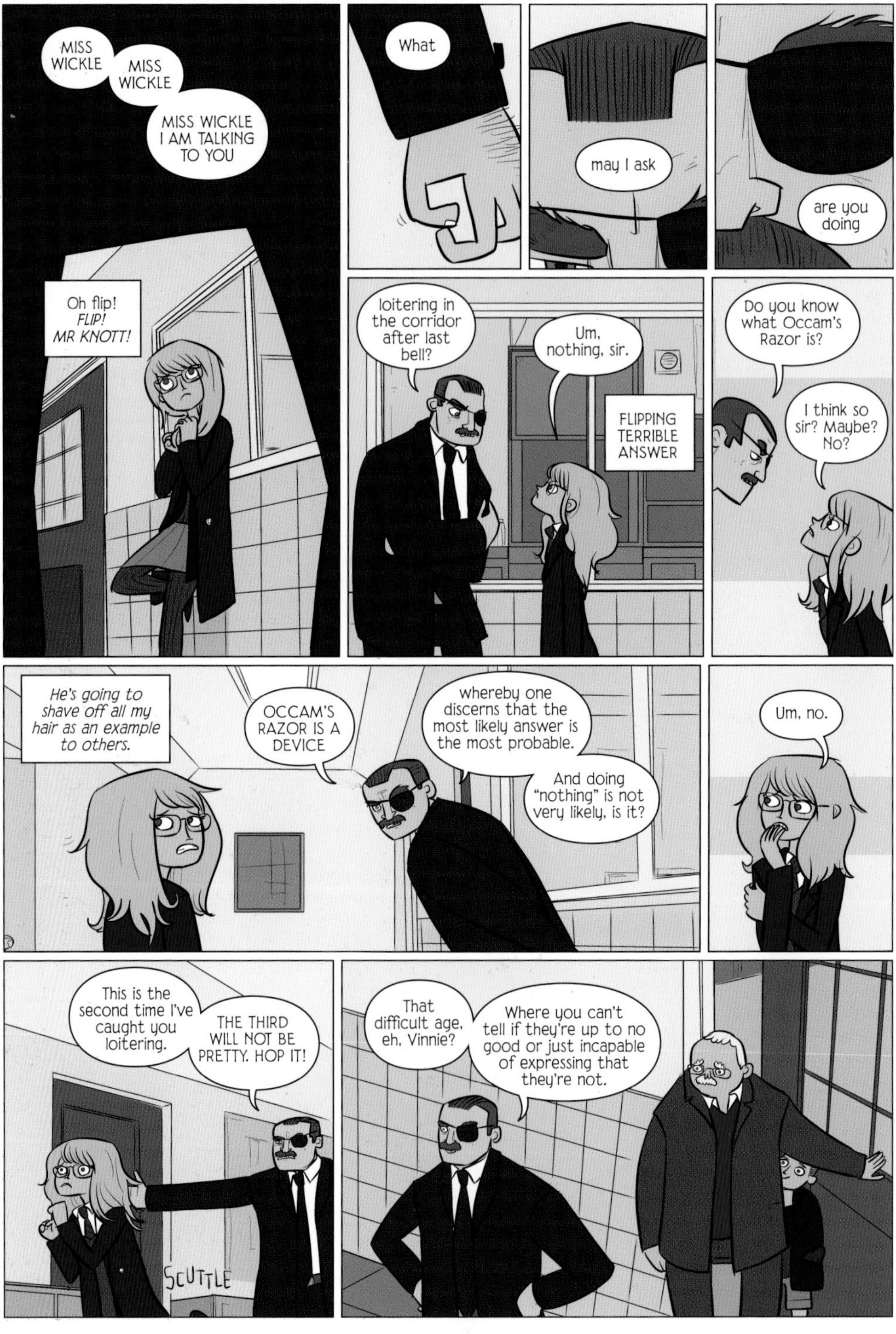
MISS WICKLE
MISS WICKLE
MISS WICKLE I AM TALKING TO YOU
Oh flip! FLIP! MR KNOTT!
What
may I ask
are you doing
loitering in the corridor after last bell?
Um, nothing, sir.
FLIPPING TERRIBLE ANSWER
Do you know what Occam's Razor is?
I think so sir? Maybe? No?
He's going to shave off all my hair as an example to others.
OCCAM'S RAZOR IS A DEVICE
whereby one discerns that the most likely answer is the most probable.
And doing "nothing" is not very likely, is it?
Um, no.
This is the second time I've caught you loitering.
THE THIRD WILL NOT BE PRETTY. HOP IT!
SCUTTLE
That difficult age, eh, Vinnie?
Where you can't tell if they're up to no good or just incapable of expressing that they're not.

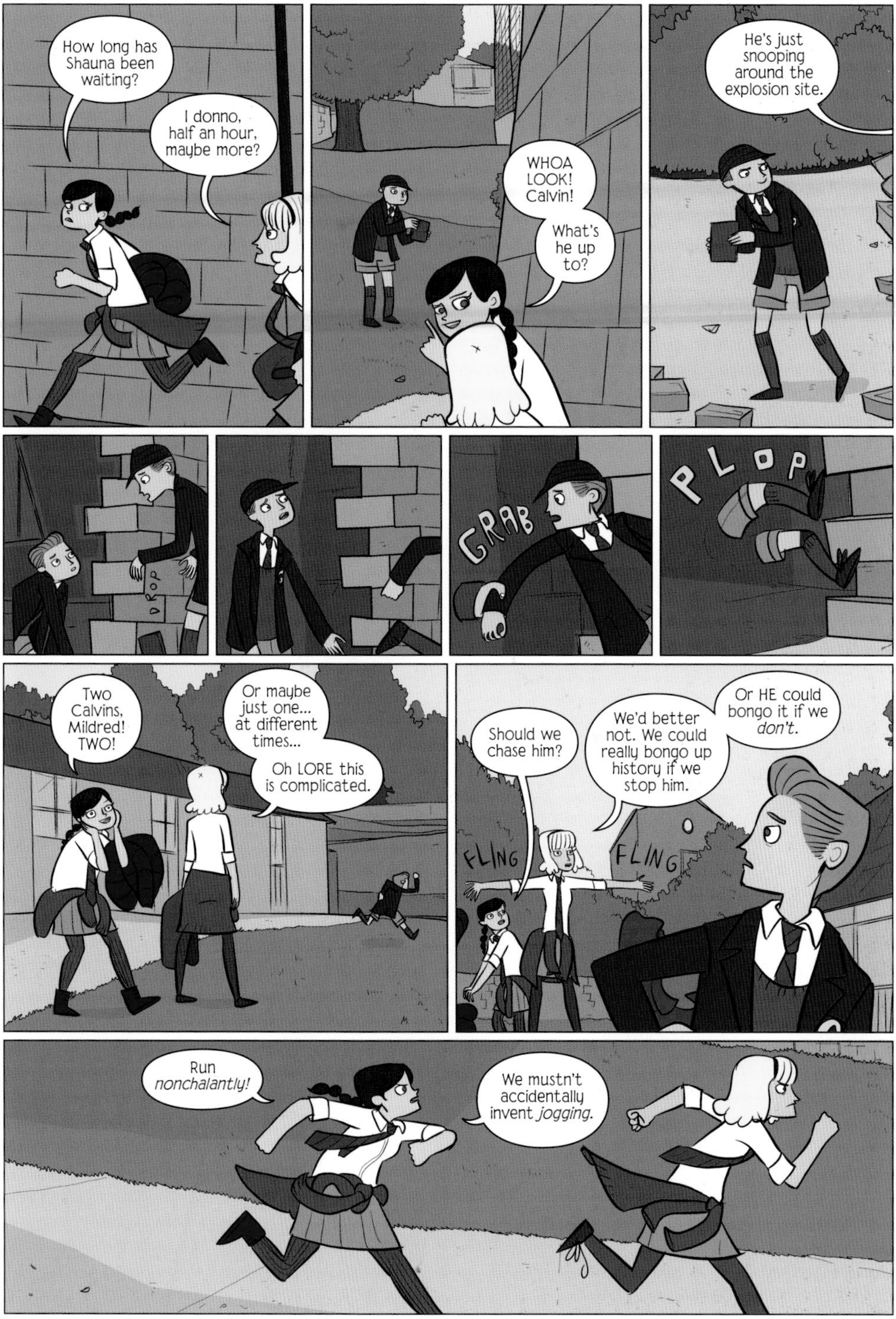
How long has Shauna been waiting?
I donno, half an hour, maybe more?
WHOA LOOK! Calvin!
What's he up to?
He's just snooping around the explosion site.
DROP
GRAB
PLOP
Two Calvins, Mildred! TWO!
Or maybe just one... at different times...
Oh LORE this is complicated.
Should we chase him?
We'd better not. We could really bongo up history if we stop him.
Or HE could bongo it if we *don't*.
FLING
FLING
Run *nonchalantly!*
We mustn't accidentally invent *jogging*.

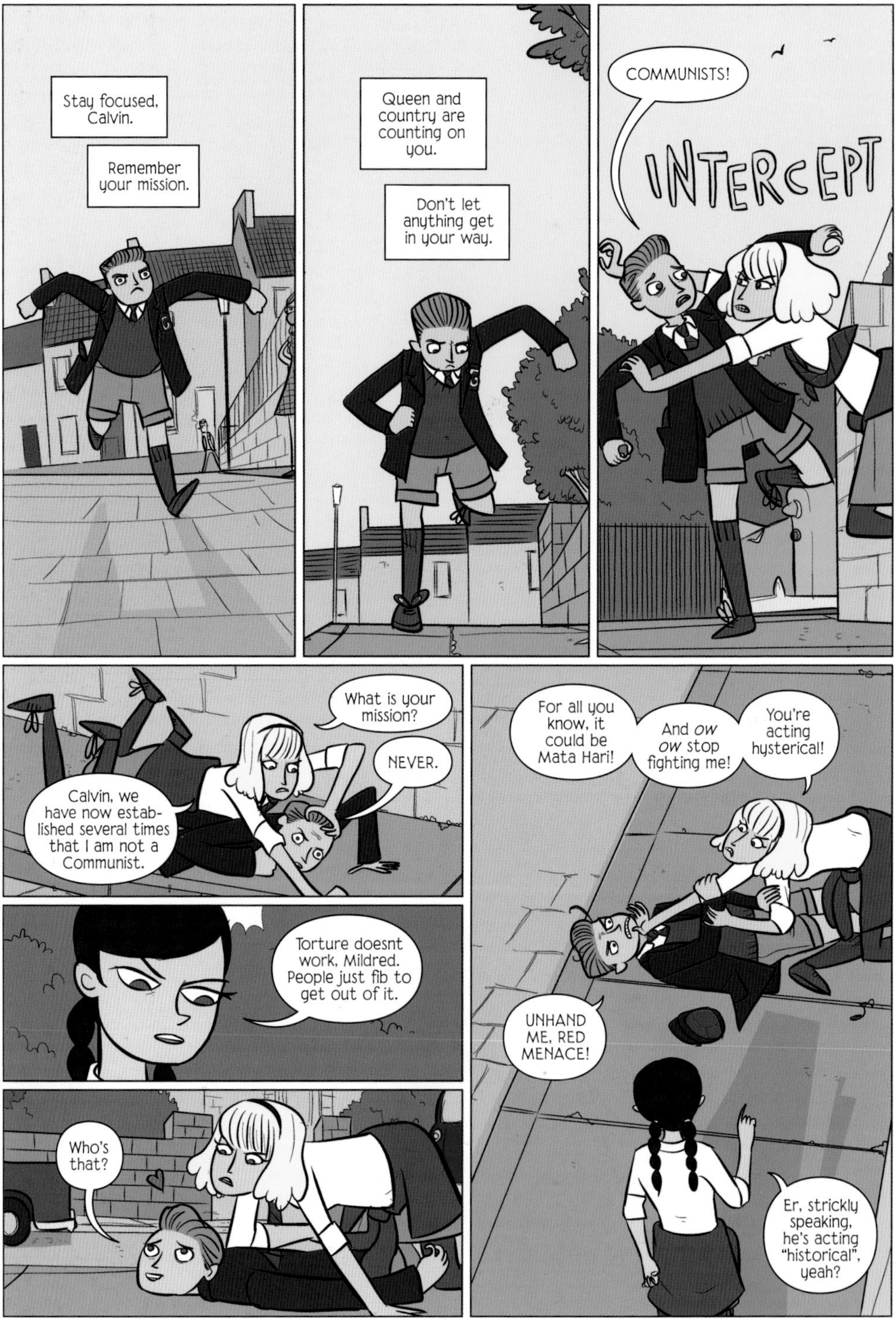
Stay focused, Calvin.
Remember your mission.
Queen and country are counting on you.
Don't let anything get in your way.
COMMUNISTS!
INTERCEPT
What is your mission?
NEVER.
Calvin, we have now established several times that I am not a Communist.
Torture doesnt work, Mildred. People just fib to get out of it.
Who's that?
For all you know, it could be Mata Hari!
And *ow ow* stop fighting me!
You're acting hysterical!
UNHAND ME, RED MENACE!
Er, strickly speaking, he's acting "historical", yeah?

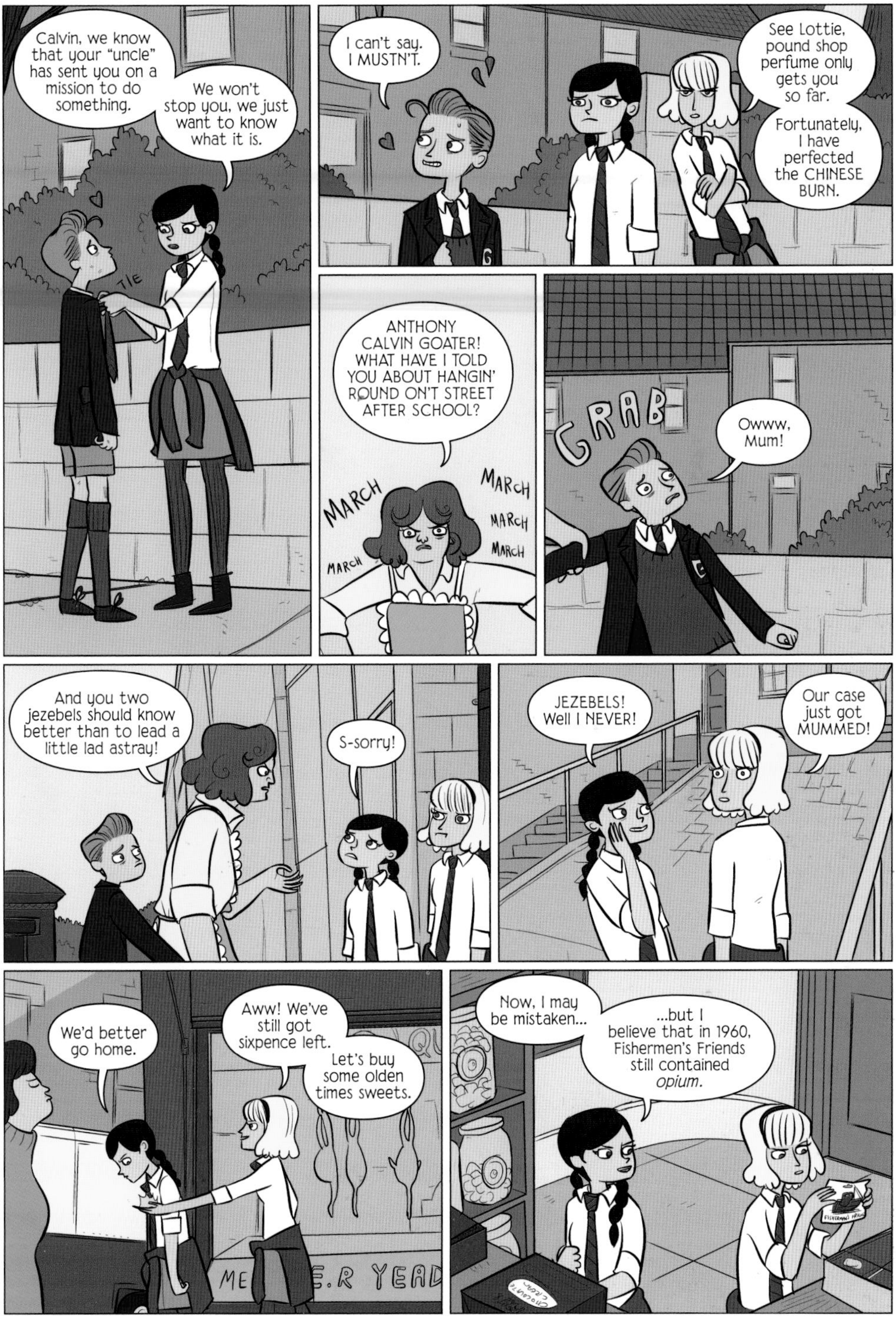
Calvin, we know that your "uncle" has sent you on a mission to do something.
We won't stop you, we just want to know what it is.
TIE
I can't say. I MUSTN'T.
See Lottie, pound shop perfume only gets you so far.
Fortunately, I have perfected the CHINESE BURN.
ANTHONY CALVIN GOATER! WHAT HAVE I TOLD YOU ABOUT HANGIN' ROUND ON'T STREET AFTER SCHOOL?
MARCH
MARCH
MARCH
MARCH
MARCH
GRAB
Owww, Mum!
And you two jezebels should know better than to lead a little lad astray!
S-sorry!
JEZEBELS! Well I NEVER!
Our case just got MUMMED!
We'd better go home.
Aww! We've still got sixpence left.
Let's buy some olden times sweets.
Now, I may be mistaken...
...but I believe that in 1960, Fishermen's Friends still contained *opium*.

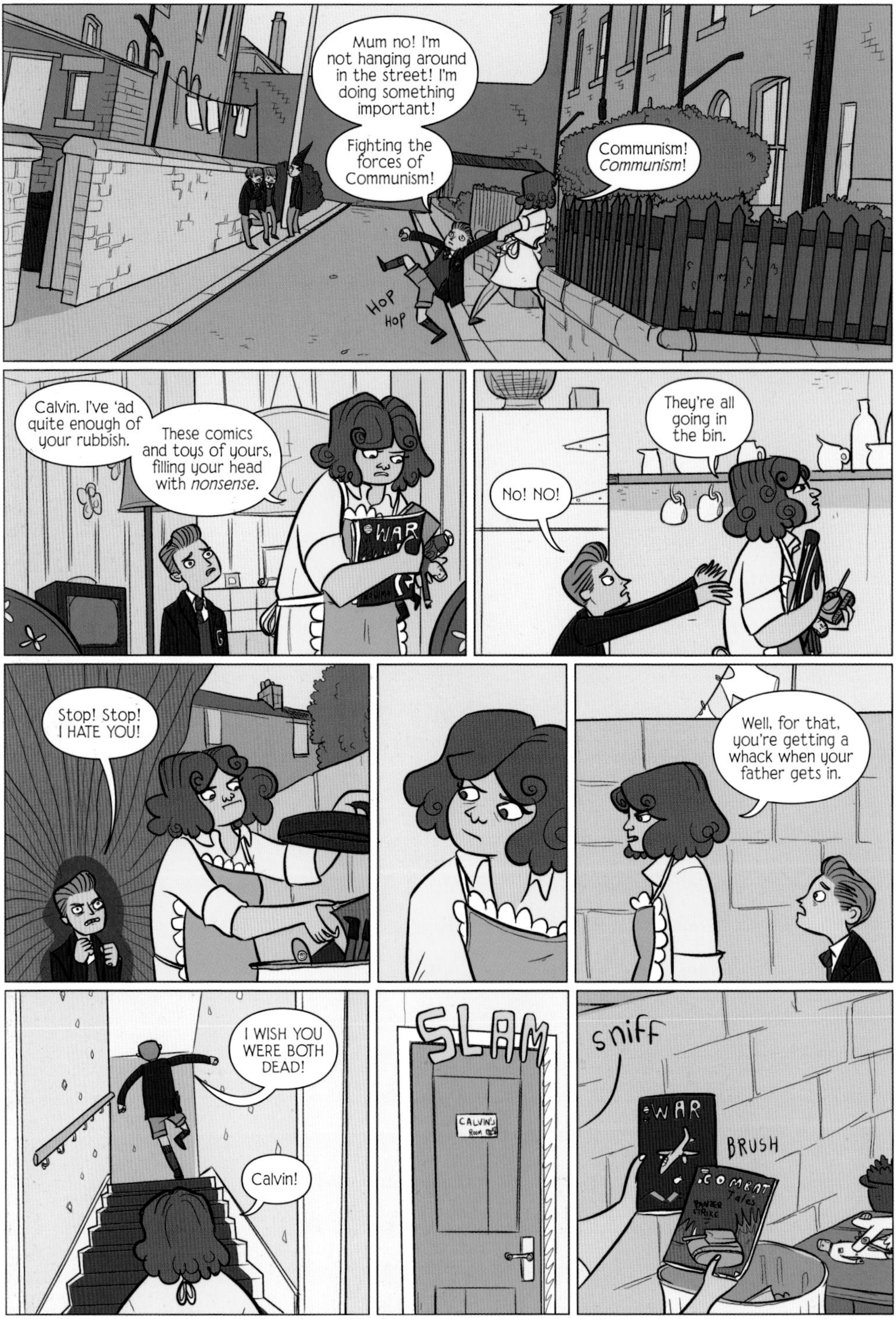
Mum no! I'm not hanging around in the street! I'm doing something important!
Fighting the forces of Communism!
Communism! *Communism*!
HOP HOP
Calvin. I've 'ad quite enough of your rubbish.
These comics and toys of yours, filling your head with *nonsense*.
WAR
They're all going in the bin.
No! NO!
Stop! Stop! I HATE YOU!
Well, for that, you're getting a whack when your father gets in.
I WISH YOU WERE BOTH DEAD!
Calvin!
SLAM
CALVIN'S Room
sniff
WAR
BRUSH
COMBAT Tales
PANZER STRIKE

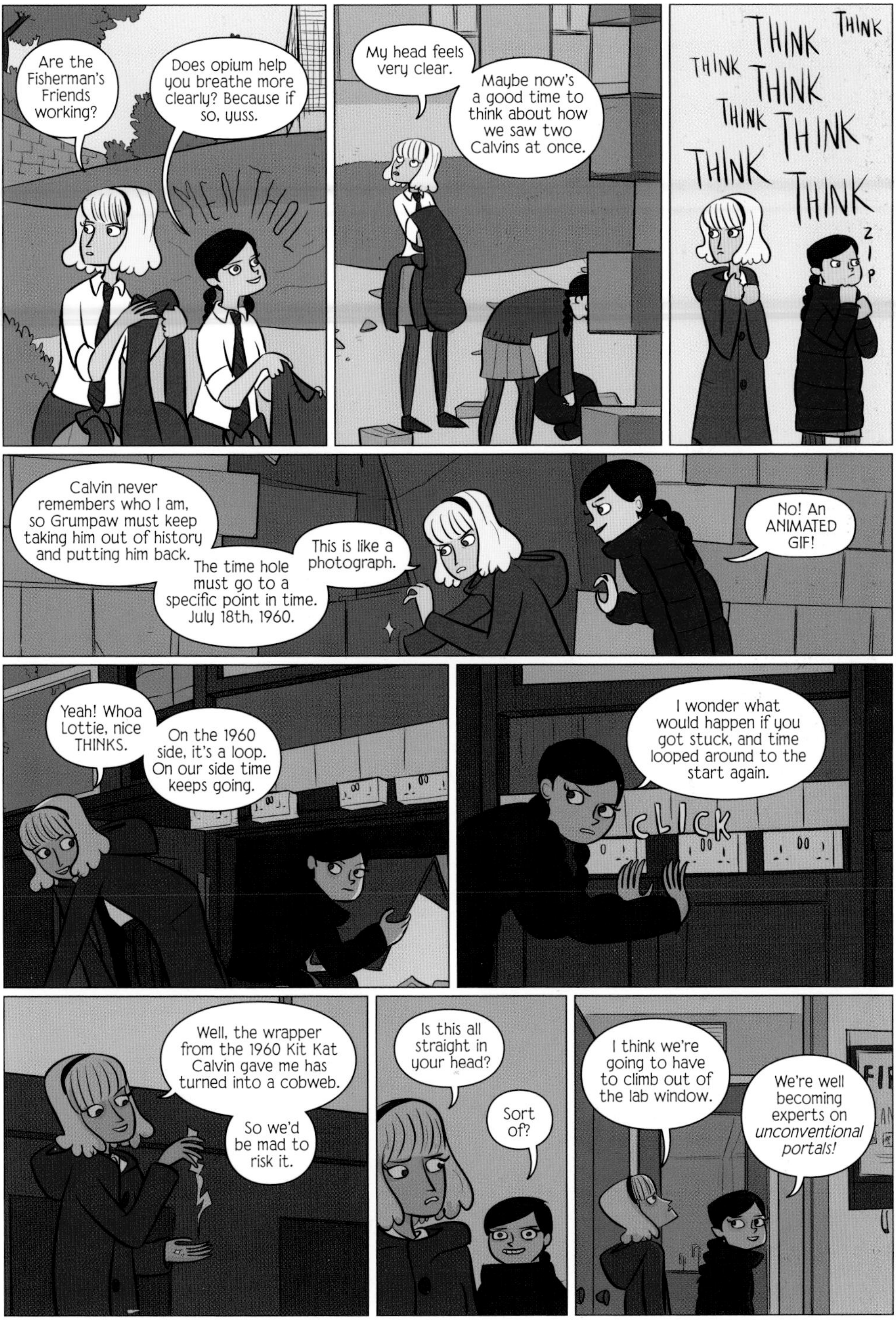
Are the Fisherman's Friends working?
Does opium help you breathe more clearly? Because if so, yuss.
MENTHOL
My head feels very clear.
Maybe now's a good time to think about how we saw two Calvins at once.
THINK THINK THINK THINK THINK THINK THINK THINK
ZIP
Calvin never remembers who I am, so Grumpaw must keep taking him out of history and putting him back.
The time hole must go to a specific point in time. July 18th, 1960.
This is like a photograph.
No! An ANIMATED GIF!
Yeah! Whoa Lottie, nice THINKS.
On the 1960 side, it's a loop. On our side time keeps going.
I wonder what would happen if you got stuck, and time looped around to the start again.
CLICK
Well, the wrapper from the 1960 Kit Kat Calvin gave me has turned into a cobweb.
So we'd be mad to risk it.
Is this all straight in your head?
Sort of?
I think we're going to have to climb out of the lab window.
We're well becoming experts on *unconventional portals!*

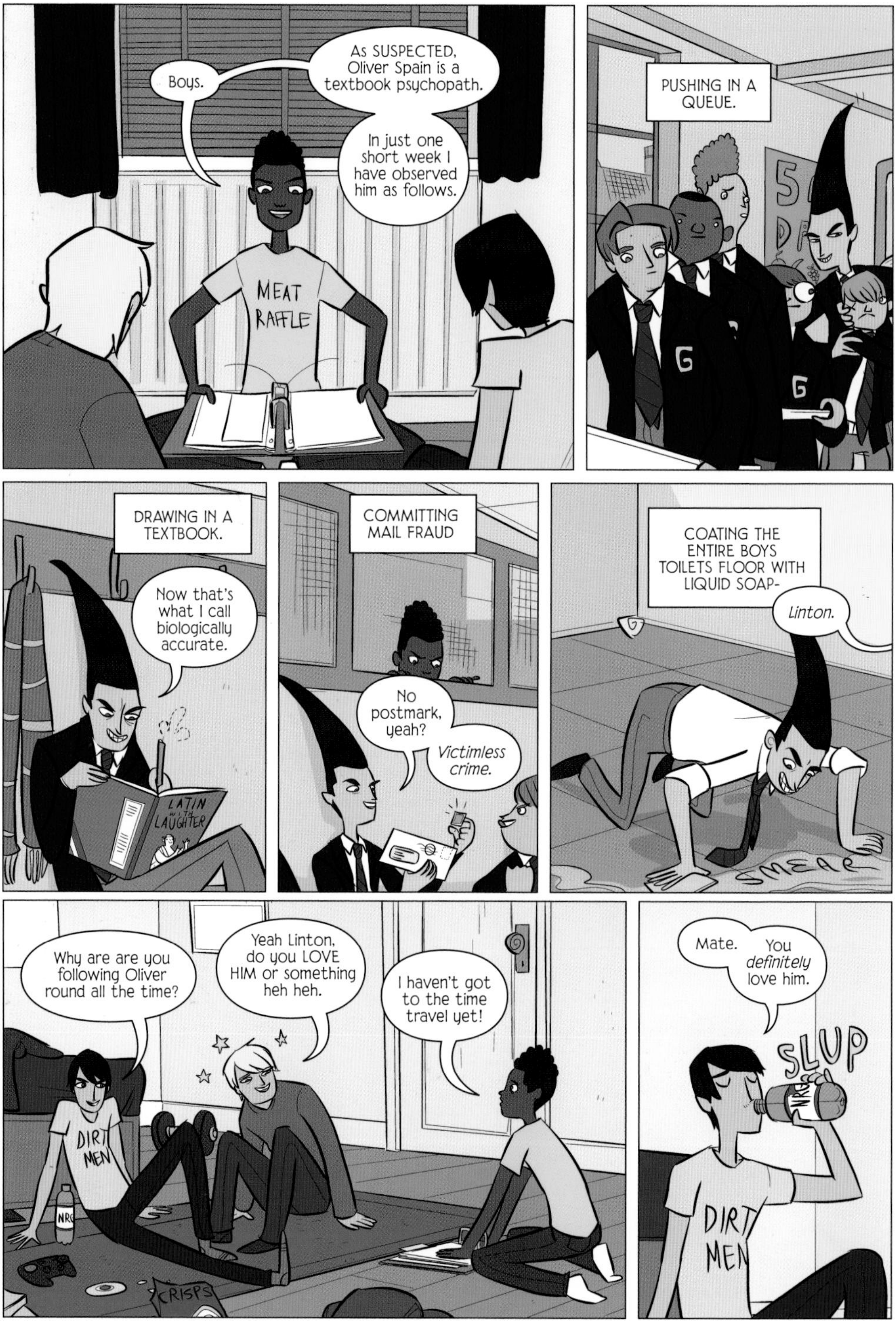
Boys.
As SUSPECTED, Oliver Spain is a textbook psychopath.
In just one short week I have observed him as follows.
MEAT RAFFLE
PUSHING IN A QUEUE.
DRAWING IN A TEXTBOOK.
Now that's what I call biologically accurate.
LATIN WITH LAUGHTER
COMMITTING MAIL FRAUD
No postmark, yeah?
Victimless crime.
COATING THE ENTIRE BOYS TOILETS FLOOR WITH LIQUID SOAP-
Linton.
SMEAR
Why are are you following Oliver round all the time?
Yeah Linton, do you LOVE HIM or something heh heh.
I haven't got to the time travel yet!
DIRT MEN
CRISPS
Mate.
You definitely love him.
SLUP
DIRT MEN

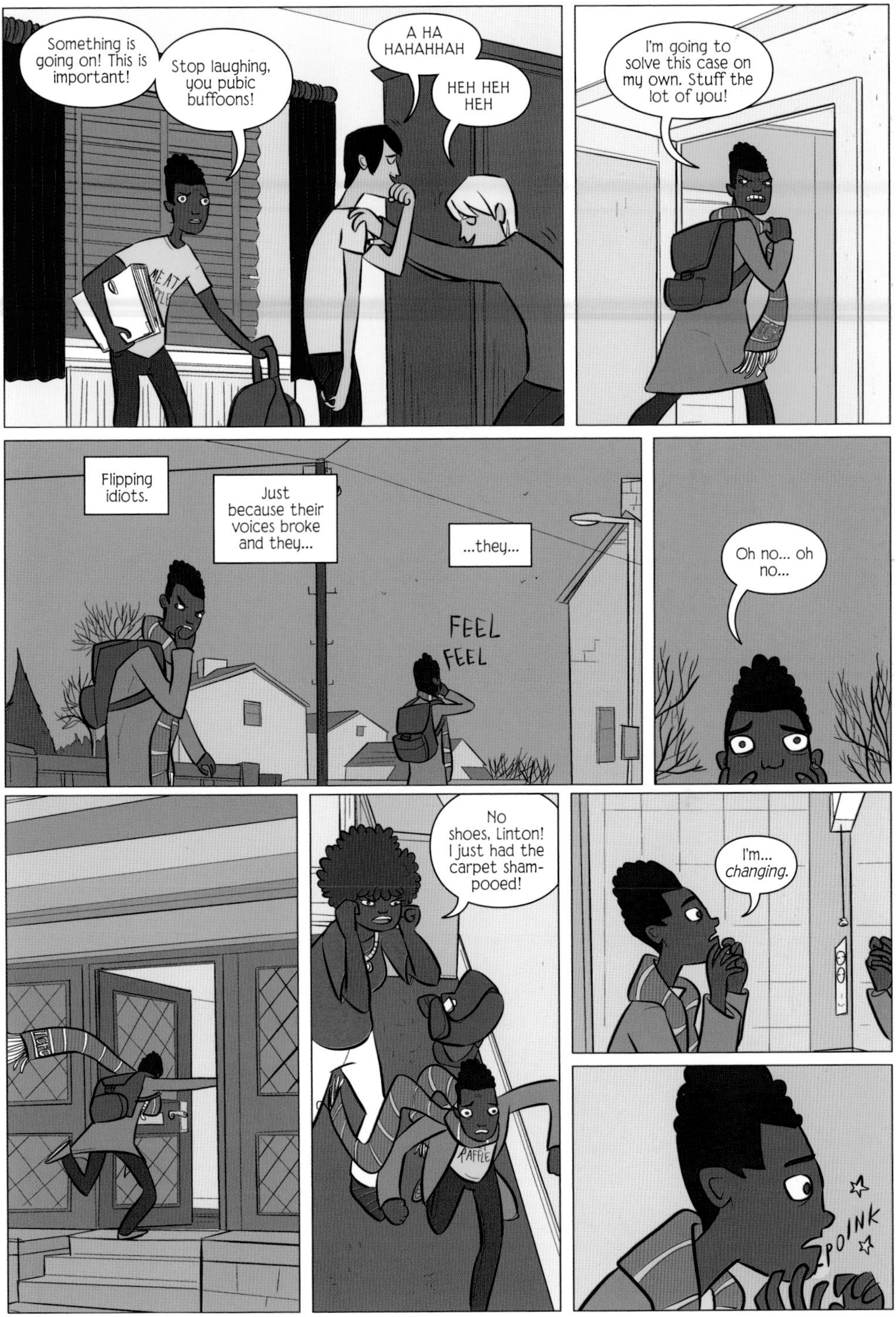
Something is going on! This is important!
Stop laughing, you pubic buffoons!
A HA HAHAHHAH
HEH HEH HEH
I'm going to solve this case on my own. Stuff the lot of you!
Flipping idiots.
Just because their voices broke and they...
...they...
FEEL FEEL
Oh no... oh no...
No shoes, Linton! I just had the carpet shampooed!
I'm... *changing.*
POINK

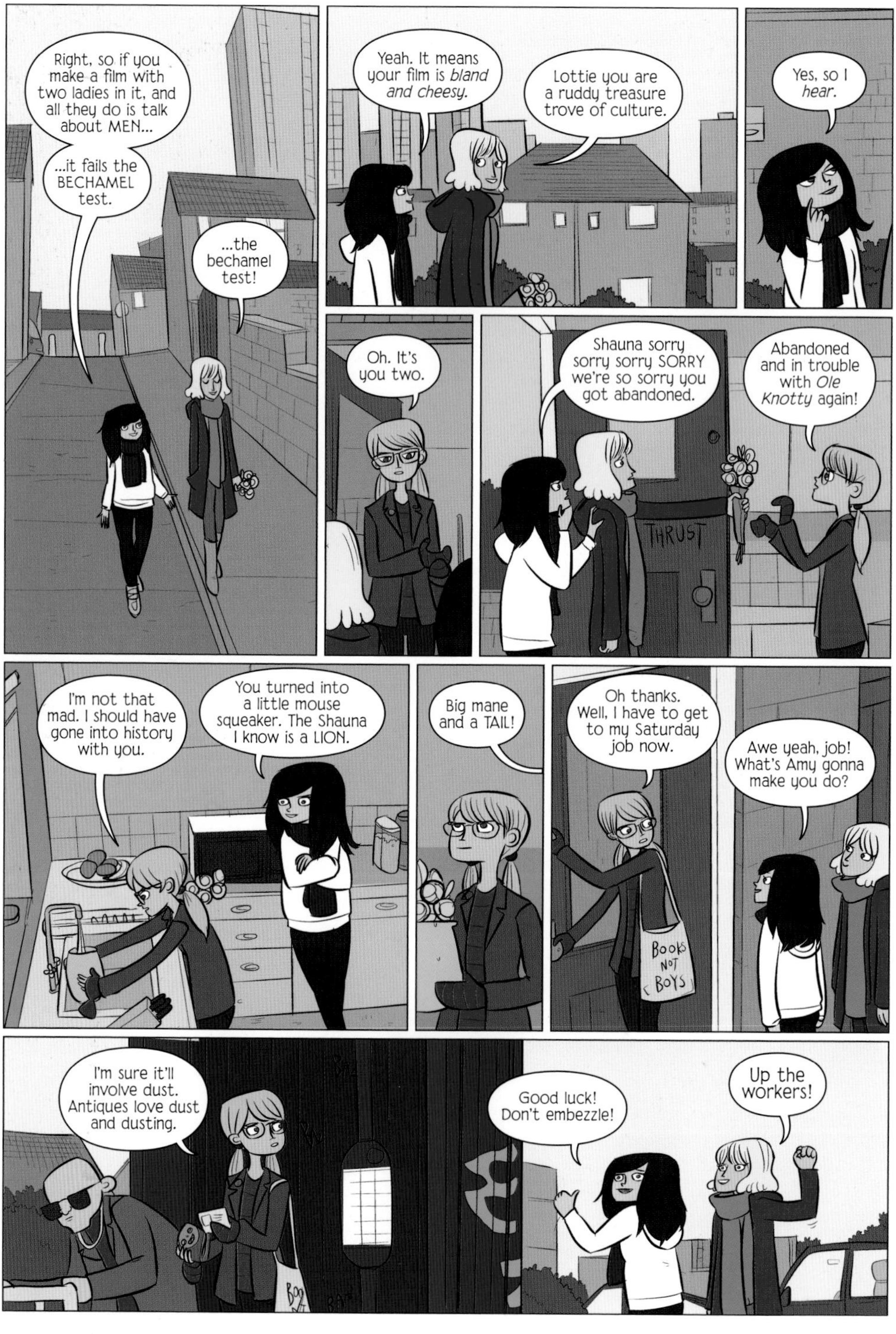
Right, so if you make a film with two ladies in it, and all they do is talk about MEN...
...it fails the BECHAMEL test.
...the bechamel test!
Yeah. It means your film is *bland and cheesy.*
Lottie you are a ruddy treasure trove of culture.
Yes, so I *hear.*
Oh. It's you two.
Shauna sorry sorry sorry SORRY we're so sorry you got abandoned.
Abandoned and in trouble with *Ole Knotty* again!
THRUST
I'm not that mad. I should have gone into history with you.
You turned into a little mouse squeaker. The Shauna I know is a LION.
Big mane and a TAIL!
Oh thanks. Well, I have to get to my Saturday job now.
Awe yeah, job! What's Amy gonna make you do?
BOOKS NOT BOYS
I'm sure it'll involve dust. Antiques love dust and dusting.
Good luck! Don't embezzle!
Up the workers!

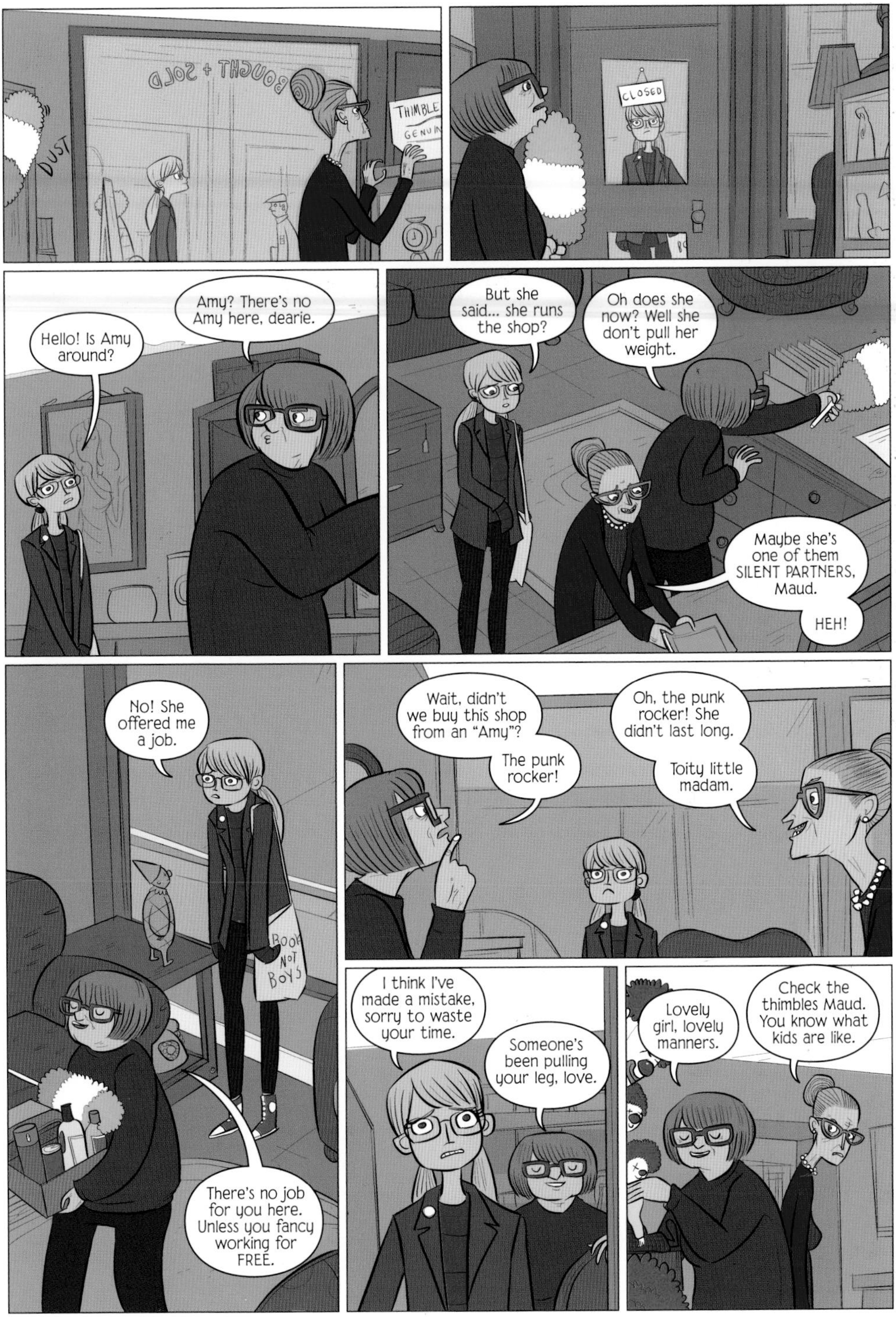
BOUGHT + SOLD
DUST
THIMBLE
GENUIN
CLOSED
Hello! Is Amy around?
Amy? There's no Amy here, dearie.
But she said... she runs the shop?
Oh does she now? Well she don't pull her weight.
Maybe she's one of them SILENT PARTNERS, Maud.
HEH!
No! She offered me a job.
BOOKS NOT BOYS
There's no job for you here. Unless you fancy working for FREE.
Wait, didn't we buy this shop from an "Amy"?
The punk rocker!
Oh, the punk rocker! She didn't last long.
Toity little madam.
I think I've made a mistake, sorry to waste your time.
Someone's been pulling your leg, love.
Lovely girl, lovely manners.
Check the thimbles Maud. You know what kids are like.

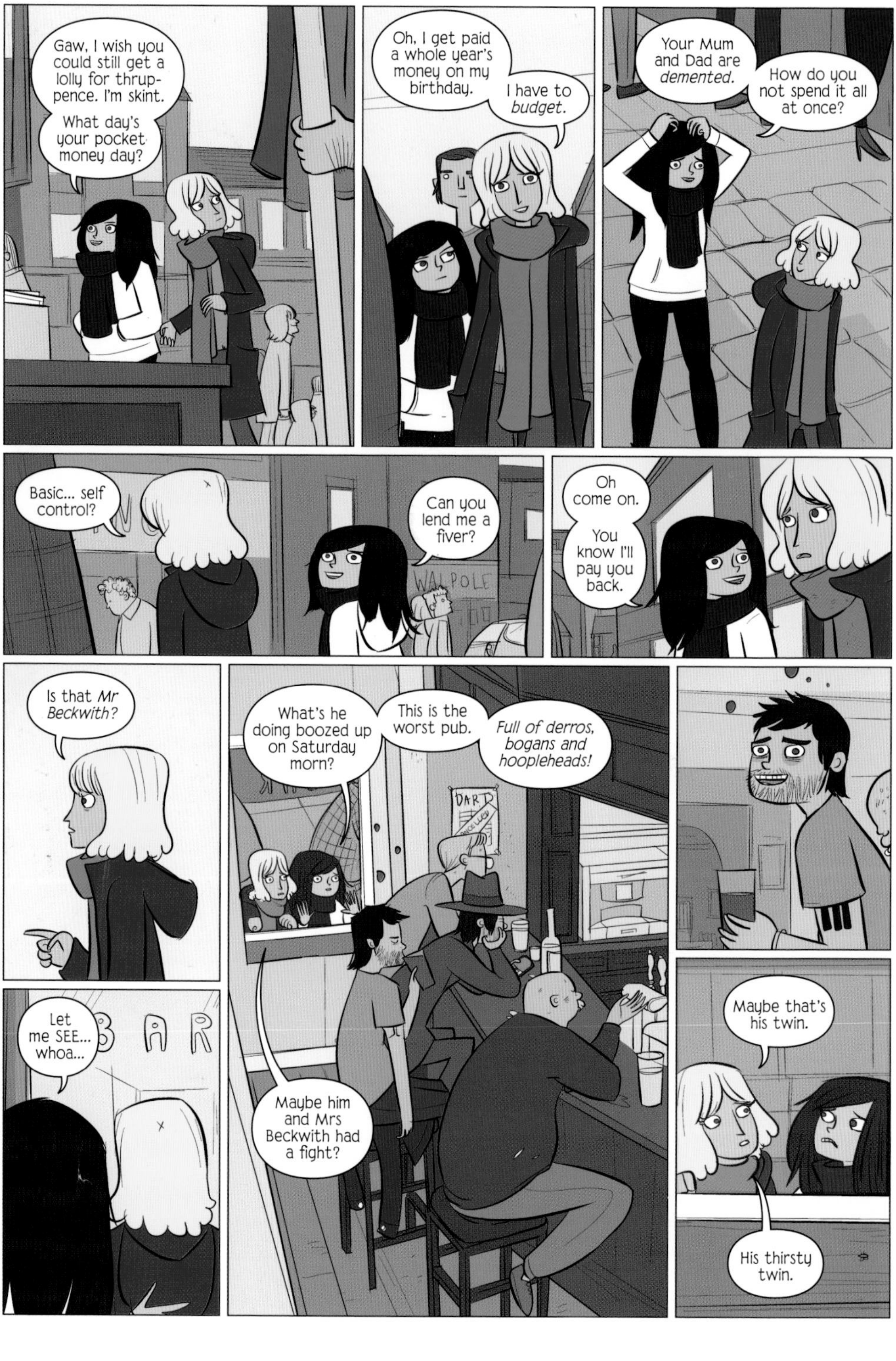
Gaw, I wish you could still get a lolly for thrup-pence. I'm skint.
What day's your pocket money day?
Oh, I get paid a whole year's money on my birthday.
I have to *budget.*
Your Mum and Dad are *demented.*
How do you not spend it all at once?
Basic... self control?
Can you lend me a fiver?
WALPOLE
Oh come on.
You know I'll pay you back.
Is that *Mr Beckwith?*
Let me SEE... whoa...
BAR
What's he doing boozed up on Saturday morn?
This is the worst pub.
Full of derros, bogans and hoopleheads!
DARTS
Maybe him and Mrs Beckwith had a fight?
Maybe that's his twin.
His thirsty twin.

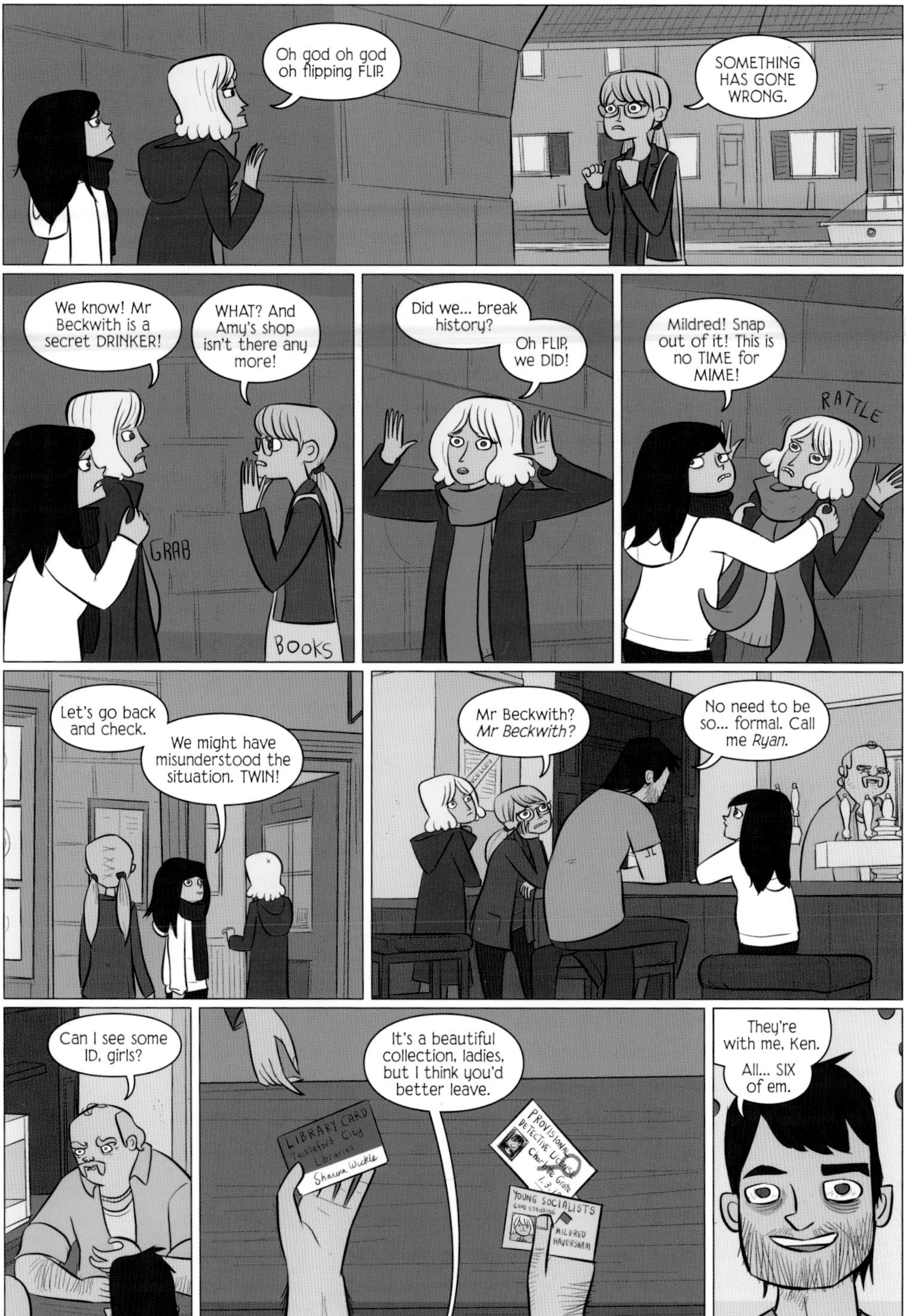
Oh god oh god oh flipping FLIP.
SOMETHING HAS GONE WRONG.
We know! Mr Beckwith is a secret DRINKER!
WHAT? And Amy's shop isn't there any more!
GRAB
BOOKS
Did we... break history?
Oh FLIP, we DID!
Mildred! Snap out of it! This is no TIME for MIME!
RATTLE
Let's go back and check.
We might have misunderstood the situation. TWIN!
Mr Beckwith? *Mr Beckwith?*
No need to be so... formal. Call me *Ryan*.
Can I see some ID, girls?
It's a beautiful collection, ladies, but I think you'd better leave.
LIBRARY CARD
Tackleford City Libraries
Shauna Wickle
PROVISIONAL DETECTIVE LICENSE
YOUNG SOCIALISTS
GOOD STANDING
MILDRED HAVERSHAM
They're with me, Ken.
All... SIX of em.

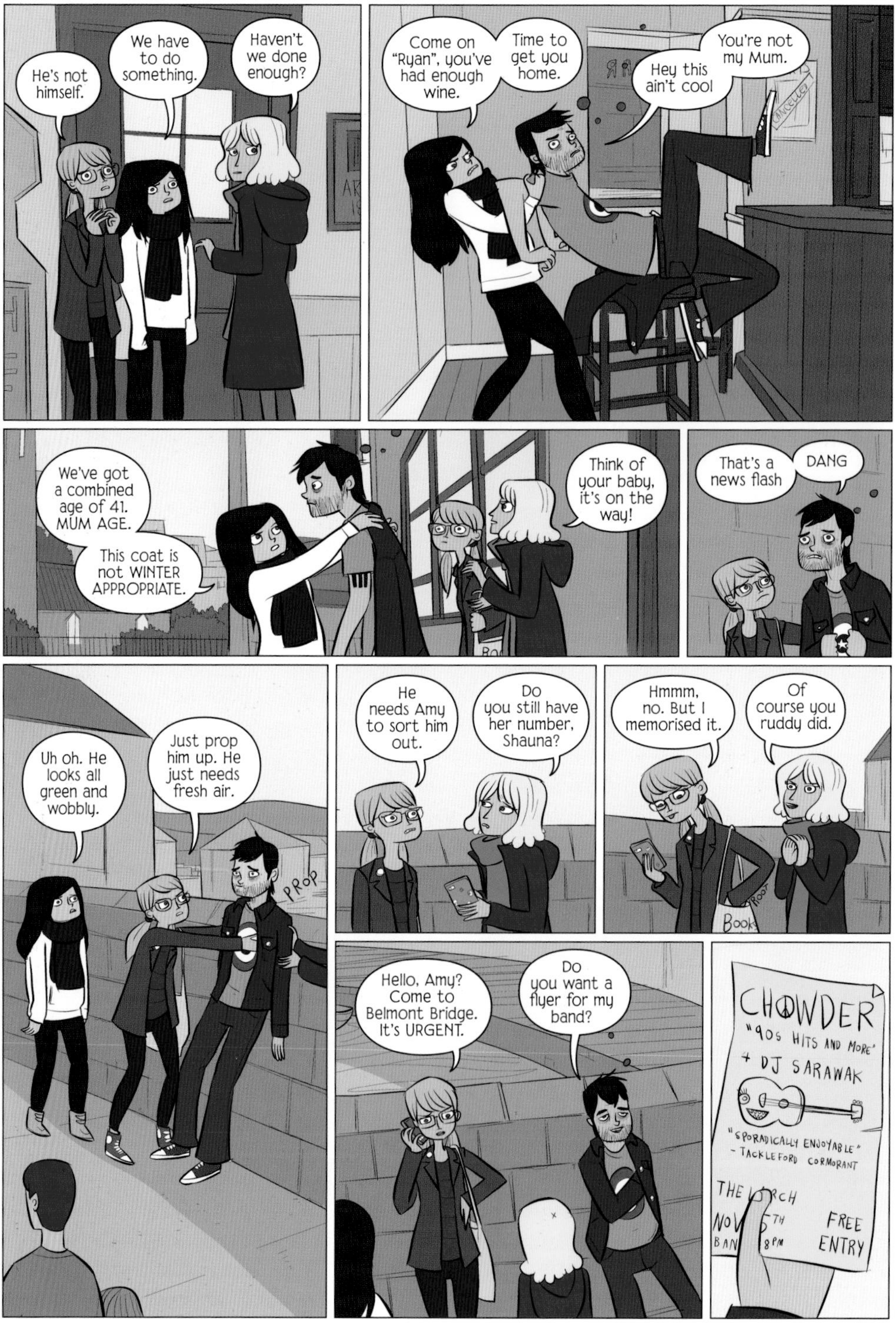
He's not himself.
We have to do something.
Haven't we done enough?
Come on "Ryan", you've had enough wine.
Time to get you home.
Hey this ain't cool
You're not my Mum.
We've got a combined age of 41. MUM AGE.
This coat is not WINTER APPROPRIATE.
Think of your baby, it's on the way!
That's a news flash
DANG
Uh oh. He looks all green and wobbly.
Just prop him up. He just needs fresh air.
PROP
He needs Amy to sort him out.
Do you still have her number, Shauna?
Hmmm, no. But I memorised it.
Of course you ruddy did.
Hello, Amy? Come to Belmont Bridge. It's URGENT.
Do you want a flyer for my band?
CHOWDER
"90s HITS AND MORE"
+ DJ SARAWAK
"SPORADICALLY ENJOYABLE"
- TACKLEFORD CORMORANT
FREE ENTRY

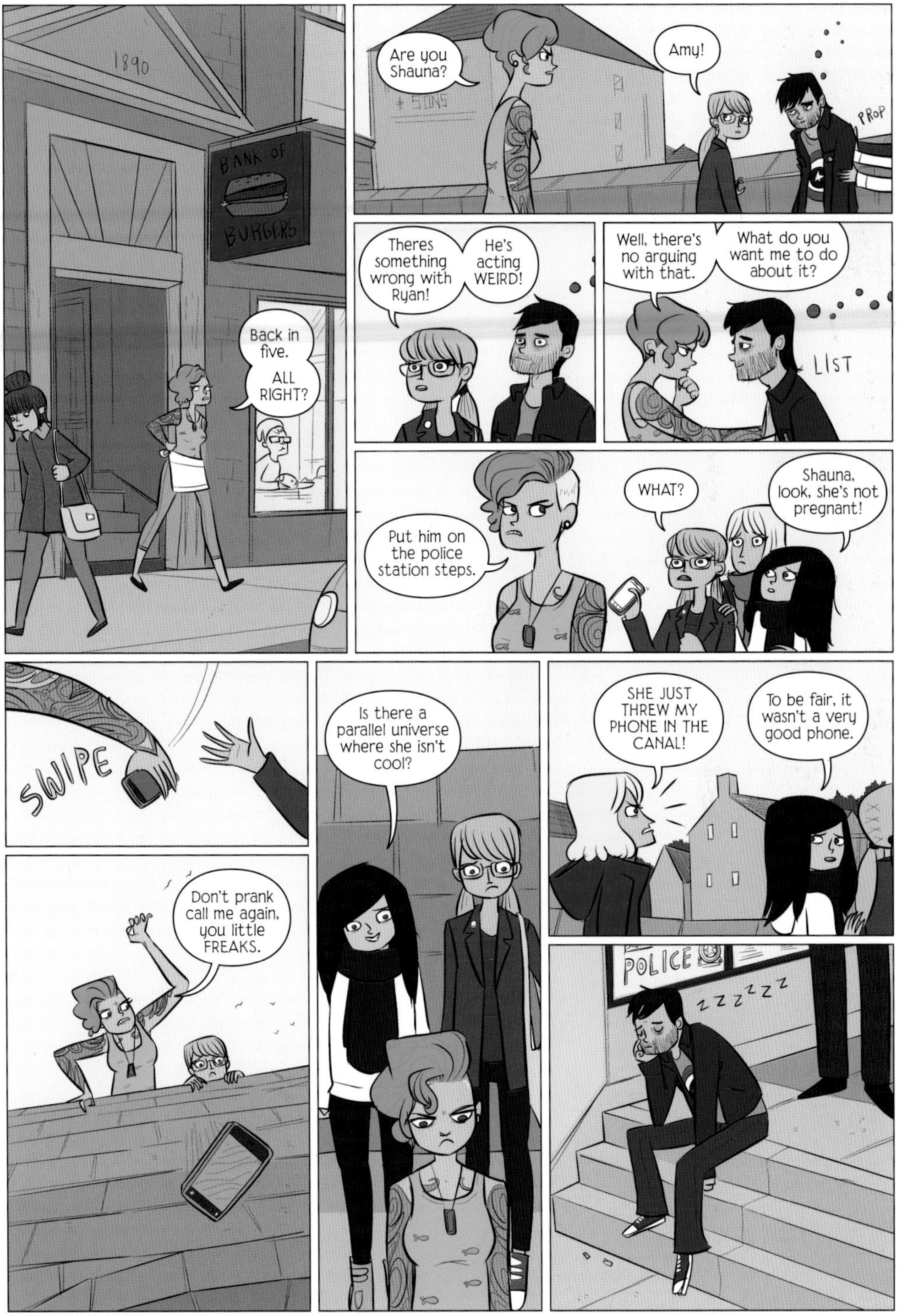
1890
BANK OF BURGERS
Back in five.
ALL RIGHT?
Are you Shauna?
Amy!
PROP
Theres something wrong with Ryan!
He's acting WEIRD!
Well, there's no arguing with that.
What do you want me to do about it?
LIST
Put him on the police station steps.
WHAT?
Shauna, look, she's not pregnant!
SWIPE
Don't prank call me again, you little FREAKS.
Is there a parallel universe where she isn't cool?
SHE JUST THREW MY PHONE IN THE CANAL!
To be fair, it wasn't a very good phone.
POLICE
Z Z Z Z Z Z

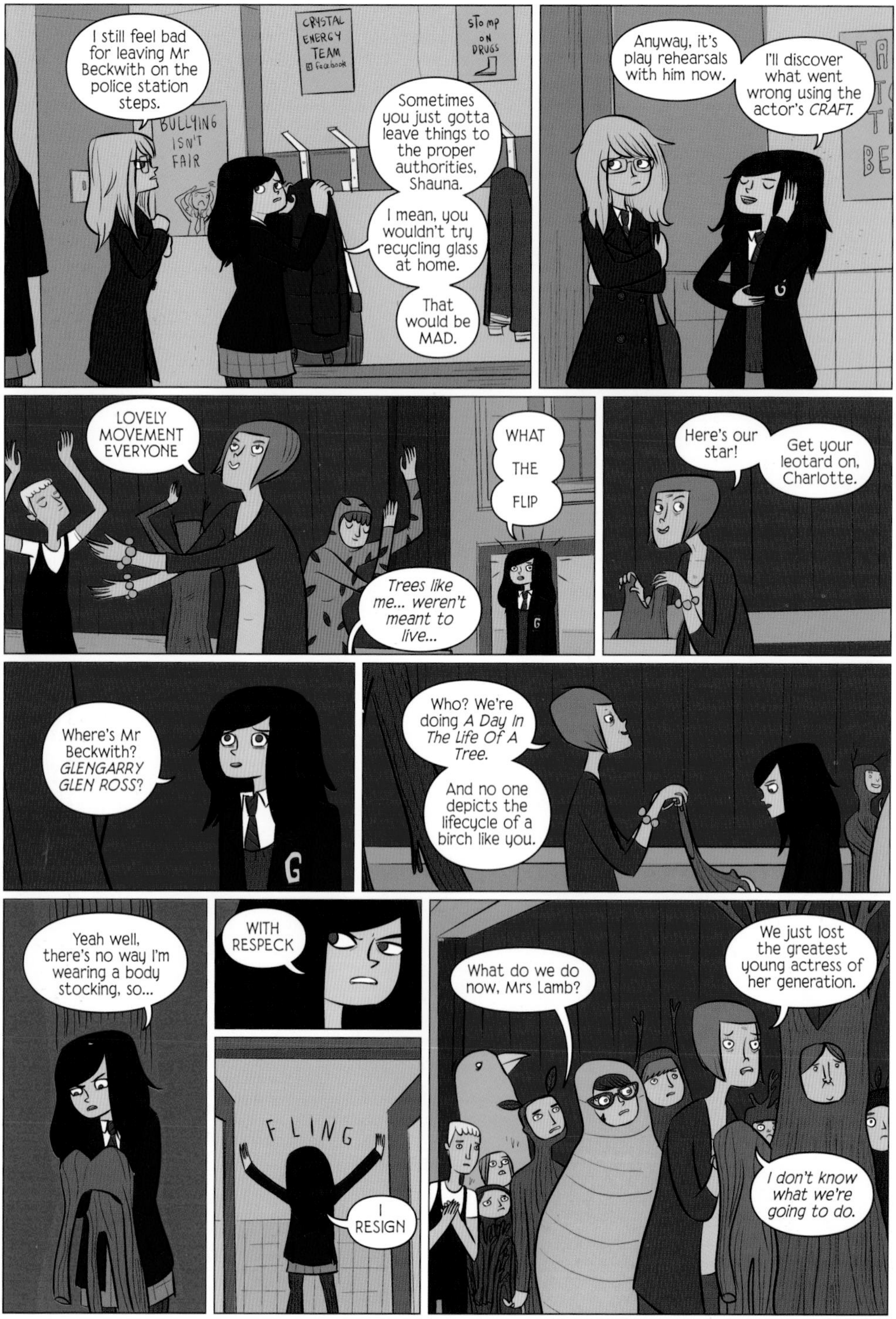
I still feel bad for leaving Mr Beckwith on the police station steps.
CRYSTAL ENERGY TEAM facebook
STOMP ON DRUGS
BULLYING ISN'T FAIR
Sometimes you just gotta leave things to the proper authorities, Shauna.
I mean, you wouldn't try recycling glass at home.
That would be MAD.
Anyway, it's play rehearsals with him now.
I'll discover what went wrong using the actor's *CRAFT.*
LOVELY MOVEMENT EVERYONE
WHAT THE FLIP
Trees like me... weren't meant to live...
Here's our star!
Get your leotard on, Charlotte.
Where's Mr Beckwith? *GLENGARRY GLEN ROSS*?
Who? We're doing *A Day In The Life Of A Tree.*
And no one depicts the lifecycle of a birch like you.
Yeah well, there's no way I'm wearing a body stocking, so...
WITH RESPECK
FLING
I RESIGN
What do we do now, Mrs Lamb?
We just lost the greatest young actress of her generation.
I don't know what we're going to do.

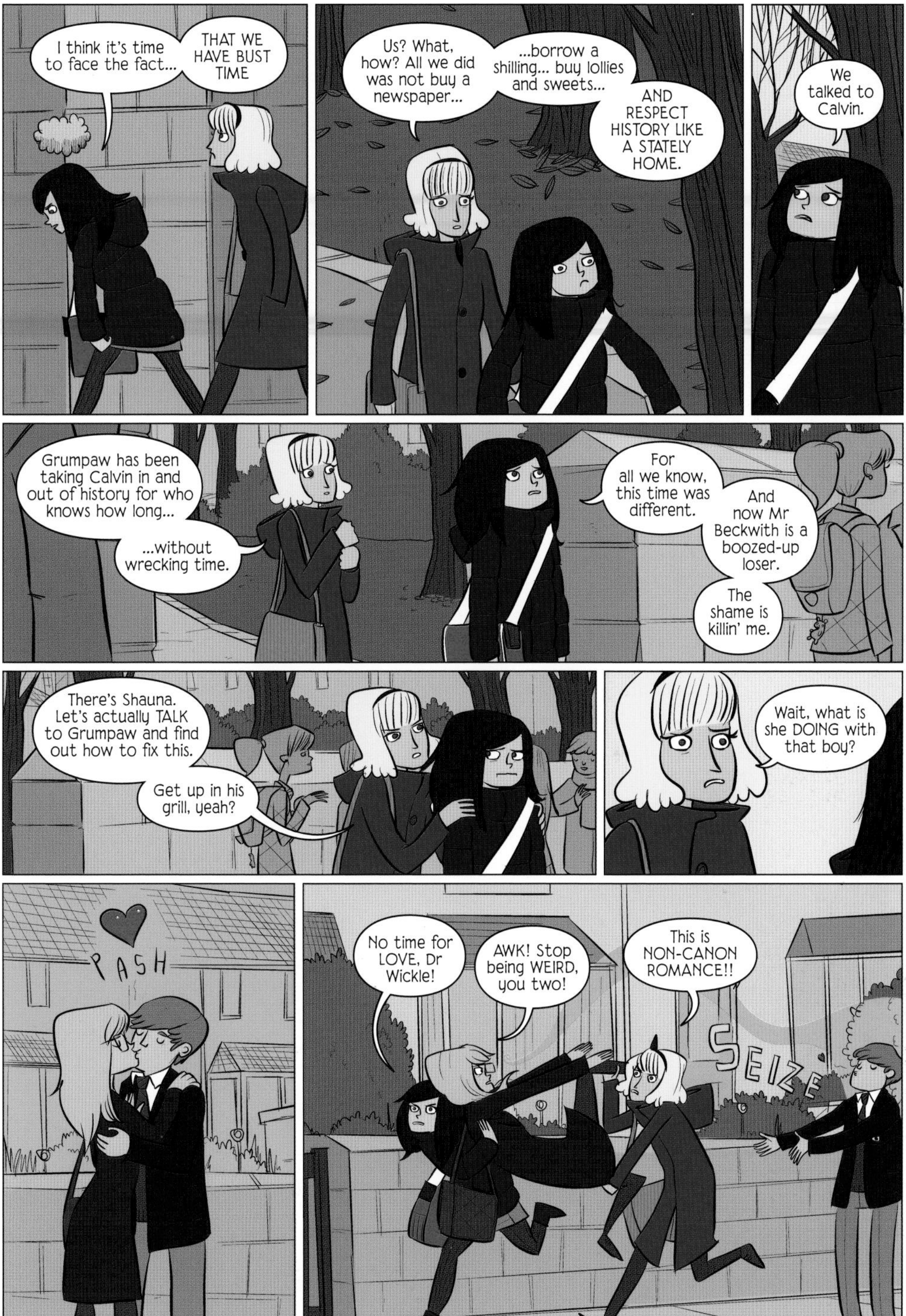
I think it's time to face the fact...
THAT WE HAVE BUST TIME
Us? What, how? All we did was not buy a newspaper...
...borrow a shilling... buy lollies and sweets...
AND RESPECT HISTORY LIKE A STATELY HOME.
We talked to Calvin.
Grumpaw has been taking Calvin in and out of history for who knows how long...
...without wrecking time.
For all we know, this time was different.
And now Mr Beckwith is a boozed-up loser.
The shame is killin' me.
There's Shauna. Let's actually TALK to Grumpaw and find out how to fix this.
Get up in his grill, yeah?
Wait, what is she DOING with that boy?
PASH
No time for LOVE, Dr Wickle!
AWK! Stop being WEIRD, you two!
This is NON-CANON ROMANCE!!
SEIZE

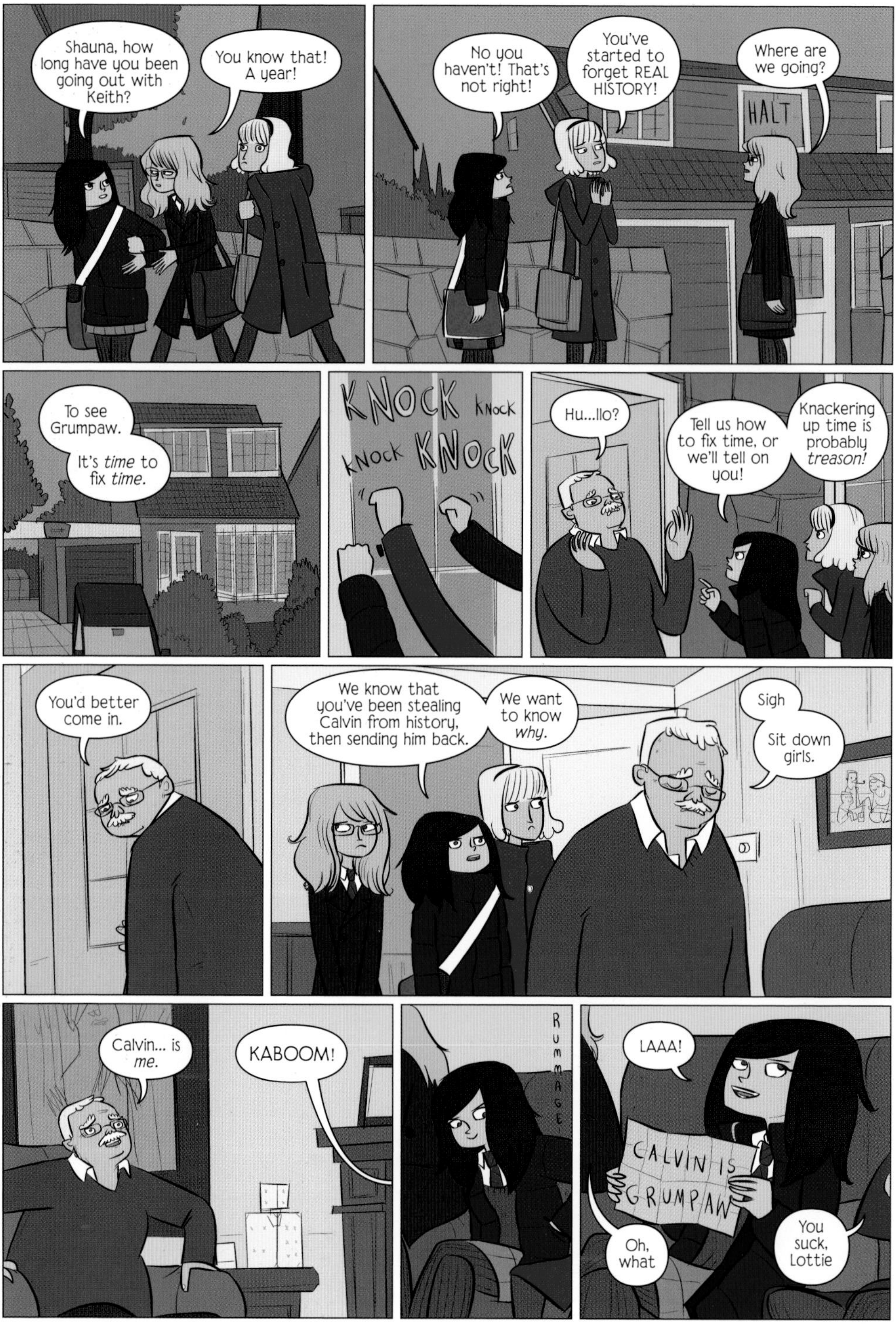
Shauna, how long have you been going out with Keith?
You know that! A year!
No you haven't! That's not right!
You've started to forget REAL HISTORY!
Where are we going?
HALT
To see Grumpaw.
It's *time* to fix *time*.
KNOCK KNOCK KNOCK KNOCK
Hu...llo?
Tell us how to fix time, or we'll tell on you!
Knackering up time is probably *treason!*
You'd better come in.
We know that you've been stealing Calvin from history, then sending him back.
We want to know *why*.
Sigh
Sit down girls.
Calvin... is *me*.
KABOOM!
RUMMAGE
LAAA!
CALVIN IS GRUMPAW
Oh, what
You suck, Lottie

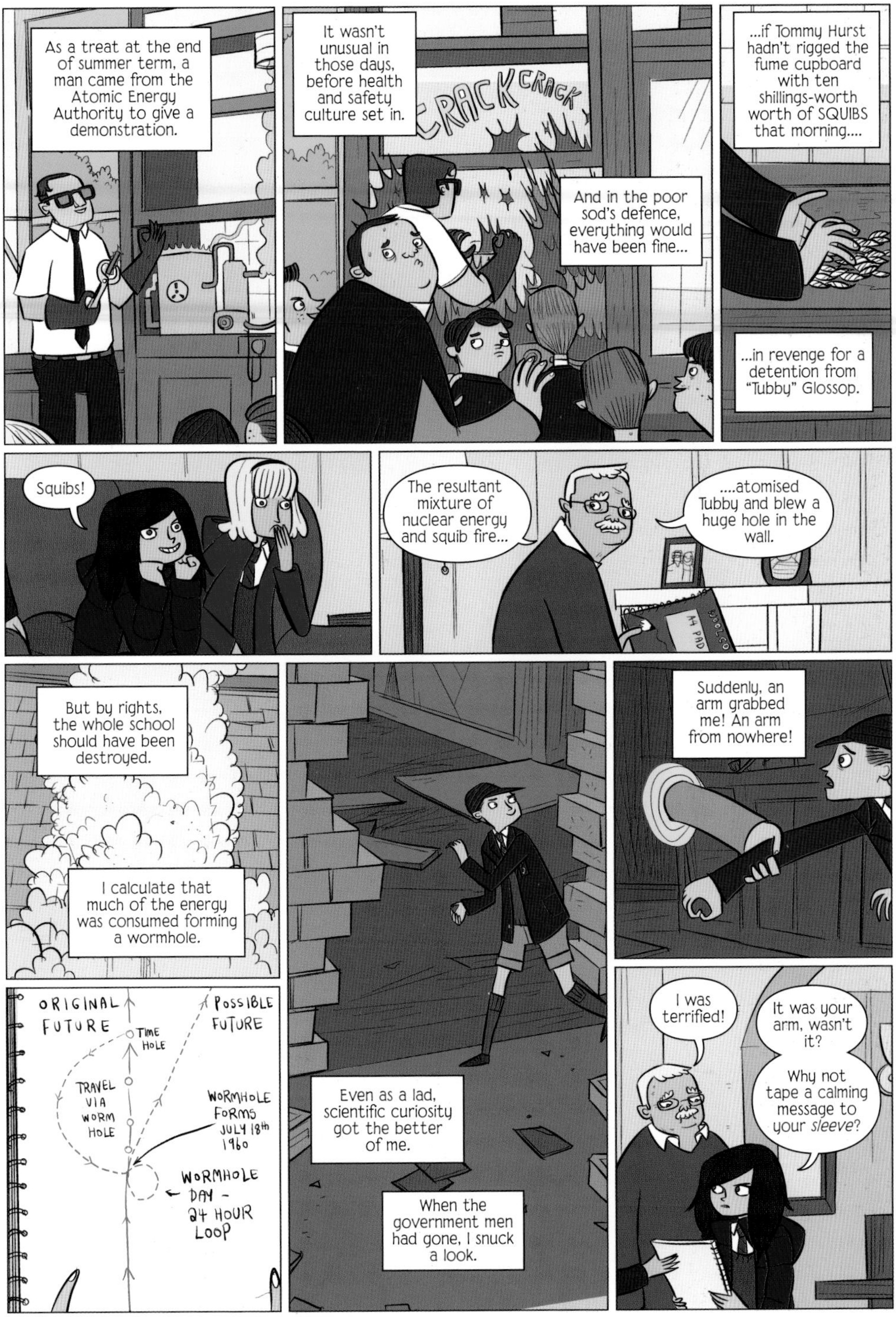
As a treat at the end of summer term, a man came from the Atomic Energy Authority to give a demonstration.
It wasn't unusual in those days, before health and safety culture set in.
CRACK CRACK
And in the poor sod's defence, everything would have been fine...
...if Tommy Hurst hadn't rigged the fume cupboard with ten shillings-worth worth of SQUIBS that morning....
...in revenge for a detention from "Tubby" Glossop.
Squibs!
The resultant mixture of nuclear energy and squib fire...
....atomised Tubby and blew a huge hole in the wall.
A4 PAD
But by rights, the whole school should have been destroyed.
I calculate that much of the energy was consumed forming a wormhole.
ORIGINAL FUTURE
POSSIBLE FUTURE
TIME HOLE
TRAVEL VIA WORM HOLE
WORMHOLE FORMS JULY 18th 1960
WORMHOLE DAY - 24 HOUR LOOP
Even as a lad, scientific curiosity got the better of me.
When the government men had gone, I snuck a look.
Suddenly, an arm grabbed me! An arm from nowhere!
I was terrified!
It was your arm, wasn't it?
Why not tape a calming message to your *sleeve*?

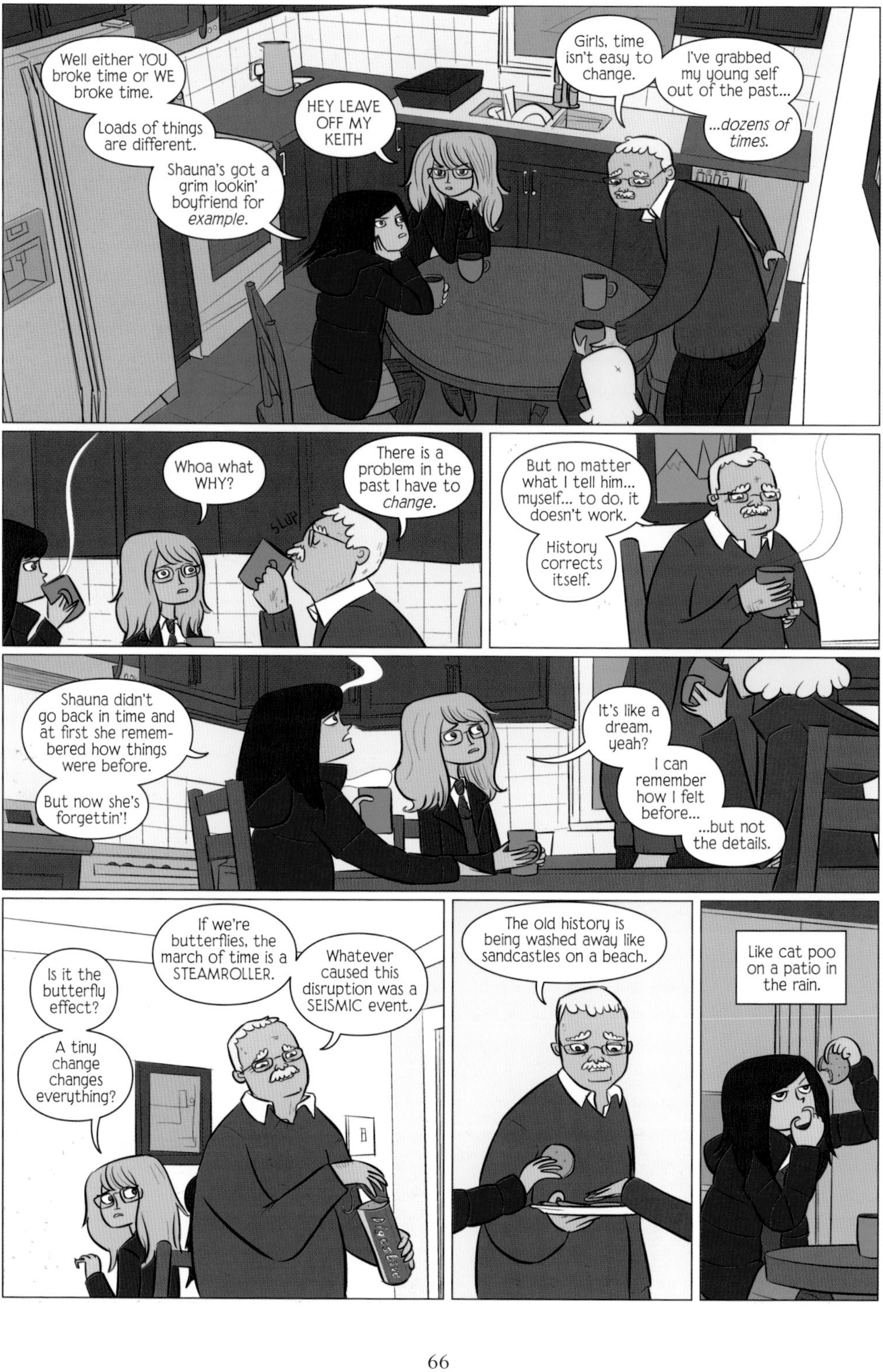
Well either YOU broke time or WE broke time.
Loads of things are different.
Shauna's got a grim lookin' boyfriend for *example.*
HEY LEAVE OFF MY KEITH
Girls, time isn't easy to change.
I've grabbed my young self out of the past...
...*dozens of times.*
Whoa what WHY?
SLUP
There is a problem in the past I have to *change.*
But no matter what I tell him... myself... to do, it doesn't work.
History corrects itself.
Shauna didn't go back in time and at first she remembered how things were before.
But now she's forgettin'!
It's like a dream, yeah?
I can remember how I felt before...
...but not the details.
Is it the butterfly effect?
A tiny change changes everything?
If we're butterflies, the march of time is a STEAMROLLER.
Whatever caused this disruption was a SEISMIC event.
Digestive
The old history is being washed away like sandcastles on a beach.
Like cat poo on a patio in the rain.

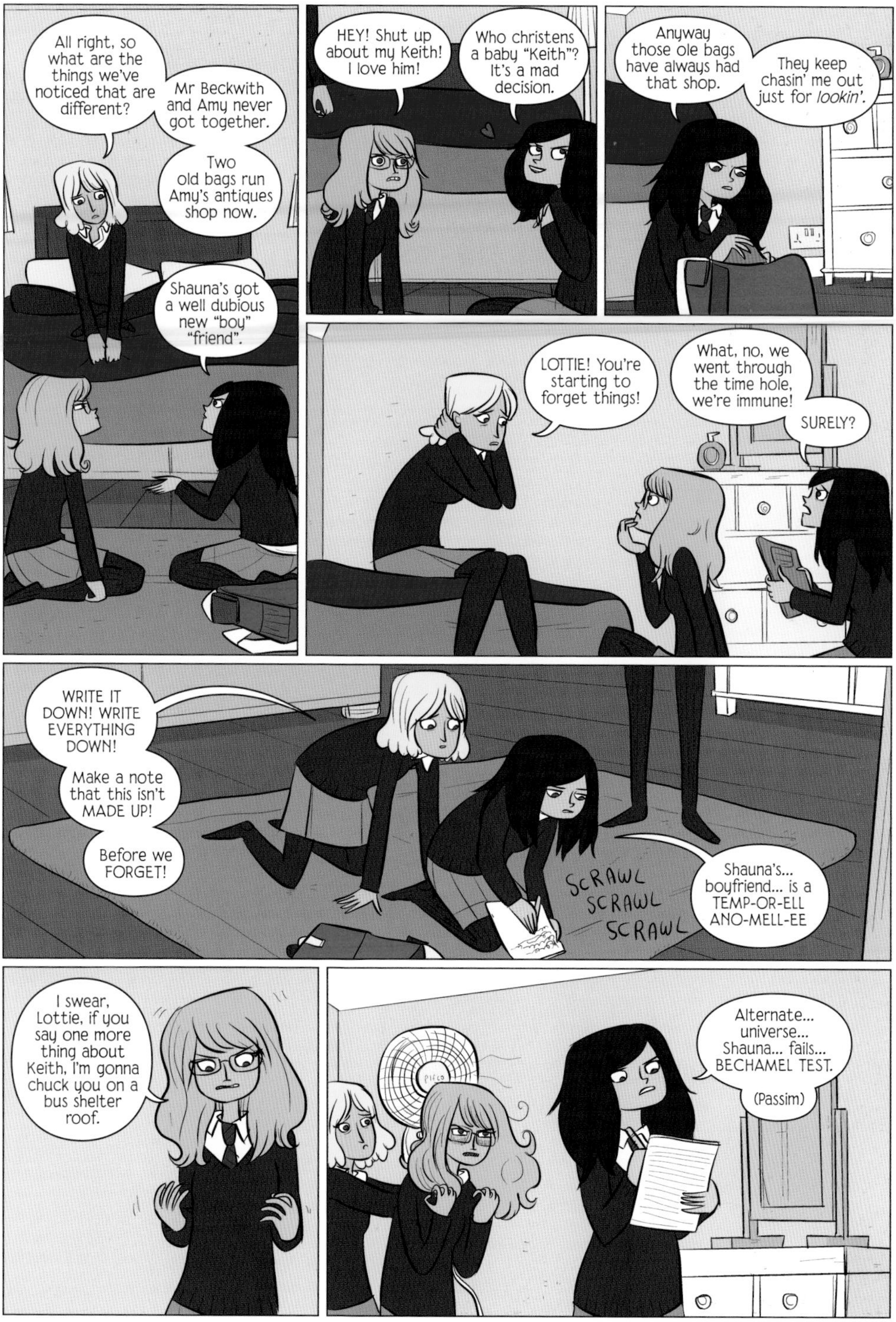
All right, so what are the things we've noticed that are different?
Mr Beckwith and Amy never got together.
Two old bags run Amy's antiques shop now.
Shauna's got a well dubious new "boy" "friend".
HEY! Shut up about my Keith! I love him!
Who christens a baby "Keith"? It's a mad decision.
Anyway those ole bags have always had that shop.
They keep chasin' me out just for *lookin'*.
LOTTIE! You're starting to forget things!
What, no, we went through the time hole, we're immune!
SURELY?
WRITE IT DOWN! WRITE EVERYTHING DOWN!
Make a note that this isn't MADE UP!
Before we FORGET!
SCRAWL SCRAWL SCRAWL
Shauna's... boyfriend... is a TEMP-OR-ELL ANO-MELL-EE
I swear, Lottie, if you say one more thing about Keith, I'm gonna chuck you on a bus shelter roof.
Alternate... universe... Shauna... fails... BECHAMEL TEST.
(Passim)

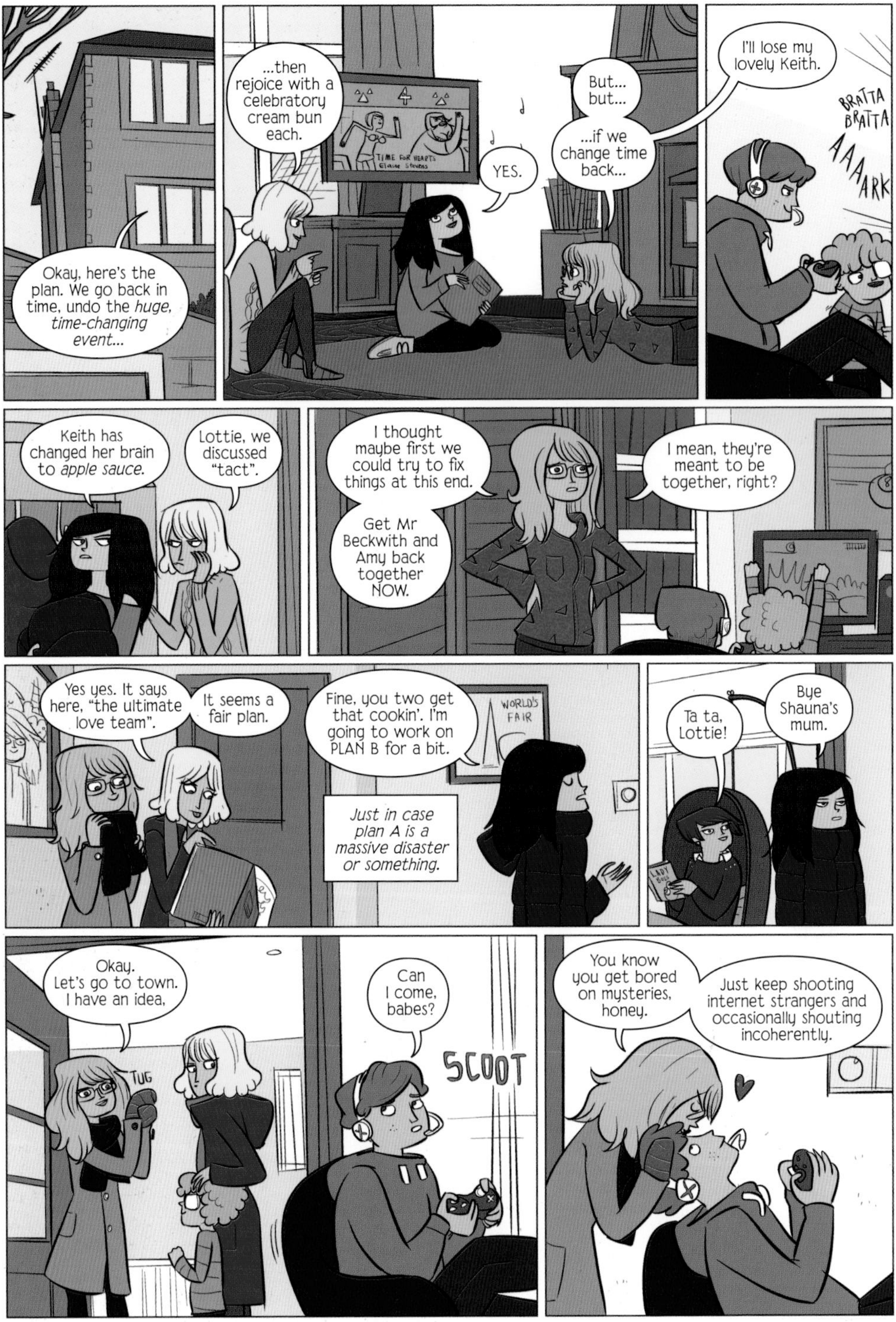
Okay, here's the plan. We go back in time, undo the *huge, time-changing event*...
...then rejoice with a celebratory cream bun each.
TIME FOR HEARTS
Elaine Stevens
YES.
But... but...
...if we change time back...
I'll lose my lovely Keith.
BRATTA BRATTA
AAAARK
Keith has changed her brain to *apple sauce*.
Lottie, we discussed "tact".
I thought maybe first we could try to fix things at this end.
Get Mr Beckwith and Amy back together NOW.
I mean, they're meant to be together, right?
Yes yes. It says here, "the ultimate love team".
It seems a fair plan.
Fine, you two get that cookin'. I'm going to work on PLAN B for a bit.
WORLD'S FAIR
Just in case plan A is a massive disaster or something.
Ta ta, Lottie!
Bye Shauna's mum.
Okay. Let's go to town. I have an idea.
TUG
Can I come, babes?
SCOOT
You know you get bored on mysteries, honey.
Just keep shooting internet strangers and occasionally shouting incoherently.

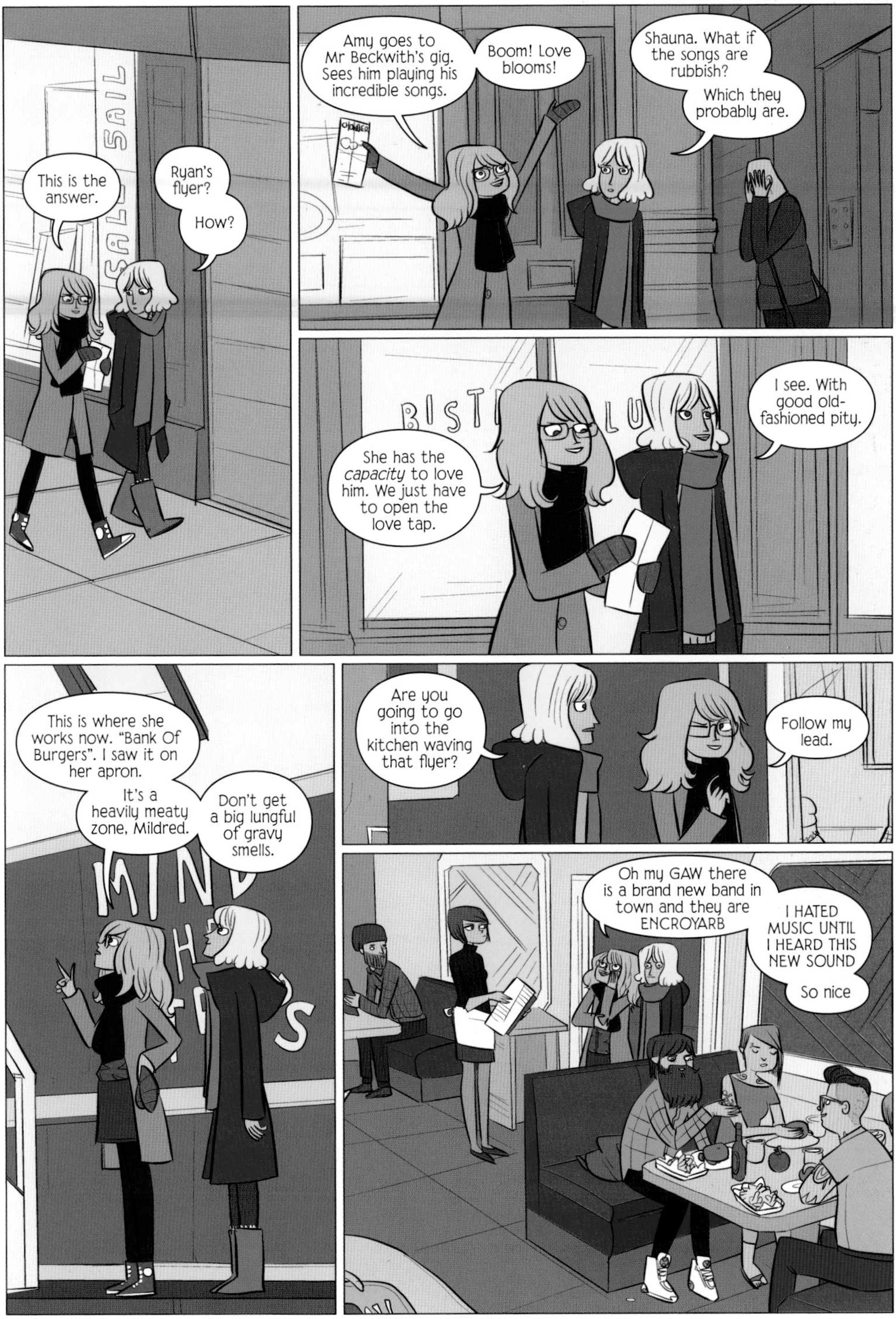
This is the answer.
Ryan's flyer?
How?
Amy goes to Mr Beckwith's gig. Sees him playing his incredible songs.
Boom! Love blooms!
Shauna. What if the songs are rubbish?
Which they probably are.
She has the *capacity* to love him. We just have to open the love tap.
I see. With good old-fashioned pity.
This is where she works now. "Bank Of Burgers". I saw it on her apron.
It's a heavily meaty zone, Mildred.
Don't get a big lungful of gravy smells.
Are you going to go into the kitchen waving that flyer?
Follow my lead.
Oh my GAW there is a brand new band in town and they are ENCROYARB
I HATED MUSIC UNTIL I HEARD THIS NEW SOUND
So nice

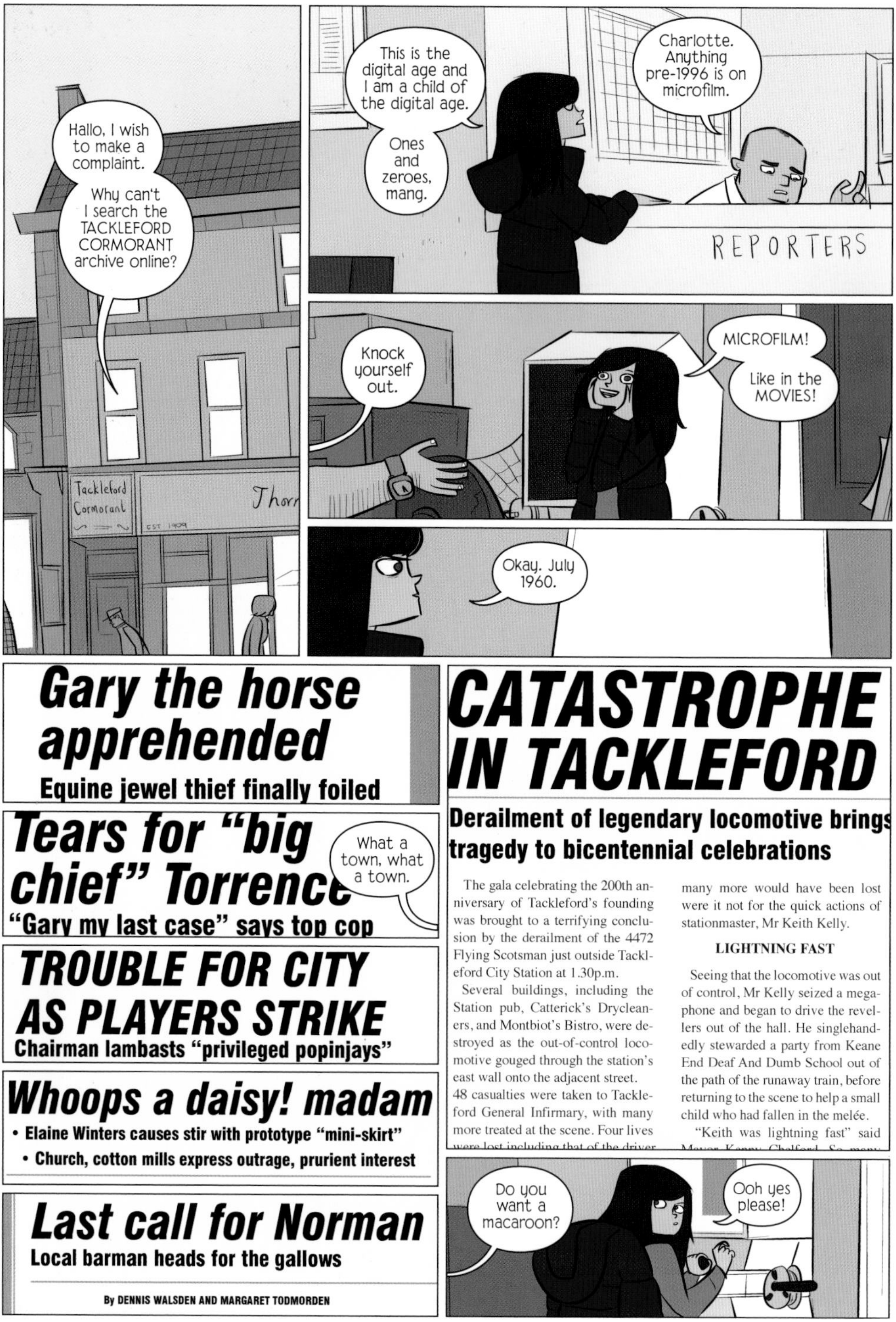
Hallo, I wish to make a complaint.
Why can't I search the TACKLEFORD CORMORANT archive online?
Tackleford Cormorant
Thorn
EST 1909
This is the digital age and I am a child of the digital age.
Ones and zeroes, mang.
Charlotte. Anything pre-1996 is on microfilm.
REPORTERS
Knock yourself out.
MICROFILM!
Like in the MOVIES!
Okay. July 1960.
Gary the horse apprehended
Equine jewel thief finally foiled
Tears for "big chief" Torrence
"Gary my last case" says top cop
What a town, what a town.
TROUBLE FOR CITY AS PLAYERS STRIKE
Chairman lambasts "privileged popinjays"
Whoops a daisy! madam
• Elaine Winters causes stir with prototype "mini-skirt"
• Church, cotton mills express outrage, prurient interest
Last call for Norman
Local barman heads for the gallows
By DENNIS WALSDEN AND MARGARET TODMORDEN
CATASTROPHE IN TACKLEFORD
Derailment of legendary locomotive brings tragedy to bicentennial celebrations
The gala celebrating the 200th anniversary of Tackleford's founding was brought to a terrifying conclusion by the derailment of the 4472 Flying Scotsman just outside Tackleford City Station at 1.30p.m.
Several buildings, including the Station pub, Catterick's Drycleaners, and Montbiot's Bistro, were destroyed as the out-of-control locomotive gouged through the station's east wall onto the adjacent street.
48 casualties were taken to Tackleford General Infirmary, with many more treated at the scene. Four lives
many more would have been lost were it not for the quick actions of stationmaster, Mr Keith Kelly.
LIGHTNING FAST
Seeing that the locomotive was out of control, Mr Kelly seized a megaphone and began to drive the revellers out of the hall. He singlehandedly stewarded a party from Keane End Deaf And Dumb School out of the path of the runaway train, before returning to the scene to help a small child who had fallen in the melée.
"Keith was lightning fast" said
Do you want a macaroon?
Ooh yes please!

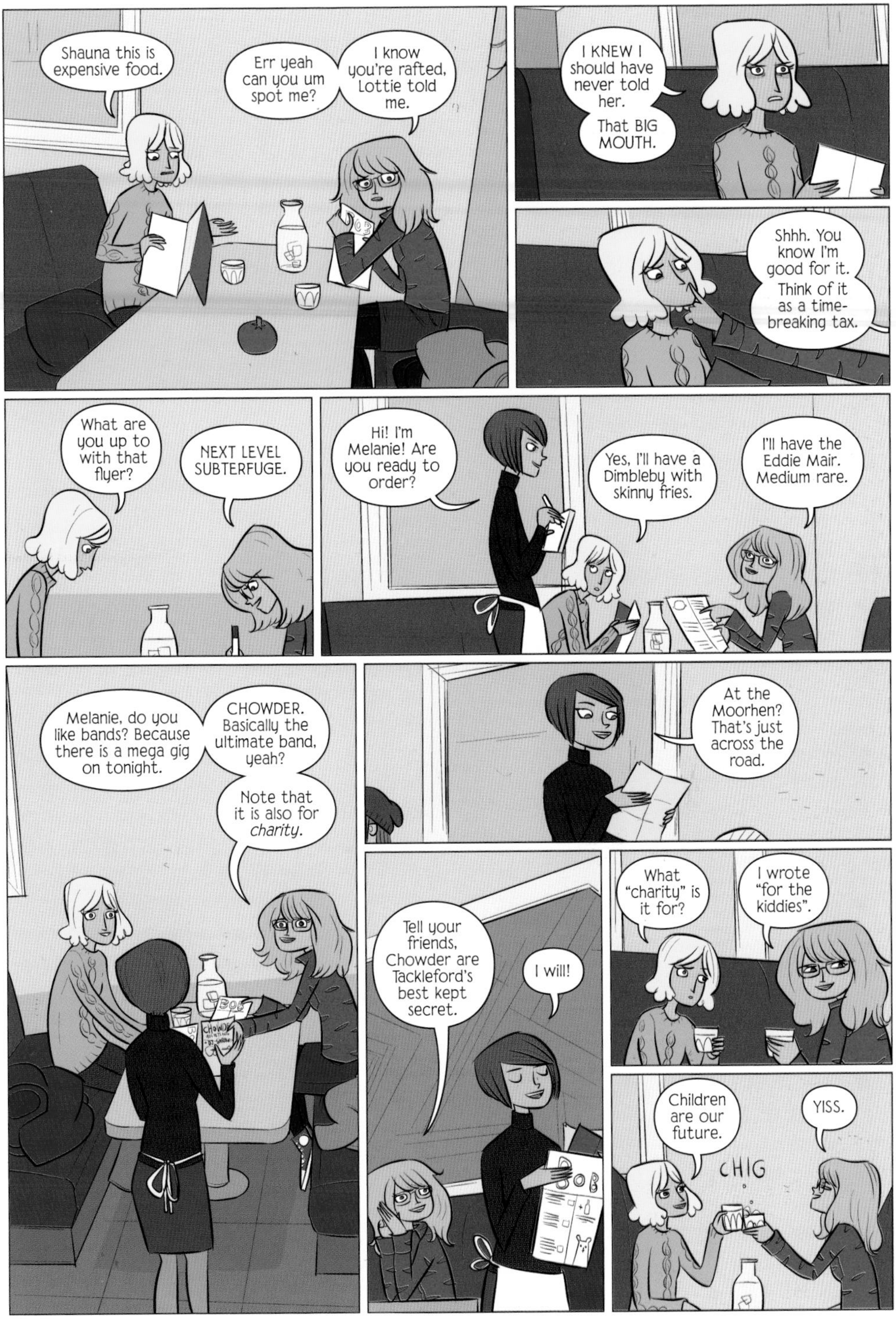
Shauna this is expensive food.
Err yeah can you um spot me?
I know you're rafted, Lottie told me.
I KNEW I should have never told her.
That BIG MOUTH.
Shhh. You know I'm good for it.
Think of it as a time-breaking tax.
What are you up to with that flyer?
NEXT LEVEL SUBTERFUGE.
Hi! I'm Melanie! Are you ready to order?
Yes, I'll have a Dimbleby with skinny fries.
I'll have the Eddie Mair. Medium rare.
Melanie, do you like bands? Because there is a mega gig on tonight.
CHOWDER. Basically the ultimate band, yeah?
Note that it is also for *charity*.
At the Moorhen? That's just across the road.
Tell your friends, Chowder are Tackleford's best kept secret.
I will!
What "charity" is it for?
I wrote "for the kiddies".
Children are our future.
YISS.
CHIG

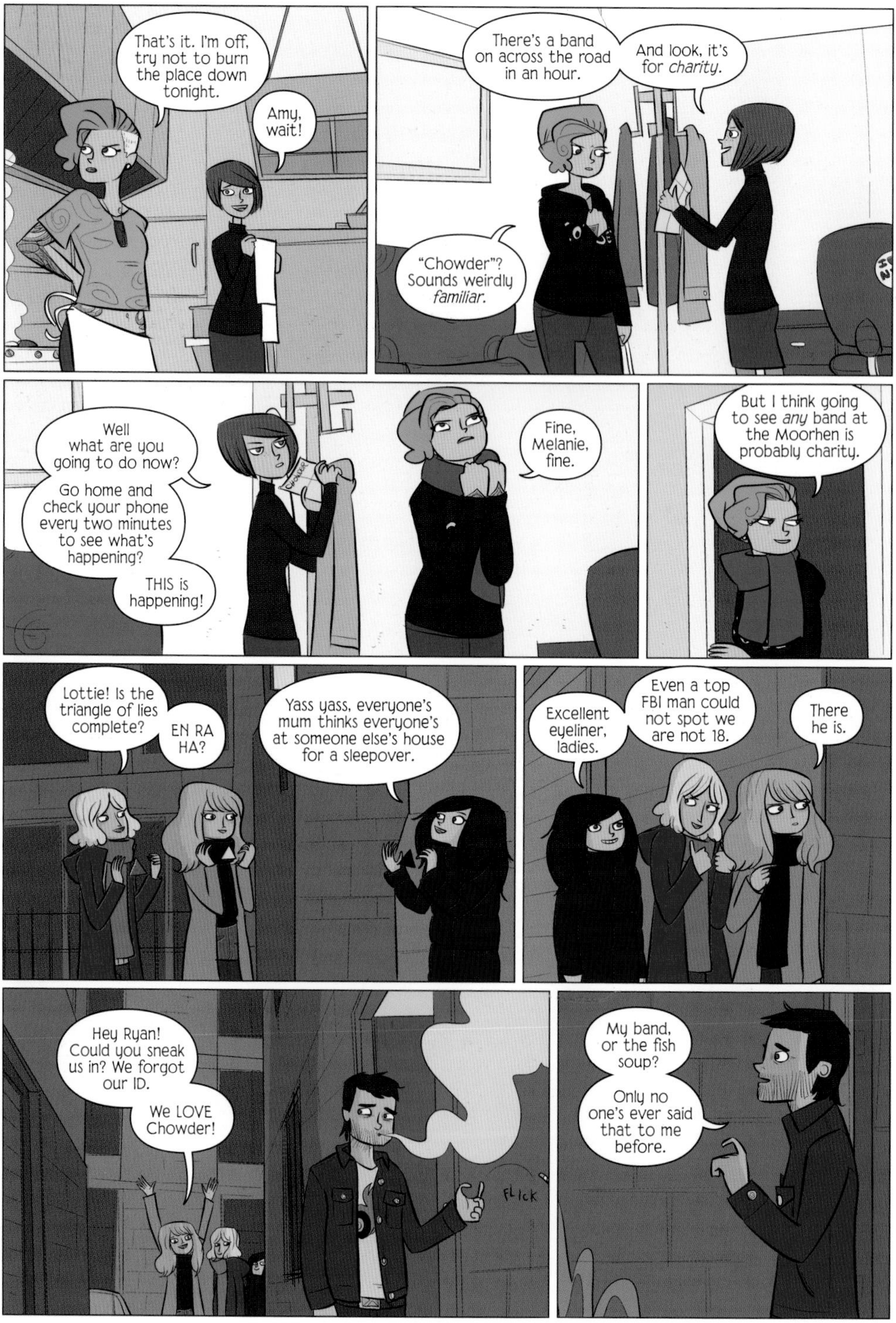
That's it. I'm off, try not to burn the place down tonight.
Amy, wait!
There's a band on across the road in an hour.
And look, it's for *charity*.
"Chowder"? Sounds weirdly *familiar*.
Well what are you going to do now?
Go home and check your phone every two minutes to see what's happening?
THIS is happening!
Fine, Melanie, fine.
But I think going to see *any* band at the Moorhen is probably charity.
Lottie! Is the triangle of lies complete?
EN RA HA?
Yass yass, everyone's mum thinks everyone's at someone else's house for a sleepover.
Excellent eyeliner, ladies.
Even a top FBI man could not spot we are not 18.
There he is.
Hey Ryan! Could you sneak us in? We forgot our ID.
We LOVE Chowder!
FLICK
My band, or the fish soup?
Only no one's ever said that to me before.

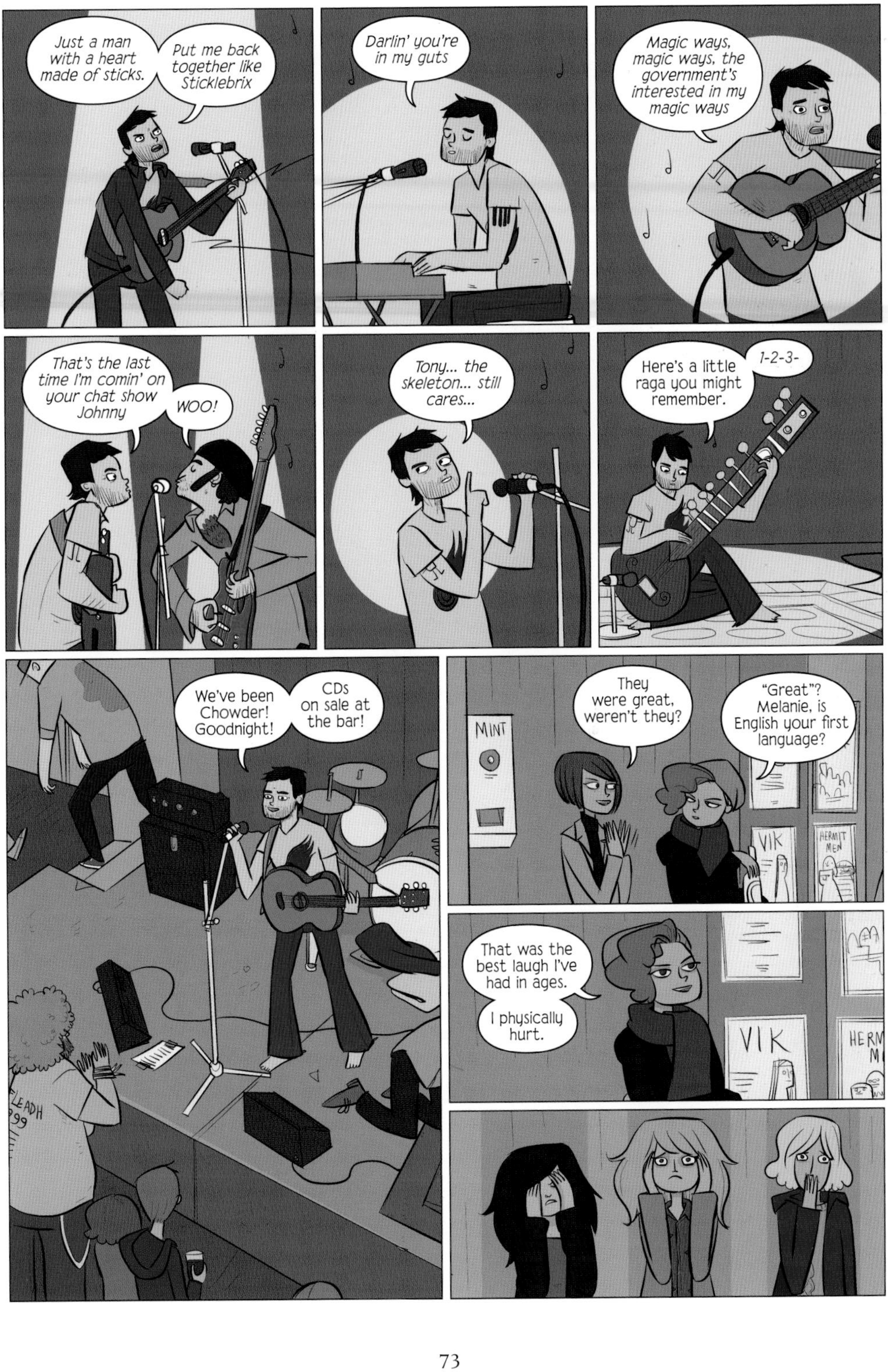
Just a man with a heart made of sticks.
Put me back together like Sticklebrix
Darlin' you're in my guts
Magic ways, magic ways, the government's interested in my magic ways
That's the last time I'm comin' on your chat show Johnny
WOO!
Tony... the skeleton... still cares...
Here's a little raga you might remember.
1-2-3-
We've been Chowder! Goodnight!
CDs on sale at the bar!
MINT
They were great, weren't they?
"Great"? Melanie, is English your first language?
VIK
HERMIT MEN
That was the best laugh I've had in ages.
I physically hurt.
VIK

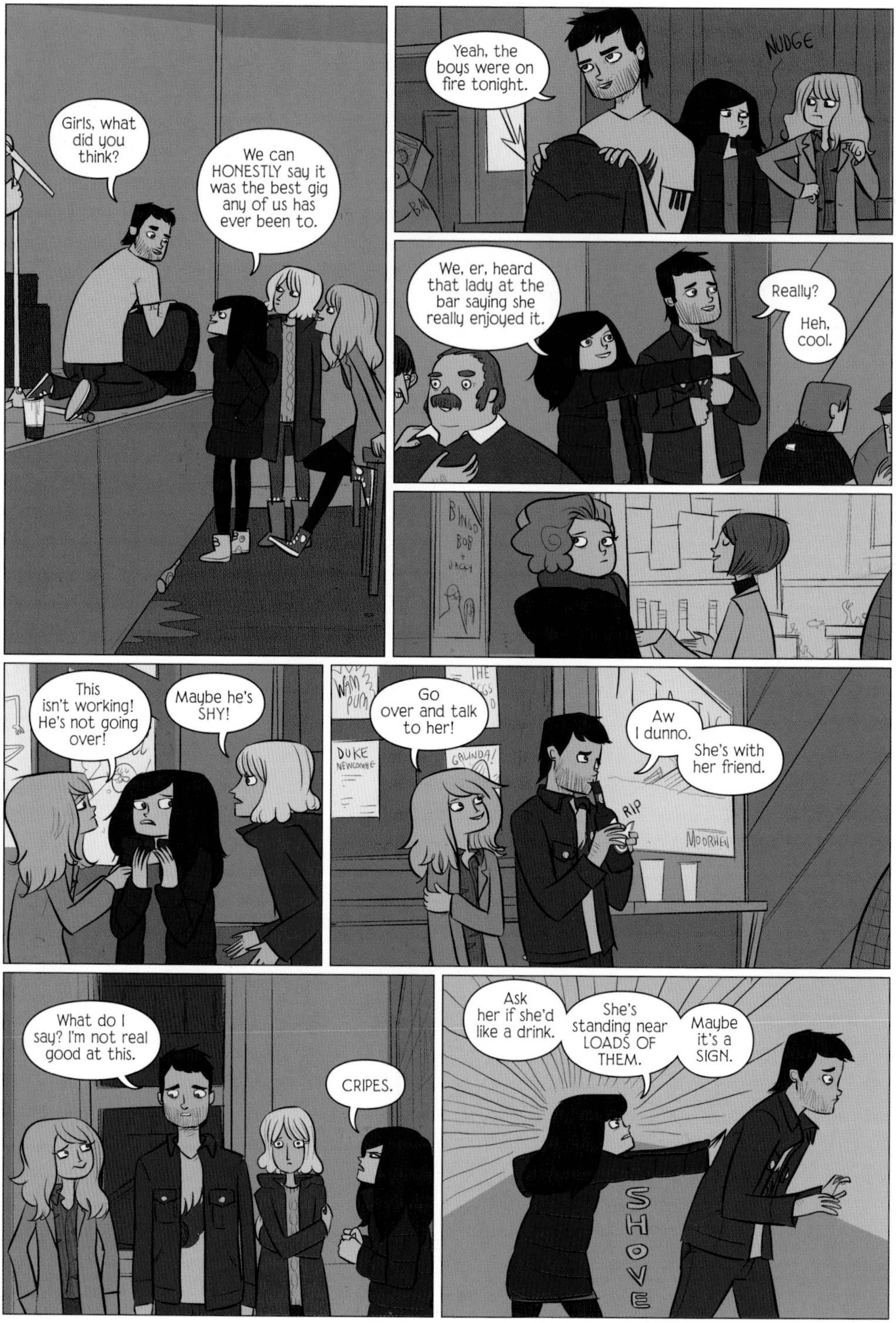
Girls, what did you think?
We can HONESTLY say it was the best gig any of us has ever been to.
Yeah, the boys were on fire tonight.
NUDGE
We, er, heard that lady at the bar saying she really enjoyed it.
Really?
Heh, cool.
This isn't working! He's not going over!
Maybe he's SHY!
Go over and talk to her!
Aw I dunno.
She's with her friend.
What do I say? I'm not real good at this.
CRIPES.
Ask her if she'd like a drink.
She's standing near LOADS OF THEM.
Maybe it's a SIGN.
SHOVE

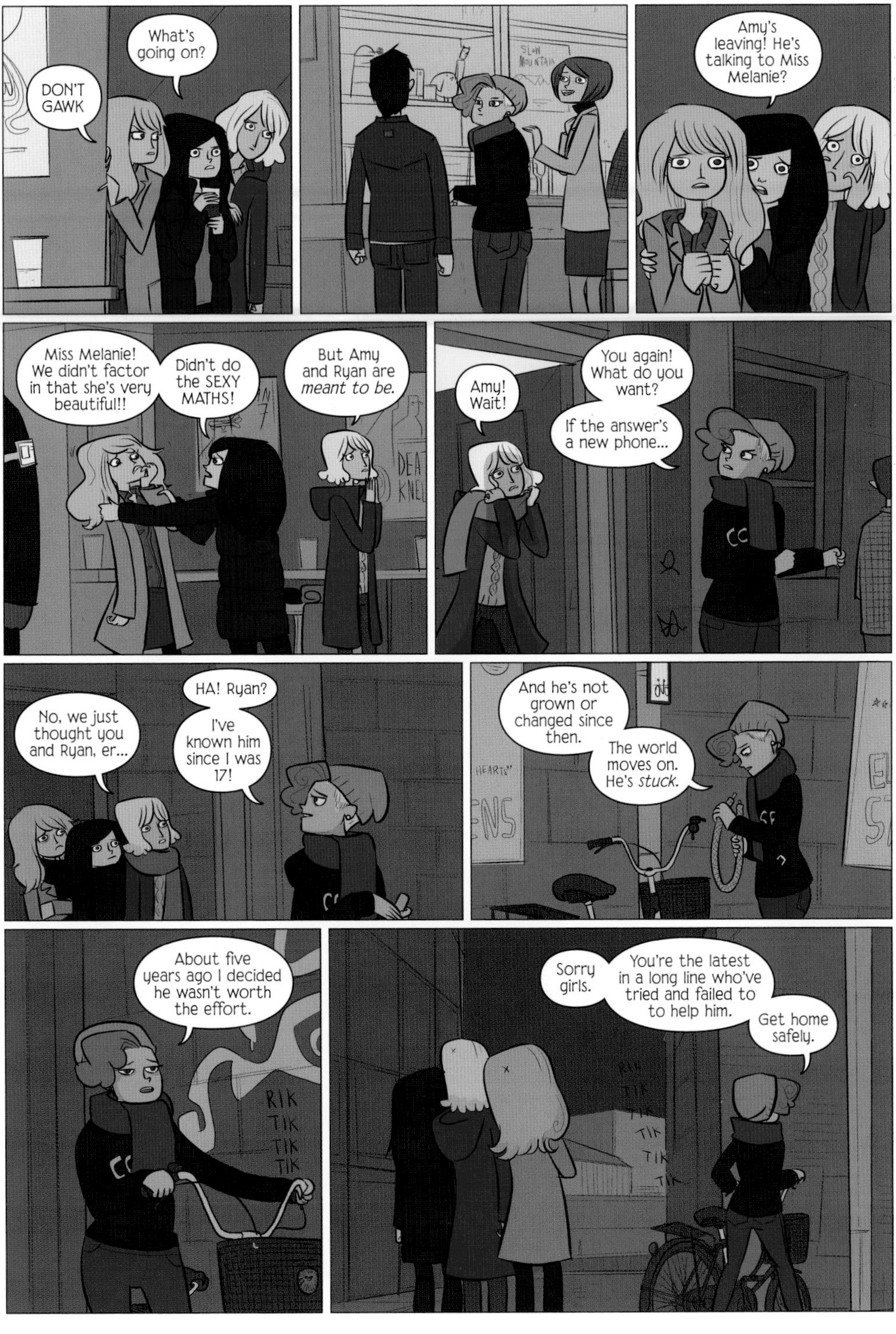
DON'T GAWK
What's going on?
SLOW MOUNTAIN
Amy's leaving! He's talking to Miss Melanie?
Miss Melanie! We didn't factor in that she's very beautiful!!
Didn't do the SEXY MATHS!
But Amy and Ryan are *meant to be.*
Amy! Wait!
You again! What do you want?
If the answer's a new phone...
No, we just thought you and Ryan, er...
HA! Ryan?
I've known him since I was 17!
And he's not grown or changed since then.
The world moves on. He's *stuck.*
About five years ago I decided he wasn't worth the effort.
RIK TIK TIK TIK
Sorry girls.
You're the latest in a long line who've tried and failed to to help him.
Get home safely.

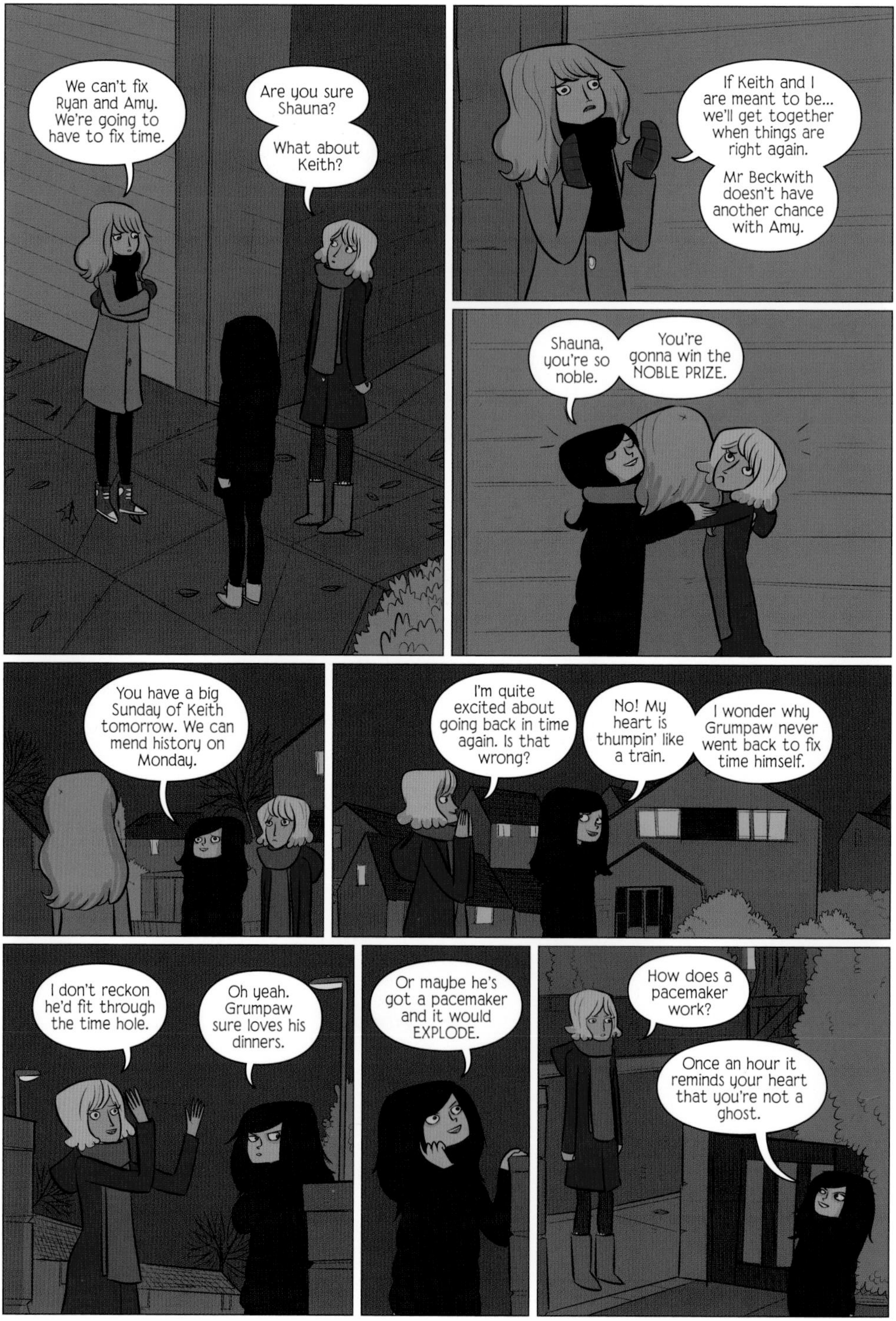
We can't fix Ryan and Amy. We're going to have to fix time.
Are you sure Shauna?
What about Keith?
If Keith and I are meant to be... we'll get together when things are right again.
Mr Beckwith doesn't have another chance with Amy.
Shauna, you're so noble.
You're gonna win the NOBLE PRIZE.
You have a big Sunday of Keith tomorrow. We can mend history on Monday.
I'm quite excited about going back in time again. Is that wrong?
No! My heart is thumpin' like a train.
I wonder why Grumpaw never went back to fix time himself.
I don't reckon he'd fit through the time hole.
Oh yeah. Grumpaw sure loves his dinners.
Or maybe he's got a pacemaker and it would EXPLODE.
How does a pacemaker work?
Once an hour it reminds your heart that you're not a ghost.

3

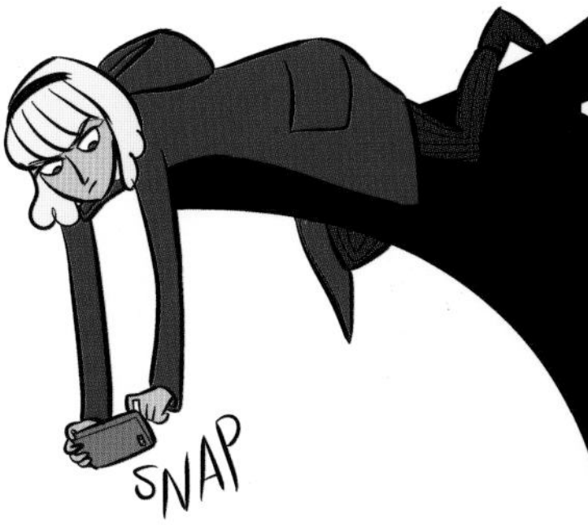
SNAP

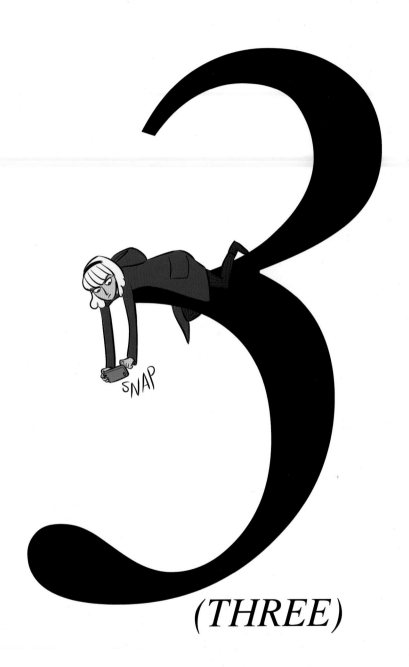

(THREE)

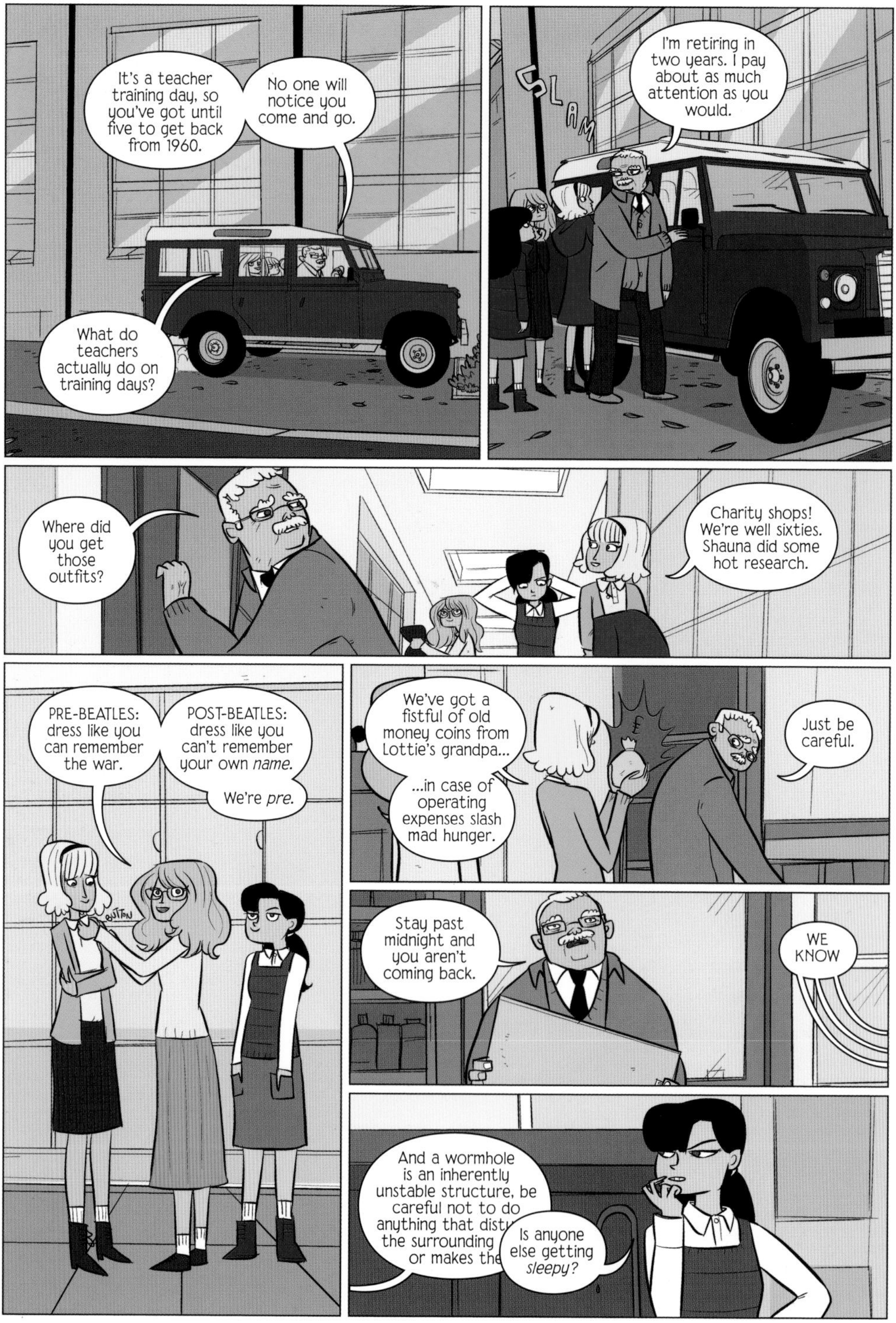
It's a teacher training day, so you've got until five to get back from 1960.
No one will notice you come and go.
What do teachers actually do on training days?
SLAM
I'm retiring in two years. I pay about as much attention as you would.
Where did you get those outfits?
Charity shops! We're well sixties. Shauna did some hot research.
PRE-BEATLES: dress like you can remember the war.
POST-BEATLES: dress like you can't remember your own *name*.
We're *pre*.
BUTTON
We've got a fistful of old money coins from Lottie's grandpa...
...in case of operating expenses slash mad hunger.
£
Just be careful.
Stay past midnight and you aren't coming back.
WE KNOW
And a wormhole is an inherently unstable structure, be careful not to do anything that dist the surrounding or makes the
Is anyone else getting *sleepy?*

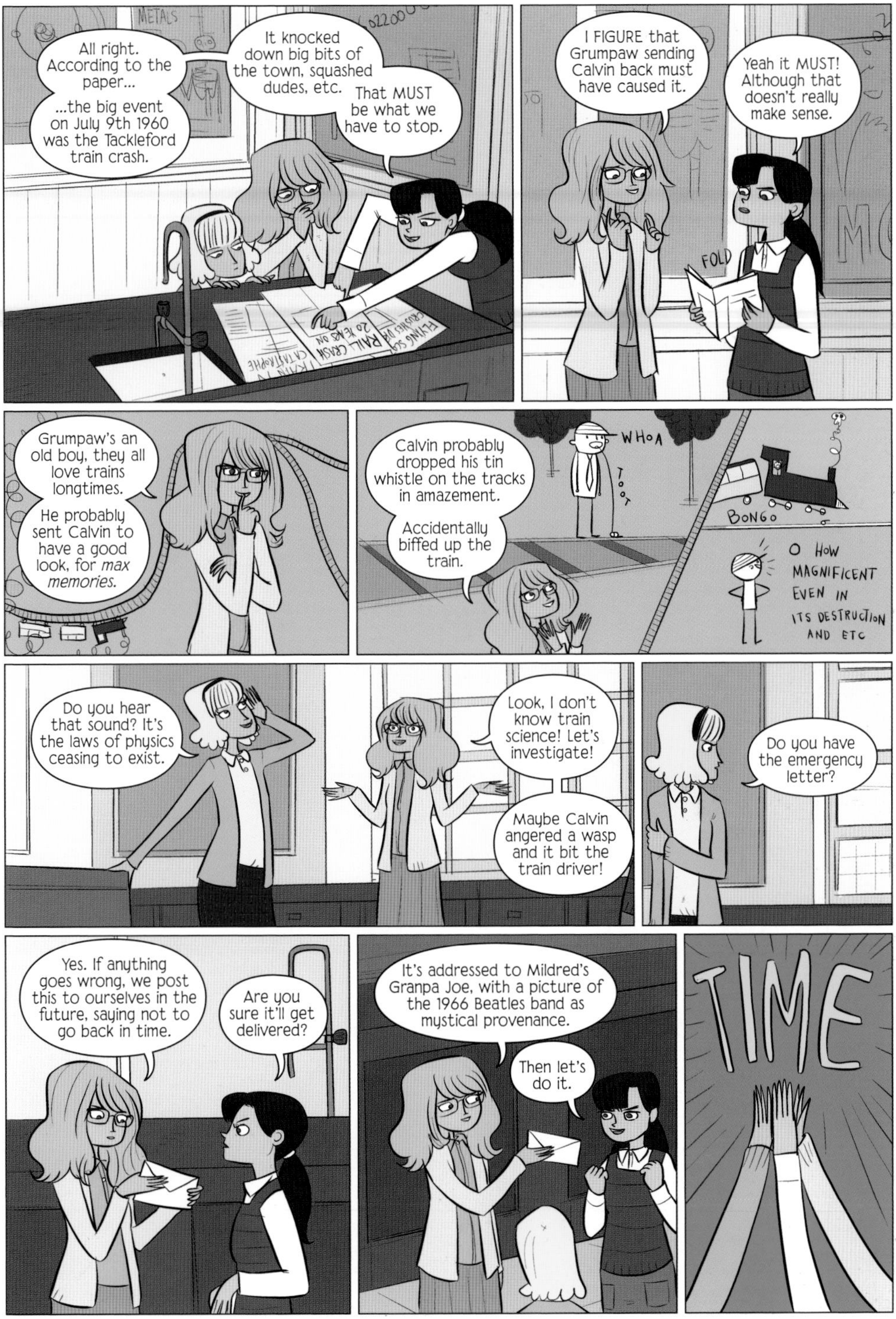
All right. According to the paper...
...the big event on July 9th 1960 was the Tackleford train crash.
It knocked down big bits of the town, squashed dudes, etc.
That MUST be what we have to stop.
RAIL CRASH
CATASTROPHE
I FIGURE that Grumpaw sending Calvin back must have caused it.
Yeah it MUST! Although that doesn't really make sense.
FOLD
Grumpaw's an old boy, they all love trains longtimes.
He probably sent Calvin to have a good look, for *max memories.*
Calvin probably dropped his tin whistle on the tracks in amazement.
Accidentally biffed up the train.
WHOA
TOOT
BONGO
O HOW MAGNIFICENT EVEN IN ITS DESTRUCTION AND ETC
Do you hear that sound? It's the laws of physics ceasing to exist.
Look, I don't know train science! Let's investigate!
Maybe Calvin angered a wasp and it bit the train driver!
Do you have the emergency letter?
Yes. If anything goes wrong, we post this to ourselves in the future, saying not to go back in time.
Are you sure it'll get delivered?
It's addressed to Mildred's Granpa Joe, with a picture of the 1966 Beatles band as mystical provenance.
Then let's do it.
TIME

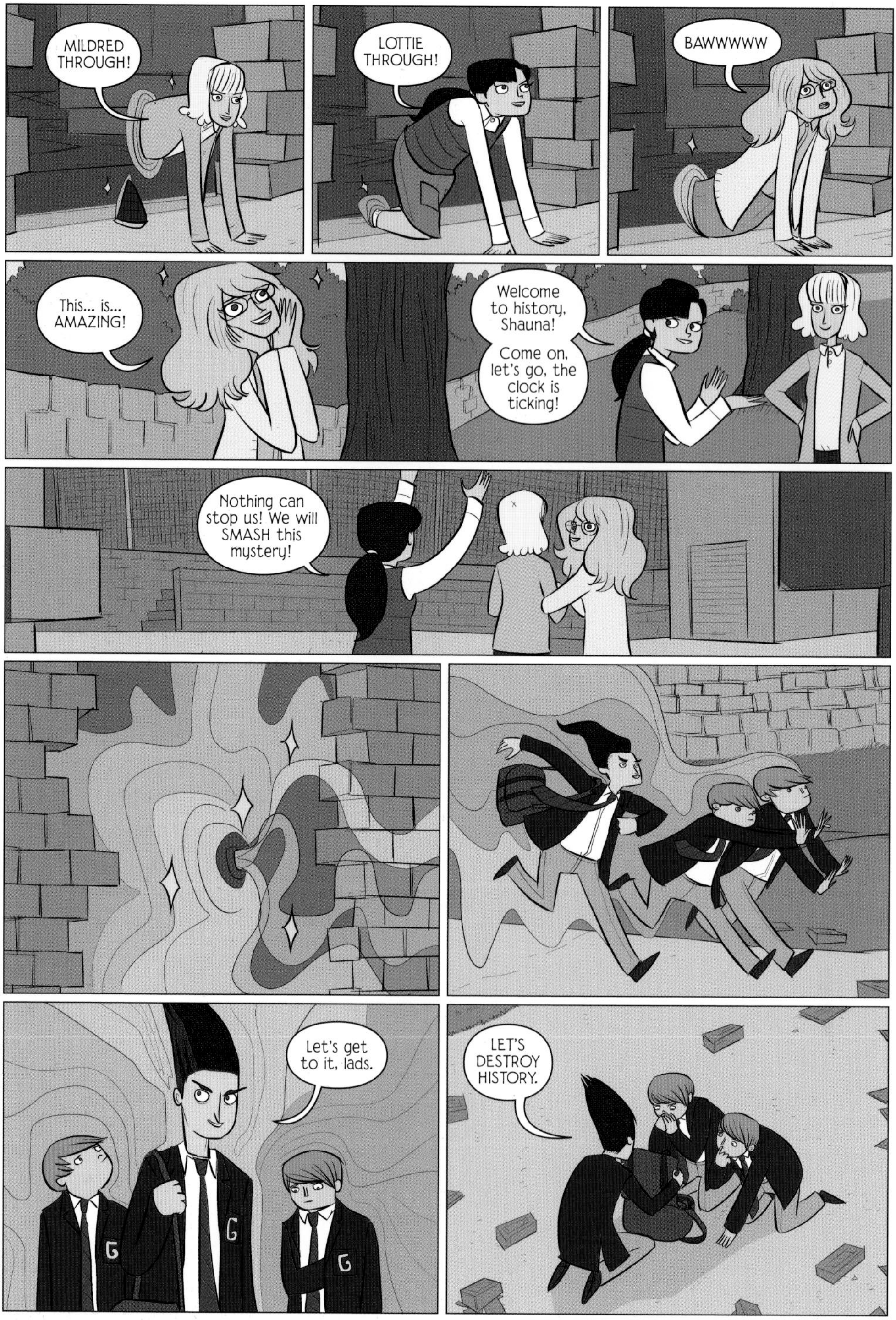
MILDRED THROUGH!
LOTTIE THROUGH!
BAWWWWW
This... is... AMAZING!
Welcome to history, Shauna!
Come on, let's go, the clock is ticking!
Nothing can stop us! We will SMASH this mystery!
Let's get to it, lads.
LET'S DESTROY HISTORY.

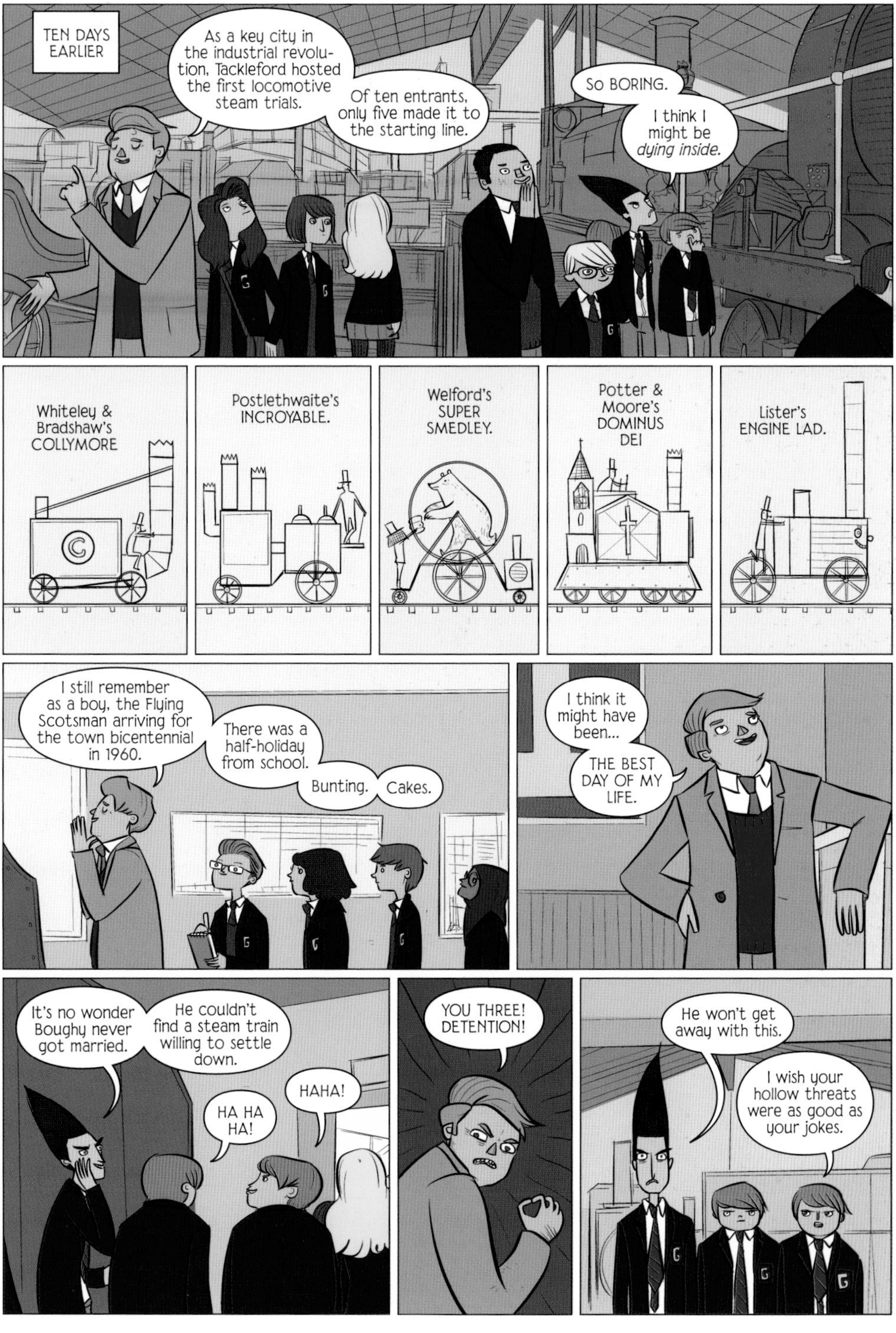
TEN DAYS EARLIER
As a key city in the industrial revolution, Tackleford hosted the first locomotive steam trials.
Of ten entrants, only five made it to the starting line.
So BORING.
I think I might be *dying inside.*
Whiteley & Bradshaw's COLLYMORE
Postlethwaite's INCROYABLE.
Welford's SUPER SMEDLEY.
Potter & Moore's DOMINUS DEI
Lister's ENGINE LAD.
I still remember as a boy, the Flying Scotsman arriving for the town bicentennial in 1960.
There was a half-holiday from school.
Bunting.
Cakes.
I think it might have been...
THE BEST DAY OF MY LIFE.
It's no wonder Boughy never got married.
He couldn't find a steam train willing to settle down.
HA HA HA!
HAHA!
YOU THREE! DETENTION!
He won't get away with this.
I wish your hollow threats were as good as your jokes.

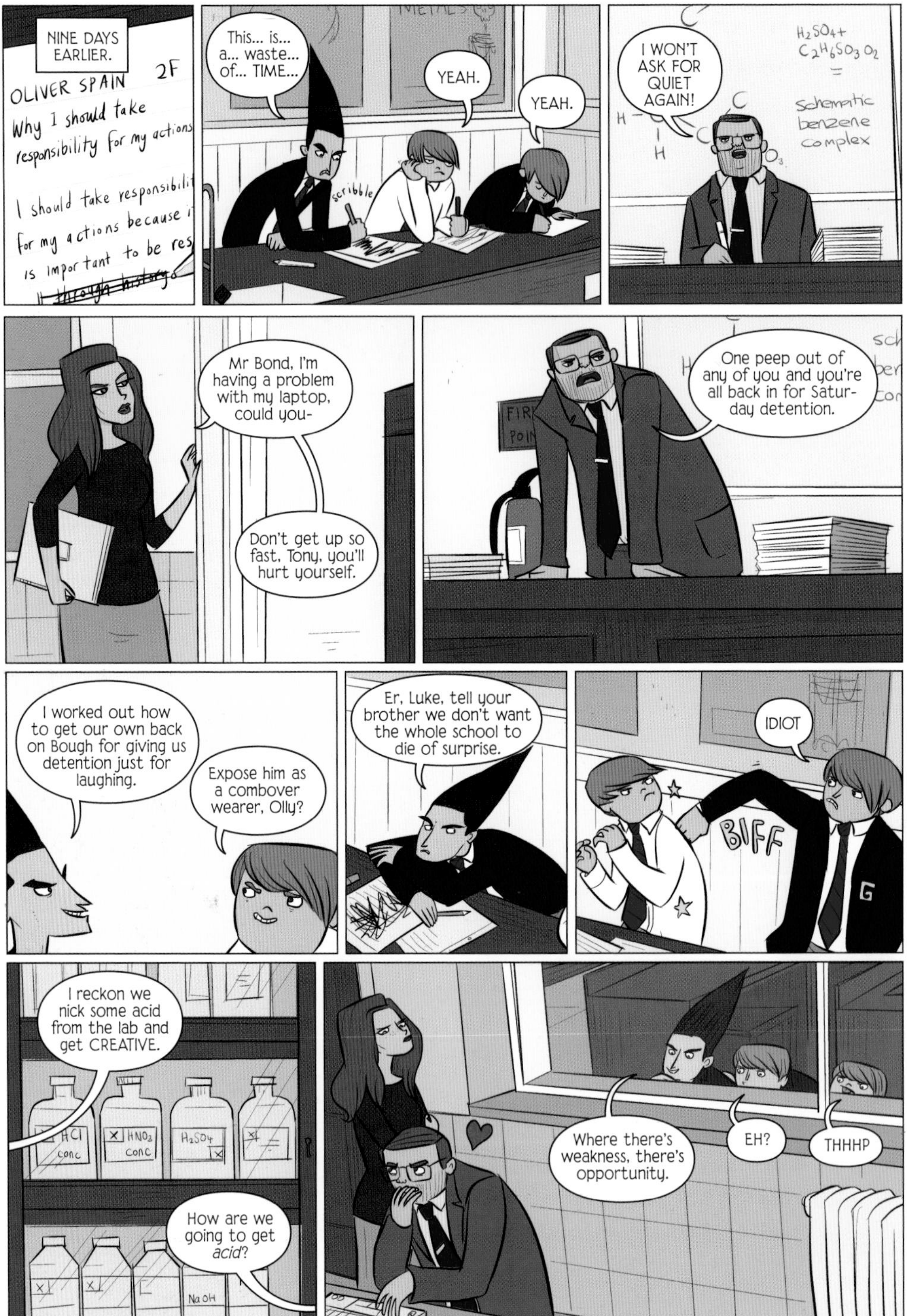
NINE DAYS EARLIER.
OLIVER SPAIN 2F
Why I should take responsibility for my actions
I should take responsibilit
for my actions because i
is important to be res
through history
This... is... a... waste... of... TIME...
scribble
YEAH.
YEAH.
I WON'T ASK FOR QUIET AGAIN!
H2SO4+ C2H6SO3O2 =
Schematic benzene complex
Mr Bond, I'm having a problem with my laptop, could you-
Don't get up so fast, Tony, you'll hurt yourself.
One peep out of any of you and you're all back in for Saturday detention.
I worked out how to get our own back on Bough for giving us detention just for laughing.
Expose him as a combover wearer, Olly?
Er, Luke, tell your brother we don't want the whole school to die of surprise.
IDIOT
BIFF
I reckon we nick some acid from the lab and get CREATIVE.
HCl conc
HNO3 conc
H2SO4
NaOH
How are we going to get *acid*?
Where there's weakness, there's opportunity.
EH?
THHHP

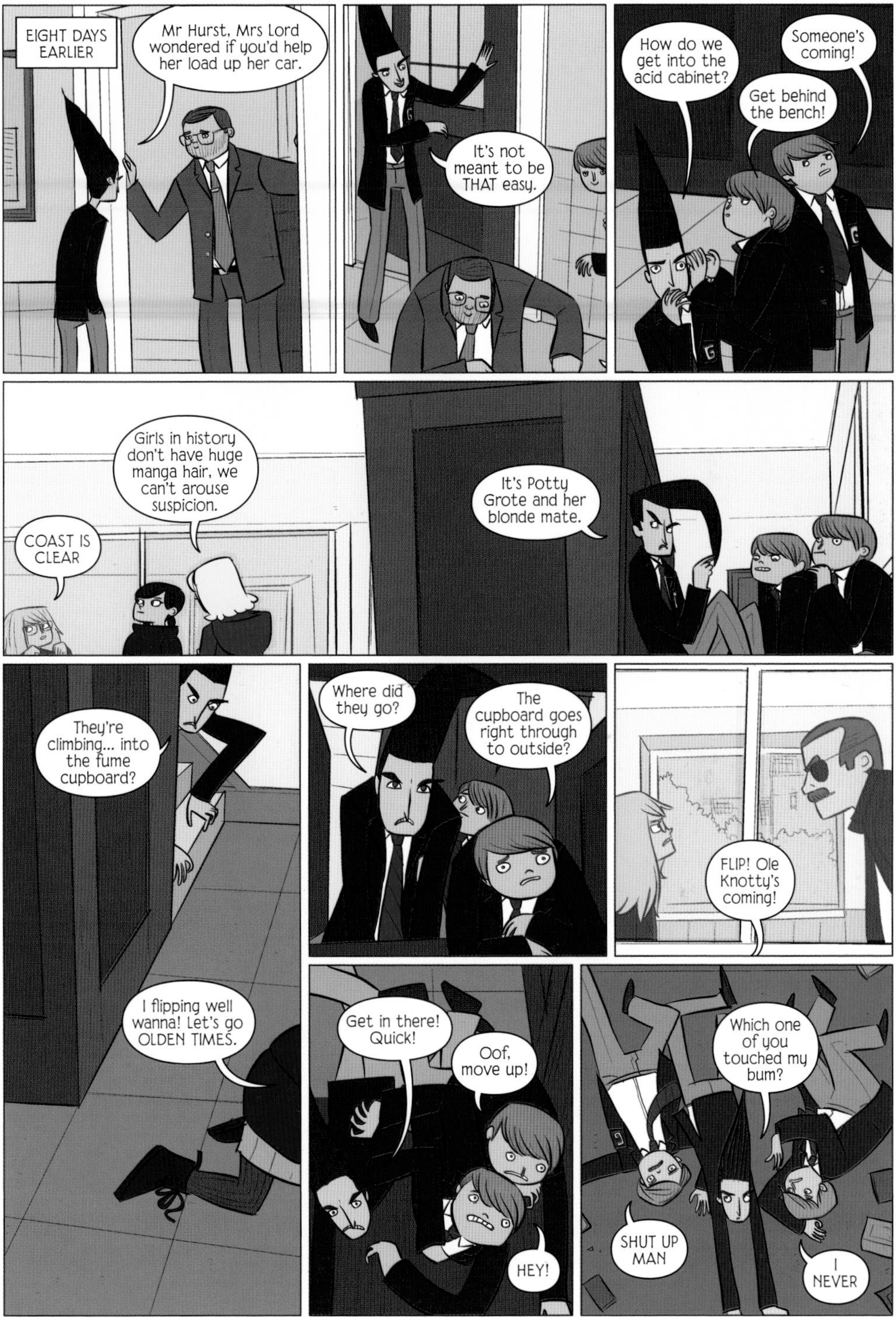
EIGHT DAYS EARLIER
Mr Hurst, Mrs Lord wondered if you'd help her load up her car.
It's not meant to be THAT easy.
How do we get into the acid cabinet?
Someone's coming!
Get behind the bench!
Girls in history don't have huge manga hair, we can't arouse suspicion.
COAST IS CLEAR
It's Potty Grote and her blonde mate.
They're climbing... into the fume cupboard?
Where did they go?
The cupboard goes right through to outside?
FLIP! Ole Knotty's coming!
I flipping well wanna! Let's go OLDEN TIMES.
Get in there! Quick!
Oof, move up!
HEY!
Which one of you touched my bum?
SHUT UP MAN
I NEVER

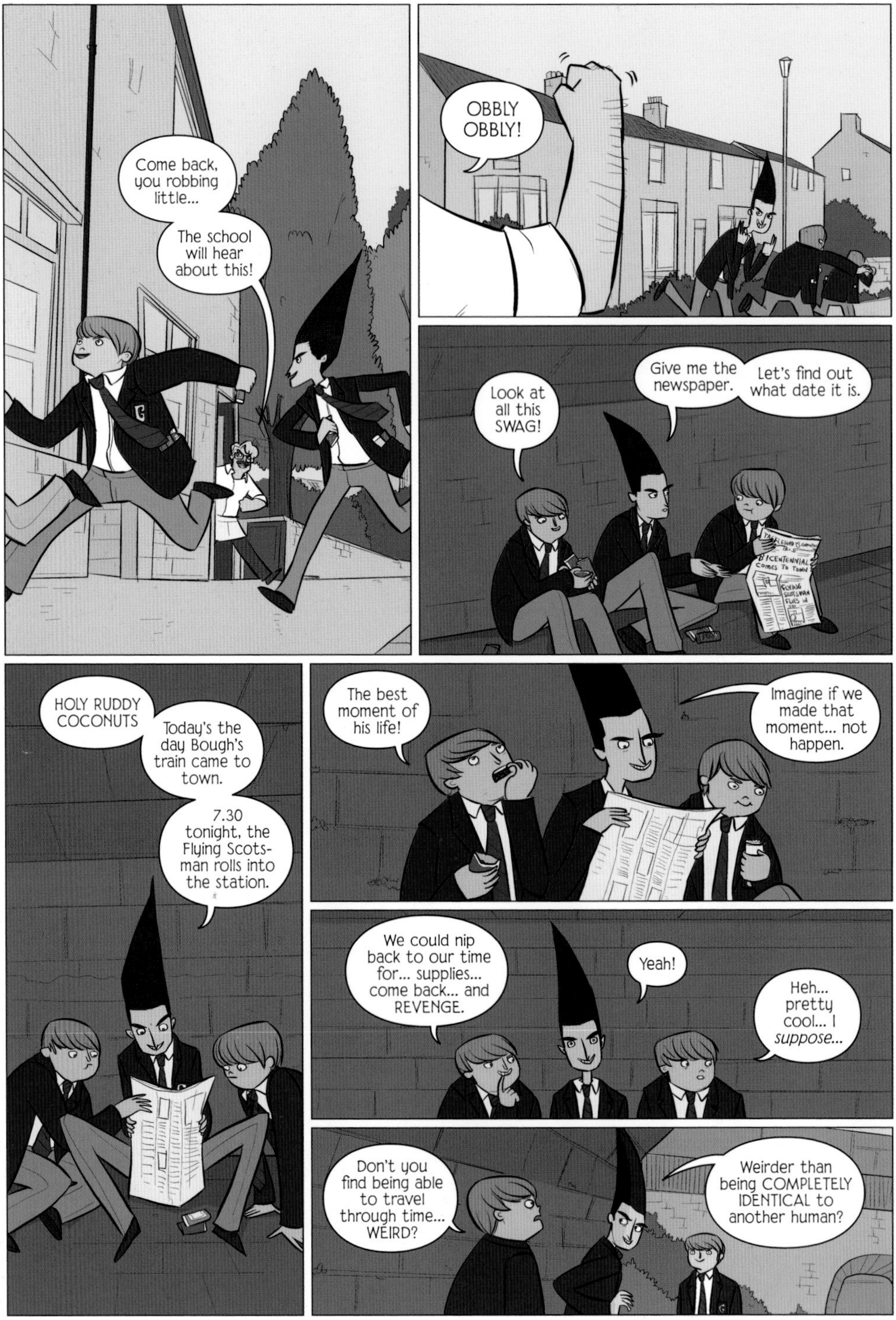
Come back, you robbing little...
The school will hear about this!
OBBLY OBBLY!
Look at all this SWAG!
Give me the newspaper.
Let's find out what date it is.
HOLY RUDDY COCONUTS
Today's the day Bough's train came to town.
7.30 tonight, the Flying Scotsman rolls into the station.
The best moment of his life!
Imagine if we made that moment... not happen.
We could nip back to our time for... supplies... come back... and REVENGE.
Yeah!
Heh... pretty cool... I *suppose...*
Don't you find being able to travel through time... WEIRD?
Weirder than being COMPLETELY IDENTICAL to another human?

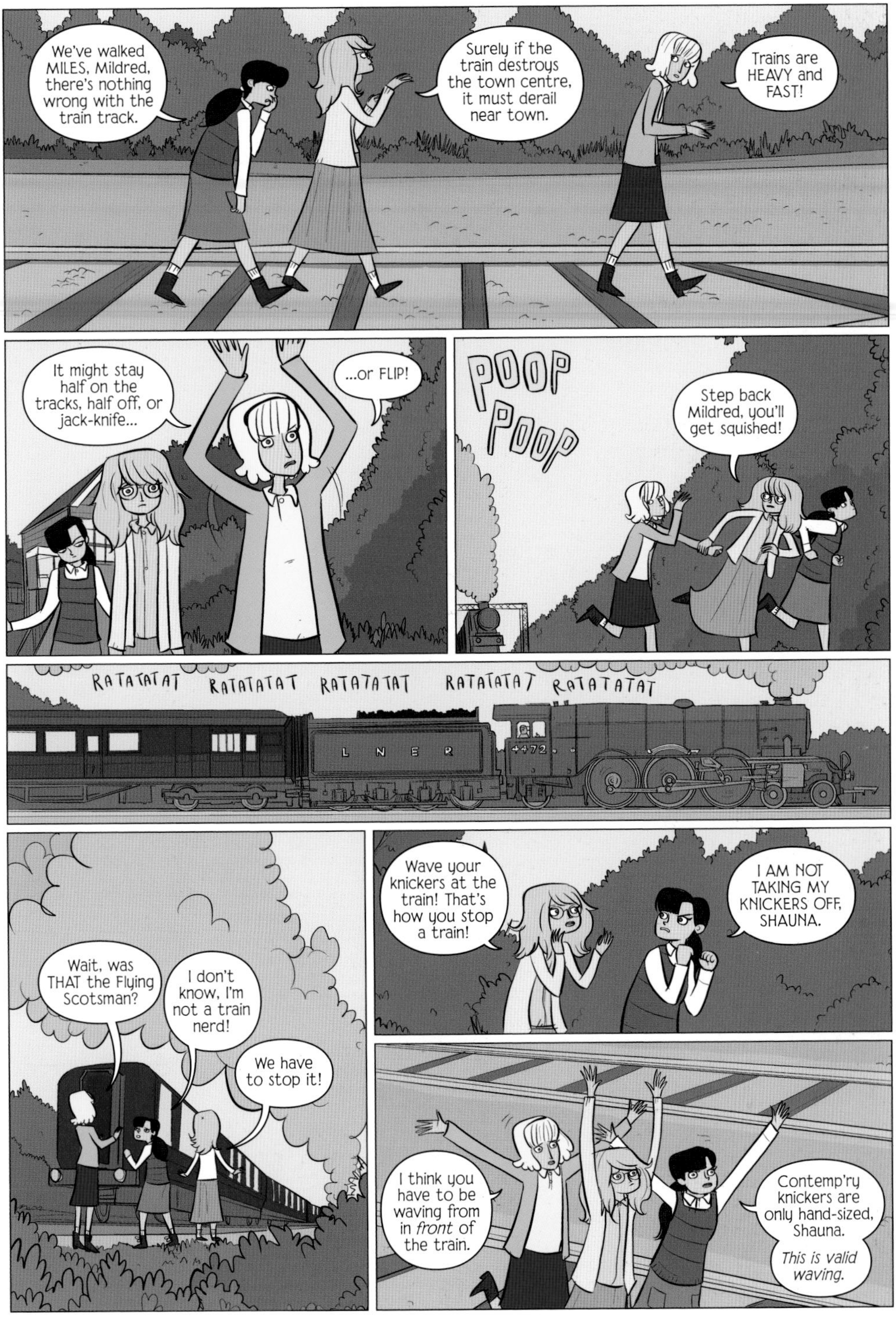
We've walked MILES, Mildred, there's nothing wrong with the train track.
Surely if the train destroys the town centre, it must derail near town.
Trains are HEAVY and FAST!
It might stay half on the tracks, half off, or jack-knife...
...or FLIP!
POOP POOP
Step back Mildred, you'll get squished!
RATATATAT RATATATAT RATATATAT RATATATAT RATATATAT
L N E R
4472
Wait, was THAT the Flying Scotsman?
I don't know, I'm not a train nerd!
We have to stop it!
Wave your knickers at the train! That's how you stop a train!
I AM NOT TAKING MY KNICKERS OFF, SHAUNA.
I think you have to be waving from in *front* of the train.
Contemp'ry knickers are only hand-sized, Shauna.
This is valid waving.

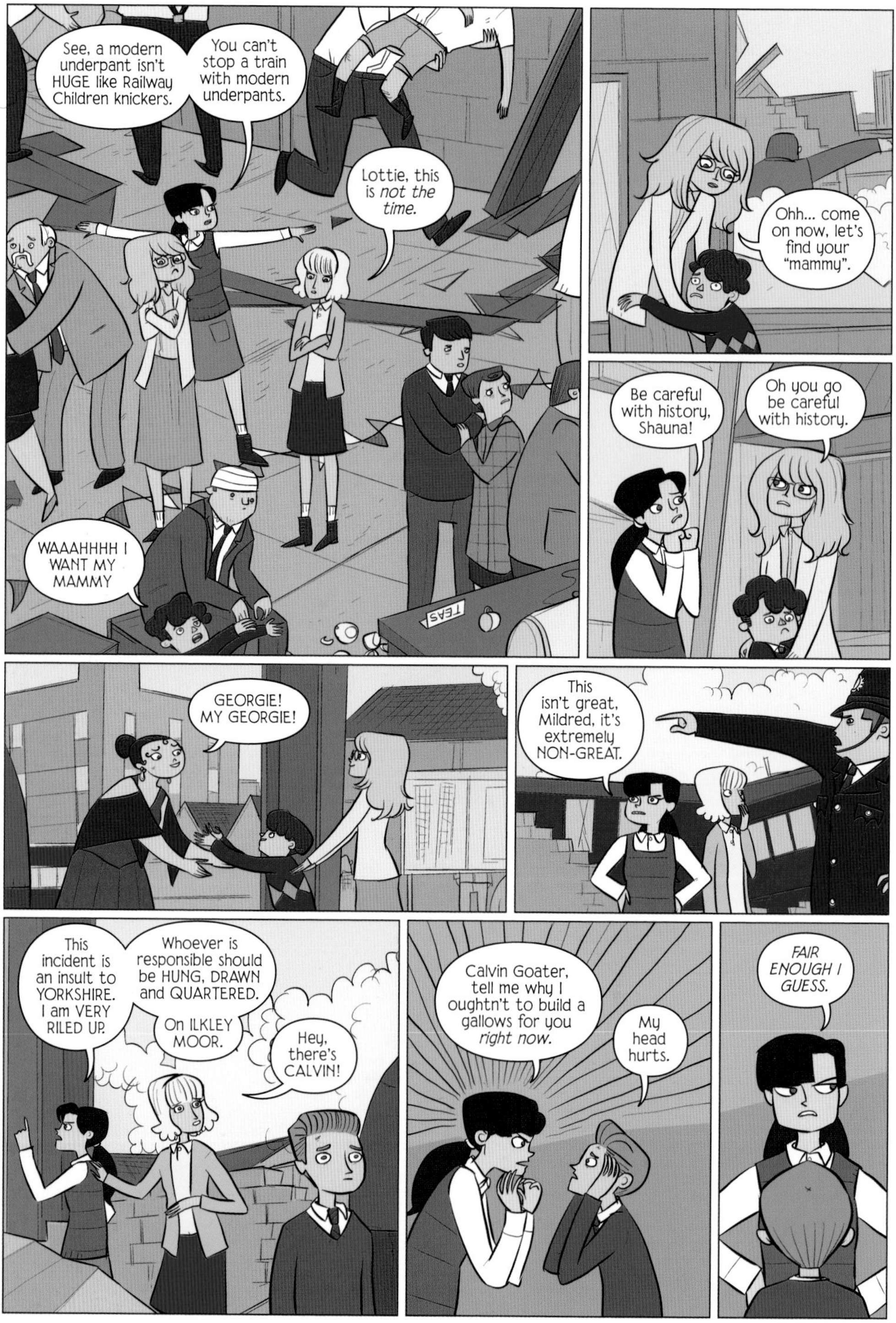
See, a modern underpant isn't HUGE like Railway Children knickers.
You can't stop a train with modern underpants.
Lottie, this is *not the time.*
WAAAHHHH I WANT MY MAMMY
TEAS
Ohh... come on now, let's find your "mammy".
Be careful with history, Shauna!
Oh you go be careful with history.
GEORGIE! MY GEORGIE!
This isn't great, Mildred, it's extremely NON-GREAT.
This incident is an insult to YORKSHIRE. I am VERY RILED UP.
Whoever is responsible should be HUNG, DRAWN and QUARTERED.
On ILKLEY MOOR.
Hey, there's CALVIN!
Calvin Goater, tell me why I oughtn't to build a gallows for you *right now.*
My head hurts.
FAIR ENOUGH I GUESS.

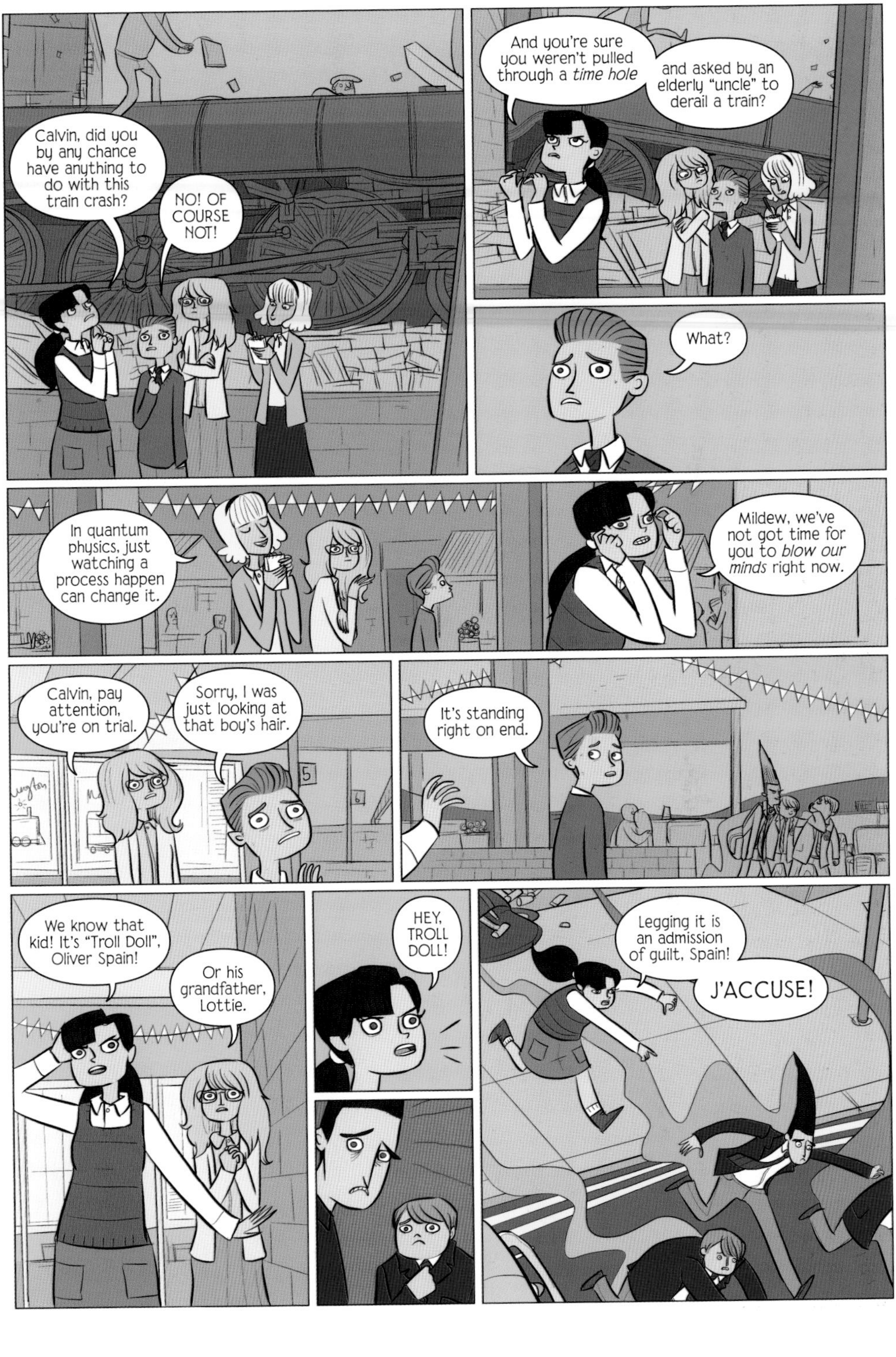
Calvin, did you by any chance have anything to do with this train crash?
NO! OF COURSE NOT!
And you're sure you weren't pulled through a *time hole*
and asked by an elderly "uncle" to derail a train?
What?
In quantum physics, just watching a process happen can change it.
Mildew, we've not got time for you to *blow our minds* right now.
Calvin, pay attention, you're on trial.
Sorry, I was just looking at that boy's hair.
It's standing right on end.
We know that kid! It's "Troll Doll", Oliver Spain!
Or his grandfather, Lottie.
HEY, TROLL DOLL!
Legging it is an admission of guilt, Spain!
J'ACCUSE!

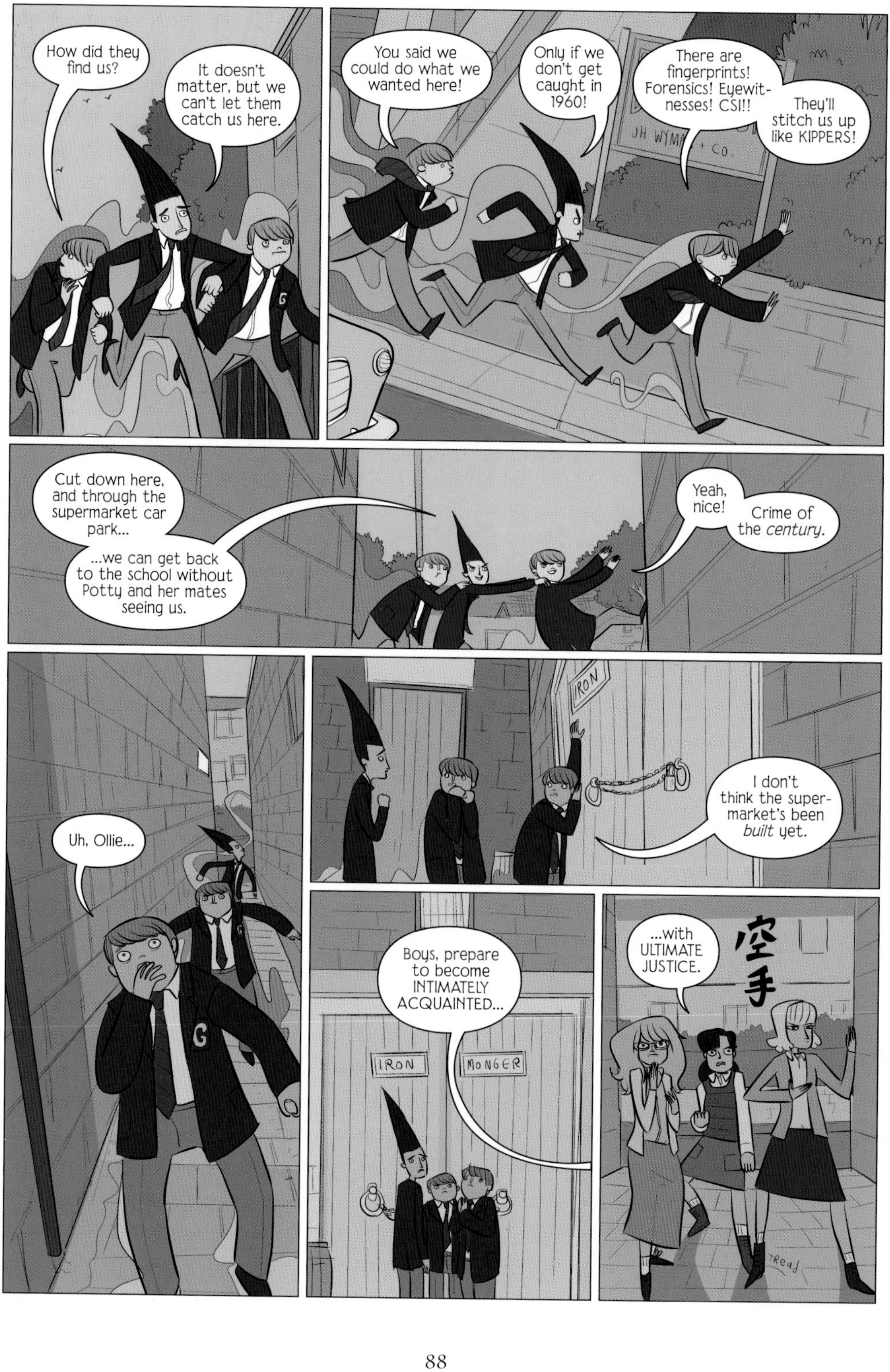
How did they find us?
It doesn't matter, but we can't let them catch us here.
You said we could do what we wanted here!
Only if we don't get caught in 1960!
There are fingerprints! Forensics! Eyewitnesses! CSI!!
They'll stitch us up like KIPPERS!
JH WYM + CO.
Cut down here, and through the supermarket car park...
...we can get back to the school without Potty and her mates seeing us.
Yeah, nice!
Crime of the *century*.
Uh, Ollie...
IRON
I don't think the supermarket's been *built* yet.
Boys, prepare to become INTIMATELY ACQUAINTED...
IRON
MONGER
...with ULTIMATE JUSTICE.
空手

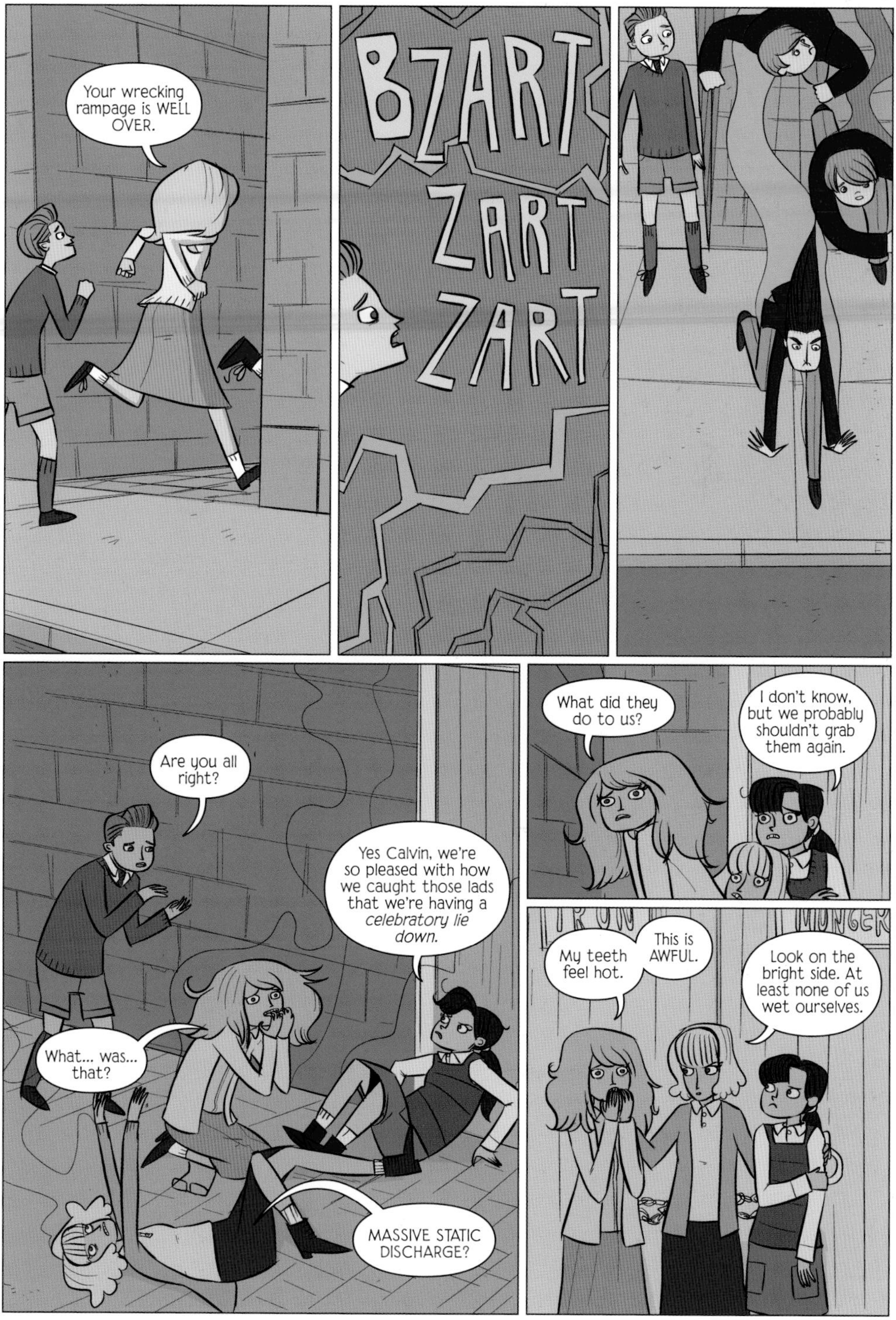
Your wrecking rampage is WELL OVER.
BZART
ZART
ZART
Are you all right?
Yes Calvin, we're so pleased with how we caught those lads that we're having a *celebratory lie down.*
What... was... that?
MASSIVE STATIC DISCHARGE?
What did they do to us?
I don't know, but we probably shouldn't grab them again.
My teeth feel hot.
This is AWFUL.
Look on the bright side. At least none of us wet ourselves.

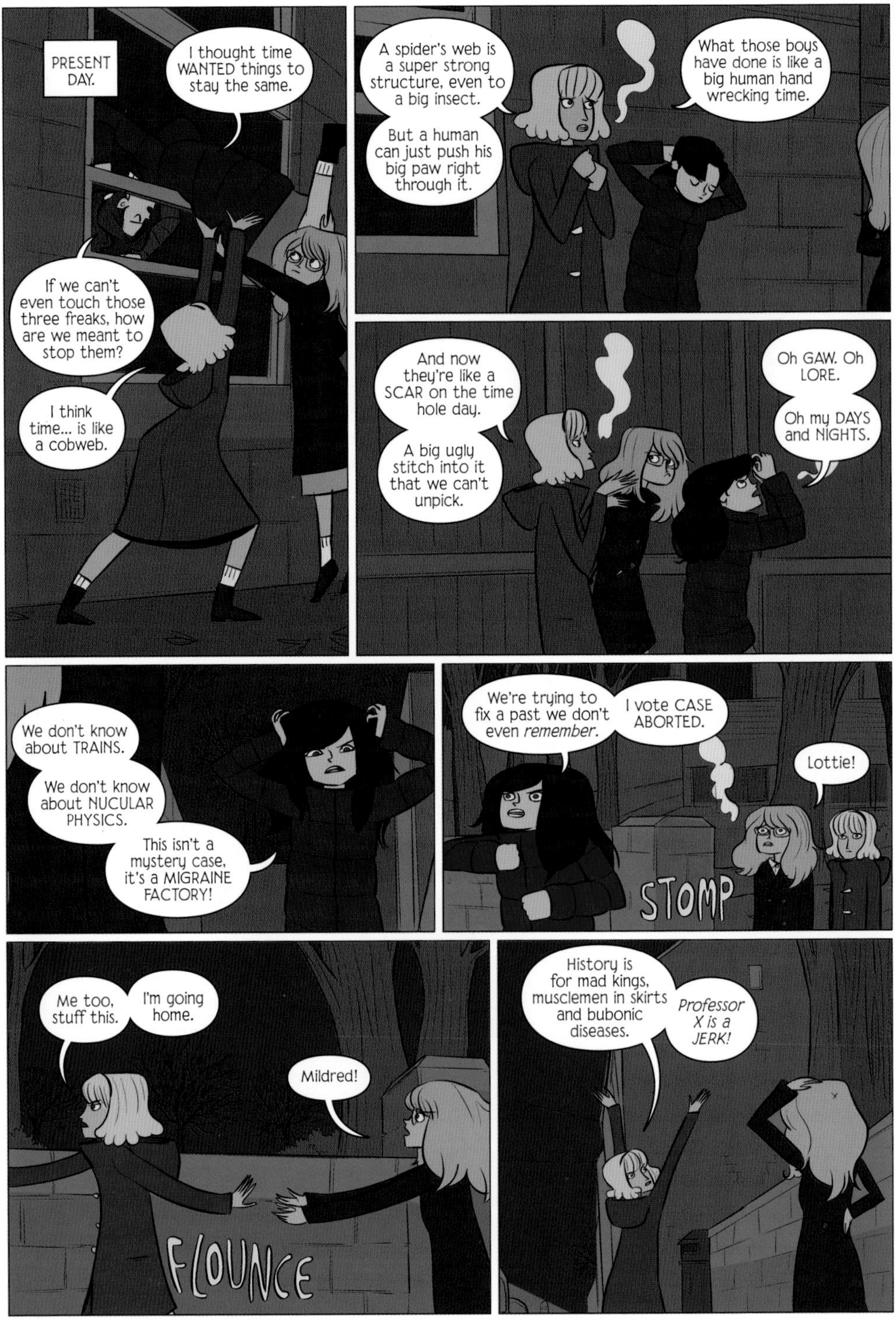
PRESENT DAY.
I thought time WANTED things to stay the same.
If we can't even touch those three freaks, how are we meant to stop them?
I think time... is like a cobweb.
A spider's web is a super strong structure, even to a big insect.
But a human can just push his big paw right through it.
What those boys have done is like a big human hand wrecking time.
And now they're like a SCAR on the time hole day.
A big ugly stitch into it that we can't unpick.
Oh GAW. Oh LORE.
Oh my DAYS and NIGHTS.
We don't know about TRAINS.
We don't know about NUCULAR PHYSICS.
This isn't a mystery case, it's a MIGRAINE FACTORY!
We're trying to fix a past we don't even *remember*.
I vote CASE ABORTED.
Lottie!
STOMP
Me too, stuff this.
I'm going home.
Mildred!
FLOUNCE
History is for mad kings, musclemen in skirts and bubonic diseases.
Professor X is a JERK!

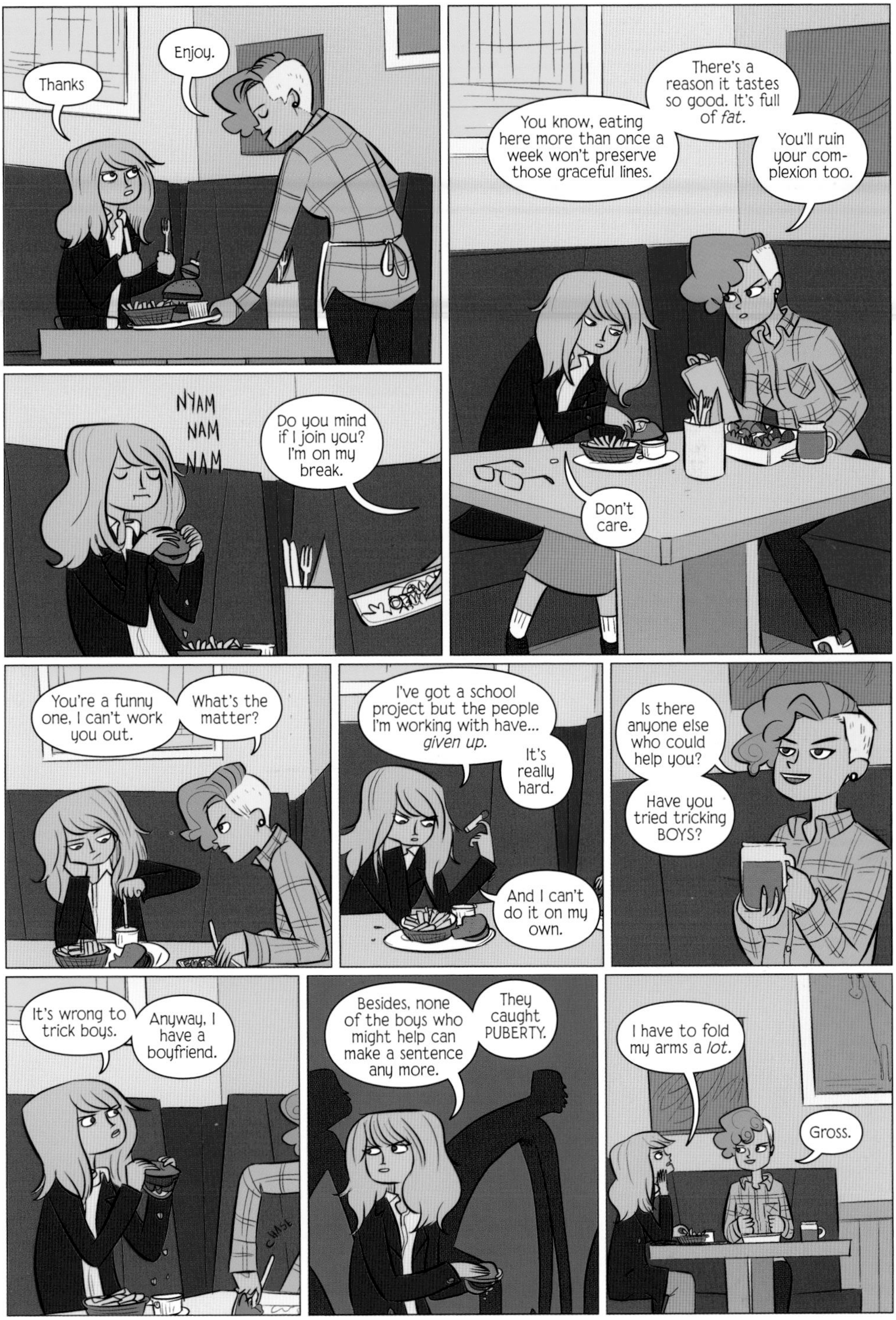
Enjoy.
Thanks
There's a reason it tastes so good. It's full of *fat.*
You know, eating here more than once a week won't preserve those graceful lines.
You'll ruin your complexion too.
Don't care.
NYAM NAM NAM
Do you mind if I join you? I'm on my break.
You're a funny one, I can't work you out.
What's the matter?
I've got a school project but the people I'm working with have... *given up.*
It's really hard.
And I can't do it on my own.
Is there anyone else who could help you?
Have you tried tricking BOYS?
It's wrong to trick boys.
Anyway, I have a boyfriend.
Besides, none of the boys who might help can make a sentence any more.
They caught PUBERTY.
I have to fold my arms a *lot.*
Gross.

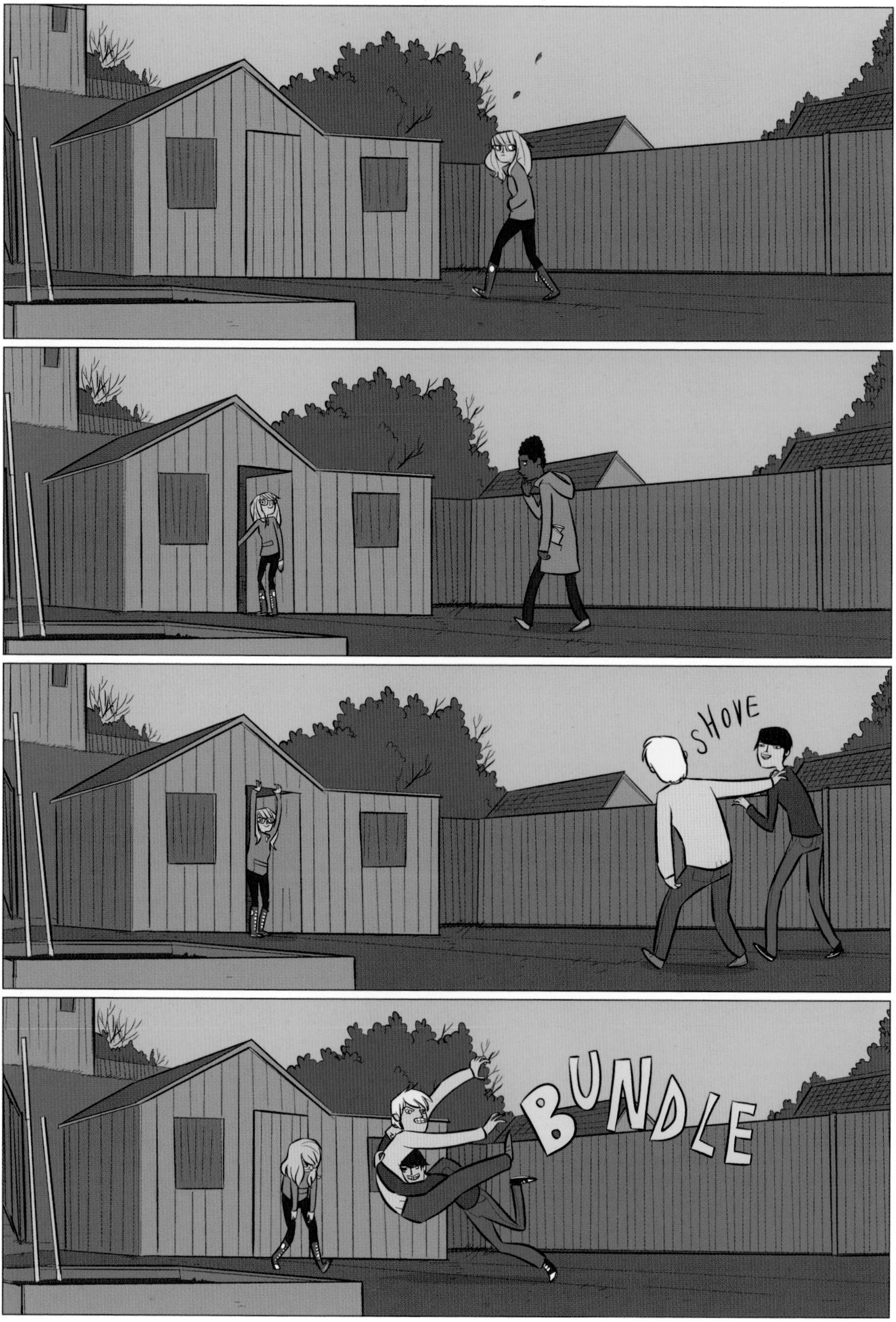
SHOVE
BUNDLE

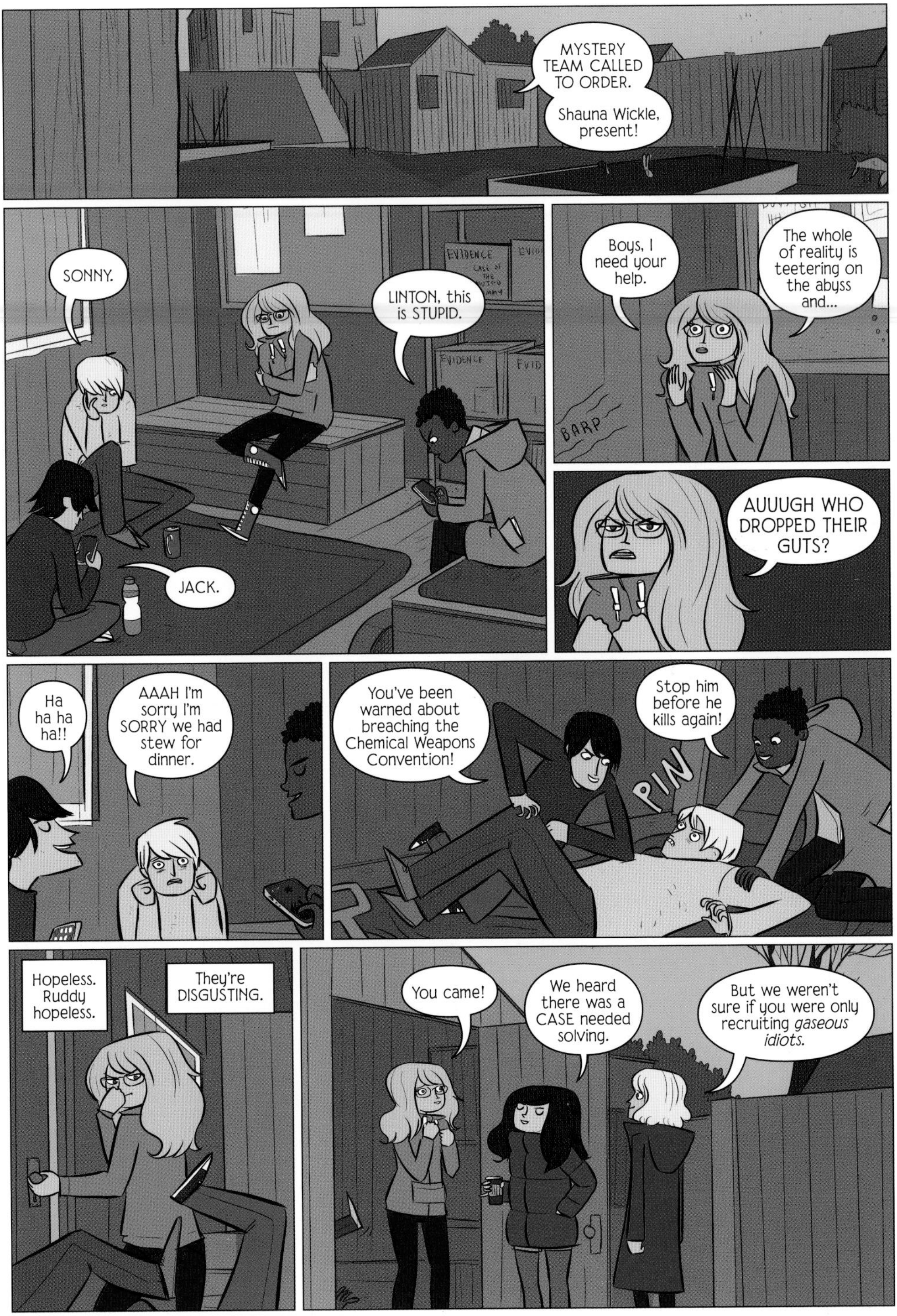
MYSTERY TEAM CALLED TO ORDER.
Shauna Wickle, present!
SONNY.
JACK.
LINTON, this is STUPID.
Boys, I need your help.
The whole of reality is teetering on the abyss and...
BARP
AUUUGH WHO DROPPED THEIR GUTS?
Ha ha ha ha!!
AAAH I'm sorry I'm SORRY we had stew for dinner.
You've been warned about breaching the Chemical Weapons Convention!
Stop him before he kills again!
PIN
Hopeless. Ruddy hopeless.
They're DISGUSTING.
You came!
We heard there was a CASE needed solving.
But we weren't sure if you were only recruiting *gaseous idiots.*

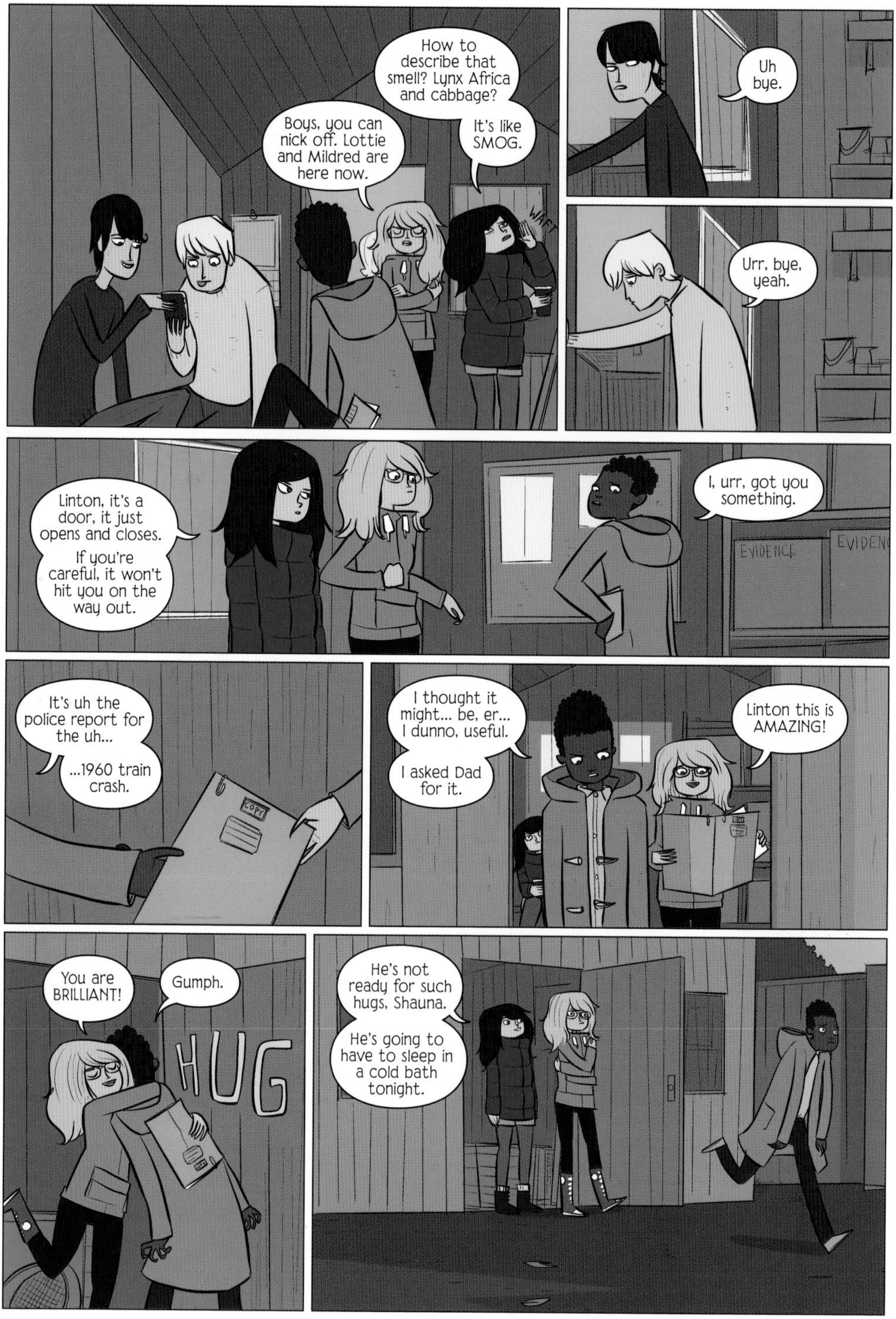
How to describe that smell? Lynx Africa and cabbage?
Boys, you can nick off. Lottie and Mildred are here now.
It's like SMOG.
WAFT
Uh bye.
Urr, bye, yeah.
Linton, it's a door, it just opens and closes.
If you're careful, it won't hit you on the way out.
I, urr, got you something.
EVIDENCE
EVIDENC
It's uh the police report for the uh...
...1960 train crash.
COPY
I thought it might... be, er... I dunno, useful.
I asked Dad for it.
Linton this is AMAZING!
You are BRILLIANT!
Gumph.
HUG
He's not ready for such hugs, Shauna.
He's going to have to sleep in a cold bath tonight.

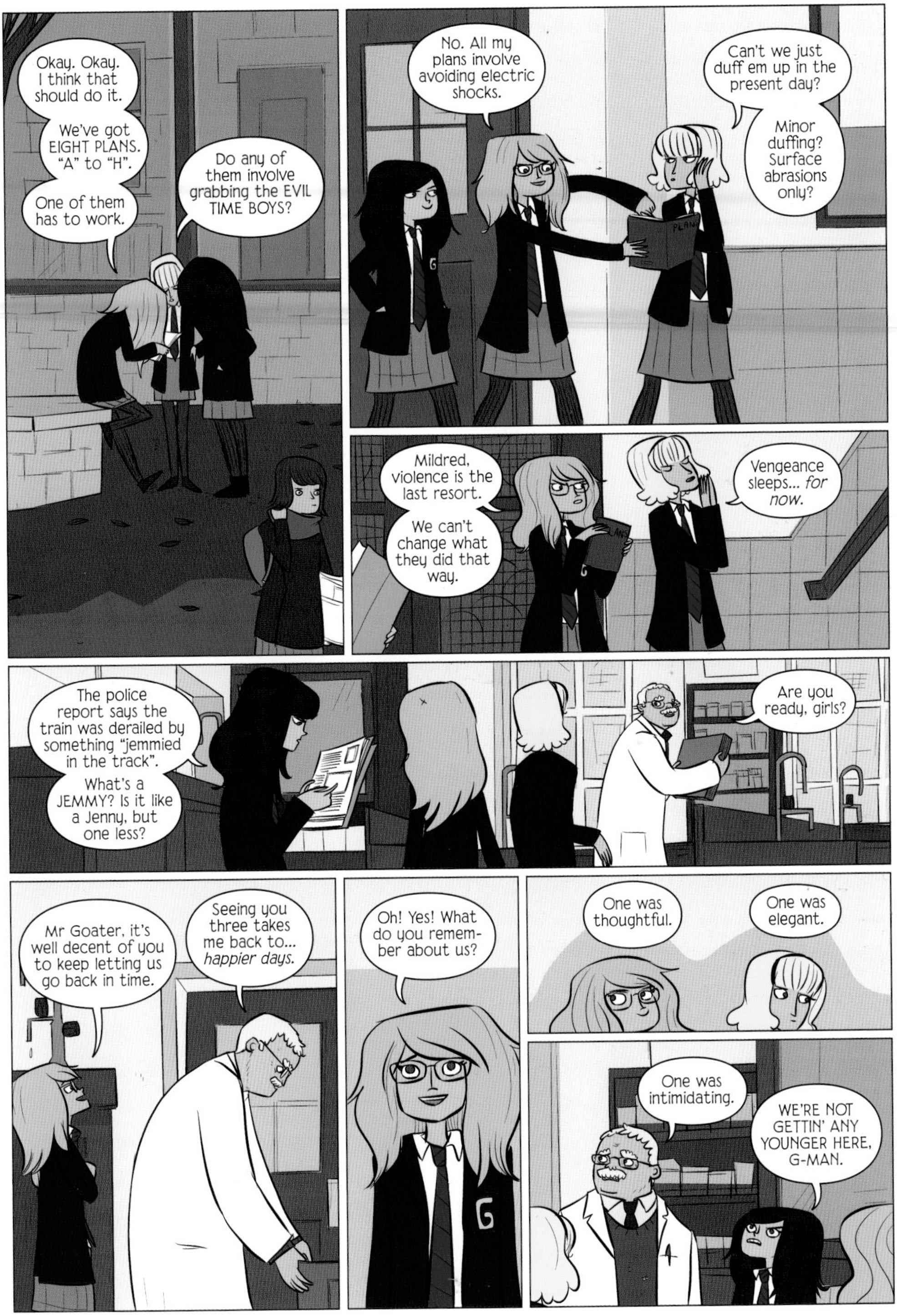
Okay. Okay. I think that should do it.
We've got EIGHT PLANS. "A" to "H".
One of them has to work.
Do any of them involve grabbing the EVIL TIME BOYS?
No. All my plans involve avoiding electric shocks.
Can't we just duff em up in the present day?
Minor duffing? Surface abrasions only?
PLANS
Mildred, violence is the last resort.
We can't change what they did that way.
Vengeance sleeps... *for now.*
The police report says the train was derailed by something "jemmied in the track".
What's a JEMMY? Is it like a Jenny, but one less?
Are you ready, girls?
Mr Goater, it's well decent of you to keep letting us go back in time.
Seeing you three takes me back to... *happier days.*
Oh! Yes! What do you remember about us?
One was thoughtful.
One was elegant.
One was intimidating.
WE'RE NOT GETTIN' ANY YOUNGER HERE, G-MAN.

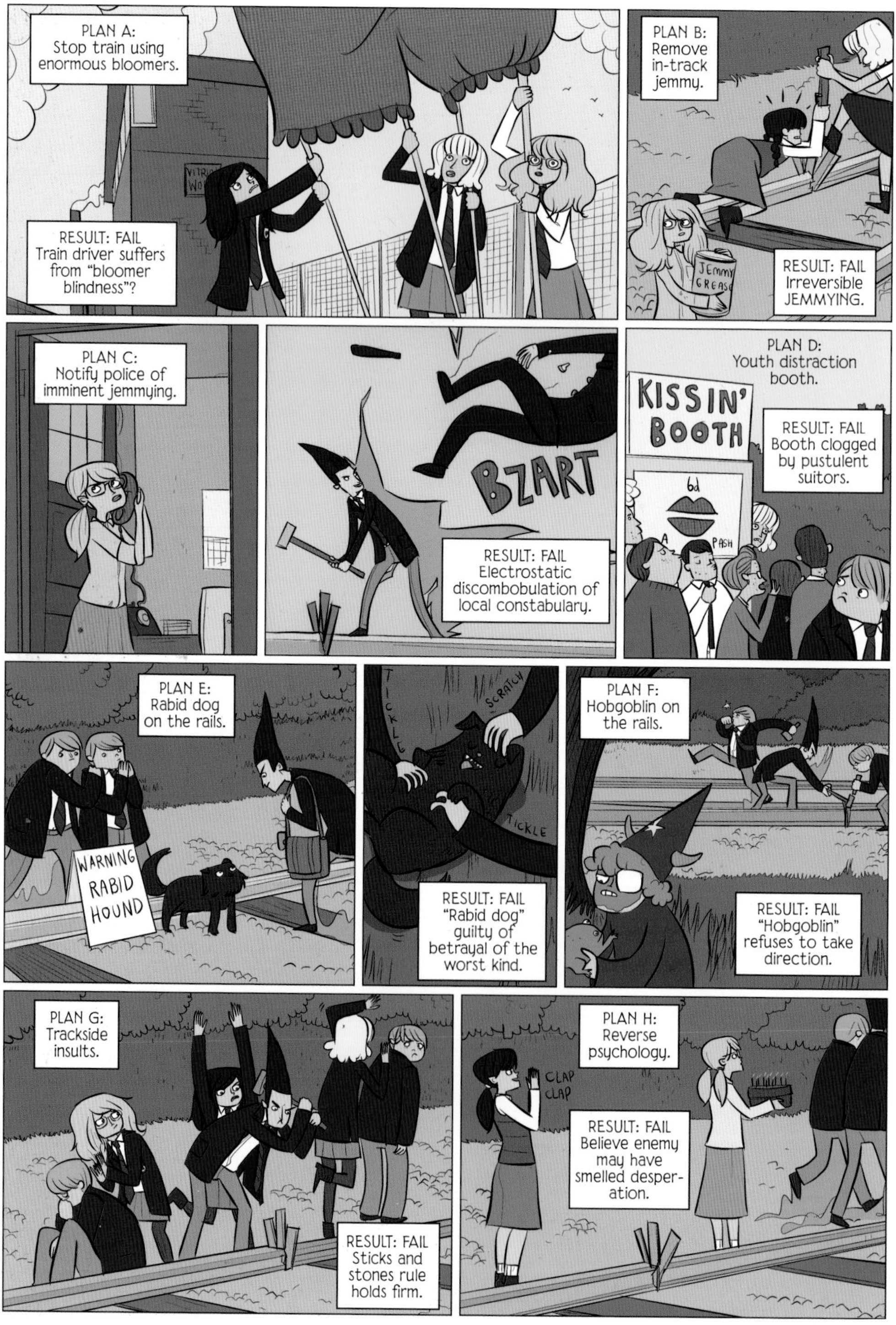
PLAN A:
Stop train using enormous bloomers.
RESULT: FAIL
Train driver suffers from "bloomer blindness"?
PLAN B:
Remove in-track jemmy.
RESULT: FAIL
Irreversible JEMMYING.
PLAN C:
Notify police of imminent jemmying.
BZART
RESULT: FAIL
Electrostatic discombobulation of local constabulary.
PLAN D:
Youth distraction booth.
KISSIN' BOOTH
RESULT: FAIL
Booth clogged by pustulent suitors.
PLAN E:
Rabid dog on the rails.
WARNING RABID HOUND
TICKLE
SCRATCH
TICKLE
RESULT: FAIL
"Rabid dog" guilty of betrayal of the worst kind.
PLAN F:
Hobgoblin on the rails.
RESULT: FAIL
"Hobgoblin" refuses to take direction.
PLAN G:
Trackside insults.
RESULT: FAIL
Sticks and stones rule holds firm.
PLAN H:
Reverse psychology.
CLAP
CLAP
RESULT: FAIL
Believe enemy may have smelled desper-ation.

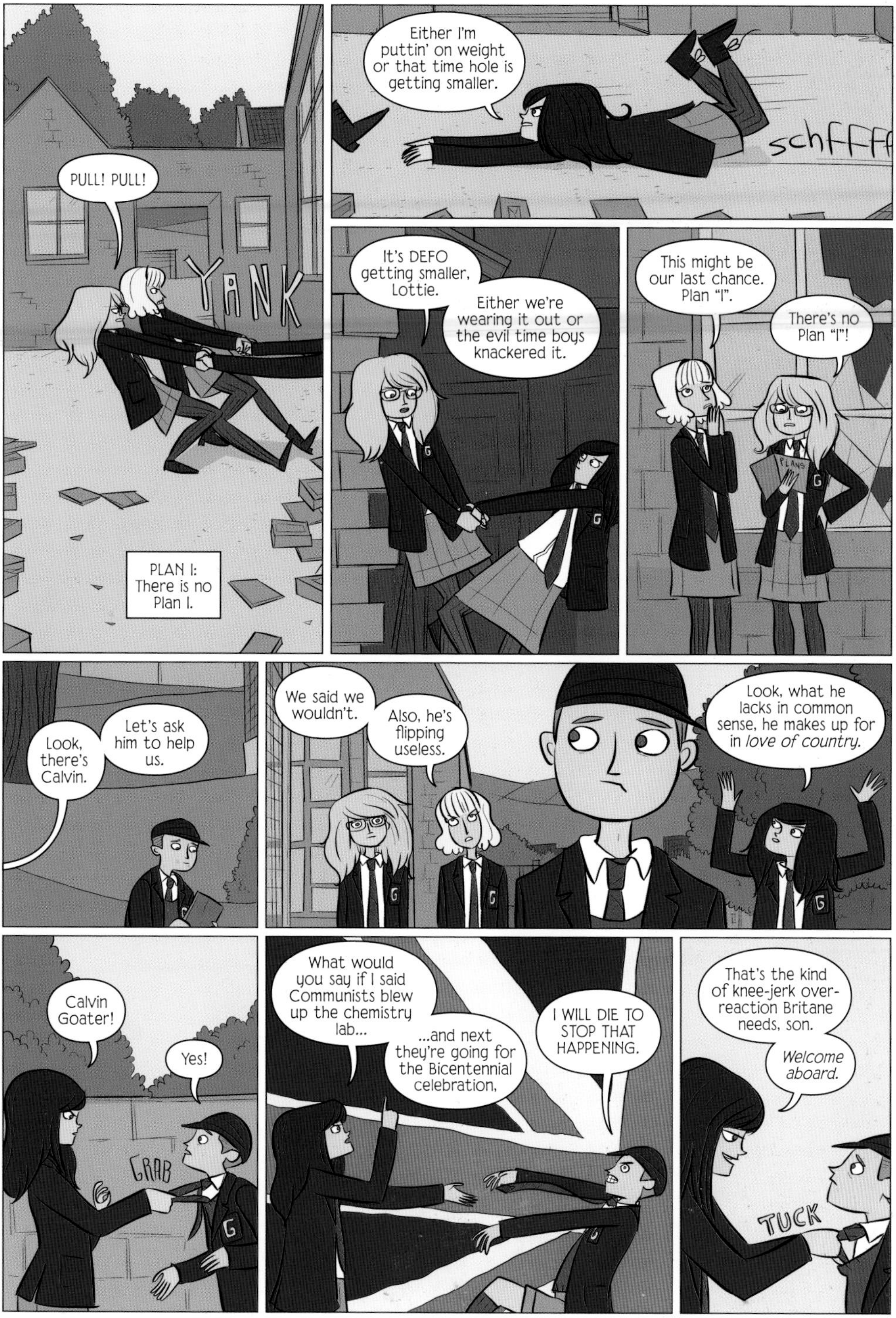
PULL! PULL!
YANK
PLAN I: There is no Plan I.
Either I'm puttin' on weight or that time hole is getting smaller.
schffff
It's DEFO getting smaller, Lottie.
Either we're wearing it out or the evil time boys knackered it.
This might be our last chance. Plan "I".
There's no Plan "I"!
PLANS
Look, there's Calvin.
Let's ask him to help us.
We said we wouldn't.
Also, he's flipping useless.
Look, what he lacks in common sense, he makes up for in *love of country.*
Calvin Goater!
Yes!
GRAB
What would you say if I said Communists blew up the chemistry lab...
...and next they're going for the Bicentennial celebration,
I WILL DIE TO STOP THAT HAPPENING.
That's the kind of knee-jerk over-reaction Britane needs, son.
Welcome aboard.
TUCK

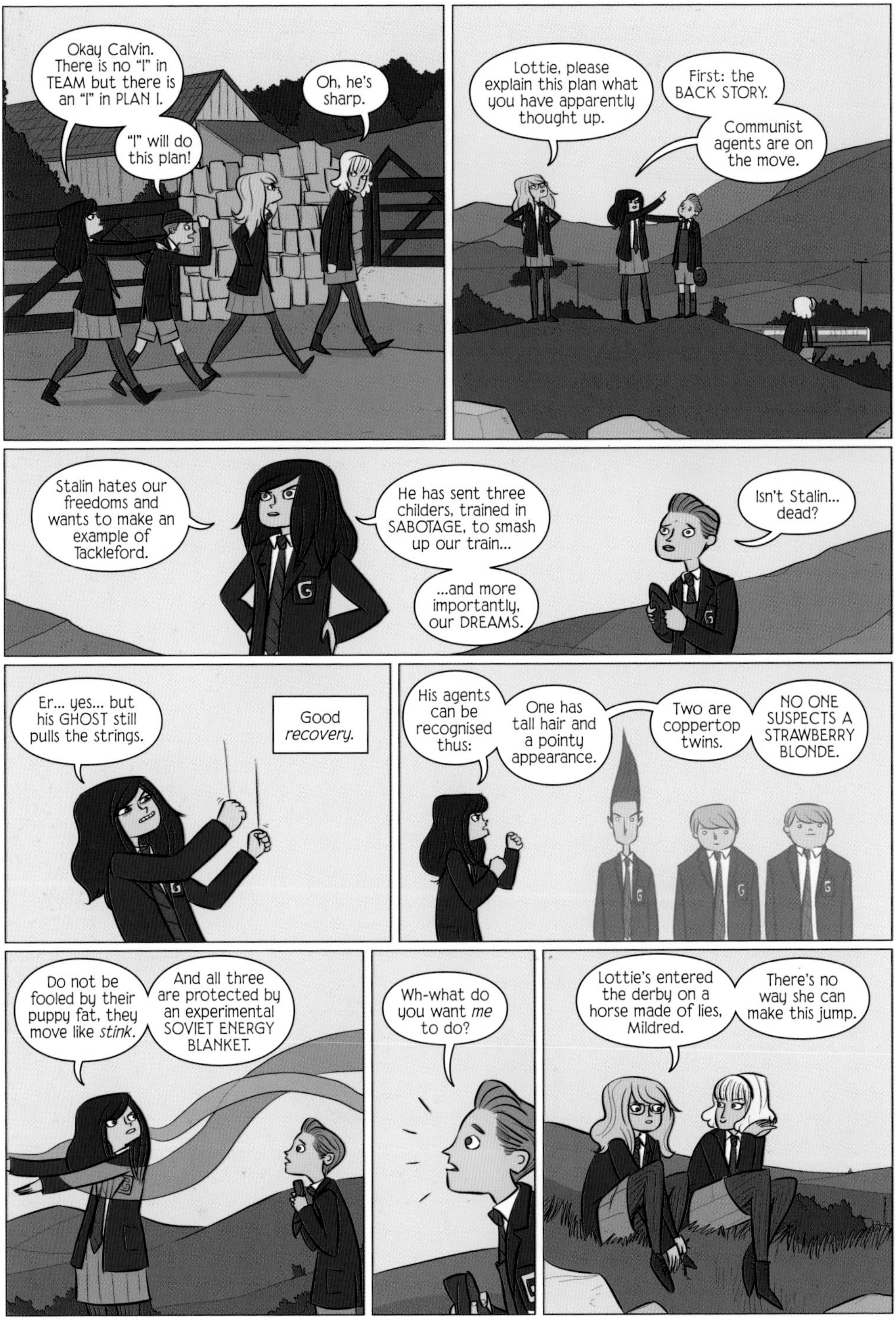
Okay Calvin. There is no "I" in TEAM but there is an "I" in PLAN I.
"I" will do this plan!
Oh, he's sharp.
Lottie, please explain this plan what you have apparently thought up.
First: the BACK STORY.
Communist agents are on the move.
Stalin hates our freedoms and wants to make an example of Tackleford.
He has sent three childers, trained in SABOTAGE, to smash up our train...
...and more importantly, our DREAMS.
Isn't Stalin... dead?
Er... yes... but his GHOST still pulls the strings.
Good *recovery.*
His agents can be recognised thus:
One has tall hair and a pointy appearance.
Two are coppertop twins.
NO ONE SUSPECTS A STRAWBERRY BLONDE.
Do not be fooled by their puppy fat, they move like *stink*.
And all three are protected by an experimental SOVIET ENERGY BLANKET.
Wh-what do you want *me* to do?
Lottie's entered the derby on a horse made of lies, Mildred.
There's no way she can make this jump.

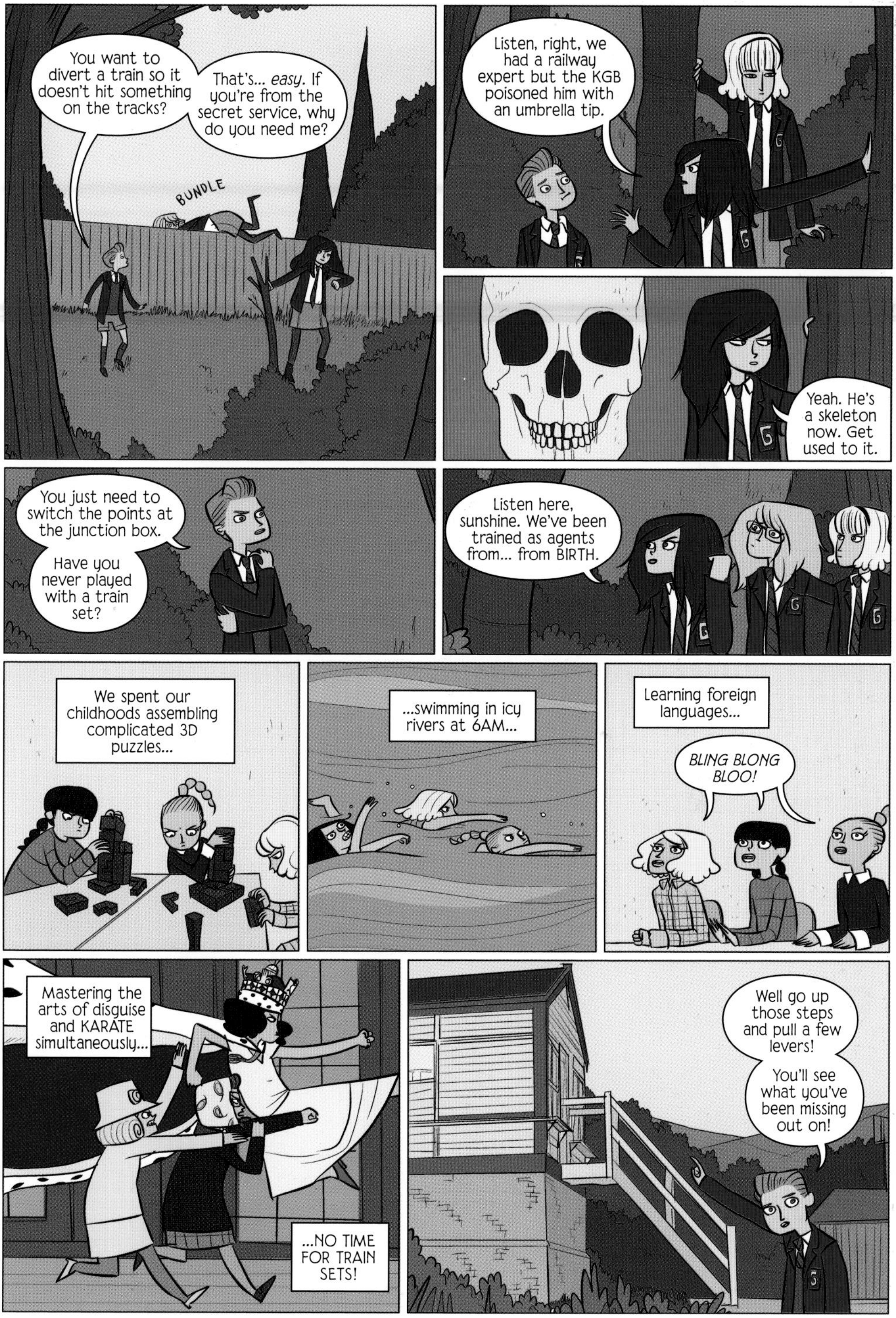
You want to divert a train so it doesn't hit something on the tracks?
That's... *easy*. If you're from the secret service, why do you need me?
BUNDLE
Listen, right, we had a railway expert but the KGB poisoned him with an umbrella tip.
Yeah. He's a skeleton now. Get used to it.
You just need to switch the points at the junction box.
Have you never played with a train set?
Listen here, sunshine. We've been trained as agents from... from BIRTH.
We spent our childhoods assembling complicated 3D puzzles...
...swimming in icy rivers at 6AM...
Learning foreign languages...
BLING BLONG BLOO!
Mastering the arts of disguise and KARATE simultaneously...
...NO TIME FOR TRAIN SETS!
Well go up those steps and pull a few levers!
You'll see what you've been missing out on!

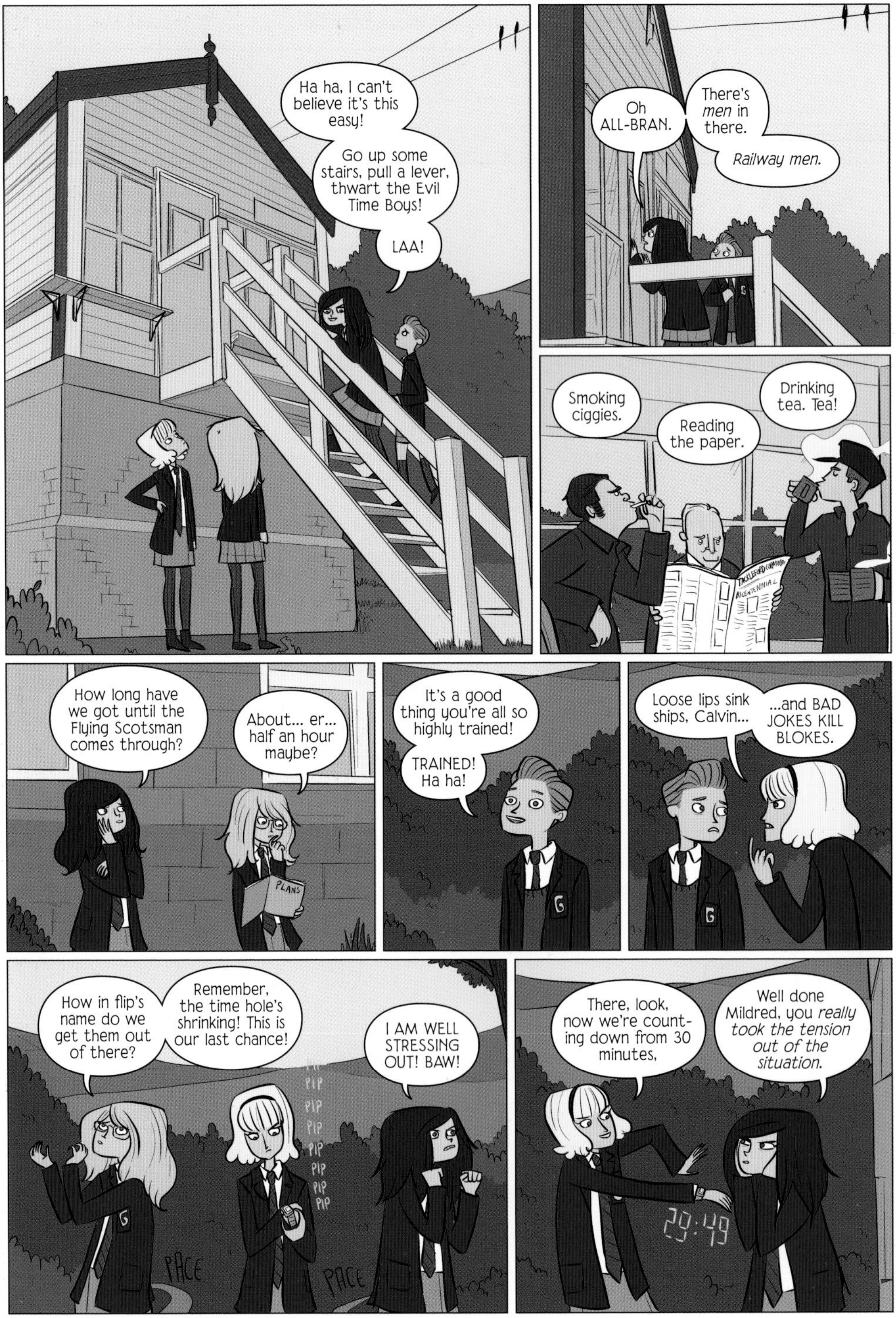
Ha ha, I can't believe it's this easy!
Go up some stairs, pull a lever, thwart the Evil Time Boys!
LAA!
Oh ALL-BRAN.
There's *men* in there.
Railway men.
Smoking ciggies.
Reading the paper.
Drinking tea. Tea!
How long have we got until the Flying Scotsman comes through?
About... er... half an hour maybe?
PLANS
It's a good thing you're all so highly trained!
TRAINED! Ha ha!
Loose lips sink ships, Calvin...
...and BAD JOKES KILL BLOKES.
How in flip's name do we get them out of there?
Remember, the time hole's shrinking! This is our last chance!
I AM WELL STRESSING OUT! BAW!
PIP PIP PIP PIP PIP PIP PIP PIP
PACE
PACE
There, look, now we're counting down from 30 minutes,
Well done Mildred, you *really took the tension out of the situation.*
29:49

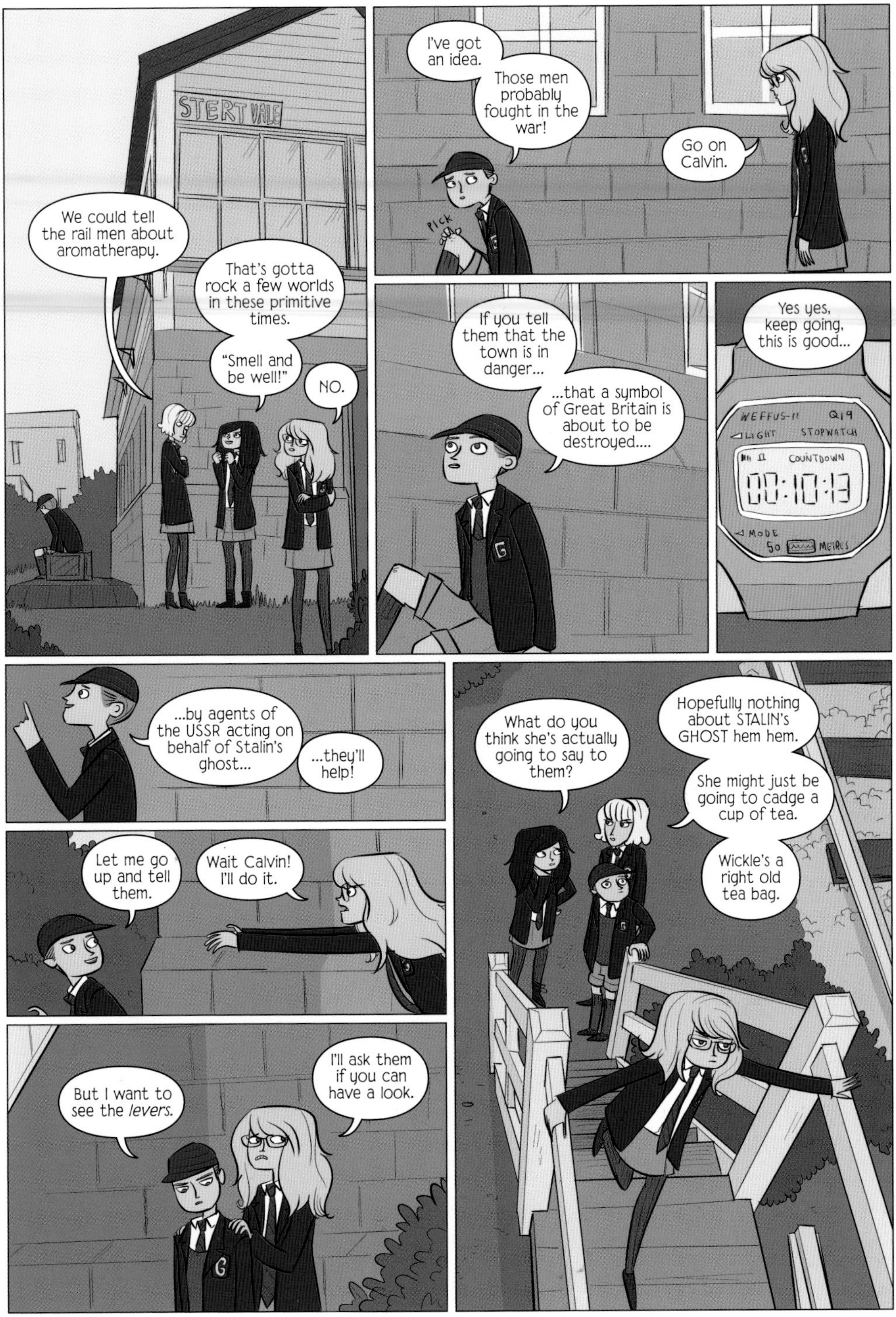
STERT VALE
We could tell the rail men about aromatherapy.
That's gotta rock a few worlds in these primitive times.
"Smell and be well!"
NO.
I've got an idea.
Those men probably fought in the war!
PICK
Go on Calvin.
If you tell them that the town is in danger...
...that a symbol of Great Britain is about to be destroyed....
Yes yes, keep going, this is good...
WEFFUS-11 Q19
LIGHT STOPWATCH
COUNTDOWN
00:10:13
MODE
50 METRES
...by agents of the USSR acting on behalf of Stalin's ghost...
...they'll help!
Let me go up and tell them.
Wait Calvin! I'll do it.
But I want to see the *levers*.
I'll ask them if you can have a look.
What do you think she's actually going to say to them?
Hopefully nothing about STALIN's GHOST hem hem.
She might just be going to cadge a cup of tea.
Wickle's a right old tea bag.

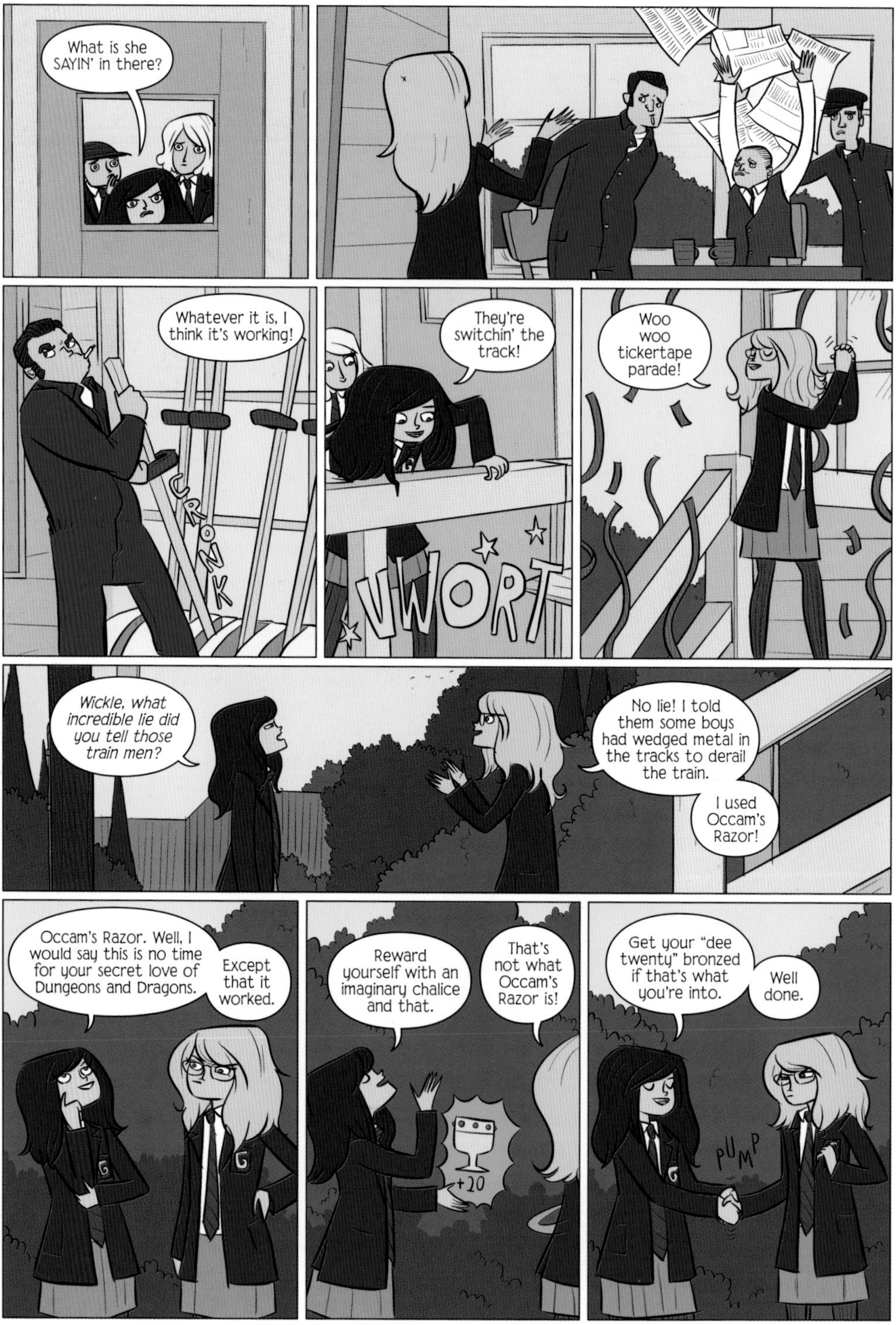
What is she SAYIN' in there?
Whatever it is, I think it's working!
CRONK
They're switchin' the track!
VWORT
Woo woo tickertape parade!
Wickle, what incredible lie did you tell those train men?
No lie! I told them some boys had wedged metal in the tracks to derail the train.
I used Occam's Razor!
Occam's Razor. Well, I would say this is no time for your secret love of Dungeons and Dragons.
Except that it worked.
Reward yourself with an imaginary chalice and that.
+20
That's not what Occam's Razor is!
Get your "dee twenty" bronzed if that's what you're into.
Well done.
PUMP

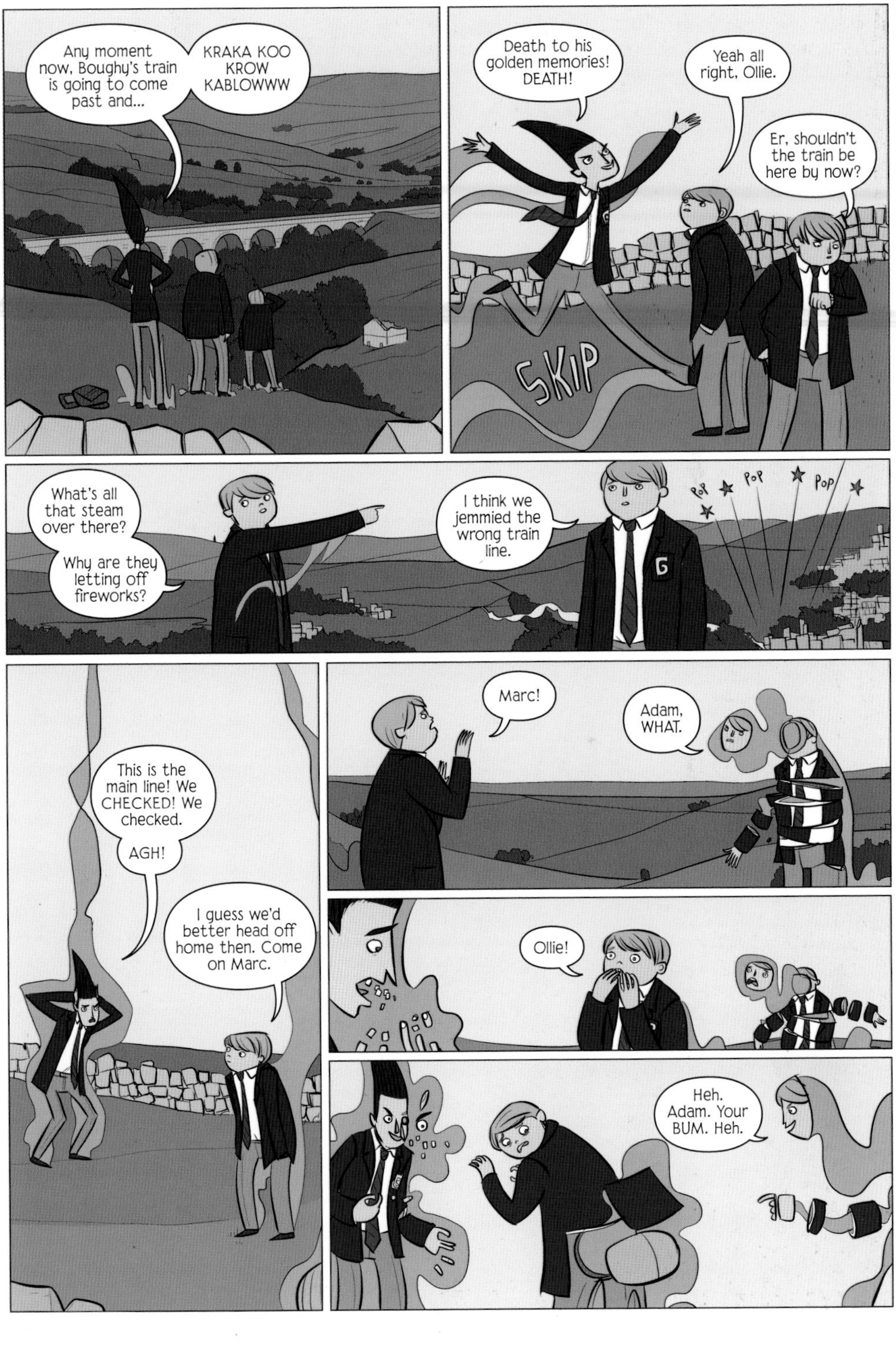
Any moment now, Boughy's train is going to come past and...
KRAKA KOO KROW KABLOWWW
Death to his golden memories! DEATH!
Yeah all right, Ollie.
Er, shouldn't the train be here by now?
SKIP
What's all that steam over there?
Why are they letting off fireworks?
I think we jemmied the wrong train line.
POP
POP
POP
This is the main line! We CHECKED! We checked.
AGH!
I guess we'd better head off home then. Come on Marc.
Marc!
Adam, WHAT.
Ollie!
Heh. Adam. Your BUM. Heh.

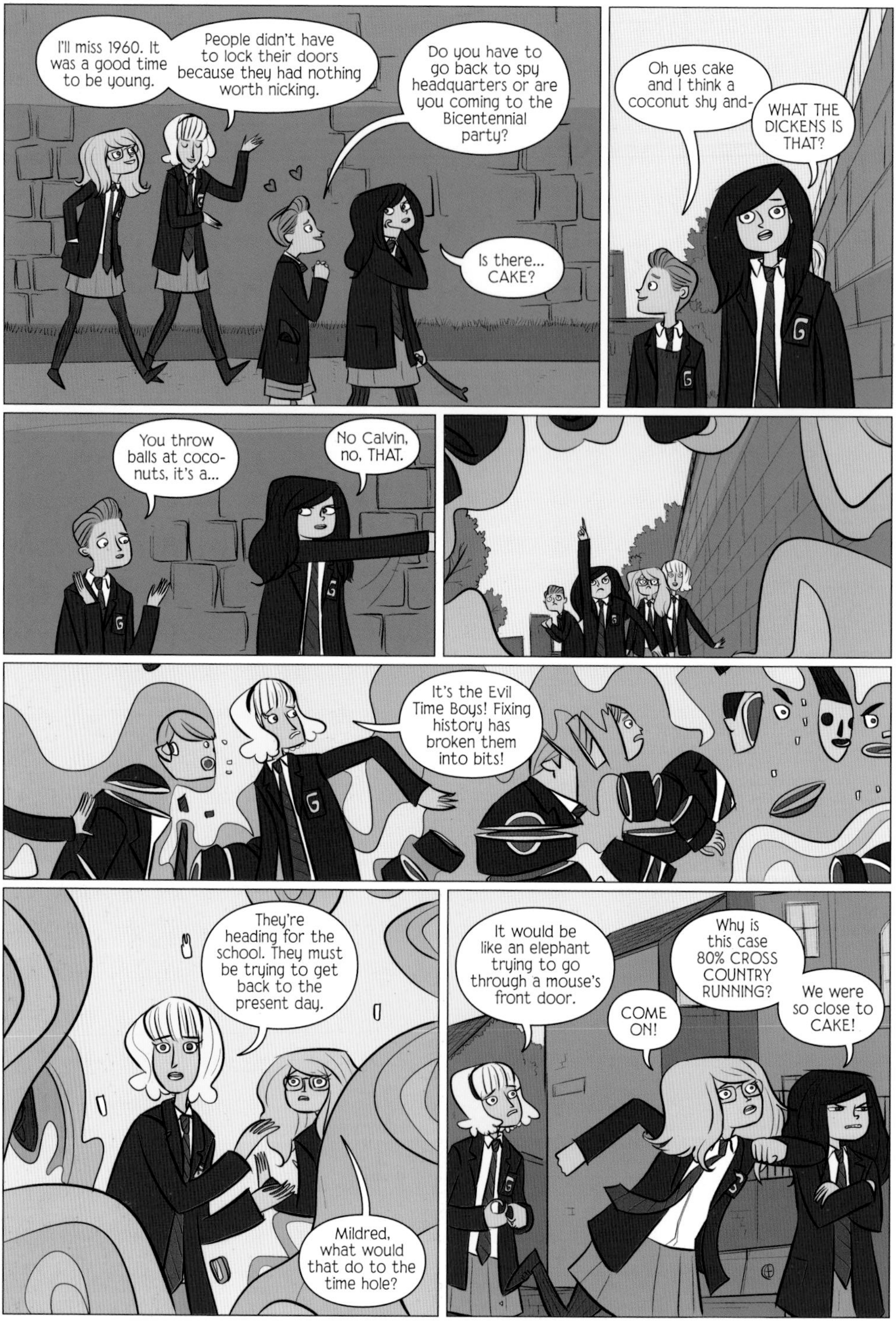
I'll miss 1960. It was a good time to be young.
People didn't have to lock their doors because they had nothing worth nicking.
Do you have to go back to spy headquarters or are you coming to the Bicentennial party?
Is there... CAKE?
Oh yes cake and I think a coconut shy and-
WHAT THE DICKENS IS THAT?
You throw balls at coco-nuts, it's a...
No Calvin, no, THAT.
It's the Evil Time Boys! Fixing history has broken them into bits!
They're heading for the school. They must be trying to get back to the present day.
Mildred, what would that do to the time hole?
It would be like an elephant trying to go through a mouse's front door.
COME ON!
Why is this case 80% CROSS COUNTRY RUNNING?
We were so close to CAKE!

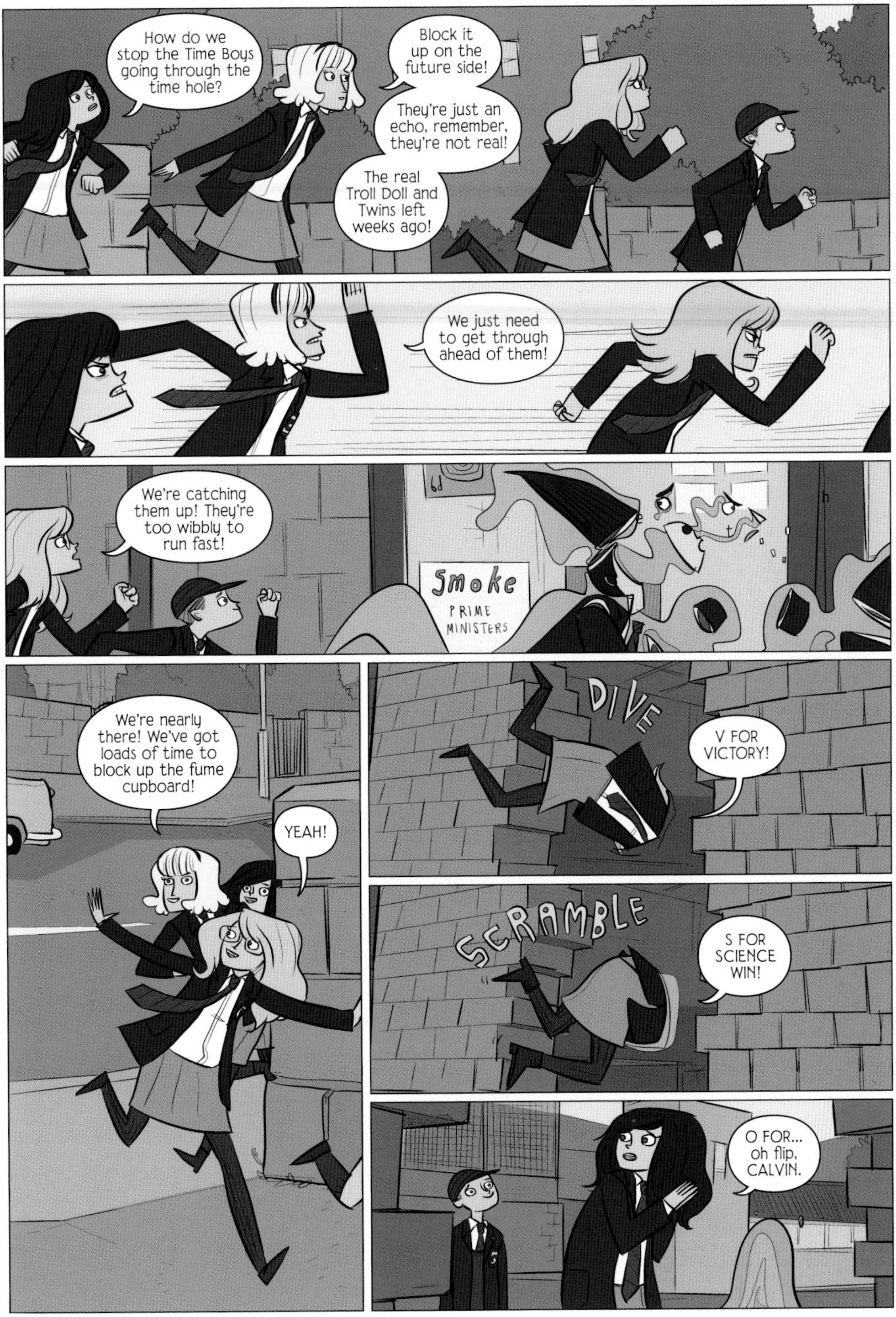
How do we stop the Time Boys going through the time hole?
Block it up on the future side!
They're just an echo, remember, they're not real!
The real Troll Doll and Twins left weeks ago!
We just need to get through ahead of them!
We're catching them up! They're too wibbly to run fast!
Smoke PRIME MINISTERS
We're nearly there! We've got loads of time to block up the fume cupboard!
YEAH!
DIVE
V FOR VICTORY!
SCRAMBLE
S FOR SCIENCE WIN!
O FOR... oh flip, CALVIN.

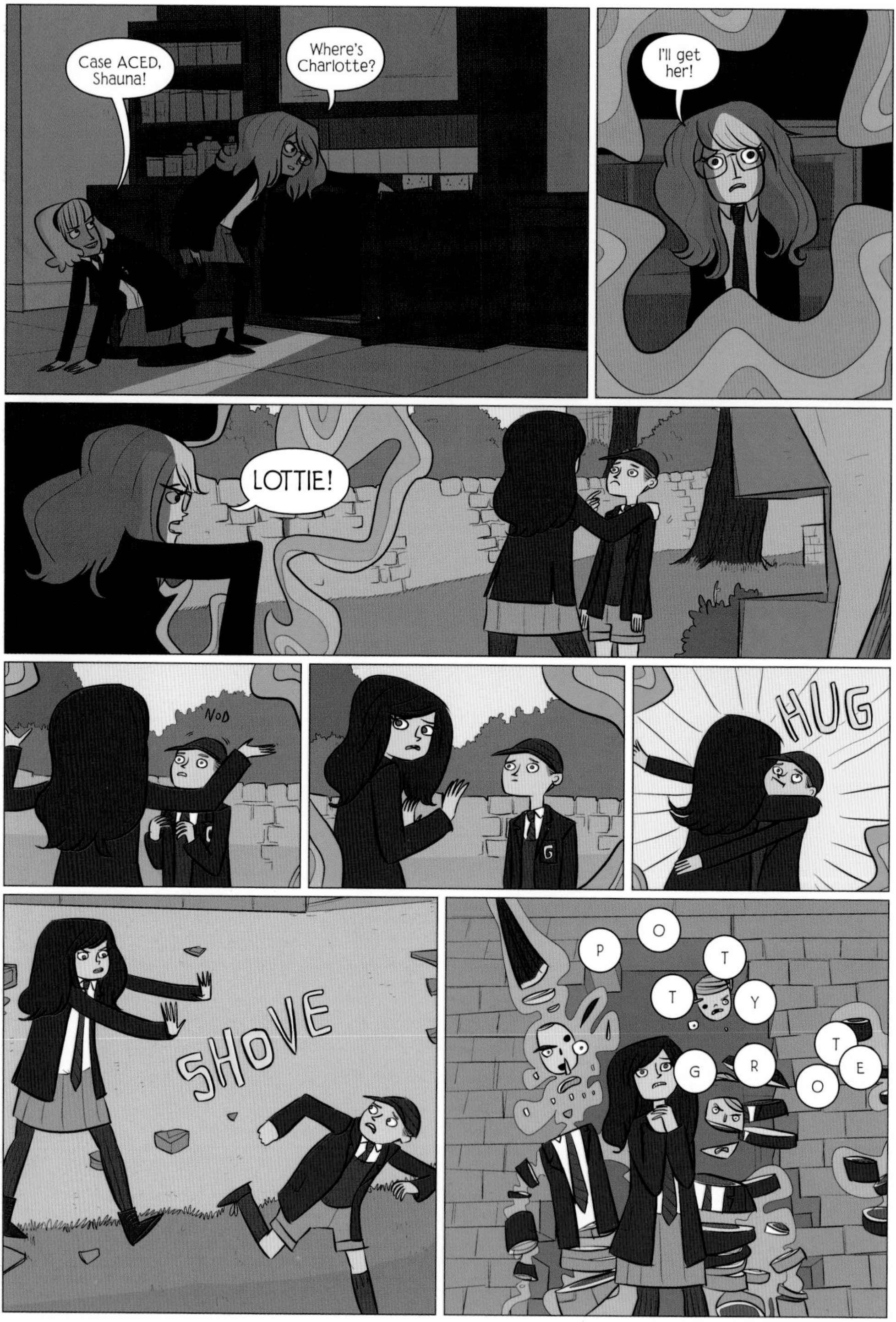
Case ACED, Shauna!
Where's Charlotte?
I'll get her!
LOTTIE!
NOD
HUG
SHOVE
P
O
T
T
Y
G
R
T
O
E

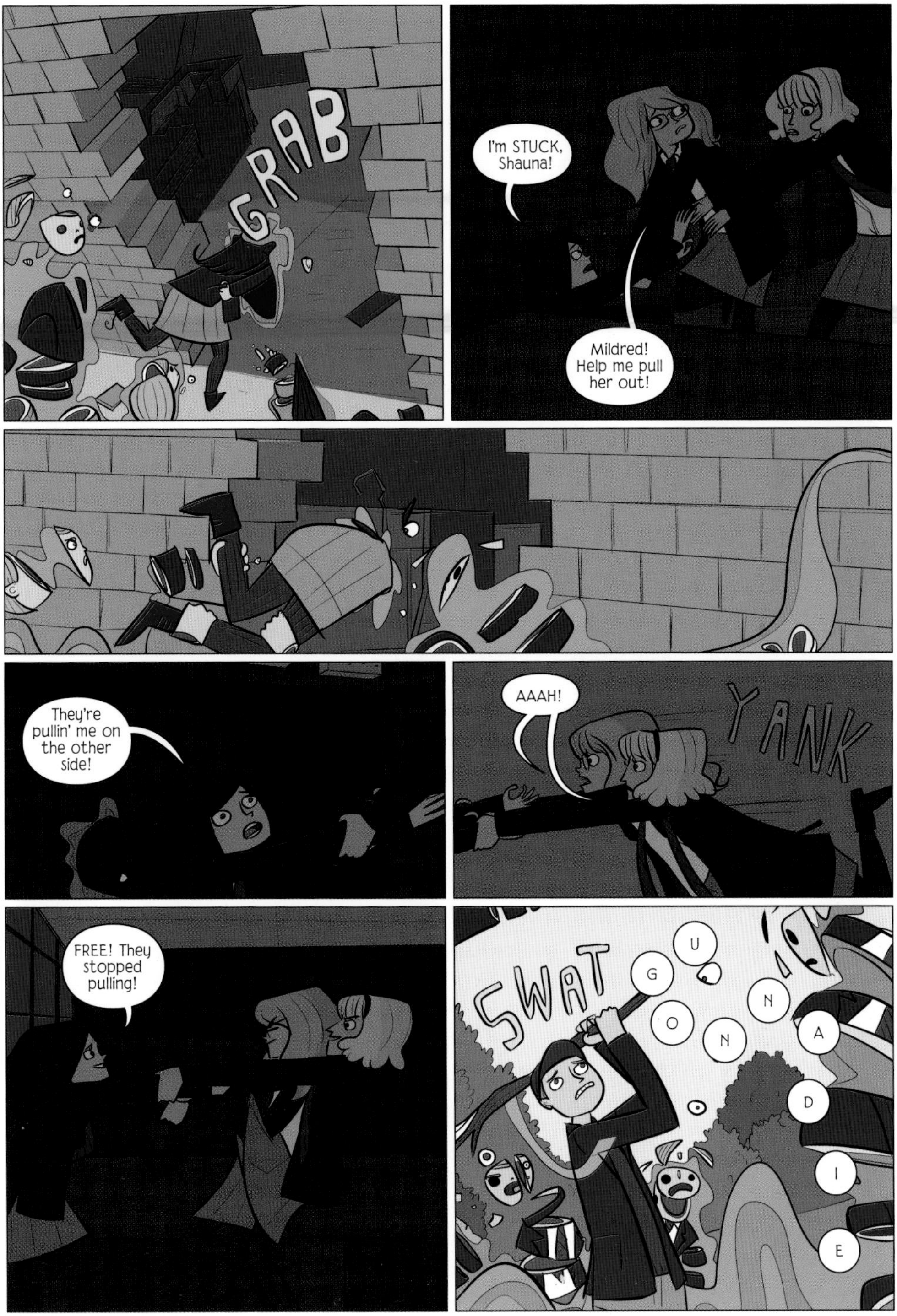
GRAB
I'm STUCK, Shauna!
Mildred! Help me pull her out!
They're pullin' me on the other side!
AAAH!
YANK
FREE! They stopped pulling!
SWAT
GONNA DIE
U
E

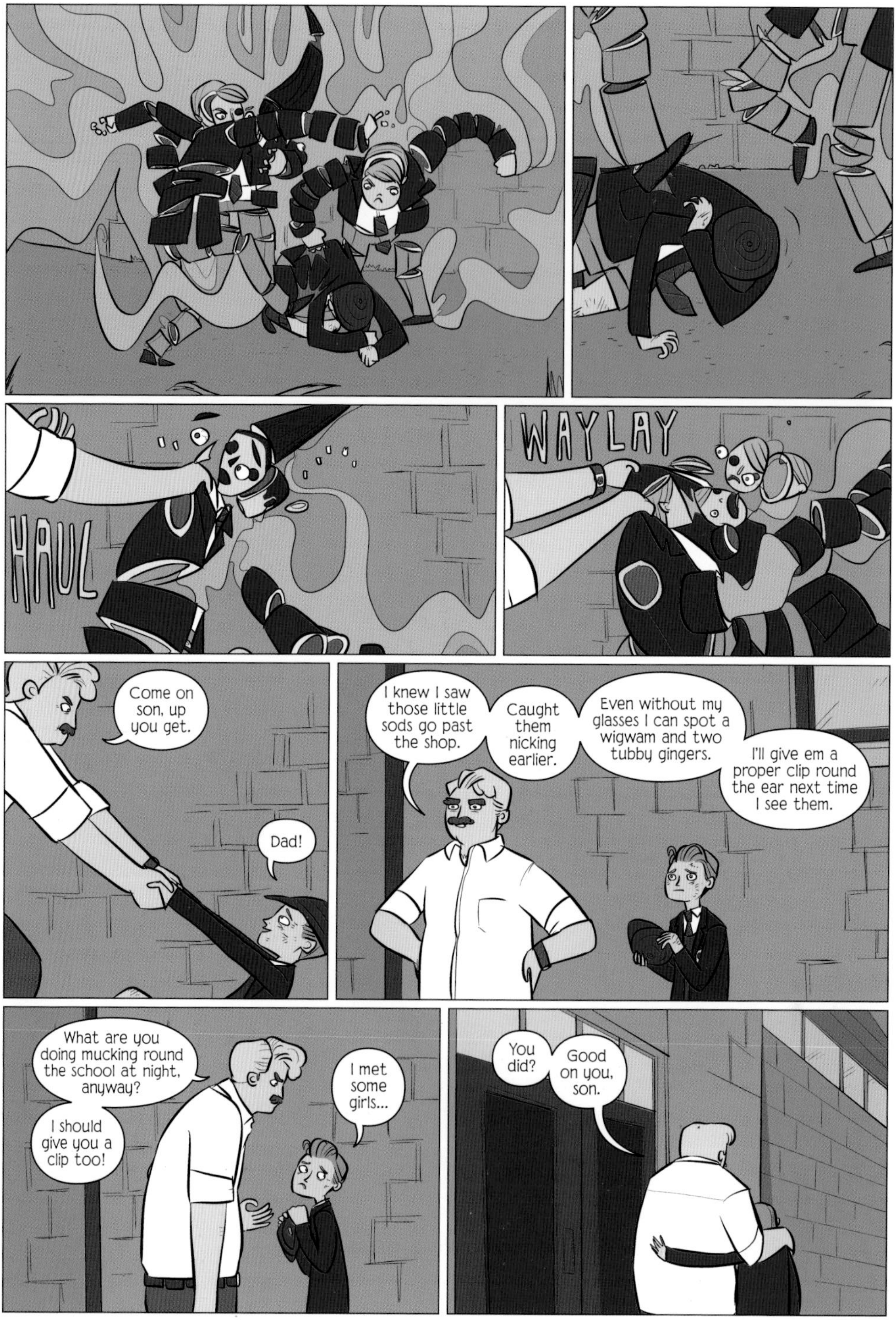
HAUL
WAYLAY
Come on son, up you get.
Dad!
I knew I saw those little sods go past the shop.
Caught them nicking earlier.
Even without my glasses I can spot a wigwam and two tubby gingers.
I'll give em a proper clip round the ear next time I see them.
What are you doing mucking round the school at night, anyway?
I should give you a clip too!
I met some girls...
You did?
Good on you, son.

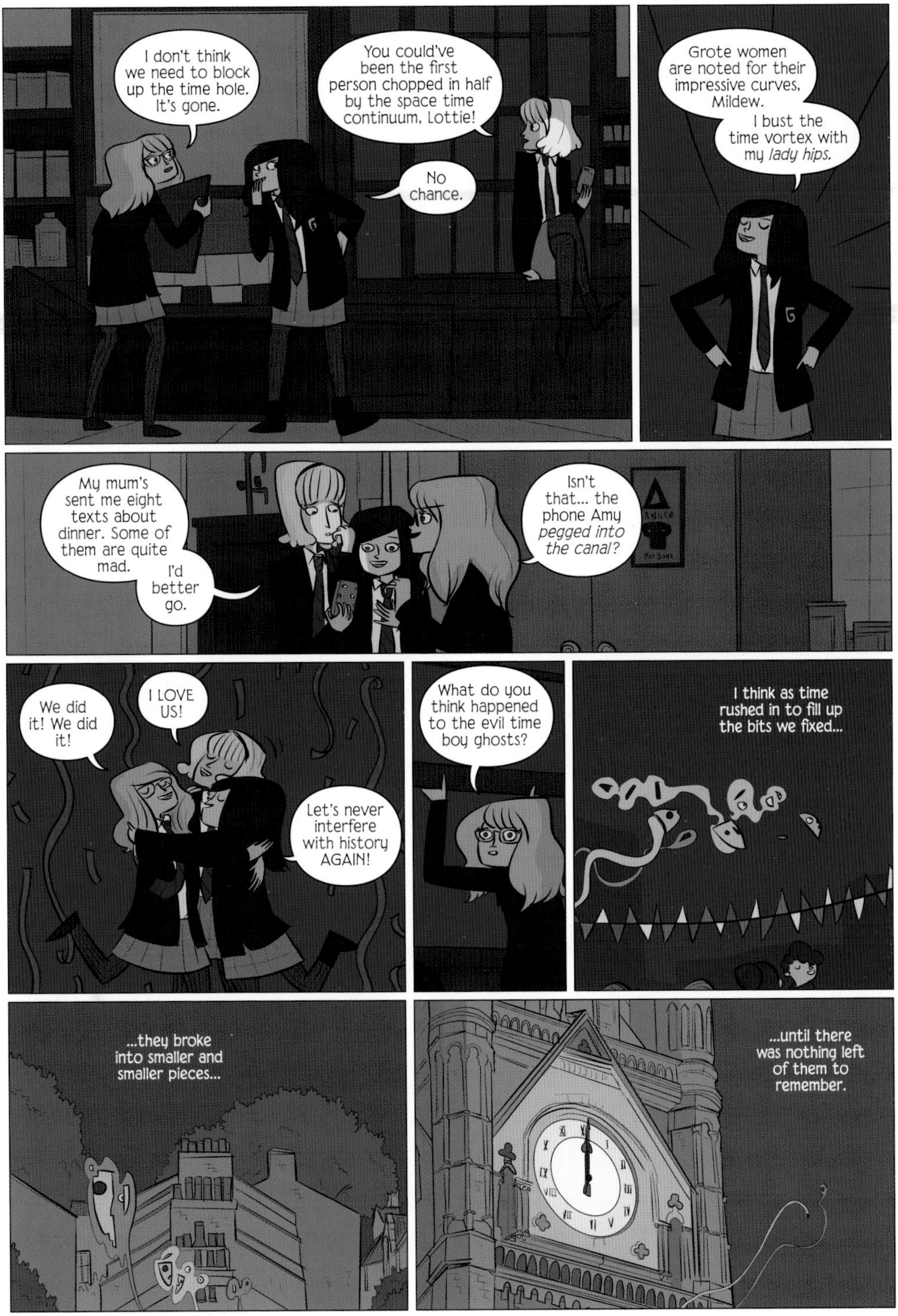
I don't think we need to block up the time hole. It's gone.
You could've been the first person chopped in half by the space time continuum, Lottie!
No chance.
Grote women are noted for their impressive curves, Mildew.
I bust the time vortex with my *lady hips.*
My mum's sent me eight texts about dinner. Some of them are quite mad.
I'd better go.
Isn't that... the phone Amy *pegged into the canal?*
We did it! We did it!
I LOVE US!
Let's never interfere with history AGAIN!
What do you think happened to the evil time boy ghosts?
I think as time rushed in to fill up the bits we fixed...
...they broke into smaller and smaller pieces...
...until there was nothing left of them to remember.

Lottie, when I looked through the time hole the last time...

...I saw you saying something to Calvin.

Yeah. Poor ole Calvin.

NEWSAGENT AND WIFE KILLED IN GETAWAY CAR SMASH

By **DENNIS WALSDEN**

Keane End newsagent Ron Goater and his wife, Nellie Goater, were killed yesterday on the A458 to Coward Cross when their car was sideswiped by a van involved in an attempted jailbreak.

Mr and Mrs Goater, were returning

HM Prison Tacklef Gary The Horse w diving at speeds in 120mph when the chance."

The Goaters are son Calvin who is

When I was looking for Tackleford disasters in the newspaper archive, I found this.

It's from a week after the time hole day.

ARRY'S BEER
THE RELIABLE PINT

Oh... oh no.

Charlotte.

Yeah yeah yeah yeah.

Grumpaw dragged his young self through time hundreds of times to fix that, and he couldn't.

He was only a little boy. Little boys can't do anything much.

So I thought about all the things I wished I said to my dad...

...and I told him it was nationally important that his mum and dad knew he loved them...

UH HER HER HER HER HERRR

Shauna I can't send you home with meatball eyes.

You can borrow my teaspoons.

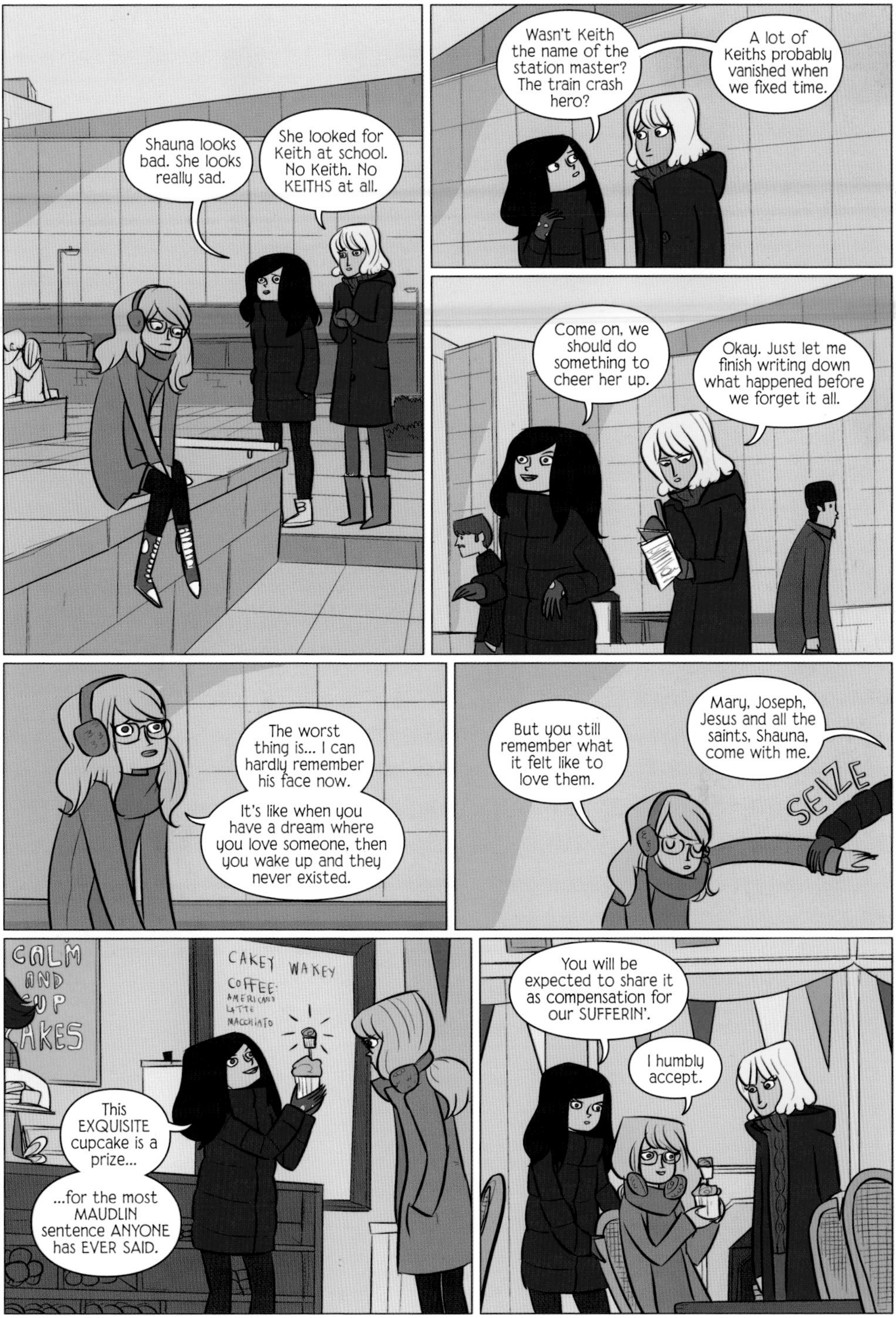
Shauna looks bad. She looks really sad.
She looked for Keith at school. No Keith. No KEITHS at all.
Wasn't Keith the name of the station master? The train crash hero?
A lot of Keiths probably vanished when we fixed time.
Come on, we should do something to cheer her up.
Okay. Just let me finish writing down what happened before we forget it all.
The worst thing is... I can hardly remember his face now.
It's like when you have a dream where you love someone, then you wake up and they never existed.
But you still remember what it felt like to love them.
Mary, Joseph, Jesus and all the saints, Shauna, come with me.
SEIZE
CALM
AND
CAKEY WAKEY
COFFEE:
AMERICANO
LATTE
MACCHIATO
This EXQUISITE cupcake is a prize...
...for the most MAUDLIN sentence ANYONE has EVER SAID.
You will be expected to share it as compensation for our SUFFERIN'.
I humbly accept.

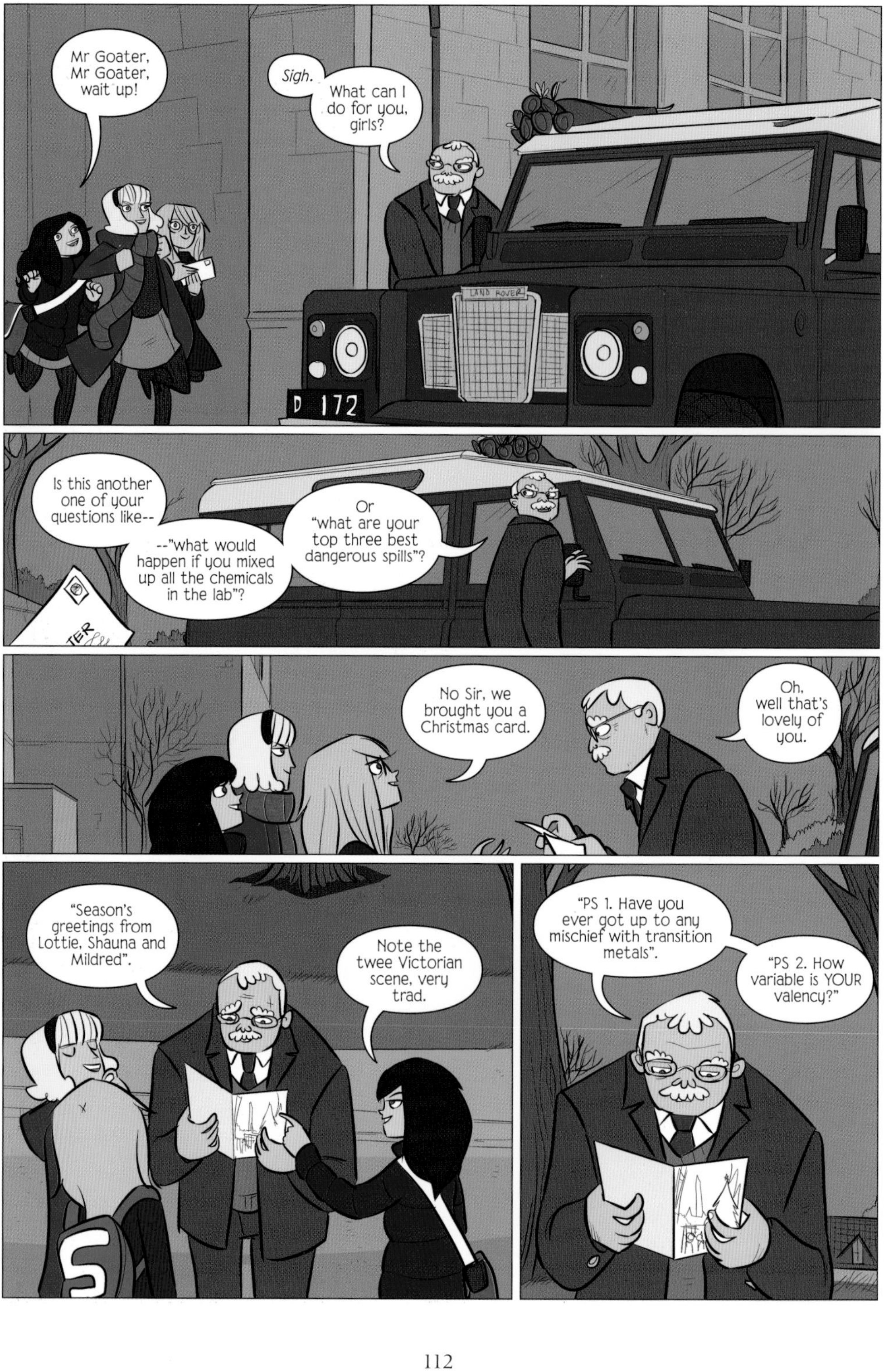
Mr Goater, Mr Goater, wait up!
Sigh.
What can I do for you, girls?
LAND ROVER
D 172
Is this another one of your questions like--
--"what would happen if you mixed up all the chemicals in the lab"?
Or "what are your top three best dangerous spills"?
No Sir, we brought you a Christmas card.
Oh, well that's lovely of you.
"Season's greetings from Lottie, Shauna and Mildred".
Note the twee Victorian scene, very trad.
"PS 1. Have you ever got up to any mischief with transition metals".
"PS 2. How variable is YOUR valency?"

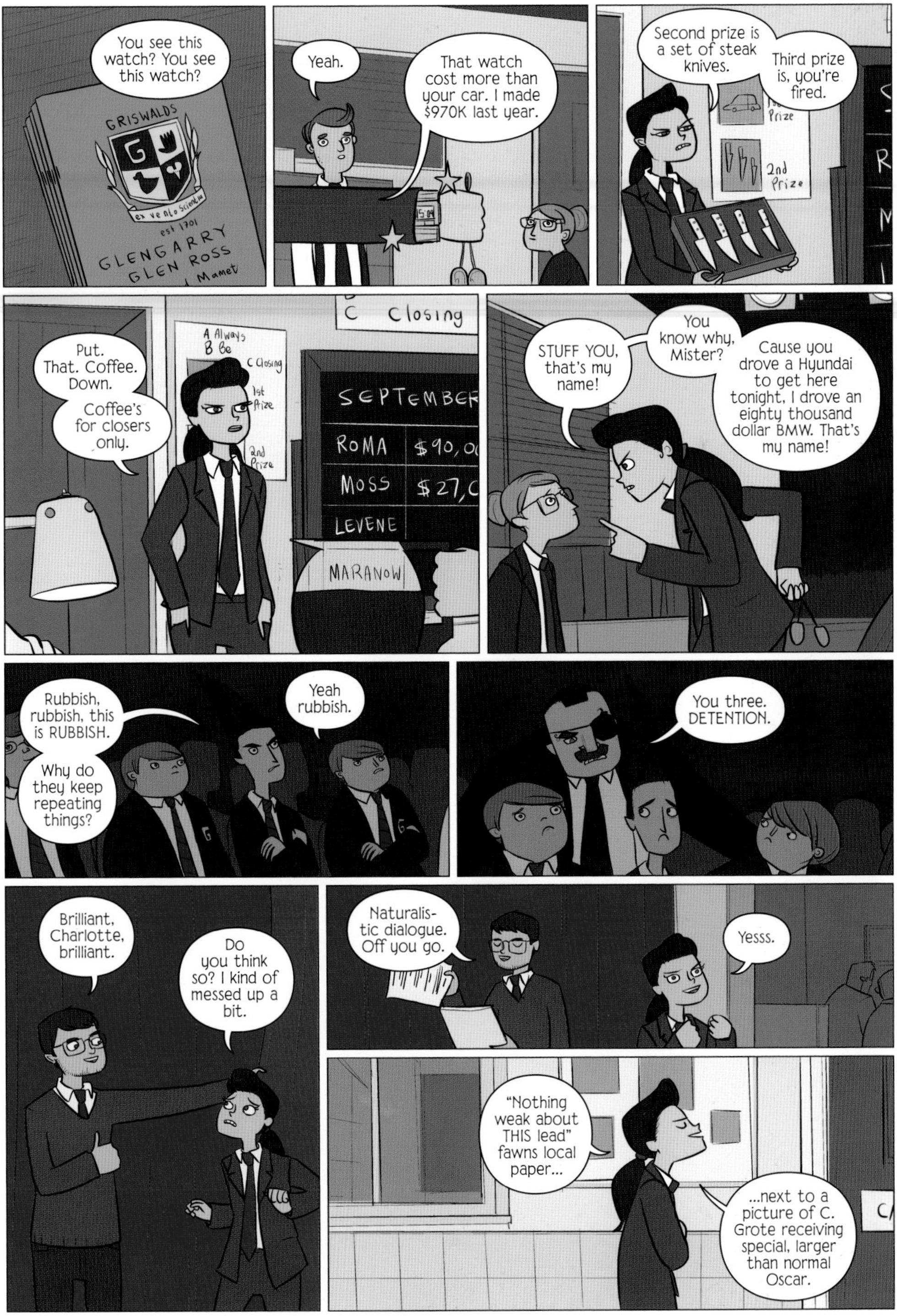
You see this watch? You see this watch?
GRISWALDS
G
ex vento scientia
est 1701
GLENGARRY GLEN ROSS
Mamet
Yeah.
That watch cost more than your car. I made $970K last year.
Second prize is a set of steak knives.
Third prize is, you're fired.
1st Prize
2nd Prize
C Closing
A Always B Be C Closing
1st Prize
2nd Prize
Put. That. Coffee. Down.
Coffee's for closers only.
SEPTEMBER
ROMA $90,0
MOSS $27,C
LEVENE
MARANOW
STUFF YOU, that's my name!
You know why, Mister?
Cause you drove a Hyundai to get here tonight, I drove an eighty thousand dollar BMW. That's my name!
Rubbish, rubbish, this is RUBBISH.
Why do they keep repeating things?
Yeah rubbish.
You three. DETENTION.
Brilliant, Charlotte, brilliant.
Do you think so? I kind of messed up a bit.
Naturalistic dialogue. Off you go.
Yesss.
"Nothing weak about THIS lead" fawns local paper...
...next to a picture of C. Grote receiving special, larger than normal Oscar.

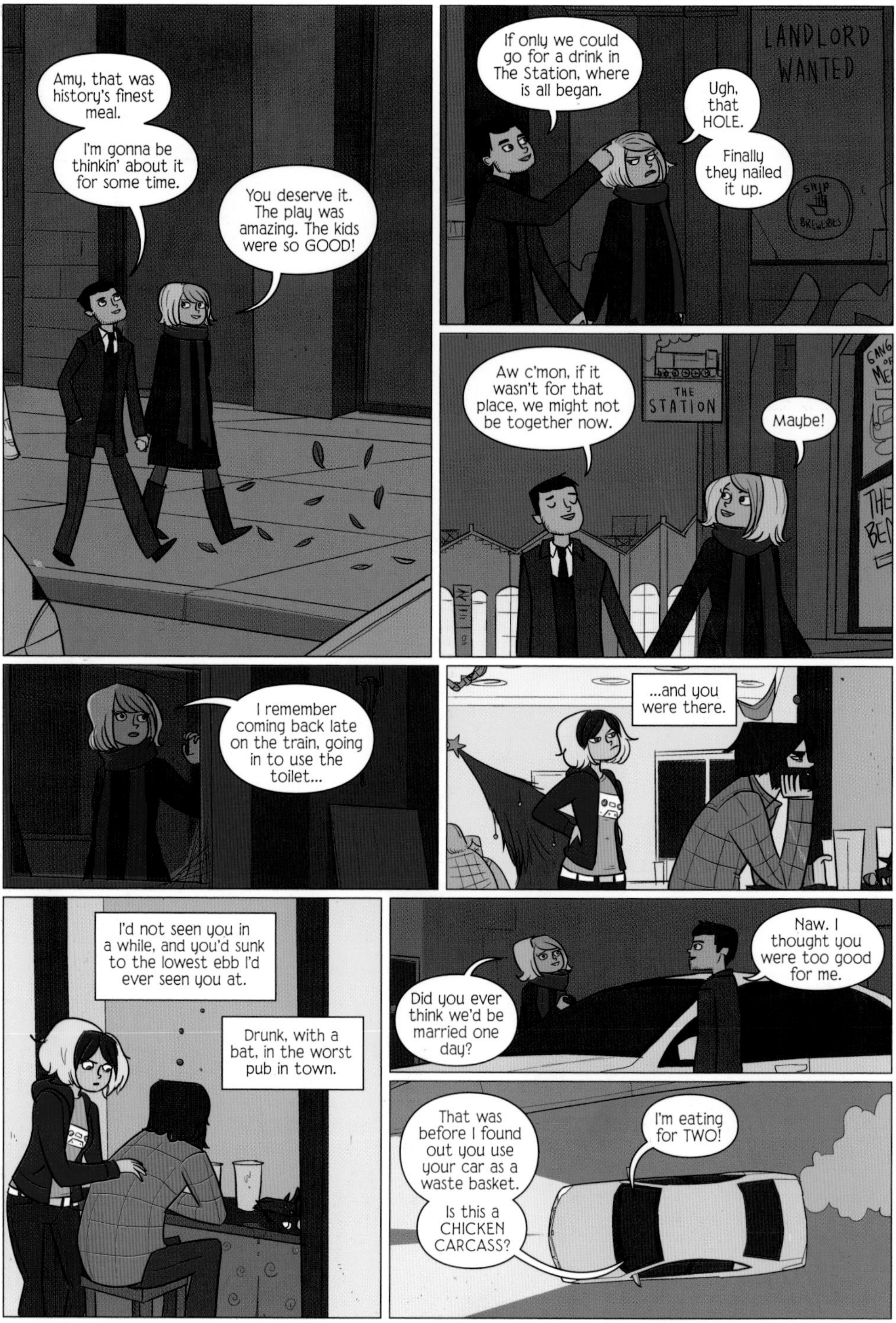
Amy, that was history's finest meal.
I'm gonna be thinkin' about it for some time.
You deserve it. The play was amazing. The kids were so GOOD!
If only we could go for a drink in The Station, where is all began.
LANDLORD WANTED
Ugh, that HOLE.
Finally they nailed it up.
Aw c'mon, if it wasn't for that place, we might not be together now.
THE STATION
Maybe!
I remember coming back late on the train, going in to use the toilet...
...and you were there.
I'd not seen you in a while, and you'd sunk to the lowest ebb I'd ever seen you at.
Drunk, with a bat, in the worst pub in town.
Did you ever think we'd be married one day?
Naw. I thought you were too good for me.
That was before I found out you use your car as a waste basket.
Is this a CHICKEN CARCASS?
I'm eating for TWO!

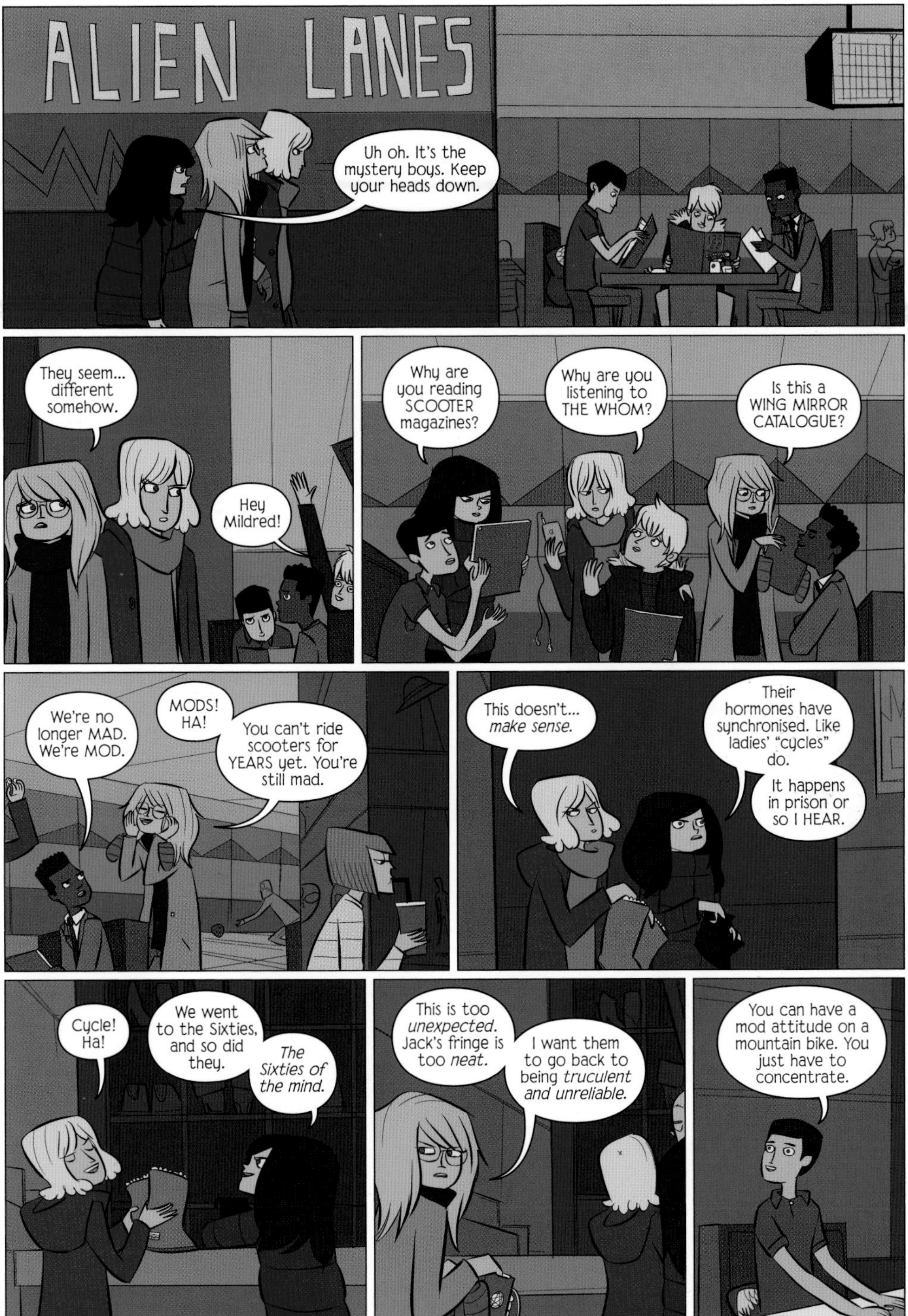
ALIEN LANES
Uh oh. It's the mystery boys. Keep your heads down.
They seem... different somehow.
Hey Mildred!
Why are you reading SCOOTER magazines?
Why are you listening to THE WHOM?
Is this a WING MIRROR CATALOGUE?
We're no longer MAD. We're MOD.
MODS! HA!
You can't ride scooters for YEARS yet. You're still mad.
This doesn't... *make sense.*
Their hormones have synchronised. Like ladies' "cycles" do.
It happens in prison or so I HEAR.
Cycle! Ha!
We went to the Sixties, and so did they.
The Sixties of the mind.
This is too *unexpected.* Jack's fringe is too *neat.*
I want them to go back to being *truculent and unreliable.*
You can have a mod attitude on a mountain bike. You just have to concentrate.

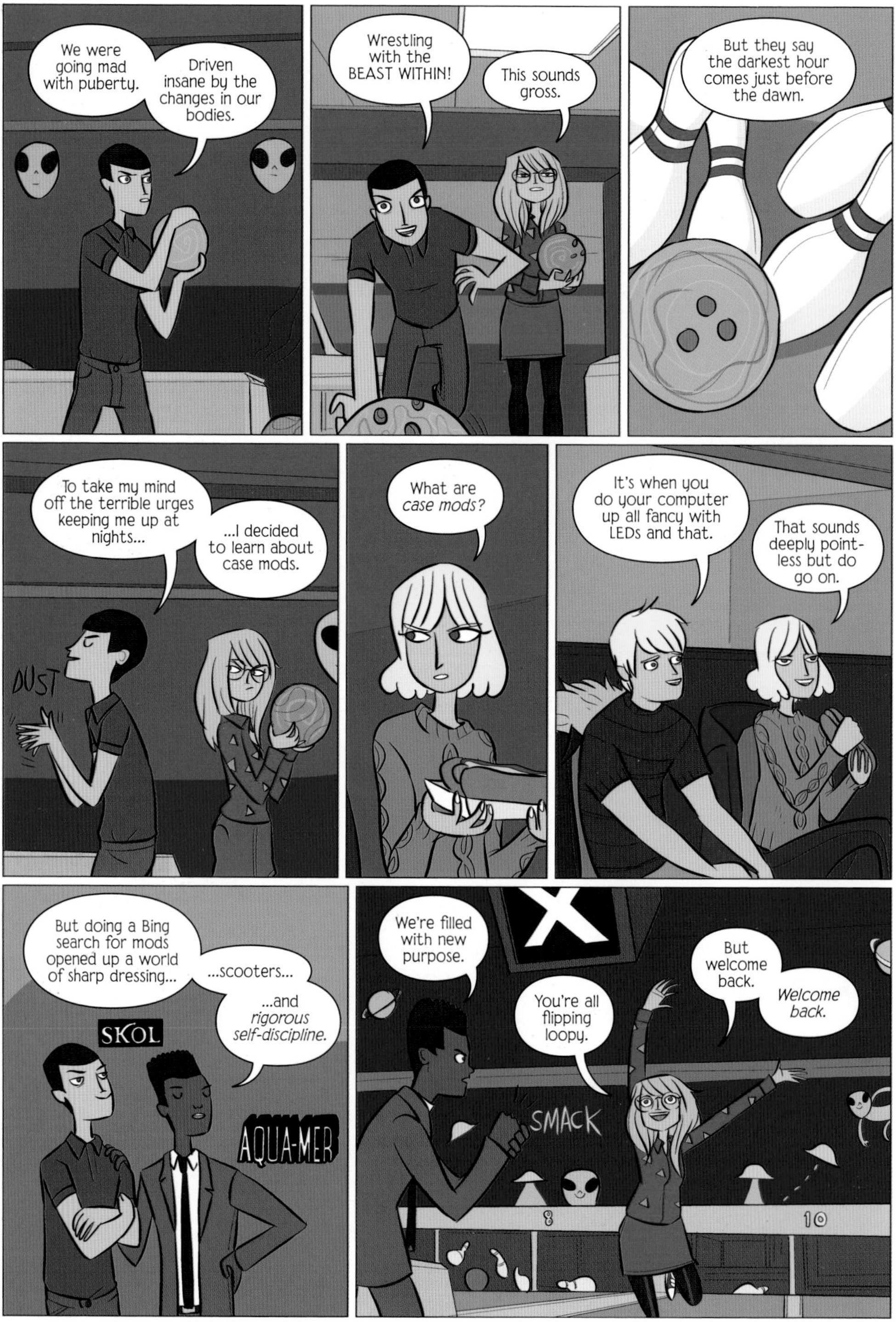
We were going mad with puberty.
Driven insane by the changes in our bodies.
Wrestling with the BEAST WITHIN!
This sounds gross.
But they say the darkest hour comes just before the dawn.
To take my mind off the terrible urges keeping me up at nights...
...I decided to learn about case mods.
DUST
What are *case mods?*
It's when you do your computer up all fancy with LEDs and that.
That sounds deeply pointless but do go on.
But doing a Bing search for mods opened up a world of sharp dressing...
...scooters...
...and *rigorous self-discipline.*
SKOL
AQUA-MER
We're filled with new purpose.
You're all flipping loopy.
But welcome back.
Welcome back.
SMACK

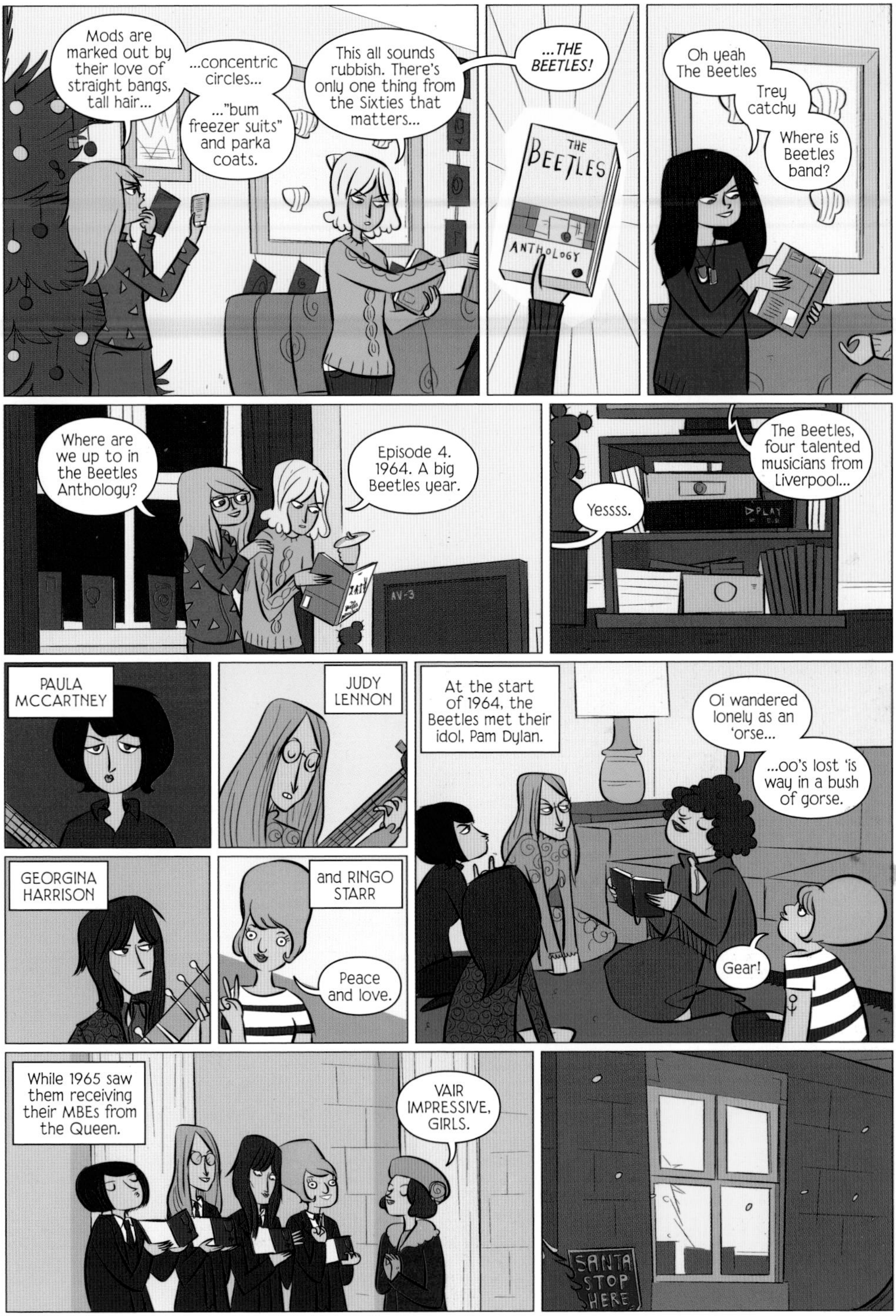
Mods are marked out by their love of straight bangs, tall hair...
...concentric circles...
..."bum freezer suits" and parka coats.
This all sounds rubbish. There's only one thing from the Sixties that matters...
...THE BEETLES!
THE BEETLES
ANTHOLOGY
Oh yeah The Beetles
Trey catchy
Where is Beetles band?
Where are we up to in the Beetles Anthology?
Episode 4. 1964. A big Beetles year.
AV-3
Yessss.
The Beetles, four talented musicians from Liverpool...
PLAY
PAULA McCARTNEY
JUDY LENNON
At the start of 1964, the Beetles met their idol, Pam Dylan.
Oi wandered lonely as an 'orse...
...oo's lost 'is way in a bush of gorse.
GEORGINA HARRISON
and RINGO STARR
Peace and love.
Gear!
While 1965 saw them receiving their MBEs from the Queen.
VAIR IMPRESSIVE, GIRLS.
SANTA STOP HERE

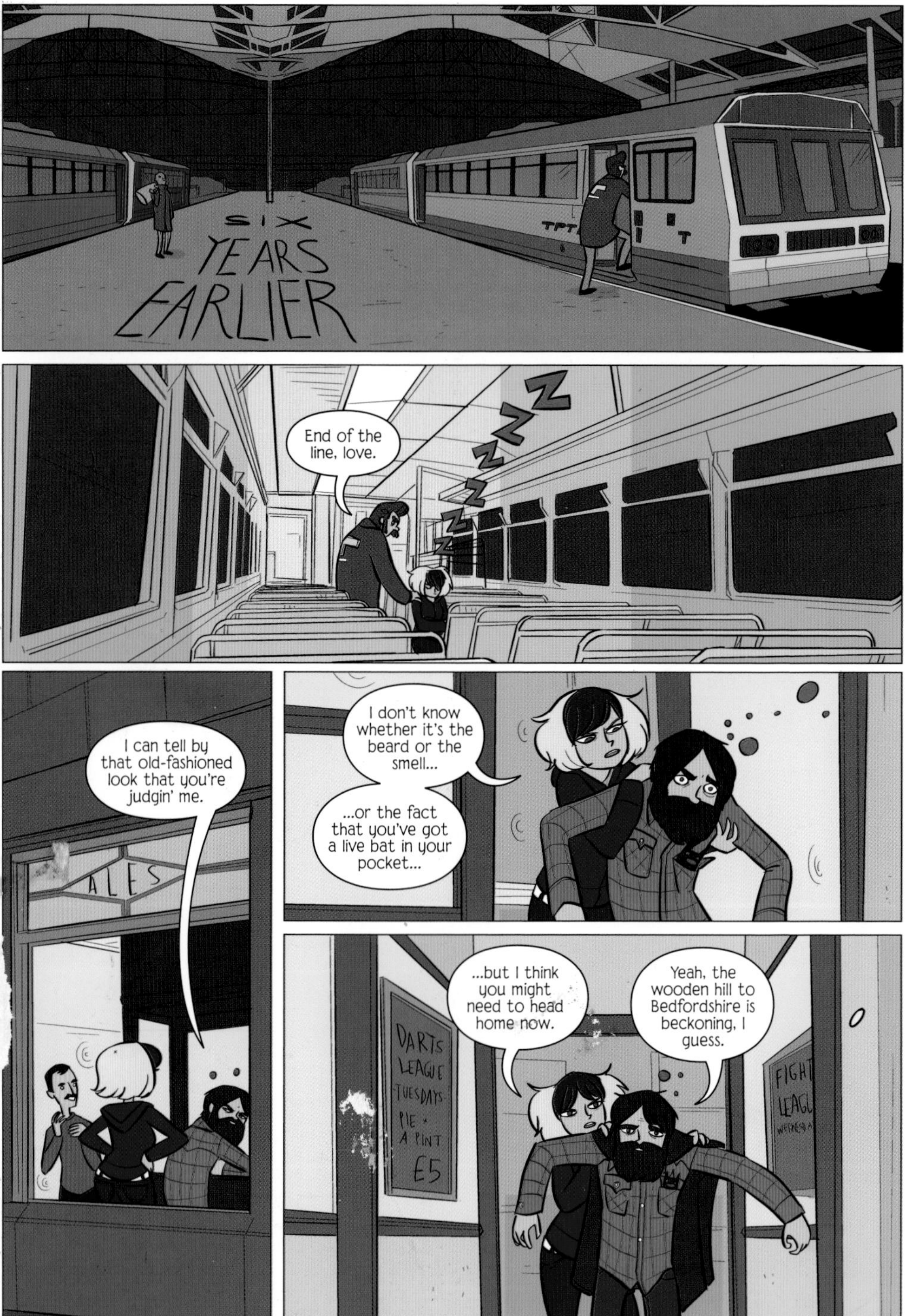
SIX YEARS EARLIER
TPT
End of the line, love.
ZZZZZZ
I can tell by that old-fashioned look that you're judgin' me.
ALES
I don't know whether it's the beard or the smell...
...or the fact that you've got a live bat in your pocket...
...but I think you might need to head home now.
Yeah, the wooden hill to Bedfordshire is beckoning, I guess.
DARTS LEAGUE TUESDAYS PIE + A PINT £5
FIGHT LEAGU

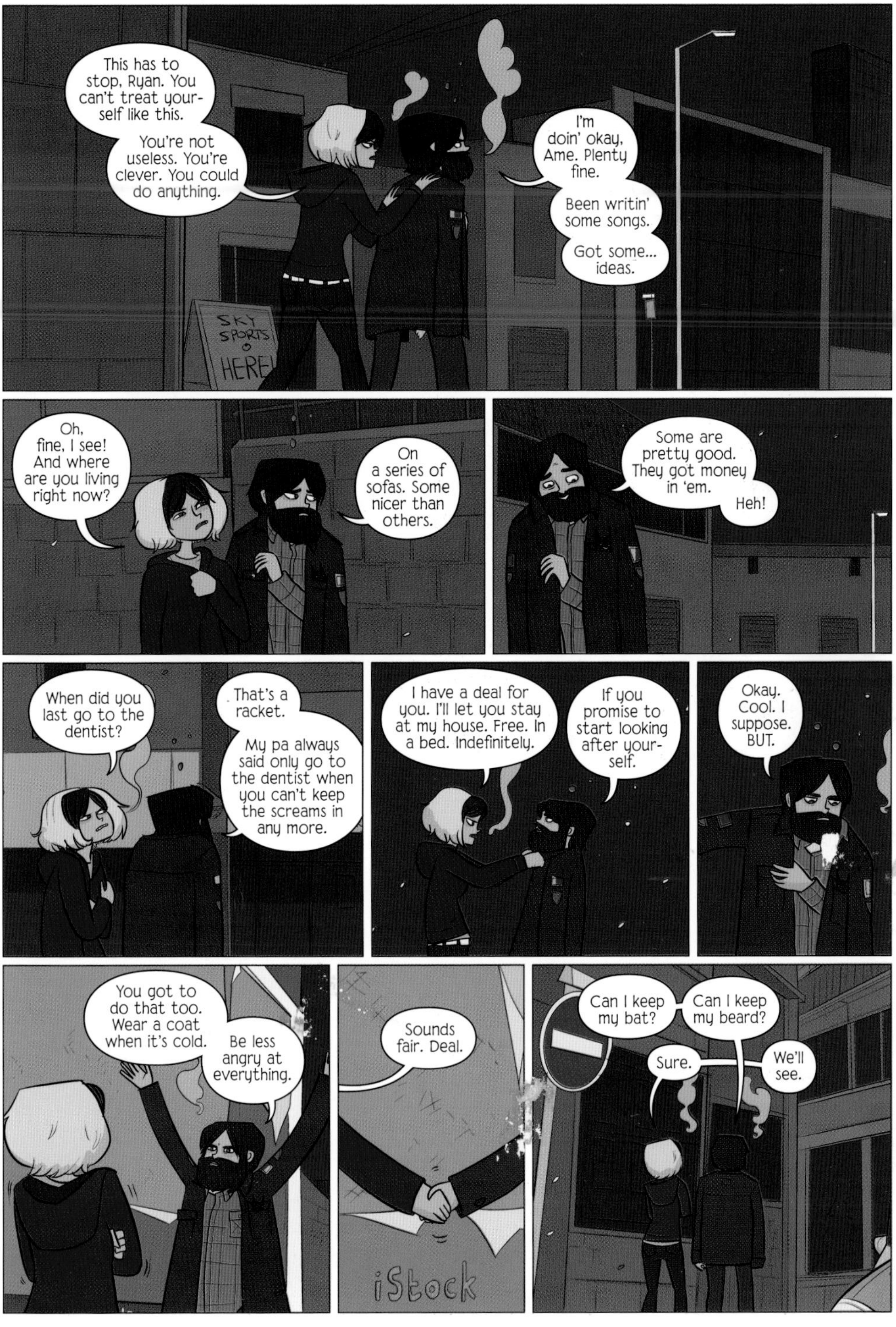
This has to stop, Ryan. You can't treat yourself like this.
You're not useless. You're clever. You could do anything.
I'm doin' okay, Ame. Plenty fine.
Been writin' some songs.
Got some... ideas.
SKY SPORTS HERE
Oh, fine, I see! And where are you living right now?
On a series of sofas. Some nicer than others.
Some are pretty good. They got money in 'em.
Heh!
When did you last go to the dentist?
That's a racket.
My pa always said only go to the dentist when you can't keep the screams in any more.
I have a deal for you. I'll let you stay at my house. Free. In a bed. Indefinitely.
If you promise to start looking after yourself.
Okay. Cool. I suppose. BUT.
You got to do that too. Wear a coat when it's cold.
Be less angry at everything.
Sounds fair. Deal.
iStock
Can I keep my bat?
Can I keep my beard?
Sure.
We'll see.

(FIN)

BACK IN TINE*: THE HISTORY OF THE FORKED ROAD

You know, like the prongs on a fork, look it up in a dictionary

Thank you for buying and reading *The Case Of The Forked Road*. I know what you are thinking. You are thinking, "I would have paid twice as much for this book" (if you bought it) or "I should buy the librarian a cream cake" if you got it from a library or "why are all the shop staff looking at me funny" if you have read the whole thing in your local book shop. It is that good.

But *Bad Machinery* number seven is not just a fun and scientifically confused journey into great acting, romance confusion, deodorant and "the timestream". It is also a tale that touches some important moments in Tackleford's past, namely the love and friendship of Mr and Mrs Ryan & Amy Beckwith-Chilton. Before they were A) a teacher with a suspicious love of elbow patches and B) a queenly antiques woman, they were just confused humans barely capable of tying their own shoelaces, or so I hear.

They had a lot of adventures, together and apart, before they decided to kiss each other's faces over and over again and do a marriage. And the critical events of this case revisit some important points that were first shown to the public in the historical and unimportant comic strip "Scary Go Round".

So over the next few pages, please enjoy a selection of the magic moments that follow Amy's fateful finding of the bearded Beckwith. It's the moment that turned them from two people who never knew where their next clean pair of socks were coming from, into the kind of upstanding humans who a bank manager would lend the money to buy a house with.

I have added some notes with my own thoughts under these comics, just a few basic opinions. Only v. mildly controversial.

NOW READ ON!

Charlotte Grote
Tackleford, UK.

THE BAT IS EATING ACORNS

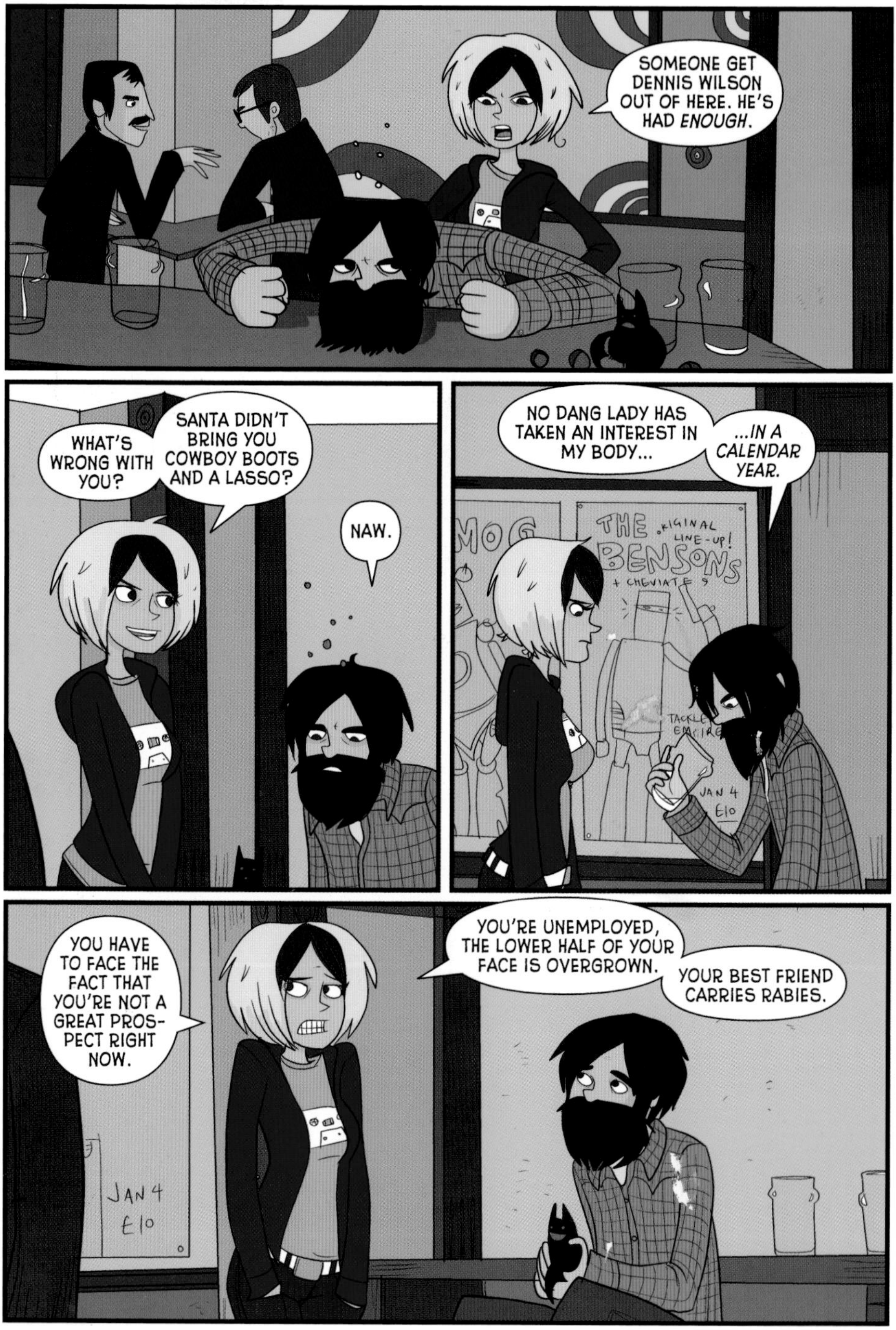

SOMEONE GET DENNIS WILSON OUT OF HERE. HE'S HAD *ENOUGH*.
WHAT'S WRONG WITH YOU?
SANTA DIDN'T BRING YOU COWBOY BOOTS AND A LASSO?
NAW.
NO DANG LADY HAS TAKEN AN INTEREST IN MY BODY...
...*IN A CALENDAR YEAR.*
THE ORIGINAL LINE-UP! BENSONS + CHEVIATES
TACKLE EMPIRE
JAN 4 £10
YOU HAVE TO FACE THE FACT THAT YOU'RE NOT A GREAT PROS-PECT RIGHT NOW.
YOU'RE UNEMPLOYED, THE LOWER HALF OF YOUR FACE IS OVERGROWN.
YOUR BEST FRIEND CARRIES RABIES.
JAN 4 £10

Dennis Wilson was the drummer in the Beach Boys. He pretty much invented the idea of being cool and having a beard. You will note that Ryan has a pet bat. This is totally against the law. That was the kind of man he was. A rebel. Or an idiot. But the bat seems to like it so I guess he knew what he was doing. Maybe they just "found each other".

A LOAD OF EXCESS

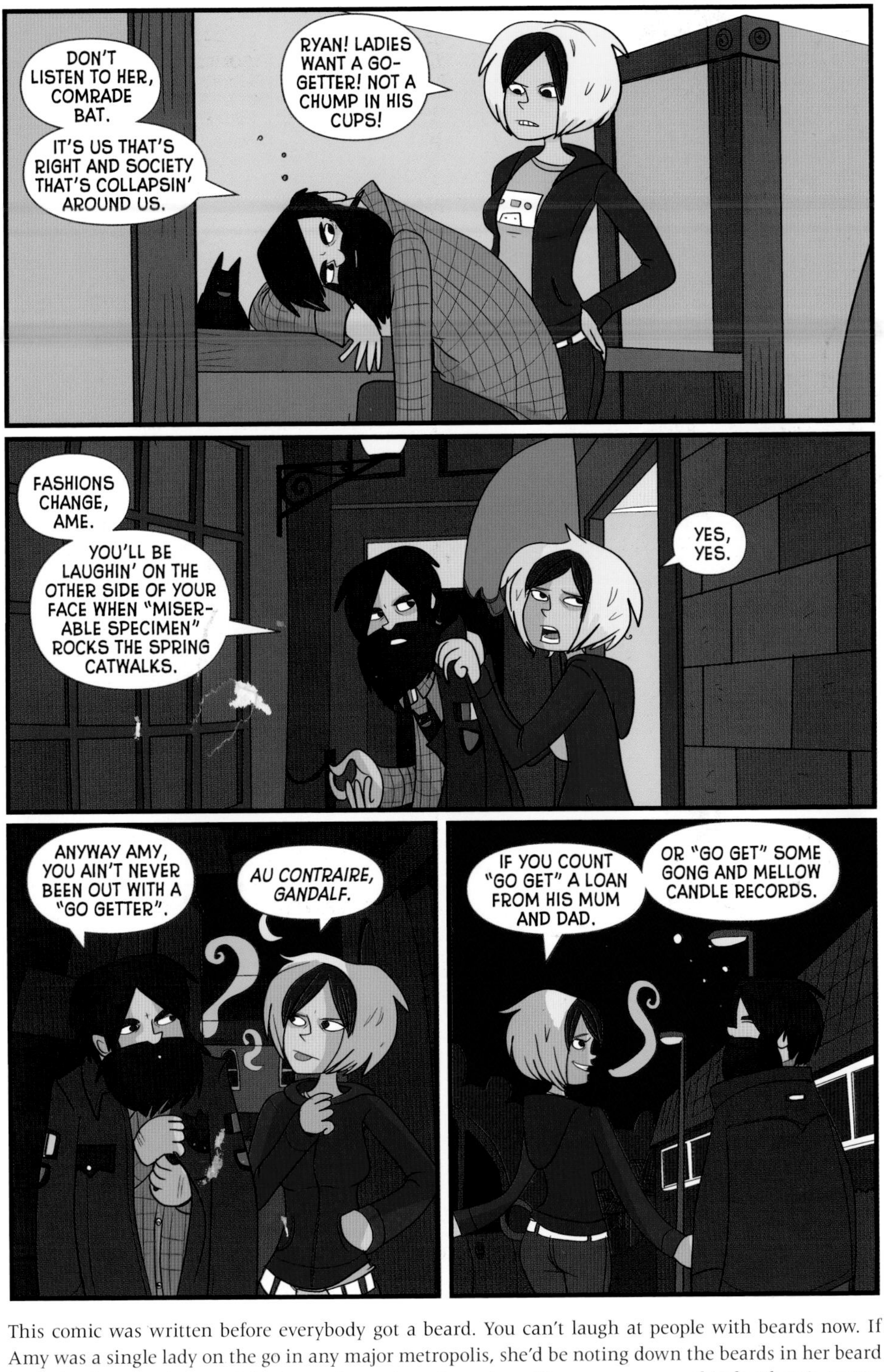

DON'T LISTEN TO HER, COMRADE BAT.
IT'S US THAT'S RIGHT AND SOCIETY THAT'S COLLAPSIN' AROUND US.
RYAN! LADIES WANT A GO-GETTER! NOT A CHUMP IN HIS CUPS!
FASHIONS CHANGE, AME.
YOU'LL BE LAUGHIN' ON THE OTHER SIDE OF YOUR FACE WHEN "MISERABLE SPECIMEN" ROCKS THE SPRING CATWALKS.
YES, YES.
ANYWAY AMY, YOU AIN'T NEVER BEEN OUT WITH A "GO GETTER".
AU CONTRAIRE, GANDALF.
IF YOU COUNT "GO GET" A LOAN FROM HIS MUM AND DAD.
OR "GO GET" SOME GONG AND MELLOW CANDLE RECORDS.

This comic was written before everybody got a beard. You can't laugh at people with beards now. If Amy was a single lady on the go in any major metropolis, she'd be noting down the beards in her beard book for future reference. It's what a dame does these days. There are so many kinds. There's greasy, disgusting, barely presentable, over-fancy, and bearable. Beards are a full time job.

THE ROAD TO SUCCESS

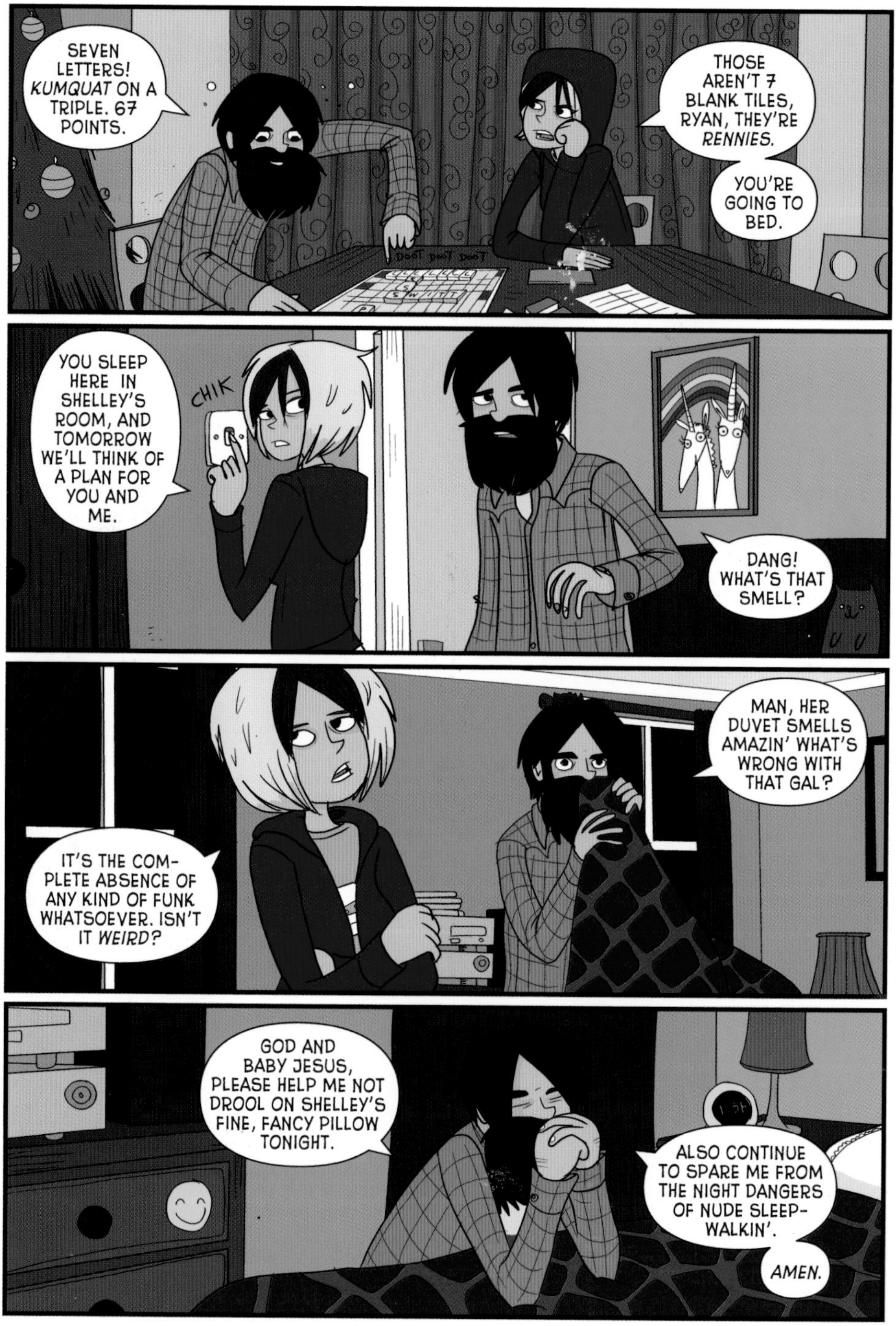

SEVEN LETTERS! *KUMQUAT* ON A TRIPLE. 67 POINTS.
DOOT DOOT DOOT
THOSE AREN'T 7 BLANK TILES, RYAN, THEY'RE *RENNIES.*
YOU'RE GOING TO BED.
CHIK
YOU SLEEP HERE IN SHELLEY'S ROOM, AND TOMORROW WE'LL THINK OF A PLAN FOR YOU AND ME.
DANG! WHAT'S THAT SMELL?
MAN, HER DUVET SMELLS AMAZIN' WHAT'S WRONG WITH THAT GAL?
IT'S THE COM-PLETE ABSENCE OF ANY KIND OF FUNK WHATSOEVER. ISN'T IT *WEIRD*?
GOD AND BABY JESUS, PLEASE HELP ME NOT DROOL ON SHELLEY'S FINE, FANCY PILLOW TONIGHT.
ALSO CONTINUE TO SPARE ME FROM THE NIGHT DANGERS OF NUDE SLEEP-WALKIN'.
AMEN.

This comic makes reference to my mentor and guide Shelley Winters, who was not around at this point, being on a global trip (I reckon, anyway). She is well a jet setter, and my idol. Weirdly she has never appeared in a mystery case, but her younger sister, Erin Winters, is in loads of them. Shelley is gentle and kind, unlike her sister, who (as you may recall), spends her days mis-spelling my name for fun. She's an awful person.

CLASSIC CRONES

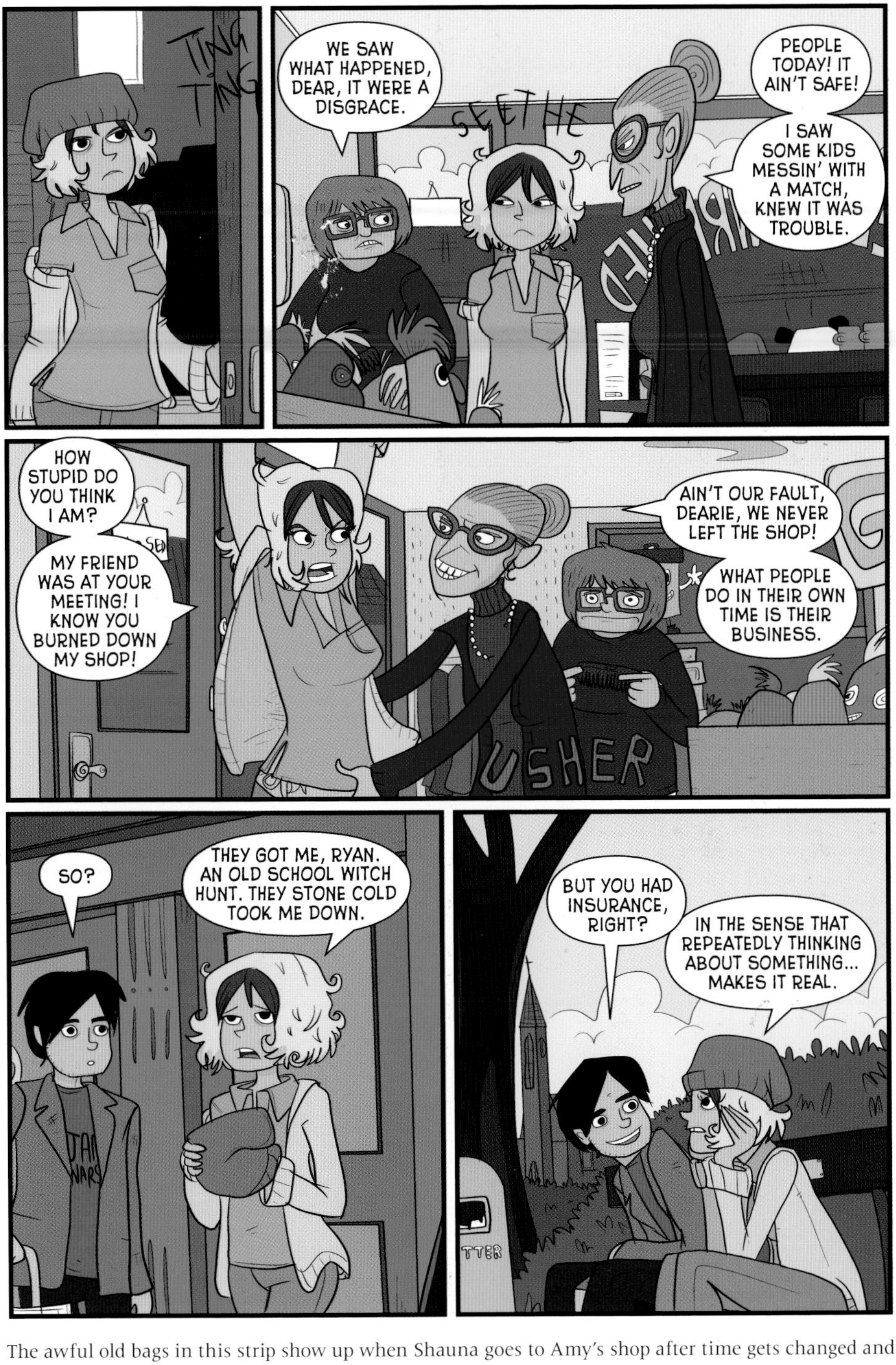

TING TING
WE SAW WHAT HAPPENED, DEAR, IT WERE A DISGRACE.
SEETHE
PEOPLE TODAY! IT AIN'T SAFE!
I SAW SOME KIDS MESSIN' WITH A MATCH, KNEW IT WAS TROUBLE.
HOW STUPID DO YOU THINK I AM?
MY FRIEND WAS AT YOUR MEETING! I KNOW YOU BURNED DOWN MY SHOP!
AIN'T OUR FAULT, DEARIE, WE NEVER LEFT THE SHOP!
WHAT PEOPLE DO IN THEIR OWN TIME IS THEIR BUSINESS.
USHER
SO?
THEY GOT ME, RYAN. AN OLD SCHOOL WITCH HUNT. THEY STONE COLD TOOK ME DOWN.
BUT YOU HAD INSURANCE, RIGHT?
IN THE SENSE THAT REPEATEDLY THINKING ABOUT SOMETHING... MAKES IT REAL.

The awful old bags in this strip show up when Shauna goes to Amy's shop after time gets changed and things go wrong. They're a right pair. Around this time they burned Amy's shop down, which I suppose made a change from selling jigsaw puzzles with missing bits and hideous porcelain clowns. They have not been seen around town for years, but sometimes you can smell them... on the breeze.

MELANIE SOAP

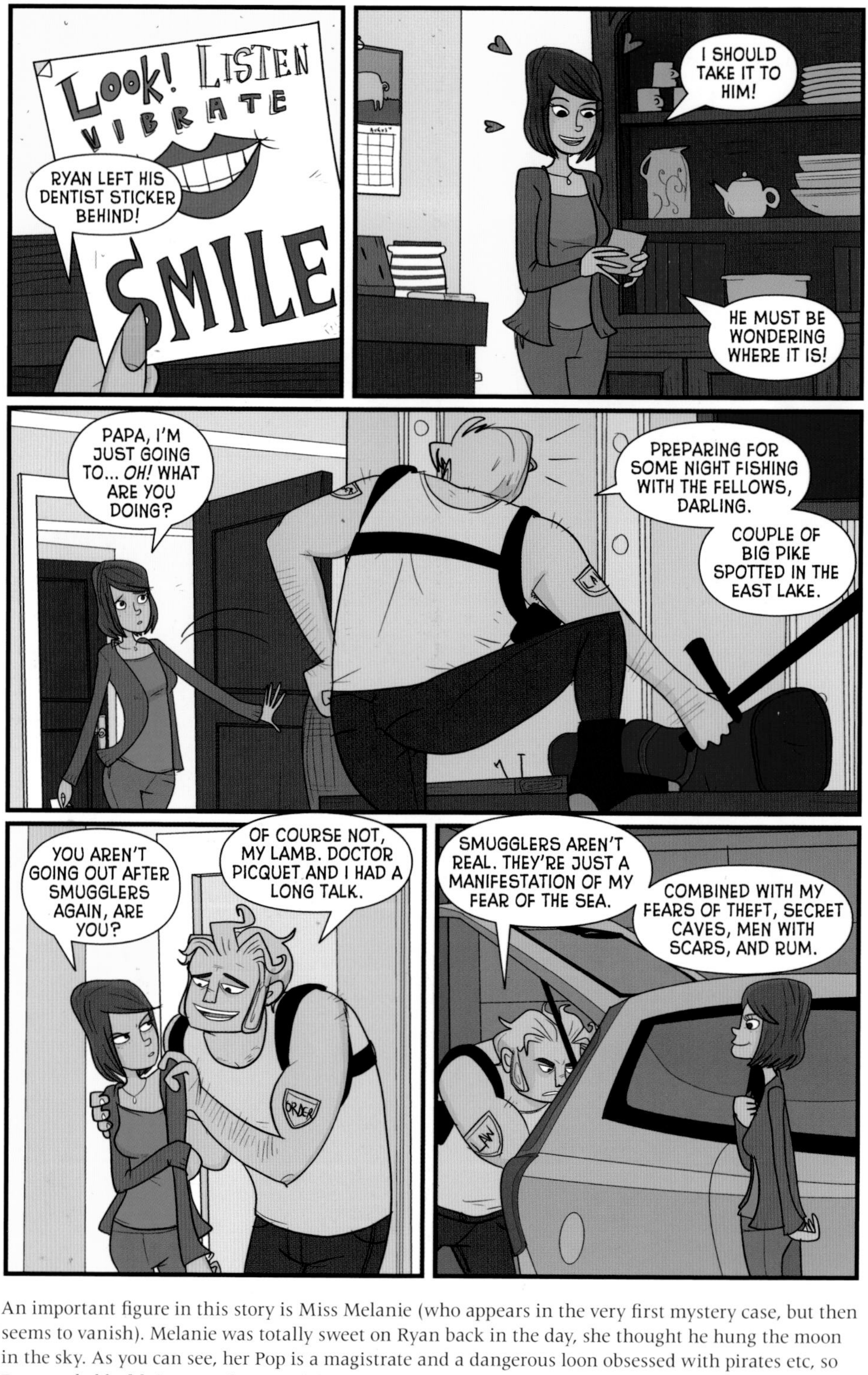
LOOK! LISTEN
VIBRATE
SMILE
RYAN LEFT HIS DENTIST STICKER BEHIND!
I SHOULD TAKE IT TO HIM!
HE MUST BE WONDERING WHERE IT IS!
PAPA, I'M JUST GOING TO... OH! WHAT ARE YOU DOING?
PREPARING FOR SOME NIGHT FISHING WITH THE FELLOWS, DARLING.
COUPLE OF BIG PIKE SPOTTED IN THE EAST LAKE.
YOU AREN'T GOING OUT AFTER SMUGGLERS AGAIN, ARE YOU?
OF COURSE NOT, MY LAMB. DOCTOR PICQUET AND I HAD A LONG TALK.
SMUGGLERS AREN'T REAL. THEY'RE JUST A MANIFESTATION OF MY FEAR OF THE SEA.
COMBINED WITH MY FEARS OF THEFT, SECRET CAVES, MEN WITH SCARS, AND RUM.

An important figure in this story is Miss Melanie (who appears in the very first mystery case, but then seems to vanish). Melanie was totally sweet on Ryan back in the day, she thought he hung the moon in the sky. As you can see, her Pop is a magistrate and a dangerous loon obsessed with pirates etc, so Ryan probably felt it was safer to seek love with Amy. I cannot argue with this decision. She's a total peach! But I hope Miss Melanie has found a special someone, somewhere. She's a peach too.

ALSO FROM JOHN ALLISON & ONI PRESS

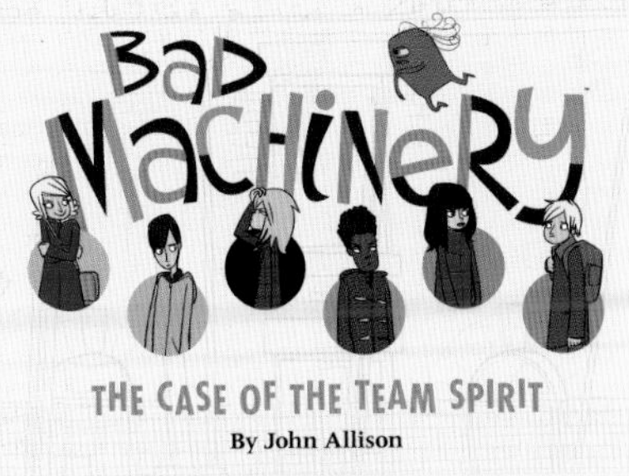

BAD MACHINERY
THE CASE OF THE TEAM SPIRIT
By John Allison

BAD MACHINERY, VOLUME 1:
THE CASE OF THE TEAM SPIRIT
By John Allison
136 pages, softcover, color
ISBN 978-1-62010-084-4
Pocket Edition also available!

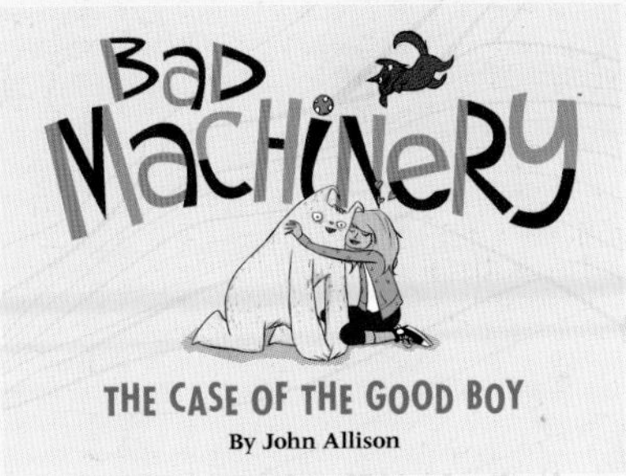

BAD MACHINERY
THE CASE OF THE GOOD BOY
By John Allison

BAD MACHINERY, VOLUME 2:
THE CASE OF THE GOOD BOY
By John Allison
144 pages, softcover, color
ISBN 978-1-62010-114-8
Pocket Edition available August 2017!

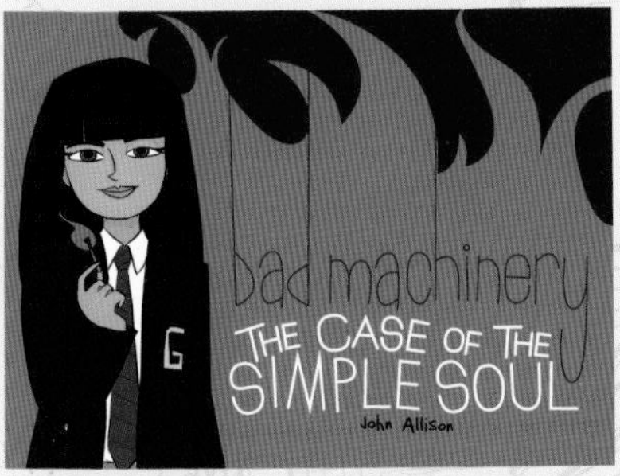

bad machinery
THE CASE OF THE SIMPLE SOUL
John Allison

BAD MACHINERY, VOLUME 3:
THE CASE OF THE SIMPLE SOUL
By John Allison
136 pages, softcover, color
ISBN 978-1-62010-193-3

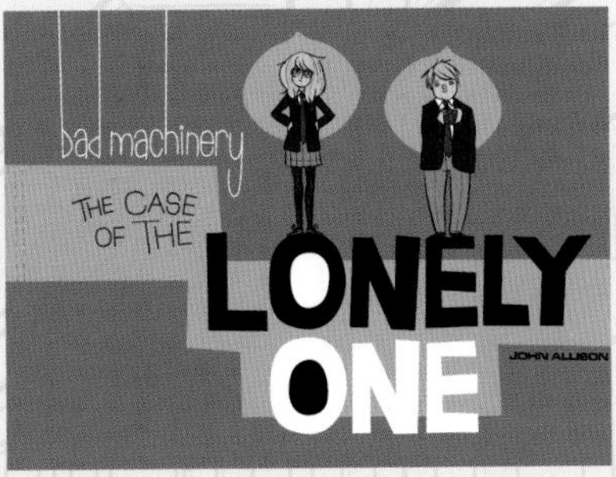

bad machinery
THE CASE OF THE
LONELY ONE
JOHN ALLISON

BAD MACHINERY, VOLUME 4:
THE CASE OF THE LONELY ONE
By John Allison
136 pages, softcover, color
ISBN 978-1-62010-212-1

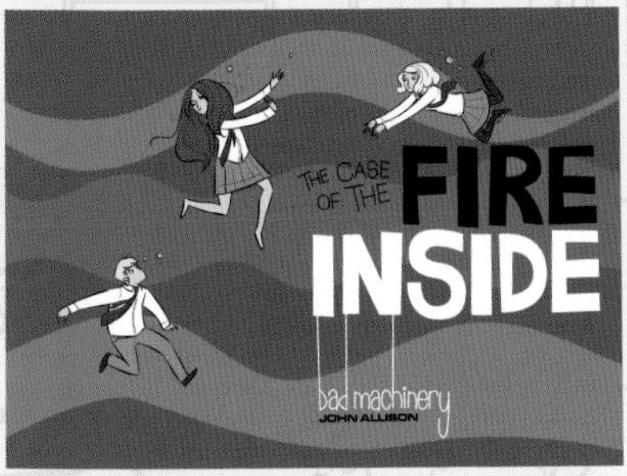

THE CASE OF THE
FIRE INSIDE
bad machinery
JOHN ALLISON

BAD MACHINERY, VOLUME 5:
THE CASE OF THE FIRE INSIDE
By John Allison
128 pages, softcover, color
ISBN 978-1-62010-297-8

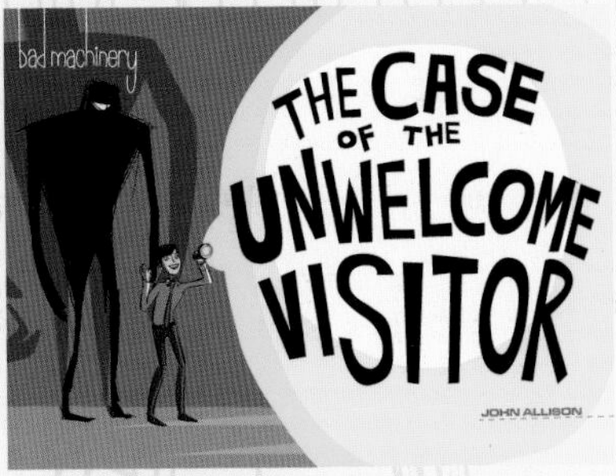

bad machinery
THE CASE OF THE
UNWELCOME VISITOR
JOHN ALLISON

BAD MACHINERY, VOLUME 6:
THE CASE OF THE UNWELCOME VISITOR
By John Allison
144 pages, softcover, color
ISBN 978-1-62010-351-7

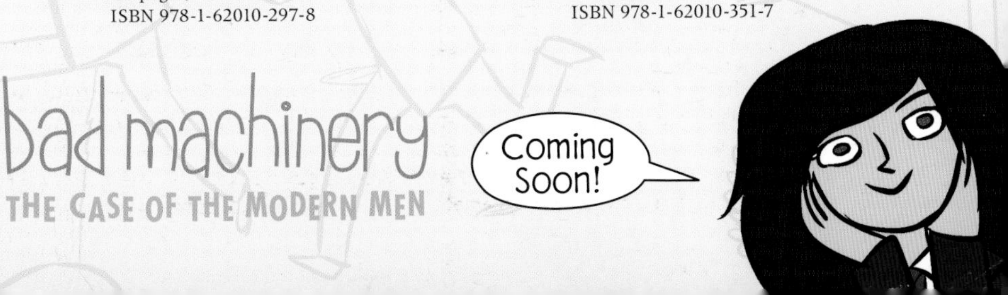

bad machinery
THE CASE OF THE MODERN MEN
Coming Soon!

EVEN MORE BOOKS FROM ONI PRESS!

BUZZ!
By Ananth Hirsh & Tessa Stone
176 pages, softcover, 2-color
ISBN 978-1-62010-088-2

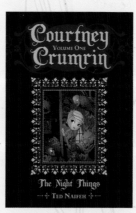

**COURTNEY CRUMRIN,
VOLUME 1: THE NIGHT THINGS**
By Ted Naifeh
136 pages, hardcover, color
ISBN 978-1-934964-77-4

HOPELESS SAVAGES: BREAK
By Jen Van Meter, Meredith
McClaren, and Christine Norrie
152 pages, softcover, b&w
ISBN 978-1-62010-252-7

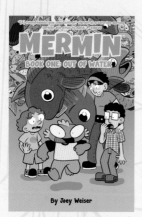

**MERMIN BOOK 1:
OUT OF WATER**
By Joey Weiser
152 pages, softcover, color
ISBN 978-1-62010-309-8

**PRINCESS PRINCESS
EVER AFTER**
By Katie O'Neill
56 pages, hardcover, color
ISBN 978-1-62010-340-1

**SPACE BATTLE LUNCHTIME,
VOLUME 1: LIGHTS, CAMERA,
SNACKTION**
By Natalie Riess
120 pages, softcover, color
ISBN 978-1-62010-313-5

ONI PRESS
www.onipress.com